Aliens & Mafia Susegaad

# Aliens & Mafia Susegaad

T. M. Konni

PARTRIDGE

A Penguin Random House Company

**To order additional copies of this book, contact**
Partridge India
000 800 10062 62
orders.india@partridgepublishing.com

www.partridgepublishing.com/india

*To all the straight forward government officials who stood for the people of India to eradicate corruption, jingoism, apartheid and sacrificed even their profession for the sake of their consciousness and principles in life.*

# Authors Note

Accidently I met Dr. Alexander Philip during a train journey on his way to his home town. He was on his last trip to his home town, he said, after spending more than three decades as an alien in the land of sun and sand, the beautiful Goa. Throughout the long journey he looked sad and gloomy. I could read frustration and disgust on his face. I was returning from the same land after one month's visit as a tourist. My intention was to write a book on beautiful Goa. My broken information about Goa was filled up by Dr. Alexander Philip. He shared his experiences, especially his official life, life in beaches, cultural scenario, about tourist places, festivals, churches and temples. I found his observations were fascinating and interesting. I appreciated his encounter with the underworld gangs, unethical politicians and corrupt officials. I already read the local news papers about the police drug mafia nexus, crimes against women and children, mining mafia, land mafia, human trafficking. Susegad is a Portuguese word for free lazy life without any stress. Though it was not growth oriented laws many people even now remember the strict Portuguese law and its proper implementation by them. I was told by locals that people were afraid of breaking law; crime rate was very less compared to present days. People were afraid to take even unclaimed or forgotten things in public places or on beaches, because of fear of strict law and order. Waste disposal system and drainage system were perfect in cities. Though there was religious discrimination, religious persecution was not much during Portuguese regime. Many people I met were unhappy about the present criminal politicians who encourage drug mafia and crime in the state. In one month stay I could read news about drug mafia, mining mafia, human trafficking and increasing rate of crime against girls. It was interesting to hear about the education mafia. Alexander Philip, who became a victim of jingoism, informed me that about thirty five years ago such news was very rare and never heard about. After that accidental meeting we met on several occasions and finally I decided to write about his life in Goa.

T M Konni

# Prologue

## Drug Lord arrested in Peru

Deputy DGP on Sunday informed that the wanted drug lord from Israel has been arrested in Peru on Saturday night. He informed thwat he has received a fax message informing about the arrest in Peru and added that the state police with the help of CBI would expedite proceedings to him to Goa. He was arrested by the crime branch after a video footage which revealed a nexus between cops attached to the anti narcotic cell and drug mafia. Investigations into the case by crime branch headed to the arrest of six police men attached to the ANC who were later suspended.

## CM seeks report on police-drug mafia nexus

Chief Minister has said that he has sought a report from the Home Department to the nexus between police and drug dealers even as SP has placed under suspension a head constable of the Police station in drug related case...

## City sex racket: DGP assures strict action

The Director General of Police has promised strict action against anybody found guilty in the City sex racket case. Once we get the reports, the role of everyone will be investigated. The inquiry is still going on, and not yet completed. Police sources say that the City police have filed a case against the victim girl saying that she was soliciting customers at a nearby bus stand, while she was actually picked up from the city. Sources also say that the girl was brought at the police station before being taken back to the City station, allegedly molested and abused there and then taken to the village police station, where she recounted her ordeal to a NGO volunteer and gave a signed statement. The report also says that there was a male constable who was watching the oral sex being performed while a lady constable even gave water to the victim after she vomited after the oral sex act. The girl has identified the guilty constable. It is more than two weeks since this heinous act was committed allegedly at the City police station. According to records; this is not the first case wherein the police have tried to exploit the victim. In another case, a victim of prostitution was picked by the police patrol car from north beach and while she was in the police jeep, a constable allegedly forced the victim to perform oral sex on him while two other police constables filmed the act on a mobile phone. Records about another incident in the village police station show that, a police constable posted at that police station received information that a girl from Mumbai was being trafficked to Goa and the trafficker was operating from a village. The constable approached the trafficker, threatened him and took the victim with him. Instead of following the procedures, he took the victim to a hotel in City and along with his friend had sex with her. The girl was later dropped in another village by the same constable. The incident came to light when the victim's statement was recorded in the presence of an NGO. The constable was later suspended and a departmental inquiry instituted against him.

# Drug cases: Co-operation from public

Having taken over the probe into drug related cases involving two Israeli drug peddlers and their nexus with some of the state police officials, the Central Bureau of Investigation (CBI) has sought co-operation from general public and others for an in-depth and exhaustive investigation to reach to the bottoms of the cases as early as possible.

# PSI arrested in fake currency racket

One police sub-inspector was arrested on Sunday in connection with the fake currency racket by the investigating police inspector. The fake currency racket came to light when a casino owner lodged a police complaint alleging that the casino management discovered fake currency notes of 1000 denominations worth Rs.21000 used by two persons in the casino. The police had suspected the involvement of the police officer attached to the City police station. They interrogated him and after fake currency notes were seized from his possession.

# Class XII Marks Goof: Officials indicted

There was a systematic failure on the part of Secondary and Higher Secondary Education that led to errors in computation of marks of Class XII students that saw over 1500 students being erroneously declared to have failed last year.

"There appears to be a systematic failure in the entire operation of preparation of results which has led to the said lapses," the 117-page report prepared by Education Secretary, the one-man probing the fiasco, states.

# The Controller has withdrawn all the mark sheets

The Controller of Exam within, less than 48-hours after he declared results of the HSSC examination conducted in March, has started the process of rechecking the internal assessment marks as added to the mark sheets of the students who had appeared for this examination. He has withdrawn all the mark sheets and postponed the evaluation as well as verification processes until issuance of corrected mark sheets.

Taking cognizance of the error that has crept in the mark sheets, the Minister said that the inconvenience caused to the students, their parents and the schools is the result of the gross negligence by the officials of the Controller. "A strict action would be initiated against those found guilty," he added. The decision of the Secretary comes in the wake of several complaints received from students that the internal assessment marks given to them by their schools are either not added to the mark sheets, or are much lesser than actually given. The number of students, who noticed this discrepancy on the very next day of the declaration of results, is very high.

## The Assault

The news about the attack on Andrew Akbar- created mixed reaction in Goapuri. Someone spread the news that he was murdered. Since his dead body was not found till morning many did not believe his death. Johnny who survived the serious attack could not say who the attackers were. He did not even remember what happened on the previous night. The severe blow on his head incapacitated him severely. He only knew that along with others he went to Zuari Nagar area for distributing free saris and other articles to the slum dwellers during day time. His friend and others tried to question him repeatedly, but he gave all senseless answers. He did not even know that he was been attacked by someone on the previous night. Port city witnessed the anger of Club Susegaad. They torched selected shops before dawn and burned many vehicles and buses. They moved in groups with swords, sticks, acid bombs, and petrol to torch the rivals' shops and vehicles. They declared total bandh in the city and forced everyone to close the shops. Black flags were flown everywhere. People remained inside their home out of fear.

The new DGP who had vowed to clear the gangs in Goapuri reacted swiftly. His mission was to clear the beaches of Goa from Russian Mafia. But soon he realised that the Russian mafia had a strong hold on the Government and a parallel mafia is run by the Ministers through, Fatima and Andrew Akbar- the Paklo dada- the blue eyed Portuguese descendent. He also realised that most of his subordinates are members of Susegaad club and they are the drug agents. He was in dilemma. He found it difficult to control a force that was fully corrupt and having deep roots in drug trafficking and human trafficking. He was forced to believe the opposition leaders words "A government of the criminals, by the criminals and for the criminals." But he thought "the woods are thick, dark, strong and deep with full of thorns, but I had promised to my boss to clear the thorns, and hours to work before I sleep… and hours to work before I sleep." When he heard the news about the fire in Zuari Nagar he immediately rushed to the site in the mid night itself to supervise the rescue work. He was astonished to see the huge fire engulfing the entire area that guttered hundreds of huts. The fire tenders reached after two hours in the mid night, but they could not do much since there was no approachability to that area. By morning the fire ceased as its own. Then DGP heard the port city is on fire. He witnessed the sluggish and lethargic attitude of his own police men in controlling the arson. He noticed even in his presence his subordinates were showing slow and apathetic in action to control the mob which is ransacking the properties. He stood there helplessly.

Alexander Philip, the alien, was away from the city on that fateful day. He dropped his family away out of fear and reached the Port city in the early morning hours. He noticed a very deserted look everywhere. On the way to the city he saw guttered shops; all were of aliens, there was no one on the streets, no taxis, no auto rickshaw. Passengers from Mumbai, Mangalore and Hubli were stranded in the bus stand without knowing what happened on the previous night. They looked each other for answers. One potter while carrying luggage of a passenger informed the news to other passengers.

"Paklo dada was murdered on the previous night" he paused.

"*Harthal* today" another porter informed.

One of the Susegaad members who always respected Dr. Alexander Philip and a secret follower of him informed him over phone that Paklo Dada was murdered or attacked by some unknown persons in Zuari Nagar and the Mafia gang was on the move to revenge on the attackers. Since, they were attacking all suspicious and rival gang members ruthlessly, he advised Dr. Alexander Philip to move to a safer place to escape from the attackers. Since the attack happened after midnight, daily news paper could not publish the news. There was only rumour that the Mafia Don Paklo Dada is dead.

One motor cycle pilot agreed to transport Alexander Philip to his place. But he asked five hundred rupees for the service. Unwillingly he agreed to pay the exorbitant rate. He would have walked that one kilometer distance if had no luggage with him. He noticed grave silence on the streets. Only a few motor cycle pilots, members of the mafia gang, were on the street. He noticed many burned vehicles and guttered shops on the street. Some shops were still burning and smoke was emitting outside. In front of railway station some miscreants burned a heap of discarded tyres and that was burning continuously. Thick black suffocating smoke filled the air announcing the victory of the anarchy and pandemonium. On the way he noticed passengers were walking to reach their destinations with the luggage on their head. They have arrived in the city by Nizamuddin Express from Delhi in the early morning.

Alexander Philip received many telephone calls from his friends and informed him the updated news in the city. Over phone he was informed that some rag pickers found the naked body of Paklo dada on a heap of garbage little away from Zuari slums with all his private parts severed and he was in an unconscious state. After a while he also got information that Paklo was shifted to a Madgao Hospital by the police. Alexander Philip looked outside and noticed a group of people moving with swords, knives, *koithas*, cycle chain, petrol bombs and long sticks in their hands and they were shouting slogans in anger. In front of his eyes they caught one man, a migrant labour and thrashed him mercilessly and left the bleeding man on the road and they moved on. While moving they threw one petrol bomb into one grocery shop that was kept opened and the flame licked up the walls and engulfed the roof. The shop keeper who ran out of his shop was followed by the Susegaad members and caught him by the collar and pushed him into a gutter and kicked by three members mercilessly for two minutes. Soon a military truck with fifteen soldiers reached the sight. Susegaad members ran in different direction after leaving their weapons on the road. Three Jawans jumped out of the truck and followed the running Susegaad members. Some of the Susegaad members ran towards the Gama beach and escaped. The jawans caught one of the strikers and locked him to the truck. The appearance of naval police jeep and soldiers in trucks gave confidence to the people. The soldiers stormed the barricades set up by the strikers on the roads and cleared the road for vehicles. But no vehicles were seen on the streets. Paulo de Silva informed Alexander to move to a safer place to escape the attack. Alexander Philip decided to move to the navy area for protection and safety. The crowded streets become deserted overnight.

# Part One

# Chapter 1

The land of caterpillars' butterflies, grasshoppers, spiders, frogs and snakes were claimed by mongoose, peacocks, sparrows and parakeets in due courses of time. This beautiful land of Goapuri could not be claimed by anyone for more than a few centuries; however, the antagonisms between frogs and snakes, grass hoppers and frogs, snakes and peacocks continued for millions and millions of years. The land of deer's, cattle's donkeys' horses, sheep's and goats were claimed by panthers, tigers, and lions. The weaker ones were killed by the mighty. The mighty ate the flesh and drank the blood of the weaker ones for millions of years. Lions, tigers and elephants never thought or dreamt that once they would be thrown out of their kingdom, forever. They do not even dream that the forest, they and their ancestors claimed and lived for thousands of years would be handed over to some unknown creatures, one day. The forest, they and their ancestors were moving fearlessly for generations to generations for thousands of years would become their own prison cages one day; they never imagined. One day it happened. The arrival of humans, the cruelest animal on this planet changed the history of the earth forever. The entire animal kingdom decided to fight the bipedal '*the aliens without the tail*'. All the water bodies became the sole property of the bipedal. Gradually, all fertile lands were grabbed by the new settlers. The river Mandovi and river Zuari witnessed the cruelty of the new settlers, but they were forbidden to talk. The new weapons, the new traps and the nets they made were dangerous. They made their own gods. They worshiped the gods which they made. They made gods of stones, gods of copper, gods of silver and gods of gold. They offered valuables to their own gods out of mere selfishness, expecting more fortunes, wealth and power. They killed helpless animals on the altars made of stones in front of their stone gods to please the speechless dump stone gods and ate the flesh and drank the blood of the poor dump animals for the sake of gods.

On the river banks of river Mandovi and Zuari those bipedal lived inside the gargantuan ant hills made of mud and sticks, a lesson they copied from the ants and their ancestral apes, for thousands of years they lived in that mud huts made of clay. They ate crabs, oysters, snails and fish. They made rafts and canoes out of mangrove trees. The mythological river Saraswathi dried up and dead somewhere before the advent of Lord Jesus Christ, the redeemer of the world. The frightened Aryans, who made tremendous mansions out of mud and stones, who firmly believed that they and their future generations to come would surely enjoy the blessings of that river and live forever on its fertile banks, alone, without allowing anyone to share its water or sacred soil along its banks, were forced to leave, all they made, all made for them by their ancestors, for many generations. Copper and silver vessels they carried with them were simply handed over to the thugs and dacoits on their long march to the south. Those valuables, once their ancestors robbed from the dark-skinned Dravidians and hid under the muddy floors of their huts and stone mansions for generations became extremely useful to the thugs and dacoits whose lazy parents left only the stabbing knives and poverty to their children. They said good-bye to the land they captured from the migrants and nomads with tears in their eyes. They saw the skulls of the Dravidians, they and their ancestors killed or buried alive under the sacred soil of river Saraswathi, when they had dug for treasures before they left their holy land. In search of another fertile land, they moved to south. They moved with their dogs, cattle, baskets, stone and wooden gods in their hands. They moved in thousands. At the same time, more than six lakh people were about to leave Egypt under one leader: the great Mosses. They moved in search of freedom, not water. They were happy to leave their land for freedom. They never regretted. They looted the Egyptians before they plan their massive exodus. An era of immense emigration, an emigration without passports or visa. An exodus on naked foot. They were ready to face the fate waiting for them. Without a leader, the Aryans moved from north to south. Lakh of people started from the river banks in search of water. Without destination without a leader, they moved aimlessly towards south. Out of Six lakh people who started from Egypt, only two reached alive in their dream land. Even the leader Mosses could not reach Palestine. The descendants of father Jacob finally reached the land of honey and milk. The descendants of the Great Aryans without any destination or leader wandered throughout the south India. Ninety Six families reached this beautiful land of sun and sand. Later years added one more adjectives to this beautiful land that was Sex. Aryans of Goapuri did not like the number three. They considered the number three inauspicious. Future generations added one more adjectives to their cap: another S: S for Susegaad.

The land of Susegaad came into existence. The old Homo sapiens were pushed into the deep forests of Neturlim, Sanguem, Bicholim and Pernem. The tail less *Homo sapiens* joined their older rivals in the forest. The usual enmity increased. The mighty pushed the weaker. The mighty remained as mighty for some centuries till they were replaced by more powerful ones. What they had imagined of theirs became others, what they had claimed of theirs became useless. The ninety six families were fortunate enough to settle along the banks of Zuari and Mandovi. The minority became powerful. The majority had to heed the minority a difficult thing to digest. The new settlers with their holy thread across their trunk, which brought cast and creed along with them, claimed everything for themselves. The son of the soils became a minority, and they withdrew themselves to the deep forests of Bicholim, Pernem Sanguem and Neturlim. The history repeated in every part of the world. The son of the soil became the landless nomads. The enmity between the old settlers and new settlers continued for generations.

The Konkas and maunders of Goem with comparatively fewer cerebellums became the slaves and workers of the modern fair-skinned Aryans of the north. They brought their gods with them. Stone gods, mud gods, metal gods of different colors and shape with diverse powers. The nomadic Dravidians believed the stories made by the fair skinned Aryans who claimed their cerebellum is bigger than that of the old settlers. The proto-australoid Kongvans and tribal Mundars lost their identity forever. They became a minority in their own ancestral land. The Kongvans and Mundars were forced to believe that the river Mandovi and Zuari and all the fertile land in Goem belonged to New Settlers. Those innocent ones, the old settlers, the protoaustraloid (the old aliens), with fewer cerebellums, so with less cunningness, believed or made to believe by the new settlers that the Aryans were made by God himself, whereas all others were made by God's workers or his slaves.

The *chandalas* believed that the Chandore belonged to a *Chandala* king where as the people selected the Chandragupta as their King to escape from a shameful ancestry. The Emperor Asoka was highlighted, and Chandrapuri was fabricated for a decent origin. "Sacrifice everything for a divine cause" priests preached. People believed. They sacrificed everything they had. *Devdasis* sacrificed what they had for a divine cause to please god, like the nuns sacrificed their lives for Jesus Christ. Temple's priests exploited the ignorance of devdasis and people for their own lust, and Catholic priests exploited the ignorance and blind faith.

A thousand miles away south of this Golden Goem at Kapad, in Kerala, near Kozhikode a heavy built warrior cum captain with his long golden beard landed with his four hundred soldiers and traders in the year 1498. The guns and swords in their hands gave them additional power and amusement. They stared at the local fisher folks with their cruel cat eyes. The poor fisher folks looked at their immense body and gave way in fear.

"*Videshikal, kadpurathu videshikal*!! (Foreigners, foreigners, and aliens in the port) the elders yelled. The echo reached the entire Kapad village in less than one hour, and people began to gather in that port town to see the aliens. They were amazed to see their strong built and attire. They looked at their own skin and compared to the white skins of the aliens and commented "They have painted their body; it is not natural" One person said to another. "No, it is natural color; they are like that, look into their eyes; they are blue" another commented. Children began to follow the aliens at a distance in fear. Women folks ran to their huts and shut their doors and peeped through the windows. The *Paragis* marched fearlessly through the muddy roads of Kappad with their guns and long swords in their hands. They stopped at a hut where some people were standing and praying. Vasco da Gama stood outside and watched the crowd. A closer look revealed that they were standing in front of a cross engraved on a huge stone. Vasco Da Gama could not believe his eyes... The presence of the cross and Christians in Kappad? It seems to be exceedingly strange incident to them. They never knew that christens were in Kerala. They never wanted to know the existence of non Catholic Christians anywhere in the world. They could not tolerate Christians, who do not accept Pope as their ultimate high priest. Pope ordered to destroy and burn all the Christian literature and other historical evidence of Marthomites in Kerala. But a few faithful followers of St. Thomas the Mar-thomites who slipped the swords of Portuguese rulers continued their faith in Jesus Christ and the Marthoma (Mar –means holy, Saint) church still exists in Travancore. Majority joined with the powerful and powerful become more powerful and proclaimed themselves as descendants of St. Thomas. An era of superstitions begun. Catholic Missionaries distorted the true faith and wanted to elevate Pope as the only representative of God on earths, who possess the key of heaven given by Jesus Christ himself after his crucifixion and resurrection. Just like the Roman Emperor Constantine who converted to Christianity, not because of his faith but to remain on the throne of the Roman empire, a majority of people in Kerala followed and joined the powerful Catholic church, not because of faith but for personal gains and be a part of the power groups.

Vasco da Gama's voyage to Goa and Kozhikode didn't fetch much fortune to Lisbon. The king of Portugal got annoyed with Vasco da Gama. The sponsors of the Gama's voyage become bankrupt. Samudirin of Kozhikode refused to trade with Portugal. Alfonso de Albuquerque succeeded where Gama failed. He looted Kozhikode market in a day light with the might of his gun powder and presented the booty of pepper, cinnamon, nut mugs, elachi and other spices to king Manuel of Portugal. Albuquerque hated Gama and refused his entry to Goa during the second instance. The new comers and juniors hate the seniors who opened a path for their arrival or guided them in their work once. He could only see his dream land, the golden Goa, from a distance in the sea and went to south in frustration since Albuquerque denied his entry into his Goa. The Gama who thought the land he founded for his king would be his, but his successor turned him away. The land of caterpillars, butterflies, snakes and mongoose once again changed the hands from Gama to Albuquerque. The Gama's fancy imagination was not long lived. Lisbon could hold it for more than four centuries, but they had to give way for a pure Indian force in the year 1961. The Susegaad members finally realised that without India, they could not attain freedom- a fact they do not want to accept. Ram Manohar Lohia was needed to teach nationalism and true patriotism to people believed in jingoism. But soon the 'Susegaad' members conveniently forgotten the nationalism of Ram Manohar Lohia and other Indian leaders and tried to cultivate jingoism. The real leaders like Tito Braganza Cunha wanted to ban this jingoists Susegaad club but he could not. An organization of jobless simpletons became the most powerful organization within twenty years after liberation. Politicians nurtured the organization later to develop hatred among the peace-loving people of Goa. Hatred against migrants (aliens) developed slowly among the population.

*T. M. Konni*

# Chapter 2

*"Now we have a government of the smugglers, by the smugglers, and for the smugglers."*

The Opposition leader

The baton of Golden Goa was moved from Konkas to Sumerians, Chaddas, Saraswats, Mauryas, Bhojas, Satavanas, Shilaharas, Kadambas, Khilji's Portuguese, Indians and finally to 'Club Susegaad' the Mafia gang. The wickedness and treachery were not new to this land. Every successful king or ruler was toppled by mistrustfulness, jealousy and envy of their own family or friends. Jamaluddin, the nawab of Honawar was invited by a prodigal son of Kadambas, to attack the Gopakpatanam, the Golden Goa. He was happy to see his father, and the entire subjects were assassinated by a foreign ruler, to hit back his father and even promised to embrace Islam and marry the Sultan's daughter in return of destruction of Chandor. One night changed the fate of the ancient city founded by the Emperor Asoka; it was destroyed and burned by the Nawab of Honawar. On that momentous night Chaddas, the kings' most trustworthy bodyguards, became traitors, and the last Kadamba king felt the sharpness of his own sword. He was assassinated by his own sword by his own body guards. The queen was away on that fateful night and survived the massacre. The news of her husband's death made her hysteric. In utter desperation, dismay and

shock she and many of her confidantes powdered their gold
and diamonds of golden Goa, by grinding them in a huge
stone grinder and threw it in a pond belonging to chaddas and
cursed all the women folks of Chandor. The queen and her
escorts jumped into the pond and drowned. The curse fell on
the family of Dos, the Chaddas who were responsible for the
king's assassination. Even after many centuries the curse of
the Kadamba queen was still haunting the Chaddas especially
the Dos, the predecessors of Minguel Custodio Dos, the great,
great grandfather of Minguel De Silva the local president of
Club Susegaad, Vasco da Gama... To escape from the curse
of the queen Dos changed themselves into Xavier then to
Silva. But the change of a name could not help; they remain
as traitors and criminals even today. Finally the golden Goa
was fallen in the clutches of Club Susegaad and Mafia Queen
of Gama.

A new drug culture developed in every nook and corners
of Goa. The smugglers become the rulers. The Opposition
leader commented "Now we have a government of the
smugglers, by the smugglers and for the smugglers'. The
beautiful definition of Abraham Lincoln for democracy was
distorted for his own gains. The same smugglers contested
elections and become the kings and queens. A Russian mafia
was planted some were in the north. Manures were supplied
by police and ministers' sons for years. The return was
unimaginable. Tax evaders, drug peddlers, human traffickers,
pedophilic and prostitutes flourished well in sunaparanth than
anywhere in India. Gradually Goa becomes hub of many
antisocial activities. Politicians made long speeches and asked
the public for help to nab the antisocial elements, and then
they spend their dinner with the Mafia gangs. The river Zuari
did not change their path for the last many centuries but the

people they supported changed their paths a hundred times without any ethics and morality. Another great river Mandovi in south moaned and sobbed helplessly along with her sister.

After four centuries of dormancy, the mysterious members of the club Susegaad surfaced from underground and became active in the year 1962. A few old secret members of the club tried to revive it. They decided to assemble at Gama beach on every last Saturday of the month at mid night, when normal activities and regular tourists retreats. Their motto was to drive away all Indian intruders from their mother land. They feared that one day they become a minority, and they may be unable to find their identity forever. They addressed all Indian immigrants as ghatis and tried to inject venomous ideas against all aliens. Politicians supported their hidden agenda secretly. The leaders found that they cannot win without the support of the Susegaad club. Government Officials could not survive without their support. Susegaad Club demanded protection money from every shop owner and government Officials. For driving license to land registrations, people approached the members of Susegaad Club. Contractors and developers realized that it was better to pay a percentage to the local club of Susegaad and run the business without any trouble. Those who opposed were harassed by the club members, police and government Officials. All the life members of the club were supplied with Susegaad emblem as the pendent, a small German cross at the end of an 'S'. How the emblem was evolved remains as a mystery even to the oldest members? Some say it is evolved from a Roman cross; some believe it was evolved from the ancient Aryan symbol the swastika. The same symbol the Hitler, the enemy of mankind, chose for his Nazi party in the year 1919 and brought him to power in 1939.

Gradually the members of Susegaad club became exceedingly rich in few years. They made a chain of huge five-star hotels all over Goa. Members made friendships with Pakistanis and Cashmeries and trafficked drugs through their Mexican connections. They arranged rave parties in the midnight to sell the drugs. Gradually, Russians and Israelis joined the business. Dead bodies started floating in the sea, and at Baina Anjuna and Baga... Police reported all those as drowning cases. Ministers, their sons, their relatives, police officers, officers, and government doctors joined the club S and protected themselves, and the S club extended their network throughout Goa.

Times reported a news item: "Scarlette Viola, a British teenager was on her holiday along with her mother. Both the mother and the daughter could not see the hidden evil spirit in her boyfriend. They rented a room on the beach side for a month. Local police also befriended with her and enjoyed days and nights with that white-skinned foreigner beauty. Members of the club S extended their full support. The joyful days did not last long. Her body was found on the sea shore after few days. Her boyfriend's blue orange chappels were found near the dead body in the sand. First report was of drowning case. Later, Anjuna police reported rape and murder because of the media pressure."

More the liquors the, more the tourists; more the drugs the more the revenue. That was the policy of the authorities. Peace-loving locals protested the rave parties and nudism of tourists. However, the club S supported the government policy openly. Protesters were harassed by the local mafia and members of the club 'S'. Susegaad members threatened the parents of the teenage girls. Few girls were kidnapped. Protesters became silent.

In January next year Goa Express reported another news "A 25 year old Russian girl had alleged that a politician had spiked her drink on the night of first December and later raped her in his car near Gama beach. Though the police at first registered it as an assault case, later it was changed as a rape case because of public pressure. Crime branch sleuth searched his house for evidence. But the politician had already changed his T shirt, and destroyed victims' panties left in the car as well as his clothes. He absconded for some days and surrendered to police later.

# Chapter 3

Andrew Akbar had never seen his father in his life. He was born with beautiful blue eyes unnatural to Indians. He was half Indian- half Portuguese. His Muslim mother wanted to put "Andrew 'as his name in memory of the night she spent with her foreigner customer "Andrew." Though hundreds of infants were buried alive under the black sand of Gama beach, Andrews' teenager mother decided to keep him alive, against the wish of her keeper. Andrew was fortunate enough to survive. He played on the dark soil of the Gama beach alone while his mother was busy in her job. He played with street dogs that visited the Beach to eat the human excreta. Not only, the infants of Gama beach, but several wealthy Indians and foreigners met with the sandy grave on this black soil. Police scared to visit the cubicles for any search. They only went as genuine customers inside. They knew that their department won't help them in case of trouble. Police officers who made friendship with the brothel owners and Susegaad club made a good fortune in a short time. Hundreds of teenagers were trapped and brought forcefully to Gama to satisfy the customers. Thugs were appointed everywhere on the beach to recapture the innocent girls who try to escape the brothels. Hundreds of taxi drivers and motorcycle pilots were appointed as agents and pimps for handsome rewards. Taxi drivers and motorbike pilots were given fake marriage certificates of the inmates of the sporting houses to escape from the Police and NGOs. This would facilitate them to book rooms in any hotels as husband and wife.

Three-year-old Andrew Akbar was playing in the muddy sand of the beach. An ex- minister was speaking over the microphone to the few hundred audiences as a part of his election propaganda few hundred meters away from him. Andrew could not understand anything. He was busy in playing in the mud, making deep holes or wells in the wet mud until his hand reach sea water. He was unclothed. Many of his friends were also like him without any cothes. It was not an intentional act but a reflection of poverty. His hand touched some dark soft objects while he made his small wells in that wet sand very near to sea. He did not know what those objects. Even his elder friends who were playing did not give any importance to these dried excreta of humans, dogs and pigs. They played in that dirty muddy beach while their mothers were busy in treating their clients. Andrew's 15 years-old mother did not get much time to spend with her son. A patriotic politician was still barking over his microphone. He was talking about the dirty age old business going on in Gama area. He promised he would appoint many police personals to check the flesh trade in this area if re-elected.

Petty leaders sitting on the temporary stage made of a few wooden desks stolen from the neighboring schools looked at each other and nodded their heads. Public which was standing with beedis in their mouth gave a round of applause. "I will stop this flesh trade in Gama forever. Our governments' priority will be to clean up this area and made available this beach for the public use. The name of our state is being spoiled by these handful elements. At any cost, we should bring peace and harmony here. All the criminals hiding inside those cubicles would be brought… hey… Hey… Hey. He stopped yelling and wiped his face. He felt something soft sticky thing fallen on his face. He saw people were running here and there with fear. Chappels, rotten tomatoes, spoiled eggs started falling on the stage. Petty netas who were sitting on the high desks covered their faces to protect themselves from eggs and rotten tomatoes.

Mafia Queen Fatima and their goons acted violently. They pushed the desks and pulled down the temporary stage and thrown out the mike and loud speakers. Members of the gang swirled with their long cane lathis in their hand. People ran helter shelter pushing each other to escape from the attacks of the assailants. The attack was unexpected. The speaker an ex-minister, a candidate for the next assembly election from the constituency ran for his life. He was caught by the members of the Susegaad club and been battered. The candidate who fell on the ground searched for his spectacles in the sand. He was kicked from behind by another. The new nationalist fell again in the sand with his face down. The police disappeared from the scene within seconds. Two aides of the nationalist leader also received kicks and thrashes from the Fatima's people when they tried to protect their leader. Within three minutes, the crowd dispersed. The police would have taken more than thirty minutes to disperse a similar crowd.

Fatima, the Mafia Queen of Gama was running her empire of prostitution and drug trafficking through the help of Susegaad Club. She was more than six-foot tall, heavy, with projected eye balls, widely opened nostrils exhibiting the thick dirty nasal hair, thick lips and unusually short hair styled like a man. She was exceedingly bold and physically strong like a wrestler. She was a sadist and enjoyed the scream and sobbing of teenage girls entering the profession. When she laughs one could see her pink gum of the upper jaw resembling an ape. Her ancestors were from Africa. The Portuguese brought her great-great grandfather as a slave to row their big boats in Goa in the middle of AD.1600. She had an exceptionally unhappy childhood. Her father divorced her mother when she was a child and went to Kenya. She was forced to this profession by her stepfather. Since she had not received any love or mercy in her entire child hood she grew as a ruthless fearless girl. When her step father moved to Vasco from Old Goa, she accompanied and stayed at Kharewade. She helped the family in fishing. The income from the fishing was so meager, but they could afford expensive cloths, and other living style because of her mother's extra income. Gradually, she also joined her mother in a cubicle in Gama. She never knew like hundreds of her age groups in the surroundings that she was doing something unacceptable to the outside society. She had no formal education.

Her second cousin Maria received her primary education from Dhaka the present capital of Bangladesh. She worked in some private schools in Mumbai and Belgaum. Suddenly, she joined in the public service with the political influence of her cousin, the mafia queen, Fatima. The ministry was forced to change all her ACR and RR in favor of Maria, and she was promoted as a class one officer. All her colleagues wondered how she was selected to the high post without any experience or qualification. Soon she acquired a Doctorate degree from YellaLingeswara Mallappa University. People never before heard of such a university in Goa. Her colleagues knew that she had robed the Ph.D. Thesis of one Dr. Menezes from Dharwad University and got it modified. Dr. Menezes gave a written complaint to the university against Maria. Fatima her cousin sister intervened, and Mr. Menezes withdrew his complaints against Maria. The officers association and the entire teaching community baffled at her appointment. The association even demanded a probe into the entire espionage. But the power of a club Susegaad and Mafia Queen silenced them all forever.

Andrew saw the crowd running for life. Some ran over his sand castles where he was playing and stamped on it, the water holes disappeared within minutes. He moved to one safer side under a coconut tree where his friends were staying. The owner of the illegal toddy shop under the coconut tree protected them from the police. A police man arrived with cane in his hand. He shouted "Dirty bastards". He swirled with the cane in the air to frighten the little naked ones under a small coconut tree. He was afraid to swirl his cane against the "S" club members and frightened the little boys instead. He did his duty sincerely and frightened the little boys. The boys ran in fear. Andrew joined them aimlessly without knowing why he was running.

# Chapter 4

*"You will leave the village you were born,*
*And in another country you will become very rich and*
*very powerful,*
*But always you will mourn something you left behind,*
*Even though you can't say what it was and eventually*
*you will return to seek it."*

Louise Gluck

While the three-year-old Andrew Akbar was running naked in fear of the angry police men in Khaki with brown cane *lathis* in their right hands and whistles in their left hands through the sandy Gama beach in Goa, a thousand kilometers south of Goa in a calm mountainous sleepy village at Konni, in Central Travencore in Kerala a nine-year-old, angry boy was running after his untamed cow, in his oversized khaki *knickers* of his elder brother without any buttons or belt and was struggling to keep that partially worn out old *knickers* in its place with his left hand and was holding firmly one end of a thick rough coir string in his other hand, that was moving straight in front of him, after his mischievous wild black cow. He did not get enough time to change his dress before he was forcefully dragged into this action. For it was a routine work to untie the cattle from the cattle shed and tie it slackly again on a rubber tree and allow the cow to graze freely. The small rubber plantations belonging to his family was about one hundred meters away from his house. The cattle knew their way. Once their noose was free, they run directly to the nearby rubber plantations to graze at grass and legumes there. The grazing place was on a small hill side. On both sides of the rocky narrow way, there were spiny pineapple plants. The narrow way with full of rocks and stones made it very difficult for ramblers to move but not for this untamed naughty black cow with white spots on its temple. Before Alex could control the beast, it started running. It raised its tail and twisted it like a loop and ran over the newly planted tapioca fields then it entered the ginger crops and creeper cucumber. The beast spoiled enough number of tapioca plants and cucumber plants, and the boy destroyed more than that in his attempt to catch the cow. It ran near to the well and paused for a moment and again started running in full speed after noticing Alex behind it. Now it started running aimlessly here and there fooling the small boy running behind. The large *knickers* looked like modern Jamaica shorts. In power, Alex was no match to the running cow. Suddenly the cow changed direction and started running towards the small country road. While Alex was struggling to keep his oversized *Jamaican shorts* in its place, with one hand, the cow dragged him through the dusty road. In his failed attempt to control the running cow, his oversized knickers slipped down through his small delicate belly then through his buttocks exposing the private parts fully. Though he had not noticed who was watching him, his fourth standard class mate, and his neighbor was watching the rare sight with curiosity at a distance from her home through the window hole of her thatched house. In a fraction of seconds, he tucked his khaki shorts like a dhoti and again followed the advancing cow. He was lagging behind because of his loose knickers. The cow thought of taking a small break, and it stopped running. It put down its raised tail and allowed a little rest for its legs. Alex acted immediately. He circled the free end of the cord on a nearby coconut tree and tied the beast there and went home to call his elder brother for help. After getting her back to the cow shed he was informed by his mother that the beast ran because of the heat. Alex could not understand much of heat then.

The village Konni has a serene panoramic view of numerous small mountains and hills filled with plenty of pepper plants, coconut trees, coffee plants, jackfruit trees, tapioca plants and rubber plantations. The climate was singularly pleasing. The gentle breeze carried the pungent smell of spices. There were small streams and patches of green paddy fields on either side of the narrow *kacha* mud roads. People ate more tapioca the starchy underground root than rice and cultivated it in the entire village. During the rice harvesting seasons, little kids played in the heaps of dried hey kept for making stalks for cattle. Through hey they made tunnels to play. There were a few churches, temples and also a Muslim madrasa at Poovanpara, two kilometers away from Konni town. In the beginning of 1900, the whole area was forest with all kinds of wild animals and birds. The new settlers, the humans –the aliens- had driven away all the wild life into the deep forests and wanted to enjoy the beautiful valley for themselves. The human greediness and selfishness have no limitations. Known for the black fertile soil many new settlers started ventured into the river basin of Achenkovil, a small river that provided everything for the old and new settlers. The old settlers called new comers as *Varathan* (new comer, new settlers or alien) with contempt and disdain. Everyone remained as *a Varathan* in that area for many years. Thomas Philip, father of Alexander Philip, and his family remained as *Varathan* in Konni for many years. They were from a place called Kumpalampoika about fifteen kilometers north of Konni. Thomas Philip was thirty years old when he moved as a new settler in Konni. Thomas Philip was not a *Varathan at* Kumpalampoika, but his father Chacko Philip was. Every ancestor in the family of Alexander Philip had the title of *Varathan* in one or other place since they stayed only 30 to 40 years in one place. Poor new settlers were afraid of the heavy land tax. People were punished with allotting barren land in their name. Powerful families occupy the fertile lands near river banks and enjoy the fertility of the soil for themselves. *Varathan, (alien) a* second-class citizen was always been a sufferer. Even the great grandfather of Alexander Philip was a *varathan* at Kuriaynnoor village for some time. For one or the other reason every member of the family moved as a Roman.

Konni the famous place for untamed Proboscidians, spices and other forest produce is a centre for a tourist attraction now. It was the duty of Alex to show the elephant cage to any visitors in that family. The wild elephants were captured from the forest about 15 kilometers away from Konni and kept in huge wooden cages to tame them. The Mahouts are ready with their long poles and dozens of sticks, as a huge pachyderm has just arrived. The wild beast with its strong long milk white tusk and dark trunk that were a matter of terror in the forest before it fell inside the trap kept by the timid bipedal in *lungi* found himself helpless in front of that small creatures with two slender brown stick like legs below their concave stomach covered by a loincloth, exposing their green or red under wear that was not washed for a fortnight. The mahouts without any professional qualifications in the taming exercises of wild elephants were truly barbaric and brutal. They were supposed to tame one wild elephant within six months. For that, they had to follow fierce cruel methods. With the longs strong sticks and poles, they hit the animal from outside and utter some words in Malayalam: *"Ivide vaa aane"(Come here)* One trainer in his shabby *lungi* that was folded and tucked on his stomach shouts from the front, and another one hit the hungry scared animal from behind with a pole on its hind limbs just above its large nail, which was already wounded because of the continuous torture on the previous days. The animal screams out of anger and terrible pain. The giant tusker hits hard on the gigantic wooden cage, and it shudders. The visitors move back in fear. The trainer hits hard again and again on the same leg, and the animal moved a little front to escape the hitting. The trainer standing in front was happy, and in a soft tone he said *"angane vaa, ivide vaa"*. He shows a bunch of green coconuts leaves to appease the hungry animal. Immediately, the hungry beast snatches the leaves from the trainer and puts it in its large mouth. The training continued. Coconut leaves or sometime ripe bananas were given for a correct response. After teaching one command fully the untrained trainer without any professional degree in teaching would start the next command in Malayalam unlike in 'modern child centered' teaching, they taught the animal at their pace. No one called it as an elephant centered education. But here the elephant is the centre of education, not the half-naked trainer in lungi. Individual attention is given to each animal. No mass coaching. Elephant: Trainer's ratio is always 1:1 and they teach less than 10 words like *Idathottu thiri anne*(turn left) *Valathottu thiri aane*(turn right), *Edukkane Edukkane* (take), *irrikane(*sit) and it was sufficient for a life of fifty to sixty years for a civilized Proboscidian to live with an uncivilized *Homo sapiens.*

One or two mahouts may engage at one time for training one wild elephant. If the elephant turns in the right direction, the mahouts pat the animals through the huge wooden grills made of special woods and give them something to eat. The huge wooden grills won't break even though the tuskers hit it with all their strength, the animals always try to escape from the cage in the beginning, but after a few weeks they give up their attempts and try to listen to the commands of the mahouts. This process may continue for months. Some mahouts were lucky enough to get nice animals to be taught and got tamed in time, like some lucky teachers who get bright students as their disciples and bask in the fame of that student later in life. If they fail in their attempt to tame the animals in specified time they will be penalized and their pay will be cut. To show their efficiency to tame the animals faster some of the mahouts torture the animals without any mercy. Many a time Alexander Philip could not put up with the torture and plight of these helpless animals. There were no animals' lovers or animal activists, only cruel tamers. The strong smell of elephant droppings and the smell of their urine in the air can be felt hundreds of meters away from these cages.

On the way to the elephant cage there was a Government Hospital where Alexander Philip as a child used to visit for treatment. After seeing the protruded belly and mal nutritious child, the hospital nurse once gave Alexander Philip a tiny packet of white powder to eat and after that on every visit, Alexander Philip made it a practice to ask for that sweet white power to eat, but the nurse never gave it on demand of the small child. In later years, he realized that, the white powder was the glucose powder. The hospital was very dirty with few rusted iron cots. Alexander saw skinny patients lying with only bones and empty thin stomachs on the fully rusted iron cots without any mattress or mats. He also waited outside the doctor's cabin for an appointment along with his mother. The doctor was sitting behind a white soiled and torn cloth screen. After every few minutes a sister, the doctor's assistant, peep out of the cloth screen curtain and shout:"Narayani 55 years" A thin lady with a hunch went inside. She carried a green bottle in one hand. The doctor never raised his face to see the face of Narayani. Soon after she entered inside she started saying her complaints as if coming out of a tape recorder. "Both legs are paining, cannot climb or stand straight, getting tiered soon and not have any proper sleep." Before she completes her complaints the government, Doctor had already scribbled on a small chit and gave it to her. "Vasudevan 32 years" Just like a parrot peeping through its head from the small opening of her cage, the sister, the doctor's assistant, showed only her head through the cloth curtains and yelled once again "Vasudevan Nair 32 years". Narayani went out outside and in seconds Vasudevan Nair went inside. He also started saying his complaints without wasting a second. He knew that this high profile government doctor has no time to listen to the patients' complaints. Vasudevan was a regular visitor in the hospital for his asthma and stomach problems. Every time he received the same pink coloured liquid that the pharmacist gave on receipt of the chit from the Doctor. None of the doctors in that village hospital looked upon his face before prescribing the medicine. So he never waited for the doctor to look at him. Before someone starts speaking, the government doctor might have scribbled on his small chit that only his pharmacist could read, and immediately hand over the same to the Patient. The doctor was doing his obligation as a public servant.

When Thomas Philip suffered from severe malaria few years ago, Mariamma Philip went to visit the local government doctor privately at his residence. She cut a fully ripened banana from her compound and kept in a jute bag and carefully packed one dozen eggs in rice husk and walked towards the government doctor's residence. Outside the gate, the dogs welcomed her first and a thin beautiful stylish lady in pink sari appeared in front of Mariamma Philip. She was unfriendly and rude while talking. With little hesitation and fear Mariamma Philip asked whether she could see the doctor. The thin lady in pink sari said unpleasantly "Doctor is sleeping."

"My husband is suffering from malaria, and I want to see the doctor," Mariamma Philip said in her feeble voice.

"Today is Sunday, Doctor won't see any patients today" the thin stylish lady said in an impolite voice.

"Please mada… m…, please… call the doctor, my man is very sick and he could not sleep yesterday night and the whole night he was shivering". Mariamma Philip pleaded to the doctor's wife.

"No No No I won't call the doctor, he is sleeping. He is not well" Doctor's wife again said in a cheeky voice.

"Madam, I brought some bananas and eggs for the doctor, please call him, where shall I go now, please madam, please" she cried bitterly.

"What lady, what you thought, he did not get his Doctor's degree by giving bananas and eggs, my father paid thousands of rupees for his studies, get lost with your bananas and eggs, do not stand over there any more, I'll release the dogs now." She threatened. Mariamma Philip stood outside the gate of the government servant for half hour thinking; she or the doctor may come out for her help. But her hope was wrong. No one spoke to her or attended her except the barking dog. After a long wait of half an hour she walked straight to the Konni market and sold the banana and one dozen eggs and went to a private doctor in that small town. She got what she wanted. While walking back to her home she decided to teach her unborn child in her womb and make him a doctor. Her both expectations were fulfilled, but partially. She delivered a baby boy and he got the title 'doctor 'in his late forties, but not of medicine but in plant science. Whenever Mariamma Philip was sick or sad she prayed to Jesus and always prayed for her second son Alexander. But Jesus had other plans with Alexander that Mariamma Philip could not realize god's ways, then.

# Chapter 5

*"Akam kannu thurappikan ashan balliyathil yethanam"*

(To open your insight you should meet the teacher when you are young."

Alexander Philip's first book was a dried pale cream coloured palm leaf of two foot long with its tip folded and beautifully tied looked like its head. The narrow apex of that palm leaf book was tied by the *ashan* teacher himself when he gives his first or new lesson to his disciples. The future citizens of three or four years old of about twenty to twenty five move in groups with their three or four palm leaf books that resembles small swords in the hands of pigmy soldiers as if they are going to capture a land for their king. In fact these pigmy soldiers who were carrying the swords like palm leaf books or *taliola* were some of the last representatives of a melting culture that witnessed the Travancore and other parts of Kerala, in the fag end of a crisis ridden century. The dusty way to *ashan pallikudam (school) was* clean except the holi cow dung here and there like black green bubbles.

The small *pallikudam* that could accommodate a maximum of twenty five small kids had no walls, no doors, no benches and chairs. The thatched roof was on its four poles of about five feet high made of ripened areca nut stems. The raised black mud floor about one foot high from the surroundings was plastered with a paste of fine mud and fresh cow dung sometimes mixed with powdered coconut shell charcoal to give its black shade. Some mats made of thatched coconut leaf were the only stuff to sit. The sir, the *ashan* sits on the mat and teaches all his disciples at the same time. Preparation of the school on the poles, its yearly maintenances like replacements of worn out roofing all was done by the *ashan* himself. It has no recognition or affiliation to any Board, or any authority, the only recognition was given by the public. No salary to a*shan*, he is contented by the daily meals, normally the lunch, given in the residences of his loving disciples in turn or sometimes a fees of half rupee per month per child. Alexander Philip's *ashan* was a dark complexioned person from a scheduled cast family, but neither the students nor the parents treated him as scheduled caste but respected him as an *aharya or ashan*. He wore a simple dhoti and a second small towel to cover his chest. Among the students there were Christians, Hindus, Muslims, and other castes. They all sat on the same floor on the same coconut mats, drank the same water from a nearby well having no side walls or fence, a dangerous death trap for small kids, they all walked together with their long palm leaf books in one hand, and a small banana leaf on the other hand during monsoon to protect them from rain. No one came in cars or buses, no school bell, no midday meals, no computers, and all of them studied the same language, the Malayalam, the language of *mala nadu* or the land of mountains and hills. Brighter kids got new lessons every day but there were students who got new lessons only after a week or only after one month. *Ashan* never had any certificate of educational qualification nor any teaching degree but he knew the child psychology well and taught his students at their pace. Simple punishments were there. Alex the three year old kid liked his first teacher and enjoyed the walk of one kilometer along with his child hood friends. No kids cried after seeing the school as in a modern nursery school where kids are reluctant to attend the school, a new unfriendly environment, for one week or sometimes one month even, where teachers were forced to lock the children inside the room to prevent their escape, like hens were locked inside hen yard. New lessons were given on the palm leaves. *Ashan* writes the lessons for every student on the palm leaves by a pointed iron pen called *Narayam,* then he rubs a crushed green leaf called communist weed or congress weed on his freshly written letters, to make them clear and bright and the fresh smell of the plant juice on the fresh palm leaf was pleasant to kids as they smell it, as if they were kissing them. After writing the Malayalam alphabets on the palm leaves, the *Ashan* reads it aloud and Alexander and his friends repeats the same for a few minutes then he helped Alexander to write the alphabets on the white fine sand kept in front of him on the black floor. The slight pain on the fingers while writing the alphabet on the fine sand fixed the shape of it in his mind.

The primary school at Mrakuzhy was established with good intention in the past. Thousands of students got primary education because it. The school was situated on a barren a hill about two kilometers from Thomas Philip's house. The kacha dusty muddy road connecting the primary school and his house was narrow but motorable; the only motor vehicle-a Jeep belonging to the school manager may pass that road occasionally. The road also was made by the effort of the school manager for his big house on the top of a mountain. Students of age groups ranging from five to ten or twelve moved in groups playing or running all the ways without knowing the distance. While climbing the steep students pluck flowers or some medicinal leaves with pleasant aroma and crush them and smell it for fun. On both sides of the rocky roads there were plenty of lemongrass plants used for distilling oil from it. There was a belief among the small children that if they tie a long slender lemon grass leaf by using only left hand fingers, on that day they won't get pasting from the teacher. By tying the leaf it is meant that they are tying the hands of the teacher, so they cannot beat. Though it was only a superstition, almost every child tie a leaf secretly on daily basis with their left hand fingers to escape from the brutal punishments from their uncivilized teachers. Also kids believed that if they stamp on the cattle dung on the road, that was plenty on the road, a bad omen, will definitely get thrash from the teachers. So both those rituals were necessary before they enter their class rooms. Primary children normally carry a simple slate and one text book. Even examinations were conducted on the slate and marks were written on the slate in big fonts. Many poor students may carry even broken slates that become a matter of humor for the unscrupulous teachers sometimes. Kids use a fleshy herb, *kakathand*, to clean the slates; the same semi transparent herb was used to prove that the plants have continuous conducting tissues. The semi transparent herb comes under the pepper family (*Piperaceae*). The plant when kept its roots in red or blue ink become blue or red within half an hour showing the thread like continuous tissues inside. The first experiments shown there in primary classes remained in the mind of Alex for a very long time. During monsoon season a grass grown on the road side was another attraction, *kannin tholli,* the very long aerial roots of that grass accumulates a thick slimy fluid on its lower part that gleams in the early morning sunlight like diamonds, the cool water drops along with the roots were detached from the creeper and children keep them on their eyes for comfort. With these activities the way to school was with full of fun and never it was tiresome or boring.

The first primary school of Alexander Philip was in the shape of a long hall divided in to four rooms by wooden screens. But the students of one class could see what was going on the next through the slits on the screen. The school was painted white and with black bottom border of four feet. Small narrow veranda was broken here and there. It was said that when they were excavating for the school foundations on that mountains, they found large earthen coffins with human skeleton inside. Nobody was more curious than that and they thrown out that skeletons and large earthen pots without informing the authorities to investigate about the very old human settlement in that forest area in the past. An important link in the history of humankind might have destroyed forever. In the middle of the small rocky play ground there was a large jack fruit tree. Under its shade Alex played joyously after forgetting the severe punishments that he receives every day. Some smart boys wore two or three knickers one above the other to reduce the effect of the pasting on the buttocks. But teachers were smarter only because of their age and experience, and beat children on the un protected portion above the knickers or on the thigh. Students or parents never protested these brutal punishments of teachers. Students are always at the receiving end from the parents and their teachers, collective efforts of the uncivilized, now we say, elders to make their children 'good future citizens'. Those unscrupulous uncivilized teachers would have been behind the bars if they were acting the same way now.

During the half an hour recess in between the periods, boys first ran towards the projected rock in front of the school and lift one side of their knickers and make a fountain collectively together, a community pee-pee. The rock became yellowish green because of the continuous torture on it, by liquid ammonia and urea, the strong foul smell even reach the class rooms and headmaster's room without any difference. Then the kids run in groups towards the nearby stream to drink natural water, they drink water like monkeys do. While coming back to the school after the refreshments, Aex along with his friends visited the lemon grass distillation centre. He amusingly looked at the oil overflowing from the small vessel kept carelessly by the irresponsible workers below the out let of the crude distillation unit. Children never knew that the lemon grass oil that was overflowing out of the small vessel on to the ground was precious. The workers kept large bundles of lemon grass over a large steaming aluminium vessel. The steam separate the oil from the leaves that will be collected with help of an out let in another vessel. They enjoyed the fragrance of lemon grass in the air. No one knew why they are extracting the same or what the uses of it are. Only for curiosity and to enjoy the pleasant smell they spend some time over there and they return to their classes after some play and sit on the crude wooden bench without any back support.

Teaching was a leisurely job then. Teachers come and go as they like, give some homework, beat them if they do not do, ask them to read something and go out for shooting the breeze, come back, ask questions and again beat them till they cry. Alexander Philip was scared of kutty sir, who belonged to his own community and same church, known to his father Thomas Philip and his mother Mariamma well. Mathematical tables were indigestible to Alex. In the classes the benches were arranged with sufficient gaps in between and the teachers could walk in between the rows easily, to see or supervise them. Kutty sir came to class ten minutes after his usual chit-chatting with a lady teacher, his face was gloomy, may be the result of an unsuccessful dating, students stood up in fear after seeing the cane in his hand. There was no good morning or good day in that village school, only sit down, stand up, turn left or turn right was a few English words used lavishly in side that Malayalam medium school.

Kutty, the primary teacher, young and handsome, wheatish with medium height was always in white shirt and white dhoti entered his class three with his thin long brown coloured special cane to scare his children. Students got up in fear.

"Sit down" he announced in his subdued tone and observed the students one by one to check whether they are in proper dress or to check what they are doing.

Some of them closed their books and kept their things in order on the floor and crossed their tiny hands in front and sat with their tightened lips in fear, except some good looking girls and the son of the school manager, Rohan. They were not afraid of him. They were his pets always.

"Sir Alex is prompting and helping others" said Rohan.

Kutty sir looked fiercely towards Alex and asked him to stand.

"You say the table of nine" Kutty turned towards the helper prompter.

Up to nine sevens Alexander Philip recited the table of nine without break and at nine eights he paused "nine eights are... he paused for a second".

"Nine eights are..?" this time it was Kutty who yelled.

"Nine eights are...? Say…" Again Kutty yelled.

Immediately Alex felt something hitting on his buttocks that radiate severe pain deep into his muscles. Again he felt the same hit, this time on another point slightly above the buttocks on his back.

"Nine eights are…? Say... says. He roared like a lion.

Because of his fear and pain on the buttocks he could not say anything or could not think properly. Painfully he was waiting in fear expecting the next slash from his dear teacher from behind. Immediately he felt that he was been dragged in to the centre of the class and now he is up in the air as the educator Kutty lifted the small boy with his left hand and hit him again and again on his thigh, buttocks and back with his right hand that was free.

Slash, slash, one after another. An old method to teach and tame the future citizens!! After receiving the PhD degree in science from, Dr.Ibid Hussain, member of planning Commission, India Dr. Alexander Philip remembered the cruel punishment he had received when he was a small child by the hands of half literate arrogant and foolish teacher teaching in primary classes who were mostly responsible for the drop outs in schools, who were responsible for the impairment in educational standards. He remembered them with contempt and hate. Crores of students might have left school only because of their teacher's cruelty and arrogance, he thought and bemoaned. He was happy to hear that now the Supreme Court has banned all corporal punishments in schools. *A teacher who cannot teach and control the students without using his cane or his hands is not a true teacher but a shame to educational system that mars the mental development of a child for ever and deserves to be sent to jail.*

Not all teachers at *Marakuzhy Primary School* were like Mr.Kutty. One more frustrated teacher called Nair also was of the same kind. All others were kind and helpful. Even the headmaster was a kind old gentleman. He looked older even at the age of fifty. In later years Dr.Alexander Philip heard about the public outcry against those two teachers cruelty and people even organized public meeting to protest the cruelty of those two frustrated guys, but didn't hear anything about the action taken on them.

Mariamma Philip could not tolerate the thirteen lash marks on his son's tender skin. By evening the lash marks swollen up as blue lines. A time when teachers were considered as gods, Mariamma's protest or anger didn't get any momentum. Further neighbours warned her that Kutty may take further revenge and fail Alex. That fear proved true. Within a week's time the blue lines disappeared from his white tender skin of Alex, every one forgot about that incident. Though the lash marks were gone from the skin the marks were not gone from the mind of that child. That year Alex name was not found in the first promotion list to standard four. Alex's mother knew what to do. She went to Mr. Kutty's residence and handed over a green five rupees note to him. Though in the first list Alex's name was not figured in the result list in the 'final' list his name appeared. No one questioned Mr. Kutty. Not even the Headmaster. A dark age that gave full freedom to teacher gods to act as they like. When Alex secured a First class in standard ten, none of his class mates of standard three were not with him even to share the class. The Rohan the managers' son hardly got a pass class. Most of the children stopped schooling by four or five. The tall boy, Soman, whom Alexander helped in class three while telling the eighth's mathematical table and got severe punishment from the General Kutty, stopped his schooling in that year itself and started his own business of climbing coconut trees and areca nut trees and fashioned a life with that in the village Konni. Credit goes to 'general' Kutty and 'commander' Nair for improving drop outs, but they all got promotions and government salary and even pension.

# Chapter 6

Three hundred meters south of Eliyarackal Junction Dr.Shamsuddin established his small clinic. People had doubt about whether the doctor had any medical degree what he had written just after his name as a tail -BAMS. He treated for all diseases in the world. Nothing was impossible to him. Of course he served in the British army for some years and was working as a compounder or as a helper in the military hospital in Madras. When the proud British receded to England for a peaceful life without any Gandhi, Dr.Shamsuddin retreated to Eliyarackal for a livelihood, as an Ex- army Doctor. He did not hesitate to seize the old Royal Enfield bullet motor cycle from his white masters when they fled the country in disgrace. People respected him not because of his profession but because of his very attractive figure and also because of this Bullet Motor Cycle. His tall and handsome face was the talk of ladies in and around Eliyarackal junction.

Mothers used to persuade their children who refused to eat the un appetizing country food and say "look!! my son you should grow like Dr.Shamsuddin, tall and handsome!! Eat! Eat." Even Alexander Philip's mother had a habit of telling Dr.Shamsuddin's name in order to encourage him to eat when he refused. But Dr. Alexander never attained the physique of Dr. Shamsuddin at any time in his life; he remained as a lean thin person throughout his life. Dr. Shamsuddin's small country clinic with only two rooms was infamous but was useful to poor people in that locality. His clinic was behind a large bungalow that he rented for15 rupees for a month in the year 1960. The front room, that was made for a shop has no direct view from the main road and the shutters were made of strong wooden planks that could be removed individually to open it fully or partially. The central and the main plank of the shutter were kept above a groove in the main frame and this could be removed first after unlocking the shutter that was attached to other shutters by an iron bar. First the iron bar connecting the individual planks having small iron rings in the centre should be removed after unlocking the bar with a key and then the main and the central wooden plank could be removed by sliding it over the groove in the frame. Then the remaining work was easy, slowly move the individual planks horizontally over the wooden groove on the frame and when it reaches the centre it can be removed out one by one sliding over the central major groove. Since the wooden planks were very heavy only healthy and strong people could do the job easily. But the job was easily handled by the doctor himself because of his strong physique. Inside the consulting room there was a medium sized table in one corner covered by an old green cloth that was not washed for several months and over the table there were numerous glass bottles with solutions and pills of different colours. Dr. Shamsuddin sat behind this table on a wooden chair having a small cushion. Accumulated dust and cobwebs on the corners were easily noticeable. On the wall behind the doctor there was one calendar, a few cheap looking pictures of human anatomy used for students in class rooms and two clay models of deer heads painted in dull cream with black dots. In front of the Doctor there was a four feet long bench kept for the patients to sit. On one side there was a foldable cloth screen with rollers on the legs. The inside room is mainly meant for 'surgery' but actually only abortion patients are welcomed inside. A partially torn dirty curtain separated this 'operation theatre' and the front consulting room. He was the only doctor in that area self licensed for abortion. That was his main income. But people with other ailments also visited him.

Once Alex had a sore throat. He could not swallow anything. To treat his sore throat he went alone to Dr. Shamsuddin's clinic since the doctor was known to his father. The BAMS asked the little boy to open his mouth. Say "aah, aah" the doctor instructed.

Alex said 'Aah, Aah".

After an observation of his sore throat for one minute the doctor took one slender broom stick made out of a coconut leaf mid-rib and made one small bud out of cotton. Then he dipped the bud in a thin narrow bottle. The white cotton became purple. Again he asked Alex to open the mouth. Alex followed the instructions of the BAMS doctor obediently. While he was saying "Aah, aah, Aah the doctor inserted the cotton bud in to his opened mouth and applied the purple liquid on his throat. Again he dipped the bud into the purple solution and again rubbed it to the other side of his throat. Alexander felt a burning sensation inside the throat and when he breathed he felt a cold sensation inside his throat. He felt relieved and the pain subsided significantly. He was happy. The first encounter with Dr. Shamsuddin was satisfying and rewarding.

On another occasion after a few months he went to the doctor with another complaint. This time it was skin irritation behind his knee folding. Doctor was sitting behind the green cloth screen that hindered the direct view of the doctor from outside world.

"Turn back" the doctor ordered the boy who was standing in front of him.

"Lift your knickers and show me where it is itching" he demanded again. The doctor examined the skin where Alex pointed out.

He felt the doctor's hand touching above the rashes. The doctor asked "Are you getting itching here?"

"No, it is there down behind the knee." Alexander responded.

"Okay… turn front" he demanded.

The doctor's investigation continued for quite some time with the same question and same answer.

The doctor stood up and opened one bottle and dipped one cotton bud made of coconut leaf mid rib into a pale cream coloured liquid and rubbed it on the knee folding of the both of legs. Alexander Philip now felt a burning sensation on his knee folding as if boiling oil fell on the skin. He looked at his leg and found the entire area became reddish.

"Is it burning?" The Doctor asked.

"Yaa… Yes, Yes", Alexander Philip answered in a painful voice. He started crying.

'Don't worry boy, it will be alright". The doctor consoled the crying boy. Alexander paid Rs.5 for burning his knee folding and with the paining knee folding he walked to his home. On the way he tried to look at his burning knee folding. It became more reddish. The next day the entire area became slightly dark and swollen as water started accumulating inside the burnt area. The terrible pain continued. Within a week time the entire area became a terrible looking wound that emits the sticky body fluid. Alexander Philip thought of visiting the doctor again. When the doctor saw this he did not utter a single word and he dipped a handmade cotton bud into one of the jar in front of him on the table and applied the solution similar to shining violet ink on the oozing wound that spread about more than three inches diameter on both the knee folding. Now the wound looks more horrible. But the indifferent Dr.Shamsuddin said it will be alright soon and the itching will not be repeated. He also said that was the only treatment for that type of itching. But the prophecy was wrong many layers of skin got affected because of the strong acid treatment and without proper follow up, the wound worsens further. Alexander Philip's ordeal continued for months.

In later ages, when Alexander became an adult he remembered his experience with that fake doctor who exploited his ignorance. He felt sorry for that adult community in his village for tolerating such a fake doctor for many years without any complaints.

# Chapter 7

The distance between Shamsuddin's, BAMS' clinic to KKNM high school was only three hundred meters. One cannot see the school building form the Eliyarackal junction but the name of the school that was written in black paint above the main

entrance was easily visible from there. One road from Kalleli
and Oottupara joins the main road at this Eliyarackal junction
near the peepal tree. This high school in that area with more
than one thousand students was on a hillside. One of the few
schools in Kerala that had a broadcasting system in late 1960s,
that worked for a few months or a few years. A school with a
reputation for not participating in politics or students strikes
for many years. However, a few would be future politicians
with aspirations to become future ministers tried to disturb
the peaceful atmosphere of the school once. The strike was
against the price hike of rice and other commodities-it was
against the government. As usual, after the lunch break high
school students assembled in front of the large peepal tree
where one man was making cotton sugar candy in open space
with his special machine. The man rotated the drum and put
some colour and some sugar crystals, inside; as the drum
moves the sugar transformed into a cottony mass that the man
collected at the tip of a long thin stick made out of bamboo,
and sold it to children. Alexander Philip saw the machine
that makes the cotton candy but could not buy that, he had
no money with him. He saw his friends eating the same. He
could taste the sweetness of the cotton candy after thirty years,
at the age of 43, when he visited a fair at Calcutta in front of
the Victoria Memorial along with his two children and his
brother's family. The sound of the fancy machine attracted
many children and a fat boy little taller than Alexander Philip
instigated students for strike. That boy was not a rowdy but a
good-looking smart boy of good manners. Though Alexander
had seen him on many occasions that fat boy was not a friend
of him and they never talked each other. From his external
features, like his expensive shirts and foot wears, Alex thought

he may be from a wealthy family. All of a sudden the fat boy who was standing under the peepal tree screamed at the top of his voice:

"*Vidyarthi aikam Zindabad*" (Victory for students' unity). His first lesson to become a political leader.

Some of the students repeated the same slogan. "*Vidyarthi aikam Zindabad*'.

The self styled leader raised his short flabby whitish hairless hand with a closed fist up in the air and screamed again with more vigor and passion:

"*Vidyarthi aikam… Zindabad*", while screaming his veins and the major blood vessels, the superior vena cava, on both the sides of his neck swells up. This time more and more students joined and followed their new leader. Now after three four outcry they attracted the attention of the passersby and also those who were sitting on the shops idly after their lunch, some with their newspapers some with their favorite beedy in their mouth. Mamachen the shopkeeper who sells the stationary items to students got up from his seat and looked at the shouting students with curiosity, a new development he thought in his mind. Now the number of students increased tremendously, the young leader's spirit also increased five folds, and he shouted with full strength:

"*Ari evide? thuni evede? parau, paru sarkare*"? (Where is rice? Where is cloth? You tell –the leaders) the followers repeated in their full voice as if they are angry with someone.

"*Ari evide? thuni evede? parau, paru sarkare?*" (Where is rice? Where is cloth? Say say you rulers).

Alexander Philip also joined the slogan shouting against the government. All these years they heard about the students' strikes all over the state of Kerala but never got a chance to participate in it. Immediately a red coloured government transport bus, mockingly people called it aana *vandi* (Elephant bus) because of elephant emblem on its side in red and yellow paint, reached the Eeliyarckal junction and the strikers moved in front of the bus and blocked its way and shouted with raised fists.

"*Eenquilab Zidabad, VidyarthiAikam Zindabad*"

"*Eenquilab Zidabad, VidyarthiAikam Zindabad*" the fellow students repeated with more vigor and energy.

"*Eenquilab Zidabad, VidyarthiAikam Zindabad*"

"*Ari evide? thuni evede? parau, paru sarkare*"

"*Ari evide? thuni evede? parau, paru sarkare*".

Students who were returning from their homes after the lunch and those who were playing "*Kudu Kudu*" and "*Kilithattu*" also joined the strike without knowing for what the strike was. The driver switched off the engine and smiled at the little innocent children with sympathy. He, a Marxist worker enjoyed the strike and supported the students' internally as he was getting some relief from his tiresome job.

At 2' o' clock when the school bell rang half of the children went back to their classes. However, Alexander Philip and his friend George continued to join the strike for another ten more minutes. George becomes a priest in later years. Though the road was blocked by the children, Dr.Shamsuddins' motor cycle found its way through the striking children. Students hauled at the fake doctor and called his nick name loudly to tease him. He ignored the screaming and proceeded through the sides as if he had not heard anything. Among the crowd he identified his patient Alexander and stared at him. Alexander pretended he had not seen him and looked at the opposite side of the road. He was afraid that this doctor may report about his involvement in the strike to his father Thomas Philip. So he wanted to escape from the gaze of the doctor, Shamsuddin. Some of the passengers alighted and requested the strikers to leave the bus, after a little argument the student leader allowed the bus to proceed. Now almost all students withdrawn their solidarity to strikers and ran to attend the classes. The student leader moved back near to the cotton candy maker and announced: "my dear friends tomorrow we will continue our strike... this is my plan" He paused for a moment and took a deep breath and coughed to clear his throat. Then he announced with confidence: "Tomorrow I am expecting many students from the neighboring schools from Konni town and they may join us... this is my plan... he continued while observing the facial expressions of his fellow beings. "Tomorrow soon after the school prayer and singing of our national anthem you all should boycott the classes, immediately after the national anthem I will shout "*Vidyarhti Aikam Zindabad*". Then you all should follow me and should repeat the slogan and should come out of the classes in masses. Now the number of strikers was reduced to nine and Alexander and George were there to give moral support to their leader. "Now you go, tomorrow we may meet" the leader assured and left to his class room. Thinking about the tomorrow's events and the strike Alexander Philip returned to his own class. George accompanied him.

Next day10.00 Am: The second bell rang as usual. The school prayer was broadcasted. All students were standing in their own classes. Alexander looked eagerly outside to see any movements are there at the veranda or in the school compound. He could not see a single sole wandering outside or any unusual sounds. Then he heard the announcement to start the national anthem. Along with the thousand children he also sang the national anthem. Alexander was eagerly waiting for the slogan, "*Vidyarhti Aikam Zindabad*' from the other classes. But a chilling silence was the answer. Not a single sole shouted, not even the yesterdays student leader from another higher class. Alexander wanted to meet the leader during the recess. He could not meet him. He was not seen in the school for another three days. Thus the strike died in the womb itself. The price of the rice remained the same. Some students remained in their classes, some with hungry stomach; some remained at their homes with no food to eat. Politicians did not do any wonder. The strike throughout Kerala did not help anyone but some student leaders emerged all of a sudden and some become ministers in Kerala, in later years of their life. Alexander got lost in thoughts and did not hear anything from George his friend. It took many years for Alex to realize the fact that the politicians are not working for the public but for themselves only to grab the public money and increase their assets. He was ashamed of himself for believing in student leaders who cheated the fellow friends on many occasions. He felt ashamed later for participating in that picketing at Eliyarackal junction at one occasion and also for shouting slogans through the streets of Konni town in another occasion, that also against the government policy. A slight wish to become a leader in politics was lying in the subconscious mind of 13 year old Alex while participating in that small strike. But later his father advised the need of financial support for any politicians' success and also informed him that a politician is a person with double standard who speaks one thing publically and does just opposite in actual practice and a sincere person has very little chance in politics. Though it was very difficult to understand the wisdom of his father at that time he decided to concentrate on his studies. His ambition to become an army man or a business man also turned down by his wise father. He advised his son to become a teacher just like many of his cousins since the money a teacher earns is 'pure' without any fraud and we need only that money he urged. Alexander Philip followed his fathers' advice.

Thomas Philip was happier than Alexander when his son got a first class at SSLC. Only three students got that award Alexander was one among them. Alexander himself calculated his own possible marks after the public examinations to check the possibility of getting a first class. Whenever he calculated there was a deficiency of three to four marks for a first class. But his examiners were more liberal than himself and he got five marks more than what he calculated and received a first class what he remembered with pride throughout his life. The student leader who was instigating him for joining the strike against government started a stationary shop in Konni town with the help of his father's blessings and joined in the process of *Bharat Nirman* by putting bricks after bricks one above the other and slowly he established his own empire with the help of local politicians' help. Alexander never visited him in his life though he passed in front of his stationary shops a hundred times.

A hundred kilometers away at Trivandrum city, the reporters of the leading news papers while searching the house of the first rank holder in that SSLC exam, at Poovanpara, five hundred meters away from Eliyarackal junction and KKNM High school, where Thomas Philip was running his grocery shop, an informer was send specially by the school Head master to announce the result of Alexander Philip, a day before the official announcement. Immediately after receiving the information, at about five thirty in the evening, Thomas Philip started to close his shop, two hours early than usual time. Simon's father who was sitting on an old bench made of mango tree wood of four foot length with a bend in the middle of it was requested by Thomas Philip to get up in order to keep the bench inside before locking the shop. Simon's father raised his head with doubt and asked "*Innentha nerathe?*" ee nerathe?'(Why are you closing the shop so early?)

A smile of pride appeared slowly on the face of Thomas Philip. A smile of pride mixed with satisfaction. A rare of rarest smile that was unusual on the gloomy face of Thomas Philip emitted and while smiling he announced.

"See... He passed SSLC... with first class"

"Who?"

"My son, Alex" "Ooo, good, First Class?"... Very good, very good" Simon's father appreciated the news. "So?" He asked.

"Going to pass the message to him, now" Thomas Philip said. "Hi, Joshua, you heard what did he say? "His son got a first class". "Then we will have party... to celebrate." Joshua responded casually.

Thomas Philip as usual did not answer anything when they say about party to celebrate it. He remained silent and was busy in closing his shop. He removed the heavy wooden shutters from the ceiling hooks one by one and closed the shop by fixing the paneled shutters in its place. The long ceiling hooks hit each other and made rhythmic sounds for some time. First, he joined all the shutters by passing an iron bar through the small strong hooks from inside. Then he locked the last wooden shutter from outside using a key. He checked once again by pulling strongly the last shutter to confirm that the lock is in position. He did not take his two feet long small baton and kerosene lantern today because of day light. He carried only the lunch box made of brass. On the way back to home he was planning for his future. He was thinking only about his son Alex. He dreamed of his son becoming a Doctor, establishing a clinic in Konni, marrying to a rich lady or sending him to USA. He dreamed of posh bungalow with fans and AC in all rooms and a new car to travel. Then he thought how to raise money for his sons education, college education was very costly especially for science that he learned from his elder son. There was no end for his thoughts. Different ideas reached his mind one after another. When thought about the financial implication he started worrying more. The excitement about his son's success in exam was short lived.

The life in college was not as he expected. The importance what he received in his school could not even be dreamed in a class of eighty to ninety students. He became one among the crowd. The lecturers were not friendly, but most of them were arrogant except a few. The college was just recovering from student turmoil against the strict authoritarianism of the young principal. Gradually Alexander Philip's outlook towards studies also changed. He could not understand most of the subject taught in a different language –English. The sudden change in medium, unfriendly community, rowdy students, and arrogant teachers changed his frame of mind and he began to revolt against the authority. He lost his interest in studies since his expectation about the college was entirely different. He hated his chemistry teacher and could not understand Physics fully, though he liked that subject. What he expected was freedom in doing the experiments, which was denied fully. He realised that there is a large gap in his knowledge and most of the basic concepts were not included in his school syllabus and that lacunae made his studies more and more difficult days after days. He lost his desire to become a doctor because of his poor percentage at the qualifying exam. The result made him almost mad for a week. He cursed himself. Neighbors wondered. Parents became frustrated. Alexander Philip had no answers. The only choice was go for graduation with life sciences, which he liked from the very early days. The results at graduation brought back his lost glory and again he was declared as a first class student. He liked his post graduation classes though he could not grasp Biochemistry and Biophysics. He spent most of his time in plant taxonomy, which many disliked, in his group. A very small group of nine students, most them spend the whole day in the Botany laboratory of Catholicate College Pathanamthitta, Kerala. What he had expected when he joined in college as a Std XI student -the freedom to experimentation- is materialized during his post graduation classes.

# Chapter 8

"My eyes are dim with childish tears,
My heart is idly stirred,
For the same sound is in my ears
Which in those days I heard"

William Wordsworth

That year cold was unbearable in Ooty especially for the village students. The hotel woodlands on the top of the hill could be seen from a distance. A group of eight students along with their professor was on their compulsory study tour. Alexander Philip noticed the large reception area of the hotel woodlands with huge brass pots with beautiful palm trees and other valuable paintings with curiosity. One attender was busy in cleaning the floor and dusting the furniture that was arranged elegantly in the lobby. Alexander and his friends moved towards the fireplace in one end of the reception room to warm up themselves while Prof. Ramaswamy was talking to the receptionist. The receptionist wore a dark grey woolen coat. All other employees were in warm clothes except Alexander and his friend Ravi. Both of them were shivering in cold that they never expected nor prepared for that, though Professor informed them in advance to carry warm clothes with them. Alexander looked at his own old clothes and felt little ashamed. He never had a pants or a woolen cloth to wear. He was in his dothi and shirt. The old completely torn sweater was borrowed from an ex-service man who settled in his own village Konni. When his friends and Professor reminded him of the severe cold in Ooty, he never expected such a cold climate. But on the previous day of the journey he began to hunt for a sweater. He had to satisfy with the old torn sweater from that ex-service man. Mariamma Philip could not tolerate the horrible smell of that olive green sweater that was not washed for two seasons at least. Against the owners wish she washed the heavy smelling sweater and given to her son. But now Alexander felt ashamed to expose his torn old sweater in front of his friends who were in expensive bright coloured new sweaters. An inferiority complex governed his pride and he preferred to remain away from his friends and moved to the fireplace along with his close friend who was also in the same boat. The receptionist handed over three keys 412, 413 and, 403. Professor Ramaswamy kept the key No. 403 and handed over the other two keys to Alexander, whom he trusted much. One room boy appeared and took charge of the Professors' luggage. Eight MSc. students followed him with their baggage in one hand and one wooden plant press in another hand.

Professor Ramaswamy hails from Hyderabad and he was a taxonomist. He loved plants than anything. The entire plant classification of Bentham and Hooker he chants like a Sanskrit shloka because of his vast experience in teaching the subject. However, his mannerisms were funny. As soon as he enters the class he pulls the small stand to one corner and supports his heavy body on the wall by keeping one foot on the wall while keeping both of his hands on the small stand in front of him, he likes to stand on his one leg for the entire period of one hour. His heavy obese body tilts towards the wall and his shoulder supports him on the wall. He was neither friendly to students nor angry. He talked only taxonomy in his class, no jokes, and no other casual talks. He recited the entire classification monotonously in a particular tone and pause. At times, he laughs showing the entire rows of teeth to students without much expression on his fat face. Though he knew the subject well he never tried to make his teaching attractive or interesting. While walking through the passage ways after every ten steps he stops and turns back to see what is happening behind, or to check anyone following him. No one knew what made the professor to act like that, but students were smart enough to make different stories about him. One such story says that his family members were killed by dacoits when he was in the village and in that fear he looked behind to see anybody was coming to attack him from behind. Another story goes like this: when he was young, he was attacked by dogs and in that fear; even now he is looking behind whether dogs are following him. The second story had some scientific background because whenever he turns back his hands tries to protect his private parts with one hand in fear.

Like a very small political procession, the eight MSc students followed this funny professor without making any noise. Alexander Philip walked behind and he was moving little away from his friends because of his shabby dhoti and olive green army sweater. His jaws started trembling though he tried to control it. The procession now reached near a lift and half of the students with the leader professor entered and moved to fourth floor. When the lift reached the ground floor, again Alexander was surprised to see Neeta along with the room boy.

"I forgot my press," Neeta said.

"It is here, I was about to bring it up" Alexander said. Their eyes clashed and they smiled. "No sweater?" she enquired. Alexander blushed in shame. "Alex I will give my Jacket, a good one, I have another one in my bag, and I came down purposefully alone to tell you this." She looked directly into his eyes. Those eyes were telling more than what she said. Alexander hesitated to answer but he understood her concern about him.

"But Neeta...? Alexander paused without completing his words.

"What...?"

"But Neeta, he intermitted... what about Ravi?

"I Know, Alex, even Ravi has no sweater... I think I could arrange one for him also... We all girls brought spare jackets... but the parrot green Cashmere woolen jacket with red and golden embroidery that I'm giving should not be given to Ravi... Okay". While saying these three very soft fingers pinched Alexander's cheek and she smiled and her face crimsoned.

Alexander looked around to check anyone was noticing them. The room boy had already left. An unusual feeling and fear wrapped him; he felt his heart was beating faster than before but he could not utter a word. First time in his life, a girl touched his body with love. When she pinched his cheeks with an unusual childish smile, he felt as if an electric spark was passing over his entire body. "That is for you... only for you... you can keep it," She again said in a loving voice with a naughty wink.

Neeta was of medium height with a very beautiful body with perfect curves similar to imaginary pictures that anyone appreciates. She was the only daughter of a bank officer who was working abroad. She was staying with her grandparents. Most of her life was in the hostel from very tender age of ten or twelve. In various schools, she studied and shifted from hostel to hostel. Her attachments to parents were unpleasant and cold. However, she has everything in life, but was depressed and was sad.

Again, the lift moved up and stopped at the fourth floor.

In the fourth floor the students gathered near to room number 403. Professor Ramaswamy was giving instructions to students "After the breakfast exactly at 11.30 we will go for plant collection. Mr. Natarajan will be our guide and he will identify the plants for us. Bring your knife, plant press, old newspapers, spirit and mercuric chloride, formalin and plastic bags for plant collection and preservation." He briefed and went to his room.

During the breakfast Neeta took a seat very near to Alexander and sat across to him and handed a plastic bag to him and said slowly in her naughty low voice "green for you". Alexander noticed her bright face become radiant while telling that and her dimple on the chin was prominent when she smiled. Alexander returned the gratitude in his usual smile and remained silent. Though he was not courageous enough to say thanks for the help openly, Neeta could read his gratitude from his eyes.

As programmed by the professor Ramaswamy, the plant collection progressed. Nearly one hundred plants were collected from eighty families. Students wondered how Mr. Ntarajan identifies the plants with correctness. Neeta tried to move along with Alexander always. Alexander preferred to keep a distance. He was afraid because one of his friends was trying to take a permanent record of their movements by clicking photographs of them. While students were resting on the beautiful lawns in the evening, Neeta sat near to Alexander and asked, "Why my dear Alex you do not like me?"

Again, Alexander puzzled and remained calm without answering. He looked away as if he was watching some other tourists in the lake riding pedal boats. Slowly he raised his gaze from the boats in the lake and looked at Neeta and smiled first and then chuckled in a funny way and bit his lower lips to control the laugh. "What you think Neeta? How can I?"

"Means?"

"...Means how can I dislike you" Their gaze again clashed.

"Then you come and sit near to me little more... please."

"Why?'

"I want to talk to you... something more"

"I can hear you very well" Alexander replied.

"That is not, I want to sit very close to you" Neeta's face blushed and reddened while saying this.

When he changed his position, she said, "Look that rascal is coming with his camera, I hate him but he is after me, we will go somewhere else."

"Please don't move, Neeta, one snap please" in a teasing voice with cunningness in his eyes Suku shouted from a distance.

Immediately Neeta put her hand on the Shoulder of Alexander and posed for the photo". Okay you click now," she announced in a bold voice.

"We are going for boating." Suku announced.

"After boating, a horse ride" Neeta expressed her desire.

"Al right we will go for that" Suku agreed.

After the boat ride and horse ride all went to a common room where Natarajan was waiting for them. He helped the students in identifying the family and name of the plants. Natarajan raised one plant twig with flowers and fruits and asked the students to guess its family. Though most of the plants were unfamiliar to students, they could identify the genera and family with their external morphology. He gave one point for the correct answer. He also noted who identified the maximum plants. Next day again they went for plant collection and shopping. They also visited the nearby rose garden. The everlasting flowers were everywhere on the roadside. Thousands of bright yellow flowers added the beauty of the roads. For the evening tea, they again assembled in the restaurant. Most of them wanted to extend the tour one more day but professor did not agree with the students. On the final day evening, they had the campfire. Everyone sat in front of the bonfire and sang songs and danced. They ignored the falling snow. Natarajan invited Professor to announce the name of the best student taxonomist. He asked the students to name the best taxonomist among them. "Alexander Philip" They all said in one voice. Here are the points, the professor Ramaswamy stood up and read out the points scored by the students. Neeta, 13 pints, Suku 17 points, Ravi 14 points and Alexander Philip 24 points. "And the winner is... Alexander Philip." Professor announced briefly. Clapping followed. Everyone looked at Neeta since she was clapping continuously without knowing others paused a while ago. Neeta was the first one to come forward to congratulate Alexander Philip. Then Ravi shook hands with him. "Next generation Bentham and Hooker" Suku said mockingly and chuckled like a hen calling the chicks.

'Tomorrow we will say Good bye to the land of everlasting flowers." Ravi said without looking at anyone.

"Leaving behind some everlasting memories" one girl, said.

"... and some everlasting relationships" looking at Alexander Philip and Neeta; Suku said in a sarcastic tone and nictated.

Neeta shook her head in acceptance, whereas Alexander was impassive.

"He is hinting at us," Neeta murmured in the ears of Alexander.

Alexander was in deep thought and remained silent. After a pause he murmured softly and indistinctly into her eras "he may be proved wrong" and then he tightened his lips and smiled at her.

"I think he is perfectly right. You shut up" and she poked him with her elbow. A cynical smile was the reply. Alexander handed over a bunch of dried up everlasting flowers into the hands of Neeta and she accepted it with her both hands." Thank you" she said with very bright face with content and smiled. A sincere smile appeared slowly on her beautiful fat round face. As she smiled Alexander Philip noticed the prominent dimple on her both cheeks.

The next four months the romance between Alexander and Neeta grew deeper and deeper. Suku's comments were hurting but that indirectly gave some vigour to the growing relationship between them. In the beginning, Alexander was very unconcerned about the relationship since he knew that they are not a perfect match financially. Nevertheless, unknowingly he was dragged into that relationship and later he realised the need of the new friendship and found some different meaning of life. Both of them spent hours together in chatting and found joy and delight in being together. They discussed a lot on various issues whenever they were free. On many occasions Alexander wanted to return that Cashmere Wooleen jacket that he had accepted but always Neeta refused to accept it back and insisted to keep it with him. During preparatory holidays, Alexander went back to his home and Neeta remained in the hostel. Both of them felt loneliness at home and at hostel room. Both of them were lusting to see each other. Finally the most awaited exams begun. After every paper Alexander showed a dull face. None of the papers went smoothly as he expected. He was unhappy. Three of his friends decided to drop that exam before declaring the results and to appear for improvements. Alexander noticed some unusual developments in Neeta during the exam days. As usual she did not wait for Alexander to come out from the exam hall and to discuss the performance in the exam. She did not share anything about the exam to him. Head of the department approached the students on the last day of the practical examination and informed the desire of the External examiners to advance the Viva Voce for one day. Though they were not prepared for the viva voce professor Ramaswamy urged them for that and finally the viva started one day before against the schedule. Alexander Philip's presentation was excellent and he scored the maximum in that verbal exam. Neeta approached Alexander and they moved together towards her girls' hostel. She appears to be very sad and gloomy. They moved together without talking for few minutes. Alexander could sense the uneasiness in Neeta. Finally Alexander decided to break the silence.

"How was the Viva?" he asked. "It was Okay" She replied without much concern. "Shall we go to Canteen?" Without looking to his eyes she asked.

"What? My dear Neeta" Alexander asked while they were searching for a corner seat to occupy. A very few students were in that small college canteen. The canteen was near the students' mess hall of the college. It was a medium room with a few tables and folding chairs. Most of the steel chairs were old and rusted. They sat across and Neeta preferred a seat that no one could notice her easily. Her face was sad and strangely serious. Her eyes filled with tears while opening the hand bag and she pulled out a pretty cream envelope and handed over the same to Alexander with wavering hands. It was printed on the envelope in beautiful golden letters 'Invitation'. Alexander could judge the content inside. Without any hesitation or wavering he asked "Shall I open it?"

She kept her head down looking nowhere and wept without answering his question and tried to cover her face. There was an increase in moisture in her beautiful dark brown eyes. From her left eyes one drop of tears rolled over her pink cheeks and finally touched the corners of her thick lower lips and she felt the taste of her own folly.

"Calm down, calm down" Alexander tried to pacify her while trying to read the wedding invitation. He could not read the letters properly. He struggled to focus on the letters but everything appeared blurred in his eyes. Finally he wiped his own tears that developed involuntarily in his eyes with his bare fingers and tried to focus on the golden letters on the card. He realised that he himself is weeping and tried to press his lips together in an attempt to control his feelings. Slowly he took his white handkerchief from his left pocket of the newly stitched brown pants and tried to wipe out his own tears, but suddenly he handed over the same to Neeta who was on the brink of outburst. Without hesitation she accepted the offer and took the white kerchief and wiped her face and looked at Alexander with swollen eyes that were filled with tears again within seconds. Both of them could not speak for a few more minutes. Though the receptionists saw the scenes he was least bothered to notice them, for him it was a daily experience during the last days of every academic year in college.

"Would you come for my wedding? She asked in a trembling voice and extended her hands with the kerchief to return it. "Please keep it for yourself" he said firmly and continued "for the sweet memory of a... a... fri... end" the last word chocked in his throat and only a murmuring sound came out. Then he wiped again his wet eyes with his bare fingers. Then he supported his unshaved chin with his left hand and pulled out his little beard in deep thought. She made circles on the table top with her fingers without knowing what to say to her friend. After sitting some more time in silence both of them raised their head and looked each other. They stood up without ordering anything to drink or eat as usual. They started to walk towards Neeta's hostel through the very familiar road through which they walked together more than a hundred times sharing their feelings and sorrows.

"Neeta, when you will be leaving the hostel?"

"Tomorrow morning."

"Okay we will remain as friends for ever... that is enough."

"Alex, don't think I cheated you."

"I never thought like that Neeta... never ever."

"Please forgive me Alex" while sobbing she said.

"For what?"

"For betraying you."

"Neeta, you never cheated me nor betrayed me... I will remember you as my best and sincere friend" Alexander said emotionally.

"Would you please come for my wedding?" While sobbing she asked.

"It will be embarrassing for both of us, better to avoid such scenes, I hope you agree." "Shall I return the jacket tomorrow?" he asked her permission with little hesitation.

"No, Alex please doesn't" She earnestly pleaded.

"Please keep those everlasting flowers as my gift to you"

"Surely in my heart... you will be there as a best friend".

When they reached near the huge hostel gate, instead of waiting for awhile as usual, Alexander walked a little ahead and then looked behind and said "That is enough... it is time to say good bye now... I forgot to say, Neeta, next week I will be going to Goa, my cousin had called me... I have to find a job... that is important... say my best wishes to your better half... hope we will meet again... somewhere in life... just like we met two years ago... Good bye Neeta... my prayers... for a very happy married life". After saying this in firm but low voice he moved ahead without looking behind whether Neeta was there waiting for him or looking at him.

# Part Two

# Chapter 9

The white ambassador car bearing a small white script-THE SECRETARIAT-under the number plate in red background took a right turn at church square at Panaji and climbed the steep in third gear for about three hundred meters and suddenly the driver lowered the gear to second and made a sharp turn to left and again he drove three hundred meters on a narrow road in Altinho and halted in front of an old Portuguese building that was not white washed for many years. One lean and tall person of about 28 years alighted out of the car. The driver raised his hand and saluted the person alighted in respect and asked his permission to leave the place. The lean person waved his hand in response and the driver fired the engine and sped to the same direction from where it had come to tell the government official who was a friend of the tall lean person who alighted just now. In that large compound there were three two storied buildings having the height of a four storied, two buildings were parallel to each other, and the third oldest buildings was on one side. There was a cemented ground in front of these buildings. Many students were roaming here and there; some students were playing the shuttle cock without any net in between. Though the students did not pay any attention to the government car and the person alighted out of it the teachers who noticed the car from the secretariat took their duster and chalk in their hands and ran to their classes in a hurry thinking that some high officials from the secretariat has come to inspect the school. In 1980's the Lyceum-the only single school in Panaji that followed the CBSE syllabus and catered the educational needs of all the transferable central government employees including the defense personals, was under the personal interest of many high profile government officials, even the secretary of education often visited this institution and interacted with the teachers and attended the teachers meetings without prior information. So the sight of a government car that belonged to Alexander Philip's friend caused some nervousness in the minds of lethargic teachers.

"Someone from the secretariat" teachers murmured each other while they were moving to their classes in an unexceptional speed. Immediately some of them closed their thermos flask immediately and kept aside the half eaten *samosas* and *pav* on the table and took their muster roll of students, chalk and duster in their oily hands and ran towards the classrooms like a cervid run for their life when they spot wild cats in the jungle.

Alexander Philip asked to one of the students who were standing in the entrance: "Principals 'Office?"

The boy without opening his mouth pointed his finger to a distant board that prominently placed in front of one of rooms in a row "Principal". He walked hurriedly to that room. The school building was very old and was on its last legs. But the huge arch doors, beautifully carved wooden railings, on both sides of the broad wooden staircase to the first floor, glorified the impressive and grand architecture of the Portuguese era. Large spacious class rooms with a platform for teachers to stand and teach, broad verandas, high roof, broken benches, broken window panes, dusty corridors with full of cobwebs, attracted the attention of Alexander Philip. The principal's room was an old class room converted for that purpose still with that platform for teachers on one end was on the ground floor. A huge and beautifully polished table with 12 drawers on both sides with shining brass decorative handles was placed in one side of the Principal's room. Six chairs with high back rest with soft cushions were positioned in front of the principals table for visitors. The Vice principals' room was on the first floor where the staircase reaches. An old Piano dusted and partially damaged was kept in the vice principals' room. This room was with full of other unwanted materials. The huge and magnificent work tables in physics and chemistry laboratory were most uncommon in any of the recent modern colleges. The laboratory was sufficient for a first grade college but the maintenance was very pitiable and poor. The buildings and the laboratories were in ruins. The Physics and Chemistry laboratories were filled with full of various apparatus that Alexander Philip had never seen. He was informed that these apparatus were imported from Paris and other European countries and now the syllabus has been changed and these apparatus were of no use to the present system. "But it has educational values" He thought. Though the building was in the capital city, under feet of the ministers and high officials, the whole building was under mismanagement and negligence. The present administration failed to realize the need of preserving the heritage. Alexander Philip noticed the utter chaos and indiscipline in the school. Students were running helter-skelter. At first he thought it was recess, but soon he noticed some teachers are engaging their classes. Next to the Principals room there was another class room converted to an office. The Head clerk a gray haired stout man was sitting on the stage supposed for teachers to stand and teach, behind his files and typewriter. On one side of his big table there was a calculating machine as big as the typewriter. The head clerk turned the handle of the machine once and looked through his bifocals at the display that was moving slowly and again typed some numbers and again turned the handle and looked at the display and he entered the figure into his thick register and looked above his glass frame to all sides of the room to other members and again continued his work with the calculating machine. The machine squeaked again and again as he rotated the handle. His face was swollen and reddish with very serious expressions. Suddenly he stopped his work with the calculating machine and started typing a new letter or something. After placing the three carbon papers in its correct position in between the four thin typing papers he adjusted the space and started to type the Office Number on the right upper corner of the paper. He typed the first line and looked around through his bifocals to all corners of the room and to other LDC s working in that room with their files one foot below him, since he occupied the stage in the old class room, and immediately stopped his typing work and got up. He lifted a Four square cigarette packet from his shirt pocket and opened it and tapped the bottom of the packet with his right pointing finger, one single cigarette jumped out, and he pressed very mildly the packet with his left hand fingers to arrest the withdrawal of that jumped cigarette back into the packet, he took the single cigarette immediately with the other hand and kept the cigarette in the right corner of his mouth and went into deep thought and remained in that position with the unlighted cigarette in his mouth. Slowly he took out his match box from his pants pocket and lit his cigarette. Though he saw Alexander Philip he looked at the other side and continued to enjoy the puff from the four square.

"Excuse me" after waiting for some time Alexander Philip thought of interrupting the smoker.

The Head clerk looked at Alexander Philip with his burning eyes like a school master looking at children to make them obedient.

"May I meet the Principal?" Alexander Philip asked in a very low voice.

'Where?" "I can't see and I don't know." The Head clerk said with annoyance.

"Where?" He repeated with the same annoyance. "I want to see the Principal." Alexander Philip asked.

"Where is He?" the head clerk asked back.

"I'm asking you"

"I don't know"

"Who knows?"

"No one knows, may be in his cabin, if not there in the bath room, or might have gone for rounds; wait, he was there ten minutes ago." The head Clerk said finally.

Another junior clerk came near Alexander Philip and said to wait there and the Principal will be coming soon. The old Head clerk returned back to his table and started to turn the handle of the calculating machine with one hand and held the cigarette on the other hand.

After half an hour the principal's cabin was opened by an old peon and the principal entered in his cabin. He was medium sized and with dark complexion. But his lips were red and one side of the cheek was swollen and appeared uneven because of pan inside his mouth. Like a ruminate animal he was chewing something in his mouth occasionally. He wore a gray pants and white slack shirt. His face with number of small pox scars was Impassive and without any moustaches. He was unwilling to open his mouth because of the pan inside and the reddish saliva appeared on the corners of his mouth. He raised his lower chin to stop the flow of saliva outside and with difficulty asked in his north Indian village accent "Whhatt?"

Alexander Philip showed his appointment order. The Principal reluctantly took the typed paper in his hand while ruminating like a mountain goat and sat on his revolving chair and started rocking it. He read it twice. Again he rocked back and forth with great pride in his yellow eyes. In between he raised his gaze from the paper and looked at Alexander Philip like a police inspector looking at a criminal, who was standing in front of him. Alexander Philip noticed the up and down movement of the Adam's Apple of the person rocking back and forth continuously as he was swallowing the great red juice of the pan masala inside his mouth. A light smile gradually spread on his small pox scarred face and he immediately stopped rocking and stood up with the appointment order in his left hand and moved his body towards the window and kept his two fingers close to his lips and spat the left over blood coloured juice from his mouth forcefully like from a jet. Some fluid fell on the window grills and when he handed over the appointment letter from his left hand to his right hand two spots of red saliva printed on that paper. The principal was least bothered to notice the pan stained saliva on the appointment order and he returned the paper back to Alexander Philip and shook his head and said in a firm voice 'No.. no... no… You cannot join today... you are late I won't allow anyone to join in the afternoon" said he and went back to his chair and began to rock.

"Afternoon?" Alexander Philip asked doubtfully.

"Look at your watch?"

"10.45 am"

"But we start the school at 8.00 am and after the recess it is after noon for us, sorry Mr. Alexander, you cannot join today… you are late... thoo late… thoo late". He announced in his Bihari accent. He paused.

A senior Officer thus got the opportunity to show his power in front of a fresh appointee. Alexander Philip could not appreciate the wickedness of that senior Officer. But he remained silent and took his appointment Order back and returned without speaking a word. The Principal who was appointed through UPSC reservation quota was expressing his frustration and tribal abhorrence to others, thinking that Alexander Philip was a local candidate. Local powerful teachers were against him and his dirty manners. Some local teachers were from ancient and rich families. And some teachers were the wives of local business men and politicians who were reluctant to accept an outsider as the head of the Institution. So, on every issue they used to insult the principal and opposed him. In turn the Principal tried to show his power by harassing the teachers. Alexander Philip became a victim of that distress. The powerful local teachers jointly met the chief minister and requested for his transfer and that acquired momentum. The Principal also was worried about his immediate transfer within one year. Lack of experience in office procedure lost Alexander Philip two more working days and he returned home. Later the old laboratory Assistant informed the wickedness of the principal to the new entrant. And he lost continuity of service. He joined Goa Government service on a Monday Morning.

Students from all parts of the country were there in his class. Children of military officers, IAS officers, transferrable police officers and a few local students who did not get an admission in other colleges. They appreciated the young and energetic Biology teacher on the very first day. Though they found the thick and flat Malayalam accent of the new teacher little funny they liked his attitude and seriousness very much. The same was expressed by one of the parents- the Ophthalmic Professor of Medical College publically in the very next PTA meeting.

"Mr. Alexander, congratulations, the boys are very much happy with your teaching". The comment that he made publically planted the first seed of malice in the hearts of senior local teachers who never received any such commendation and approval from any parent teachers' organizations. A seed of jealousy malice and ethnic hatred slowly grown in the minds of Lyceum teachers against the Alien- Alexander Philip, that slowly grown as a large tree enough to kill him professionally in later years.

The chosen profession-teaching-he liked very much. He spent most of the time inside the Biology laboratory, his workplace. The Biology Lab was in the oldest building–a Portuguese mansion originally made for some Portuguese rulers or for their relative–was on the side of the road few yards away from the two parallel buildings. Down portion was occupied by a private college for its library and class rooms. The broad wooden staircase leads to the upper biology Lab. The Lyceum management, the government, rented a major portion of this building to a private college. Five rooms on the upper floor were ear marked for Lyceum: the Biology lab a nearby class room that could accommodate nearly forty students easily with teachers' plat form, a small corner room for std. XII science students, old lyceum library with Portuguese books, and a nearby school library that was later converted to a class room for lower classes. The corridors were lofty but with full of accumulated dusts and cobwebs. The stair case railings were made of beautifully carved wooden pieces that naughty children removed for fun one by one and sold to neighboring houses or agents for money. Decades of neglect and accumulated dust inside the biology lab were his prime concern. Rarely does he spend his time in teacher's room. He was busy in cleaning the laboratory himself. Sweepers did their routine ritual in few minutes allowing most of the dust and dirt in its place for gathering size and leave the place for chit chatting in another room earmarked for that. The pigeons, the earlier settlers, who settled on the roof for ages were another menace, their castings on the tables and their fallen feathers everywhere made the cleaning very difficult. The 150 years old wooden flooring started showing old age degeneration here and there in the form of holes and depressions and shake as people move on. One could see the down library and the book shelves through those holes and cracks. In his leisure time he cleaned the dusty apparatus, dusty faded models, human skeletons-one of a male and another of a female-both imported from Paris. While saying about the past glory of Lyceum, the old lab assistant's eyes glowed with pride. He was also disappointed with the pathetic condition of the rooms because of lethargic attitude of principals and authorities of new government. He was appointed as a peon in the early 1950s and later elevated to the post of lab assistant. He liked the office works than Lab assistant's job and spends most of the time in the school office while Alexander Philip was busy in cleaning the Lab. While working in the lab Alexander Philip noticed the different models of very old microscopes of various shapes and pattern kept in a large wooden cupboard with sliding doors. Most of them were unserviceable because of fungus on the lenses and were stored separately. An old rusted rotary microtome, more than hundred years old herbarium sheets, hundreds of teaching aids like beautiful charts of butterflies, insects, birds and animals were lying on the wooden floor half spoiled and eaten by termites. All those charts and other teaching aids were labeled in Portuguese, so it cannot be used directly without translation, Alexander Philip thought. From the Assistant he learned that all those overhead projectors and hundreds of glass slides were imported from Paris or from Lisbon. The lab assistant explained how to distinguish between a male and female skeleton from their external morphology and this knowledge was new to him. Alexander Philip found it very difficult to keep the things in order and maintain it due to lack of space and manpower. There were big models showing different systems of dissected frogs, earthworms, birds and snakes kept in large glass cases, some of the cases were broken, covered with dust and were lying here and there disorderly. Though smeared with dust all the models were of good condition even in1980s. Some of the life sized models of human beings showing internal organs, nervous system, muscular system were distorted or desecrated by the nearby commerce college students who shared a portion of the campus with Lyceum. One of the human models had a garland and another one had a national flag attached to its raised hand to make more funny and some had with moustaches drawn on. As days advanced, Alexander Philip witnessed those caged humans came out against their will through the broken cages, without hand, some without head, some without their internal organs and perished to mere broken pieces of plaster of Paris. Thus the students exhibited their talents and authorities exhibited their helplessness and apathy in preserving the heritage.

An eminent scientist from National Institute of Oceanography, a biologist, visited the school to inaugurate the Iris nature club and after seeing the Biology lab in ruins said he had never seen such beautiful teaching aids anywhere in India. He lamented to see the treasure in ruins and suggested to get help from the government to preserve the treasure. When the proposal to preserve the treasure through some government agencies and make a museum, reached the ears of the new principal, a tall bald headed aristocrat Brahmin, from the mouth of an alien, his eye brows raised up unusually with a number of folding on his forehead and he looked sternly and scornfully to the eyes of the outsider sitting in front of him and scratched his for head in confusion, but kept quiet. His ego got hurt. Alexander Philip who was sitting in front of the authority could not read the feelings and calculations going through the mind of his boss. But he learnt that the proposal had negative effect after few months.

Less than three months lapsed after the proposal for a museum in the premises of the new Lyceum, exactly 23 years after the liberation of Goapuri from Portuguese rule, two middle aged persons in their newly stitched dress stepped into the principal's office, with a charming face. Alexander Philip, who was practicing a rat dissection himself before a practical class, was summoned to the Brahmin principal by a messenger. Soon he entered the old cabin of the Principal and the two persons sitting in front of the Principal stretched their lips and struggled to smile and the Brahmin said immediately "Alexander, as you know we don't have geology as a subject and I knew there are numerous geology specimens are lying in your biology lab un attended... he paused for a while. "Sir they are our teaching aids, many are priceless fossils, very difficult to get it, and we have chapters on paleontology in Biology and it..." Alexander Philip could not complete the sentence before that the principal said "Please hand over that specimens to them, they are from a nearby college... and they may make use of them and we do not have any space to keep them or money to maintain it properly. After telling these few words he started to write something on the paper in front of him.

"Sir, I was trying to make a museum in our school out of it and I talked about that a few months ago..."

"Yes, Yes you were talking about that, I know, now you accompany them and hand over that specimens to them, and keep a list of materials handed over to them and get their signature on that paper and keep that with you in the laboratory file. He said in an authoritative tone. Reluctantly with broken heart he followed the two college professors and moved towards his biology lab. The two professors looked eagerly to the glass cases dumped on both sides of the class rooms with large models inside. They waited anxiously to enter the lab while Alexander Philip turned the keys slowly and reluctantly. As they entered inside two pigeons the 'earlier settlers' inside the lab before Alexander, flew away making sound with their flapping wings expressing their annoyance and irritation. A few new small soft feathers fell on the dissecting tables here and there. The professors looked at the dissected rat on the table and turned their face showing discomposure.

All the geology specimens and rare fossils were kept neatly in specially prepared thin drawers of a large cupboard and the microscopes were stored above in the same cupboard in shelves. Each of the geology specimens were kept in small cardboard boxes doubles the size of a match boxes with proper labeling name, place of collection, year of collection etc on the small box itself. All these boxes were arranged systematically inside the narrow drawers or racks in such way that while pulling the drawers one could see different specimens with their labels inside. The labeling was done by calligraphy in black ink. The hundred years old labels were intact but were written in Portuguese. The young lecturers appreciated the method of preservation and exhibition of the specimens.

"Well preserved and neatly arranged" one of them commented.

"Very good specimens" another one said.

"Look like these fossils are original samples-some ferns… isn't?"

"Lepidodendrales of Devonian era and conspicuous throughout Carboniferous, collected from coal mines, not a fern fossil… but ancestors of them "Alexander Philip corrected.

"Okay"

"What is that some snail shells? One of the professors asked after seeing a shining shell in the shelf.

"Nautilus —Cephalopod of the Indian and pacific ocean having a spiral shell with pale pearly partitions' Alexander Philip explained briefly.

"Another fossil "One of the professors took one piece of rock like plate and commented. "What?" He looked at Alexander Philip for answer.

"This is not a real fossil but a fossil imprint of Archaeopteryx a toothed primitive bird of the Jurassic period having long feathered tail and hollow bones, usually considered the most primitive of all birds" Alexander Philip paused.

"So you have good collection of fossils and rare stones from different parts of the world" really a treasure. Alexander Philip remained silent in protest and he did not express it to them, but the professors could realize that Alexander Philip is not interested in handing over the rare specimen to another institution.

"Shall we start?" the apparently junior one asked his senior. "But how?" the senior expressed his doubt and worry. "I have brought some gunny bags, it is in the vehicle, and I shall bring it' the junior walked towards their vehicle hurriedly while the senior was examining the rock samples himself. Alexander Philip went near to the dissected Rat for final work and flag labeled it neatly for students' reference.

Large gunny bags to transport 50 kg rice to grocery shops were arrived. One junior professor opened the mouth of the gunny bag and the senior professor emptied the centuries old rock samples well identified and labeled were transferred to the gunny bags like a labourer who collect metal or crushed gravel for concrete mixture for road asphalting. Alexander Philip noticed the foolish work of the professors who mixed up all well labeled and properly identified rock samples in to one gunny bag carelessly. Another drawer was opened and the content was again transferred to the same gunny bag and mixed all the samples of various places making it difficult to identify the place of collections later. Alexander Philip tried to keep mum for some time but he could not. He asked "Oh! You mixed up all the samples carelessly, how are you going to identify it?"

"We will identify it later and sort it out in our institution". One of the professors answered.

"Even the place of collection?" Alexander Philip.

The young professors gazed each other for answer "The place of collection is not important". One of them replied after a few seconds. "We know everything, we will identify it later." Senior professor said in a proud voice.

Alexander Philip knew that these professors who could not identify a real fossil from an imitation or imprint are not going to identify the century old rock samples easily. His question was never answered by the young college professors. Alexander Philip again asked "How would you remember the place of collection or the year of collection without the label? You have mixed up all samples and labels..? The intelligent young professors were silent for some time. They were fully engrossed in dumping the rock samples from different drawers to one rice bag just like a rag picker who collect the plastic bottles, nuts, nails, cycle tubes, stolen parts of parked vehicles, iron wires, aluminium wires in to their large plastic bags. Suddenly one of them smiled and said "Do you think that we are going to exhibit it in our institution?" In our institution we do not have enough chairs for us to sit. No drawers to exhibit these rock samples. Our principal instructed us to collect it and we are collecting it. We think it will remain in this gunny bag for another ten years and then the new authority will throw it out without knowing what it is… It is going to happen."

Alexander Philip was shocked to hear this. "Then… why are you taking this from here?" he asked with little annoyance. "That you may ask your Principal" At present we do not have any infrastructure to keep it. We will ask for funds and if we get funds we may exhibit it otherwise throw it out after few years." The senior one said with aversion. "So you are destroying the priceless treasure of an institution" Alexander Philip said in irritation.

"Definitely"

"Why?"

"Ask your Principal that is better. Ask him why wanted to destroy this. We never knew that this rock collection was here with you, your principal asked us to remove these items from here". Young professor said in a defying tone.

Alexander Philip sighed and exhaled with deep thought. The bald headed tall Brahmins figure appeared in his mind. *"You're Principal asked us to remove these items from here"* The words of the young professor echoed in his ear drum. An unexplainable feeling of intense anger stormed into the blood stream of Alexander Philip. He stopped talking and continued with the flag labeling of the circulatory system of the dissected rat.

After filling four big gunny bags with fossils, rock pieces, mathematical models, and some antique collections the young professors approached Alexander Philip with a captivating face. One of them had the model of dinosaur in his hand.

Alexander Philip after controlling his repugnance tried to smile but the smile appeared only in one side of his face with a twisted lip movements from one corner of his mouth and said "Are you permitted to take all the things you like here" He asked with contempt. "This model of the dinosaur was made by me out of clay for an exhibition here few years ago. That you cannot take, if you have taken any biological specimens and models please keep it back, that DNA model also made by me with month's labor you cannot take that, that DNA model got state level prize even, I cannot depart that… that is precious to me… though not to my great Principal." He said scornfully.

One of the young professors responded immediately, "Sorry we do not know that… It looks very natural and we thought it is an imported model of Old Portuguese era. We thought of keeping it in our college show- case or in the Principals' room" He paused.` "Mr. Alexander this is only the beginning we will see that none of the Portuguese materials will remain in this institution and shortly we close down this institution permanently". His eyes were burning with hatred. He continued "Why should we preserve the nasty feelings of old Portuguese now? He asked with burning eyes. "Do you know what they did to our ancestors? They destroyed our culture and introduced dirty European culture here. Why should we preserve their heritage?" We should destroy everything they made here like what they did in the past. They destroyed our temples and constructed Churches there. They made our fore- fathers slaves and forced them to work for the construction of those famous churches there in Old Goa. They are the memories of our ancestor's hard work and slavery not monuments of Portuguese era. We should destroy everything they left here not even the memory of them". He looked furiously to Alexander Philip.

The sudden outburst was unexpected and spontaneous. A group of people who conveniently tried to forget their origin and lineage are trying to distant themselves from the western culture now. Alexander Philip thought. Alexander Philip after a moment's thought replied "If the Portuguese has conquered your land it is only because of your ancestors fault. They never had any unity among themselves. How many of the Portuguese warriors came here then, one lakh? Fifty thousand? No. Only about four hundred soldiers in a small ship. Very well your ancestors could have defeated them if they had unity among themselves. But they welcomed them to settle the competition and rivalry among themselves. They used the black foreign gun powder to finish their own brother's life, thinking that the white skinned gods will rescue them in their danger. Yes they rescued them and like the camel in Arab's tent, devoured them later. Only your ancestors and their jealous rulers have to be blamed for the deterioration of your culture, not the foreigners. Had they stood together to fight a foreigner this would not have happened. Is the situation is better now? No. Go to an Indian restaurant in Goa, and wait for the waiter for giving an order, and if there is a foreigner the waiter serves the foreigner first and you get a third class treatment. Our people even today have a respect and adoration to the white skinned people. Now we lament about the deterioration of culture. Who promote drugs? Who encourages prostitution and kidnapping? Our so called corrupt leaders… the nation builders… builder politicians… drug mafia… sex mafia et al. Do you have any courage to fight these vices? Then please do not try to contempt the Portuguese for all vices. Portuguese were bad our people were worse."

One hamal came and the gunny bags with Portuguese treasures were dumped inside a small truck and the driver fired the engine and the treasure disappeared within seconds from that heritage building. Alexander Philip, the alien in the land of Sunaparanth, looked helplessly through the half grilled window of the Biology lab overlooking the Mandovi River. His dream to preserve the heritage of an old era dissolved in the jingoistic feeling of pseudo-patriotism. The slow death of the old lyceum started there. The suggestion to start a lyceum museum was not originated in the mind of Alexander Philip, but in the mind of his predecessor another Alien, having no hatred to a foreign rule. He wanted to keep that idea alive but burned in the fire of jingoism of new generation. Every politician wanted to grab the space for themselves and they allowed dying a prestigious institution for ever. Local students instigated by unscrupulous elements gradually removed the beautifully carved wooden railings of the stair case one by one and sold it to their agents. One night the entire wooden ceiling of the biology lab fell down exposing the old broken Manglorian tiles. The very old wooden planks could not support the weight of accumulated pigeon droppings of more than a century and it fell down right on the heavy tables below. It took more than a week to clear the droppings and no one replaced the fallen ceilings and it remained naked there exposing the moss covered tiles allowing the sun directly inside through small holes from the roof. The slow death of old lyceum, the fame of the east, got momentum. The protest of some heritage lovers fell in the deaf years of authorities. Finally the entire institution was extracted and dislodged by unethical dentists to a dust bin without trying any root canal treatment to preserve it.

Thus one and a half century old heritage institution was killed mercilessly by vultures and hyenas. Only the river Mandovi sobbed. The old patriarch of Asian education, the stalwart of yester years, the fame of Goapuri, died a miserable death. The last years were more pathetic, no one to care, no one to love or protect, spend most of the time in isolation and in utter pain remembering his old prestige and the present shame, sometime cursing himself, he spend his last days. Those who loved him were some helpless, powerless *'aliens'* and a few old teachers and some ex-students. The powerful sons that he taught ignored him at his old age and repudiated him and thrown him to hyenas and wolfs allowing to tear his flesh from the living body and remained as silent spectators when his eyes were pecked by the vultures. There was no official moaning. Deserted and forgotten by everyone the Lyceum's soul wandered here and there seeking a place to rest.

Was the killing of old lyceum revenge against the already left Portuguese? Who benefitted out of it? The octogenarian Lab Assistant who spends forty years in that prestigious institution wiped his wet eyes with his trembling hands when he heard about the death of the Patriarch-Lyceum. His own Lyceum. He wept along with Altinho and river Mandovi. Centuries of fame, decades of shame. Now no one will climb 150 steps to see that old patriarch's tomb there on that hill. The descendents of old Goapuri have no chance to know about that knowledge centre of the yester years, who only wanted to wipe out everything old and all the reminiscence of everything old - good or bad. It is easy to destroy difficult to build.

# Chapter 10

Dr. Alexander Philip reached in time. The institution was not unfamiliar to him. He served as a post graduate teacher in that Susegaad Higher Secondary for three years in the past. So it was not difficult for him to find out the place where he was supposed to sit as the head of the institution now. He reached his place. The word cabin was not appropriate for that soiled dirty, dull compartment. Above the broken door it was written 'PRINCIPAL' in white paint on an eighteen by four inch brown wooden plank. The door was opened. The room was with full of cob webs and dust. It was not swept or cleaned for months. The glass table top appeared brown due to dust and dirt. The old grimy executive chair with its faded torn fabric was looking at the new comer with an unfriendly gesture, as if he was not welcomed inside. The very old royal blue furnishing cloth once decorated the principals chair was almost spotted and mottled with dull mosaic appearance. The head rest of the executive chair had become black with constant imprint of cheap hair oil and sweat from many heads in the past. The fabrication and the rubber sponge on the one of the wooden hand rests were missing exposing the thin rusted iron bar support on one side. The Principal, Dr. Alexander Philip was reluctant to sit on that old dusty chair. He dragged a plastic chair with full of dirt and cleaned it with his own handkerchief and sat on that. He pressed the buzzer twice in anger, but there was no response at the other side. It was dead. It was already disconnected decisively to welcome the newly appointed Principal Dr. Alexander Philip. Wherever there were astute peons in Government institutions the buzzer won't work its full life. Many peons can't tolerate the noise pollution. He looked at the wall clock. The cream coloured clock supplied by the AIDS society of GOA informed him that the time as 7.45 am and it was the time for the second bell then. He looked at the very old curtains, stitched unevenly, never washed after installation, and fully crumbled was hanging on a jute thread like a thin bath towel. He noticed the broken window pane. The glass window pane was well protected by an outer covering of wire mesh. The wire mesh was rusted and broken in many places. The ground floor cabin of the principal was the target for any protest or disturbances in the school. Few years ago the Principal's cabin was put on fire at night by the angry members of Susegaad club and students. The Formica table top and the old curtains were completely burned. The watch man saw the burnt table on the very next day morning. After that incident the wire mesh was fixed on all ground floor rooms including office and library. The windows were never opened after that even on day time by the next principal. After that incident no head of the Institutions were dare to take any actions against any students or any of the Susegaad staff members. The ex principal changed his sitting position in fear of Susegaad club. He kept his chair near to the wall that no attack would come from behind.

Some schoolchildren were screaming and some of them were running helter shelter in front of his room. Some small children ventured to glimpse inside his cabin to see the new Principal's face. When he looked at them they chuckled and ran away. A moderately tall lean man in worn out Khaki uniform appeared.

The principal recognized him: The watchman.

"*Namaste sir.*" He greeted in Hindi in his Nepali accent.

"*Namaste*" The Principal greeted back.

"*Kaise hai aap*" *(How* are you sir*)* he enquired.

"*Teek hai*" (I'm good) Principal replied.

"*Peon log abhi tak aaya nai sir*" (peons are not yet arrived). He expressed his complaint. "*Hum chai peene bhahar gaya*". (I went out to drink tea).

The watchman was from Nepal. He joined the service many years back and serving in the same institution for more than twenty years now. Unlike other watchmen in service, he prefers to wear his Khaki uniform. He was proud to be a watchman and he was contented and was happy. The wall clock from AIDS society of Goa again warned him about the time for the second bell: 7.50 AM. By this time the watchman started to clean the dirt covered glass table top with another murky rag. The rag left its cloudy path wherever it visited. But better now. He moved his hand with the efficiency of a carpenter's plane. Now the dust and dirt spread all over the glass top giving it a dull design on the top.

"*Yey kappada achha nai sab*" (This cloth is not clean) the watchman complained with a remorse noticing the track of his rag all over the table top. He said that he was not given any new cloth to clean the table. In reality it was not the responsibility of the watchman to clean or sweep the Principals room. He had taken the responsibility himself since others were not seen. "*aap ek kam karo, thode se pani laker aavo*" (Please bring some water) Principal requested the watch man to bring some water.

"*Latha hai Saab*" The watch man disappeared to bring water. The principal noticed his devotion to duty and respect to others. He was from Nepal. His mother tongue was Nepali, he also learned Hindi as a foreign language like any other, but was sensible to use the words in right time. He never used the word '*Tu*' when he addressed to the principal or teachers. He knew when and where to use 'Tu' *Tum*' and *Aap*'. The culture of Kongvanas reflected even today in the local language. A language having no respect or proper grammar, the principal thought. The language is the yard stick of one's culture.

Time 8.am. The newly joined principal waited for half an hour to see any teacher or peons to come. As per the timing shown on the timetable kept under the glass table top of Principal, it was time to finish the morning Assembly.

Suddenly the school bell rang. The improvised bell made of broken railway track made its peculiar sound which was familiar to students. The School corridors, verandas and staircases became active. Like herds of wild sheep, students moved down the staircases. They were screaming and hauling to express their joy. They were high school and middle school children. The principal was in Charge of both high school and Higher Secondary sections. Many of the poor students dressed in the dirty oversized or undersized discarded uniforms of a nearby private school, which they might have got free of cost from their wealthy neighbors. Some wore the uniform without removing the neatly stitched school logo of that private school. Some students wore sandals; some wore broken worn out shoes, and some with bathroom chappels. A lean teacher who was moving here and there with a plastic whistle in his mouth was trying to control the unruly students. Some students listened to him others ridiculed him from behind. The principal recognized him as the Physical Education teacher because of his style of functioning and the plastic whistle in his mouth. Single handedly he was struggling to control about three hundred students. He was trying to keep the students in line and preparing them for the morning assembly. Since there was no space for the children to stand they stood like people waiting for railway tickets in a long queue at Victoria Terminus, Bombay. Along the long stretch of narrow space he ran up and down to control each and every student. Some were intentionally creating trouble for the Physical Education Teacher to see the fun when he shouts at them. A group of ten or twelve teachers were also enjoying the fun of the morning assembly by keeping their mouth shut as if they were spectators and not a part of that institution, and were standing in a line near to the office building. Finally with great struggle the students settled themselves in front of the old shabby looking school building. Though the uniform is Navy blue and white students were in different shades of blue and white. Some were in white shorts and white shirts of physical education day and some in full blue and very few in proper school uniform. The money and stipend given by the government for school uniform would have spent by their parents to buy cashew *fenny* or vegetables. Again they would appear in the same borrowed or gifted uniform from the neighboring schools. Teachers looked at the students with contempt because they were poor and ill mannered. Students saw teachers with hatred since they were unfriendly and harsh.

By that time the Headmistress arrived in beautiful apparel. Her face was with full of fear and anxiety. The teacher in charge of the assembly did her part honestly. Students sung the school prayer in different tunes and tones. The devotional song was started by a few in one end and like a wave it spread to other end in few seconds. In three different tunes the same song was sung. The third section finalized the song after five seconds and they themselves laughed when realized that the other end of the line already reached at the final stage. Immediately the PE teacher whistled and shouted "No laugh" No Noise". Students stopped laughing. The Headmistress stood in attention position without any movements exposing her freshly waxed wheat coloured fat shank. Her mind was flying at a distance. She did not see or heard anything. She was in deep meditation, like an Indian *sannayasini*.

Then immediately the student leader shouted in his full voice: ATTENTION; Pause: "*Pledge shuru karenge; shuru KAR.*" All the students stood in attention position and kept their right hand in a horizontal position just like pope blessing his audience. "India is my country; he paused and gave time for others to repeat. Three hundred children who were standing in different blessing positions because of lack of space repeated "India is my country". Again the leader shouted "All Indians are my brother and sister". The flock repeated the same error: "All Indians are my brother and sister" "I love my country"… I love my country… and the great Indian pledge continued. In between the leader lost his memory and hesitated to continue. One teacher prompted the next word in his ear. The leader continued. The school assembly ended with national anthem.

"See the eyes of PT" One student commented. "He is struggling to stand straight" Another one said.

"Yesterday I saw them in the bar" another student said

"Where?"

"In Jesus Bar, Gama".

Jesus is a nearby bar. As a rule there should not be any bars within a radius of 300 meters of religious places and Schools. But there are at least thirteen bars near to Susegaad Higher secondary School. Most of the teachers won't visit bars during the school hours. Who could control them after office hours? Non-veg are available only in bars. Teachers cannot be blamed fully. Students are satisfied with 'Star gutka', 'GOA', 'pan parag' and other tobacco produce of India. Parents supply them at home or they rob parents' money to buy tobacco products within school premises. Some traditional vendors along with other eatable items sell all tobacco products to school children without any hesitation. At home along with parents they eat the same. Till recently only higher secondary students were using hashish, brown sugar and marijuana but now even standard X students couldn't survive without that. The club Susegaad would supply all the needs of the students.

Principal returned to his dirty cabin. He did not address the students. He was not happy with the assembly. He just attended the assembly. He did not want to interfere in the High School matters. From his cabin he could hear the sounds of hundreds of shoes and sandals climbing the stairs. There were sounds of shouting, shrieking, screaming and sounds of music on the corridors. The stinking smell of students' clothes that were not washed for many days mixed with the fresh smell of human sweat in the burning heat of the sun made Dr.

Alexander Philip nauseous throughout the day. The morning assembly had eaten up 10 minutes of the first period. Ten minutes late. The way a government school should function. Alexander Philip thought. Politicians and mass leaders always condemn the indiscipline in government offices. Bureaucrats and officials blame the politicians for the pitiable public administration. Criticism and condemnation went on for generations to generations and the state of affairs remained the same. If any officer was free of corruption he could not have survived in service long. The government officers are responsible for arranging money for the mass leaders for celebrating their birthdays and other selfish requirements. One chief minister was against teachers. He enjoyed blaming teachers for everything. But he never tried to study their problems or pretended to be ignorant like a hypocrite. Though the public noticed the deterioration of standard in government schools in Goa, the legislative assembly invented it in December. The politicians allowed death of the government schools for decades-a mercy killing, with the permission of the authorities. Those non patriotic DEOs or ADEIs who challenged the attempt of those mercy killings were demoted or transferred to distant places to teach them a lesson. Most politicians started their own schools in the vicinity of a Government schools in many places. They used their own government machinery to destroy their own schools. The patriotic politicians criticized the teachers in public meeting or whenever they got a chance. The authorities appointed only the members of the Susegaad club in government institutions. Recruitment rules (RR) and promotion rules were changed by every government to fill up the posts with the unqualified worthless Susegaad. An English graduate was compelled to teach Hindi or math, a science teacher was compelled to teach Social Science, Physical Education teachers were asked to teach math or science. For the sake of the job near their houses they taught the subjects that they did not know. Headmasters and principals struggled months together to make the time table without teachers. The schools waited for years to get one regular headmaster or a principal. The time tables in government schools were always incomplete and unsatisfactory. For the post of a single science teacher in a school there would be three or four science graduates appointed, but no language teacher. Department transferred the teachers recklessly in the middle of the academic year to satisfy the mass leaders and to please the members of the club Susegaad. Alexander Philip remembered the comments given by the apex court of the land: "Even God cannot save this country." After that many judges were caught red handed for accepting bribe or for their involvement in scams. What they commented was true.

Because of the unbearable noise from different classes even after the commencement of periods, Principal lifted himself from his plastic chair to get personal information and climbed the steps very carefully since in many places the steps were broken with loose floor tiles. The broken steps brought him on the first floor of the 20 years old building. The faded mosaic tiles looked like murky kadappa stones because of the dirt accumulated on it for the last several years. The floor was filled with chocolate wrappers, gutka covers, empty plastic wrappers of Lays & Kurkures and paper bits and bread pieces. The cement plaster of the passage walls were broken on several places and exposed the brown bricks here and there. The decolorized cheap cement paint was present only six feet and above because of the constant wear and tear on lower portion by students' activity. The wall decorations resemble the Khajrao temple arts of Madya Predesh. Some of the wall frescos were the replicas of the AIDS control palmlets. All corners of the stair cases were beautifully painted with pan dribbles contributed by visitor's students and sometimes teachers. 'Do Not Spit Here' computer print out notices were pasted here and there on the walls at a greater height to avoid the immediate attack of students. On the white washed roof there were the muddy imprints of foot balls.

Staff room looked like an ancient scrap yard. But teachers were in the mood of morning party. Some of them were slowly sipping hot coffee from their personal thermos flask while they were earnestly listening to the gossip of others. When teachers were cracking jokes inside their staffroom students were breaking tube lights and desks in their class rooms. Headmistress in the nearby room pretends to be very busy in making substitution periods. She was fully engrossed in her work. She did not hear what was going on in the nearby scrap yard were teachers were sitting and enjoying their morning party. She did not see or notice anything special than any other day. As usual she did not attend the post assembly party in the staff room. She was sitting comfortably beside a completely rusted 30 years old Ricco cyclostyling machine. In her so called cabin in one corner there was a heap of old waste question papers and used carbon papers. The empty cyclostyling black ink tubes were lying in another corner. Now the laughing and chuckling sounds from the teacher's room reached its climax. With the hands locked behind his back the Principal stood silently in front of the door. All of a sudden a grave silence engulfed the staff room. Those who did not realize the reason for the sudden silence, raised their head like cattle and looked around with curiosity, and they saw a tall lean man with his hands locked behind standing straight in front of the door with cool expressionless face. Suddenly all were on their feet. They searched for their brown coloured students register. Some closed their flasks in a hurry. Some hid their half eaten samosa under their sari folds. All moved in hurry. No one talked. Principal Dr. Alexander Philip moved to one side to give way for the emerging teachers. He stood outside the staff room till all of them disappeared.

The very first day itself Principal Dr. Alexander Philip realized that the teachers and students were out of control and very modern. After seeing the corridors and walls he realized that instead of good habits students were under all vices. Most of the teachers were not interested in teaching. Most of them were the members of the infamous club Susegaad. Some of the teachers have criminal back ground. Most of them help the students in the examination halls. Many students were pan eaters. Even small children are addicts to gutka and other tobacco products in various names. The empty sachets were the evidences of all the vices here. The sweeper was irregular and not punctual. A very few teachers were interested in the wellbeing of the students and of the institution. The mere reason was most of the students were migrant labourers' children with no motivation to study.

# Chapter 11

That evening, exactly after one month, Dr. Alexander Philip took charge as the Principal of Susegaad Higher Secondary; the local unit of Susegaad club summoned an extra ordinary meeting at Hotel Sumitra, the infamous hotel. It was right on the shore on a rocky cliff. The heavy waves of Arabian Sea constantly hit the walls of the hotel and in rainy season the sea water even splashes inside the front rooms especially the conference room No.2. People book this room mainly to enjoy the sight of the sea; people get a feeling that they are right inside the sea in a modern ship. That day the reflection of the pale golden yellow moon light made the sea more beautiful. Through the glass window they could see the reflection of the beautiful Gama beach and the clear cloudless sky with twinkling stars. Inside the hall No.2 they could hear the sounds of waves hitting the nearby rocks.

Minguel De Silva, the unit president of Susegaad Club already booked conference room No.II in advance. He instructed the floor manager not to allow anybody inside other than Hassan the room attender. All the members of the club 'S' arrived after 10 Pm as instructed. At one end of the large oval shaped wooden table Minguel De Silva sat with a gauche face. On his right was Paulo de Silva, his brother and on his left the treasurer of the club Satoskar Dhume. On the eastern wall of the conference room there hanged a full sized photograph of a beautiful south Indian film actress. It appeared that she was looking at the members through her beautiful charming blue eyes and welcoming each and every one inside with her charming smile. There were two other erotic photographs of foreign models on the other walls. In candle light the members could not see each other fully. In that dim candle light the pictures appears more beautiful and sexy. Members were talking on various subjects of their own in low voice to each other. Hassan, the room attender entered the room with three full bottles of Teaches whisky, soda and ice cubes. He opened the bottles and poured it into nine whisky glasses kept on the wooden tray. Then he gently opened Alaska soda bottles and filled the glasses and served to the members with respect. Ice cubes were placed on the table at three different places for convenience.

"I think there will be a change in Ministers' portfolios soon". Satoskar Dhume said in his hoarse base voice.

"No... No... No... there will not be any portfolio changes now, the entire ministry may collapse. Otherwise you see." Minguel De Silva announced with confidence.

"Two members of the C D P may pull down the ministry, and they may soon join the congress, I heard from reliable sources" Paulo De Silva said in his soft voice. "What their demand was?" Satoskar Dhume interrupted in his hoarse base voice with curiosity.

"Ministerial berth, what else? Paulo De Silva. He laughed.

"But yesterday Chief Minister said in a TV interview that there was no threat for his ministry".

"Definitely there was threat, otherwise he might not have made such a comment, and he was worried" Paulo de Silva said.

"If a person says that he is not afraid of any one, is really afraid of others, it is quite common; it is a practice to cover up their fear. CM is definitely worried of his post, out of sheer fear he made that statement in front of the TV crew, to fool the people, common strategies of politicians, that's all." Paulo de Silva paused.

"Certainly CM was concerned very much, he was anxious, otherwise he would not had gone to Delhi two times in this week itself, surely he was under tremendous pressure, he knew that his seat was shaking, he was afraid." Minguel De Silva supported his brother Paulo de Silva

"Delhi Baboos advised him to negotiate, I'm sure he'll negotiate and his Ministry would survive at least this time, I'm sure." Satoskar Dhume said.

"Better he does, as we had demanded, better he include CDP in his ministry, if he negotiates he could continue as CM for few more months. Our club controls about ten members in the Assembly you know and we control the government at present." Commented the local unit president of the Club 'S' in an affirming tone.

"Better to say... continue as our faithful dog"... one of the members commented.

"A faithful dog of Delhi baboos... isn't it? Another commented.

They all laughed.

"CDP wanted Education" said Fillip Francisco Gomes.

"Education for Braganza Pereira? Xavier asked with inquisitiveness.

"He is illiterate. Isn't it?" Another member expressed his doubt in a very low voice.

"Who said he is illiterate?" Fillip Francisco Gomes. "We cannot say Braganza Pereira is illiterate" "He completed his primary education and passed standard fifth from Lyceum, Panaji. And a person who can put his signature in any of the Indian languages is considered as literate" while sipping his whisky he said.

"We can't blame the CM. How could he allot that portfolio to a person with meager education" Paulo de Silva expressed his personal view with little hesitation. He noticed the anger in eyes of his brother and hesitated suddenly.

Fillip Francisco Gomes continued "Mr.Paulo, there is no relationship between education and efficiency, and there is no relationship between education and corruption. All educated people are not efficient. All well educated people are not corruption free. Mr. Braganza Pereira may be a school dropout, he might not have university degree but he is a sensible man. He is far better than many educated ones."

Dhume who was listening to his friends and was silent for a while suddenly spoke, "Do you know my dear friends the Emperor Akbar, was illiterate but he was a great ruler at Delhi.

He did better than his educated father. We hope our Braganza Pereira would be a better Minister than his predecessors."

Then Hassan, the bar boy opened the door of the seminar room No.2. The room was filled with the smell of whiskey and cigarette smoke. He kept five plates of freshly fried chicken tikka on the oval seminar table and disappeared. The members of the S club, who were participating actively in political dialogue, were the teachers of Susegaad Higher secondary. They had a very important issue to be discussed and finalized on that day. Though many members knew that it was shameful that a state claiming 80% literacy could not produce an educated minister in Education, and the educated teachers are supporting the action for mere selfish motive. Their action was sheer dangerous and self-destruction, some members thought. But they were not allowed to criticize the policy of their organization, if they want to be inside. It was the decision of the 'S' club, to support the candidature of Braganza Pereira.

Immediately Minguel De Silva started to deliver his welcome speech. "Greetings, dear comrades," he smiled wickedly through the corners of his mouth, "today we have to make some important decisions which bothers us, it is not our job to teach the ministers, in our democracy, we the people will decide who should rule us, educated ones or illiterates, smugglers or criminals that we will decide. You just compare our state with other states, do you think that all ministers in north Indian states are well educated? You might have heard that a minister in Haryana studied to put her signature after winning the election and after getting the portfolio of a minister. This is our Goapuri; this is our beautiful Goa of club Susegaad, the land of sun, sand, sex and club S.

Minguel De Silva was a swarthy faced tall guy of about 40 years. He was the great great grandson of the Minguel

Custodio dos Silva, a hard core criminal. In 1714 Minguel Custodio was picked up a quarrel during the procession of three kings in Chandore. He was convicted and sentenced to 10 years imprisonment by the supreme senate of Goa High Court. All the descendants of senior Mingul Custodio dos were criminals. The father of Minguel De Silva, who was adopted by a wealthy family in Chandor, was in Portuguese jail for 6 years for stealing church property. He was released in the year 1959 when Minguel De Silva was two years old. Soon after the liberation of Goa from Portuguese his father managed to enroll himself in freedom fighters list. When he was in Portuguese jail he met some influential members of Susegaad club and made friendship with them. With help of those members he enlisted his name in the freedom fighters list. Till his death in 19... he and his family enjoyed all the benefits allotted by the Government. Only a very few senior members of Our Lady Bethlehem Church, Chan village knew that he enjoyed the government pension for stealing church property in 1950. Minguel de Silva junior who was a student of St. Mary's Institute Chan failed six times in SSC exams. His father then a politician and renowned freedom fighter through his influence arranged a SSC passing certificate for him. He joined ITI, and passed his diploma after several attempts. Soon he joined government service under freedom fighters quota. He joined as peon and later promoted as a lab assistant in Susegaad Higher Secondary School, He became an active member of club Susegaad and became the president of the local unit.

Minguel De Silva continued his talk "and now comrades, we are in grave danger. We have to say good bye to all our freedom that we were enjoying till one month back". "I don't know how far we will succeed in our attempt and activities. I'm talking about the Principal, Dr. Alexander Philip. I knew this man for the last few years now. He is famous for his discipline and hard work. Now you might have realized the suffocation as I realized it. No principals of this institution dared to check our office timings till date. All these years we were enjoying full freedom here. Within few days he may change the school timing and time table even. As you know we were preparing the time table for us for the last ten years now. No principals dared to question our time table till date. Now this, I say this "Ghatti" is trying to change everything. He found out that we were adjusting our periods. Mr. Shenai was reaching late. Ms.Correa Carvalho has to collect her son from RM every day. There are certain reasons for going early or coming late. If that Ghatti Principal insists to follow the timings some of us have to leave the job itself. For the convenience of every one we prepared the time table. Now we have to decide whether to act or suffer like slaves". He interrupted his emotional and instigating speech for a sip of Teachers whisky. He was angry. Members of the club Susegaad listened carefully to their leader.

Anand Shenai, the math teacher was worried about the changed time table now. Minguel De Silva had adjusted the periods for his convenience. The time table submitted to the Principals office was a forged one to fool the inspectors and authorities. Every day first two periods were made free for Anand Shenai and Minguel De Silva. Further he was not a Class Councilor. He had private tuitions in two big cities. His day starts at 5 a.m. in the morning at Madgao city. Every day exactly at 8.am. he finishes his private coaching at Madgao and travels 28 km by his Honda city luxury car to his work place at Vasco city. His driver takes only 35 minutes to reach his work place. His private tuition earned him more than one lakh rupees a month when the principal takes a meager twenty thousand a month as salary. Other colleagues looked at him with jealously since no teacher or even the principal could afford a personal vehicle with a driver, in 19--s. Anand Shenai takes little rest and sleeps for some time during his journey to Vasco. Every day he reached 45 minutes late. Since he was an active member of that powerful gang Susegaad, Principals and other teachers kept a blind eye towards that. Previous principal enjoyed a free luxury return trip every day at the expense of Anand Shenai. The principal saved Rs.450 per month on the bus fare and Anand Shenai made Rs.1, 00,000 per month from his private coaching. His public exam results were never more than 15 % for the last several years. He blamed the poor results on illiteracy of parents' and students' apathy towards learning. He was worried why this new principal Dr. Alexander Philip was so keen in improving the school discipline and results. Everybody knew that this Susegaad Higher Secondary was for the migrant labourers, fish vendors and poor out-siders. No one was keen on studies who take admission in this Higher Secondary because of its very bad reputation. No good students willfully joined that school. Locals knew that the school was under the control of the infamous club Susegaad and Andrew Akbar. No one was daring to question those two authorities.

Diago Dias was the accountant working in the office of the Susegaad Higher Secondary for the last several years. The years of familiarity with the local business establishments and shops he ran the office in his own way. His brother was the personal assistant of the Director of Education. An additional post created to please the Susegaad club. He had the first hand information about any development in the department and in the government offices regarding transfers, posting, promotions etc. He was an active member of the Susegaad. He worked as an informer to this club. Though he had attended the meeting called by Minguel De Silva, he kept quiet and did not open his mouth. He was not happy with the Principal Alexander Philip. He knew that he cannot manipulate the accounts if the principal continues. He knew that he cannot leave the office before time to collect his son from RM High School every day. He was frustrated with the strict time schedule of Dr. Alexander Philip.

"I don't like ghatis, I don't respect ghatis. All these ghatis were the product of our government policy; I blame our previous governments for allowing the intrusions of all ghatis in to our golden Goa." (Ghatti is a name given disrespectfully by the members of the Susegaad to all outsiders in Goa, those who came beyond the mountains). Minguel De Silva continued his instigating and provoking speech in order to develop hatred towards outsiders. "You can see in our government organizations all the important posts are occupied by the ghatis. We are still slaves of the outsiders. Our parents were the slaves of Portuguese, now we are the slaves of these ghatis". I will not tolerate it; our club will see that every ghatis will be thrown out of this state in few years. Our government made all the dirty South Indians and North Indians as our masters. "Bloody Indians" What identities do we have in our own land? One day we will become minority and they infiltrate in politics and they rule us." The same tribal fear of the proto australoids, kongvans and mundars returned into the blood streams of the Susegaad members. He continued "If we keep quite now, these outsiders will rule our state forever. We never are able to enjoy any freedom in our own land. We will pressurize the government to transfer this ghatti principal from our institution immediately. We have to find ways to throw him out". He stopped his brief talk.

Accountant Diago Carvlho lit his third cigarette and began to smoke. He kept the smoke in his lungs for a few seconds and said "We will wait for few more days, all our movements depends on the present developments in government and who will be the next education Minister."

"If Braganza Pereira won the battle I guarantee that I will throw out this ghatti principal within three days" Minguel De Silva announced in a reassuring voice. "And I will see that no regular principals will be appointed here. We shall ask to maintain the present status with in- charge principal in this institution. And we, the club Susegaad will rule this institution as we did in the past." Minguel De Silva concluded. Members could sense the hatred in his words. Many could not justify the reason for the enmity and hatred between the principal and Minguel de Silva. But they kept quiet.

The midnight secret meeting went on till 2 AM in the morning. They have decided not to follow any instructions or any orders issued by the principal Alexander Philip. Minguel De Silva and his close aid Fillip Francisco Gomes agreed to create maximum trouble to the Principal by instigating students and parents. Accountant, Diago Carvalho was assigned the duty of meeting the Director of Education Dr. Maria, through his Brother. Paulo De Silva agreed to meet the 'Minister' in advance to brief the situation. Anand Shenai agreed to bribe all concerned Officers and the secretariat Staff to affect the transfer immediately. They also decided to publish one full page photographs with congratulations cum best wishes in all local dailies if Mr. Braganza Pereira won the game. The buffet table never seemed empty. By mid night everyone was high. There was a smell of marijuana in the room. A mixture of hash and tobacco were passed around. Members thanked the president and left. The last person to leave the hotel was the unit president of the club S. He slowly walked towards the nearby telephone booth. It was 2.30 in the morning.

# Chapter 12

*"The woods are lovely dark and deep*
*But I have promises to keep,*
*And miles to go before I sleep,*
*And miles to go before I sleep"*

by Robert Frost

Francisco Pacheco, the English language teacher was sitting in the staffroom on a broken Godrej armed chair without any back rest. The slender interlaced rattan strips of the chair were broken completely and were protruding out like the sharp erectile bristles of a porcupine. He was leaning towards the front table to support his fat body. He was sad and gloomy.

"Hi Pacheco, did you get firing today? Subaida the Hindi language teacher asked with curiosity after seeing the depressed Francisco in an off mood. However he did not respond as if he heard nothing. He was pretending. Again she asked "Are you not keeping well? He nodded his head.

"I heard that Principal observed your lesson today? Subaida Sheikh asked with more interest.

"Yes, he came to my class and sat. Let him observe. Who cares?" he briefed.

"Were you not in time?"

"No"

"Why?'

"I went out, and reached 10 minutes late"

"Did he ask you to sign the observation report?

"Yes"

"Did you sign?"

"No., I am not going to sign."

"That's brave. You did the right thing. You shouldn't sign." She instigated him.

The Hindi language teacher was under suspension for six months. She joined recently. A criminal case was filed against her by the Exam Malpractice Committee. She had reduced the marks of hundreds of students intentionally. She would not have been caught if the doctor couples had not verified the answer book of their daughter. They found their daughters' answers were miserably manipulated by the examiner without any apparent reason. The child found that her answers were made wrong only to reduce her marks. The examiner put unnecessary full stops, comas here and there and put red marks on the paper and reduced her marks. She actually lost 20 marks in the SSC public examination. The parents' complaints were not considered at the first instance. But later Chairman was convinced. He examined more than 100 papers valued by Subaida and found the same error in almost all answer papers. She had reduced the marks of hundreds of students and failed many good students without any apparent reason. She was called by the authorities and she agreed her mistakes in front of the committee. She told the committee that her own daughter who was weak in her studies eloped with her boyfriend and got married without her consent. In utter frustration she decided that no one would get better marks than her daughter. She agreed that she had reduced the marks of hundreds of students in utter frustration about her daughter. The reason was not acceptable to the committee and they recommended her suspension and removal from service. The department reluctantly suspended her from service and appointed one committee to probe the case. Since she was a secret member of Club Susegaad their members jumped into action to protect her. They suggested the names of the most corrupted officers of the Education Department for the enquiry under the leadership of Adharma Pal, who himself was an active member of the Club. The enquiry committee unnecessarily delayed the enquiry beyond six months by asking various silly counter questions to the Malpractice Committee. After six months she joined her parent institution without any hesitation or guilt.

"There were only 15 students in the class. Others, about 20 were playing outside the class." Pacheco explained the situation to his friend and advisor Subaida "I do not know whether I was supposed to go and invite the students to attend the class. Any way I'm not going to do that even in future." He said with determination. "Further" he continued, "he blamed that since I was late to the class the students went out to play. I'm not agreeing with that. Only in this school students are undisciplined, if the teacher was late for a few minutes they go out and play and never return to class. We need a Principal who understands our problems. All the ghatis are given responsible posts and we are the victims." He expressed his discontent of working under an outsider principal. Subaida sheikh was listened each and every word of Pacheco and nodded her head in support.

Within few days Dr. Alexander Philip observed that the timetable placed under his glass top was a bogus one and the teachers were following their own time table for their own reasons and personal convenience. All the periods were cut shorted by five to ten minutes. Same subjects in two divisions were engaged by the same teacher at the same time, but shown as different periods to show inflated work load. Anand Shenai the mathematics teacher was free for first two periods continuously. He noticed that even though he was coming by his personal car he always reaches after 8.35 or after the first period. Correia Alfonzo Carvalho has no last two periods. He knew that every day she leaves the school by 12.00 noon and signs register on the next day. Minguel De Silva had only 12 hrs of lecture per week instead of minimum of 18 hrs. Vice Principal is not engaging any periods at all. He realized that the class rooms had the capacity of maximum sixty students but they were combining two divisions of forty students each without the knowledge of the Head of the Institution. Every alternate day's one teacher engages the classes and the other one gossip or roam. He knew that one Satoshkar Dume was in charge of the Timetable for several years. There were no regular Principals for the last five years and the teachers were not listening to the Vice Principal. Vice Principal only wanted to protect the nearby posting of her and was not interested in the administration of the school. She never asked the reasons for late coming to anyone. Actually she was angry with the department for the heavy work load for her in the absence of a Principal. She never knew that the corrupt officials in the department are allowing the mercy killing of Susegaad Higher Secondary School for their personal benefits. She did not know that a nearby private management wanted to start higher secondary division in their institution. As per rules they cannot start a Higher Secondary Section because of another Institution in the close vicinity. They contacted the Club S and bribed them to close down this Susegaad Higher Secondary School. Officers and Director of Education promised them to kill this institution within five years. Director of Education's Bank account increased by another two lakhs and Adharma Pal booked one three bed room flat in his drop out son's name in Panaji city. The Director of Education had written "Posting may be kept in abeyance." And there were no principals for Susegaad Higher Secondary for many years.

Principal Dr. Alexander Philip summoned for Satoshkar Dhume and asked to explain why two different time tables were followed and why a bogus time table was submitted to the Principal. He informed that there were some problems in the past and he could not feed the new time table in the computer and agreed to submit the new timetable with in few days' time. Principal pretended that he accepted and believed him. Later he called the Vice principal and discussed about the grave irregularity in the time table. She informed that Satoshkar Dhume was in charge of the Time Table and she never tried to verify it. She talked as if she was not interested in the entire issue. She could not give any clarifications in respect of the clashes in timetable. She refused to accept the fact that most of the teachers were irregular and late. Vice principal did not have any explanation regarding tutorials and remedial teaching. A register was maintained by the office to show the account of the tutorials and remedial teachings by individual teachers. But in reality there were no remedial teaching by most of the teachers. The register was maintained only to show the inspecting officers. The public examinations results were exceptionally low whereas the internal results were above 90 percent. He found no justifications for the very low public examination results since the neighboring schools have excellent result in previous years. This is how government destroying the future of thousands of students to protect the personal benefits of politicians and other clubs. Chauvinism, narrow mindedness, regionalism and nepotism were the reason behind the very pathetic condition of the government institutions, he thought.

Alexander Philip was distressed and he thought about his teachers, his poor students, and the very poor condition of the institution. Everything appeared in front of him as in a dream.

Minguel De Silva the gangster and the president of the club 'S' who hate the migrants, who combines his periods and make himself free from duty for most of the days for his club activities was a frustrated man now because he found it was difficult to run his extracurricular activities within the school hours because the Principal was present in the school always. The parallel administration that he was running through the S club with the help of politicians and the officials of the department got a severe blow now.

Anand Shenai, the millionaire, the most irregular post graduate teacher who was engaging in private coaching classes, without fear, was another threat to this institution. The vice principal was scared to the talk truth, and silently supporting all indiscipline in order to continue in the same place because of her personal problems. Subaida the one with despicable mind who destroyed the future of thousands of students, moving like an angel in public was another threat to this institution, he thought. Alexander Philip remembered the words of Robert Frost "The woods are lovely dark and deep, but I have promises to keep (to the public) and miles to go before I sleep, and miles to go before I sleep".

# Chapter 13

And Jesus fasted forty days and forty nights and afterwards the devil the tempter came to him and showed all kingdoms of the world and its glory. And he said to him "All these things I give you if you fall down and worship me."

Conference Room No.2. Hotel Sumitra The room was cleaned and decorated with imported orchid flowers from

Malaysia. An important event was about to happen. Susegaad members were moving here and there like wounded pigs. Minguel de Silva was waiting anxiously to receive the chief guest, Education minister. Fatima arrived in her Benz car accompanied by Dada Auguestino, her consigliore and Minguel de Silva welcomed her with a beautiful highly expensive imported bouquet with 21 yellow roses. The number 21 represented the strength of Susegaad in the legislative assembly. Minguel fell on her feet and expressed his respect and others followed him. Then the Director Maria came in her small Marti 800 that was making abnormal vibrating sound. People could not control their laugh by the sight of the red Maruti 800 fitted with illegal gas kit.

"For whom she is saving all her money?" Satoshkar Dume asked Ms.Correa Afonso Carvalho who was standing by his side. She smiled mockingly but did not open her mouth to tell her comments.

"She has put on weight these days" Paulo de Silva commented.

"It means she is eating well... and not starving and saving for future..." Anand Shenai, the tuition baron commented looking at Correa Alfonso who was still smiling mockingly.

"She is a living example of atavism, please note her features... look like her Kenyan ancestors... with..." Xavier De Sa could not complete his sentence, before that they saw Minguel and Satoshkar running towards the gate and they saw the Braganza Pereira's white car with red beacon and the CDP flag on the bonnet. Superintendent of police ran towards his official car and opened it for him and stood in attention and saluted him. About twenty police men, who arrested him six months ago for smuggling 300kg gold biscuits to Goa, stood in attention and saluted their criminal leader. Paulo De Silva cursed the very bad state affairs of his state, and failure of

democracy. Immediately Director rushed through the crowd
and wanted to show her face to the minister. She touched the
feet of her boss with an artificial respect and stood one foot
behind with a smile of inferiority complex on her face. She
remembered the words in the Bible –the devils' words to Jesus
Christ, - and after showing him all the kingdoms of the world
and their glory the devil said: "all these things I give you if you
fall down and worship me". She was under confusion, whether
to worship the corrupt minister or to live in dignity without
licking the boots of the wicked devils on earth. But the taste
for power over-powered the desire to live with dignity. She
surrendered all her dignity for false pride and fake dignity in
public life as the Director. A lifeless artificial smile without
any originality and showing unpleasant gestures while talking
was her weakness throughout her carrier. The minister looked
on his right and then left like bulbul jerking her head suddenly
and he raised his joined hands above his nose level to greet his
supporters. Minguel moved with his bouquet and followed the
minister behind along with the director like a fox following
the goat thinking that the large testicles of the goat may
fall down and he may get it for dinner. Others followed the
minister with one or the other memorandums, thinking that
the Braganza Pereira is the messiah to solve their problems.

Braganza Pereira was of short stature with little less than
five feet with well developed muscles like a karate fighter,
a thin awkward looking moustaches that projected out of
his thin sunken cheek, thin black hair of two centimeters
length cropped like an army petty officer, he had not made
any attempt to cover his baldness in front, exceptionally long
exposed incisors that gave him an appearance of a big rat with
bristles on both sides. The little crowd moved on both sides
of the pavement and the Minister moved like a joker looking
on both sides with a jerking movement like a bulbul and was

with an artificial smile on his rat face. Occasionally he waved his hand to his supporters and gestured something that no one could understand. With this stature no one could predict the fact that he is the sole father of nine small kids. As he entered the hall no 2 of the hotel Sumitra, some other members of the Susegaad who were sitting in the hall stood up and started to clap their hands, in order to show solidarity and support. Minister himself started to clap his hands while moving. He sat on a chair especially reserved for him. Fatima sat beside her cousin sister. Susegaad local president Minguel stood up for his introductory speech and welcome.

Respected... minister of Education, Mr. Braganza Pereira, respected madam, he looked at Fatima and bowed his head in respect, respected madam Director and my dear friends..., he started his speech. As you all know we arranged the party in honor of our new education minister... we are very happy that our member becomes a cabinet member and we are here to celebrate the same. In his speech he emphasized the need of changing the medium of instruction in schools and requested the minister to discontinue the grant in aid to English medium, schools. The matter was put for discussion.

One priest who attended the celebration in plain clothes expressed his view on English education. "Sir what I feel is our education should be in local language... the mother tongue... of our children... a language that our children can understand better... and if we are not giving proper value for our language, it will gradually die."

Braganza Pereira was sitting motion less supporting his head by his own small hand. He was thinking about his own children... all are in English medium schools... and they are doing well in school... but why these people are thinking differently he thought..."

Satoshkar Dume arose and said... there is one more reason... sir, now more than twenty five percent of our population is of outsiders, they do not want our local language... if we stop the grant in aid to English medium schools... naturally their migration in to our tiny state will definitely dwindle... otherwise, one day these migrants will outnumber us and we remain as a minority in our population. We should not allow this at any cost.

The same fear of Pharaoh against Israelis, the same fear of Dravidians against Aryans, the same fear of Portuguese against Muslims kindled in the minds of Susegaad and they tried to poison the public in order to have an upper hand in public.

"I do agree with Satoshkar, but what would happened to our children... what they would do with our local language... how do they compete with others?... in future we will be promoting and producing a population having no knowledge of international language?... are we in a position to provide jobs for all our students... what type of job they are expected to do with this local language? What type of higher education you will be able to provide them? For higher education is there any single text book in our language? Are there any text books of medicine, engineering or law in our language? Paulo de Silva asked to the members with anger.

Minguel de Silva looked at his brother with anger and resentment. There was silence for a few minutes. No one talked. All eyes were on Paulo De Silva. The silence was broken by Paulo de Silva himself." I have expressed my view, you may decide what you want, but think properly before we take a decision" he said affirmatively.

Director of Education wanted to say something but because of her shyness no voice came out through her mouth, except some gestures. She was struggling to express something but only her facial expressions changed in every few seconds, in between she tried to smile in vain. Others were waiting to hear from the Director's mouth. But after a few minutes' gesture and struggle she withdrew herself and looked down and remained silent without any confidence to speak.

By that time Hassan the steward showed his face and gestured and asked Minguel what to bring. He replied in gesture and Hassan disappeared and reappeared with a tray of drinks. All types of drinks were served.

"Don't feel shy to drink" Fatima advised her sister who was sitting beside her. "In Rome you behave like Romans". Reluctantly Director took a glass of beer and sipped little and kept it on the table.

"Do you think that if we stop all English medium schools' the inflow of migrants would be reduced?" Anand Shenai expressed his doubt while putting some ice cubes in to his whisky.

"I think the idea is not clear to our members, what Mr. Minguel de Silva said was, we will withdraw the grand in aids to English medium schools, and a number of private people will jump into action and they will start private English medium schools and they will be allowed to charge fees from their students. You know most of the migrants cannot afford the fees and they will be forced to leave the state, those who want education to their children... definitely there will be many... many will leave. I know". Adharma Pal paused after telling this and sipped another sip of whiskey mixed with cocaine.

Braganza Pereira who was whispering to Dessai who was sitting near to him shook his head in appreciation of Adharma Pal's comments and clapped his hands and said "he is intelligent, he is intelligent, good, the idea is good, and I think it will work partially. After telling this he started to adjust his bristles in position with his fingers and scratched his fore head.

A young swami in his red clothing and thick black whiskers who was sitting in a corner sipped his feni that was specially brought for him and kept the glass on the table without making any sound and cleared his throat in preparation to talk and finally said in Marathi "I have a different view, my friends, all our religious books are in Marathi or Samskritham and if the next generation is not studying Marathi they would not know what our great religion is, they may not show any interest in reading our Mahabharata or Ramayana and slowly our future generation will not have any knowledge or respect for our religion." He paused for a while giving time for others to think over it. He continued "I have attended this meeting only to convey our religious sentiments to you all, you should not forget that we are more than sixty percent of the population even now and without us no one can form a government here... you decide what you want... but we will show our strength during the next election." There was anger, frustration and a tone of challenge in his voice.

Members looked each other, no one talked for a few moments and the silence was broken by Adharma Pal. 'Swamiji, do you think that this government would take a decision against the sentiments of our great religion. No, never, they can't do that, but our present problem is outsiders, migrants who is proliferating in our state like crickets or locusts and one day we will become a minority without any voice in our own state... at any cost we have to protect our own interest, our own people's interest... Swamiji you don't worry we will revert our decision when the migrants leave our land forever..."

The priest who was attending the meeting frowned in disgust and thought in mind "Oh! Then that was the hidden agenda! We never envisioned this... Why this Adharma Pal who is not belonged to Goa talks like a... and confusing the things... he could not believe the intention of Adharma Pal."

The kitchen cabinet went on till mid night and members had enough time to express their views on medium of instruction in schools. The members were instructed not to reveal the informal decision to anyone outside.

Next month a number of prominent English medium schools in the city witnessed a decline in their enrolment. All prominent personalities' children including the ministers and local Susegaad member's children took leaving certificate from their school and informed the authorities that they are moving to other reputed English medium schools in Ooty, Kodaikanal, Chandigarh and Bangalore to pursue their education. Neither teachers nor the students realised what was the real reason for these mass movement of students from their schools. Every one guessed something new is going to take place, but no one was sure why this mass movement. Before the end of the school year in the month of February government announced their decision to withdraw the grants to all English medium schools in the state. Many patriots supported the government move without knowing what the real intention behind the decision was. They praised the new policy of the Government that encourages the local language and promotion of education in mother tongue. Thousands of migrants were forced to leave their children from the schools because of the heavy fees in English medium schools. The idea of Susegaad worked well. There was an emigration of new migrants from the state. They knew that the education in local language would spoil the future of their children. Husbands send their family to their own villages for the sake of their children's education. The very busy streets of Mongore, Varunapuri and Baina showed a deserted look. The streets looked empty without any roaming children who used to play cricket in the middle of the road unmindful of the traffic once. The trains were full of departing families moving away from their loved ones. Their families were separated. The poor labourer's wives sang songs of sorrow as they moved with heavy loads of household articles on their head and departed from their husbands who were serving Municipality for years. Thousands of small children followed their mothers with luggage on their head and tried to sing the same songs the elders sang.

The Susegaad members felt relieved when they saw the exodus of migrants in thousands from their land. Uncultured dirty creatures are gone, now we can walk freely of the roads, the dirty dark skinny boys are not there to play cricket in the middle of the road- they thought. Good they are going. Our land would be free from migrants they thought. As the migrants left their make shift tin homes in Mongore and other places, Minguel de Silva and his friends were planning another plot to put an end to their return again.

"Mongore slums are under fire" Alexander Philip heard someone shouting. He moved out of his room and saw bellows of smoke rising up in the air from Mongore slums. He heard the sounds of pitiful cry of some ladies still remaining inside their huts packing their things for the next train to Bangalore. They were unfortunate. Most of the men were out for work. Many accompanied their families to send them home. A handful of slum dwellers that were still in their huts could not fight the fire. They helplessly witnessed the fire engulfing their huts made of tin and rags to protect them from rain and sun. Alexander Philip saw one more shining thing, other than the black thick smoke moving up in the sky, a jet plane flying very low but above the bellows of smoke, the plane that was carrying the Prime Minister of India, who was on a visit to Goa on that fateful day. What he might had assumed when he saw the fire below on the ground. Never might he have assumed that their own countrymen are driving their brothers and sisters, their own country men are setting fire on their own neighbour's houses or huts, a valour they failed to show against their foreign invaders for centuries. He might have thought it as an accidental fire normally happens in crowded slums. Sometimes he might not have noticed that fire on the ground.

The streets of Goa looked neat without the dirty bloody migrants for few days. Jingoists and supporters scoffed for few more days. The municipal authorities found the increased garbage on their streets with no one to clean. The accumulated and decayed garbage made the streets dirty than ever. Locals refused to accept the scavenging work while passengers closed their nose to escape from the horrible smell of the decaying garbage dumped in one corner of the fish market for weeks together. Municipal authorities expressed their helplessness to remove the garbage from the streets. Builders found it difficult to complete their projects without labourers. An anarchy and chaos developed slowly. The Susegaad refused to take the responsibility. They withdrew themselves and went to hibernation

# Chapter 14

"Hit the iron when it is hot" Minguel de Silva said and smiled smugly.

"It is a matter of prestige. There is no meaning in waiting, we should act immediately" Satoshkar Dume backed his friend. His voice had a shade of revenge.

"I'm fed up under this ghatti. It is a matter of prestige." Francisco, the English language teacher who was under treatment for psychopath joined their comrades. In every summer when the heat of the sun becomes unbearable the behaviour of Fillip Francisco also becomes unbearable to students and others. He had a habit of stripping of students for fun in shadow of punishments. He selects only the poor students for this cruel ragging who could not defend themselves. He was warned by many principals against this cruel entertainment. The victims normally leave the school or their name appears in the list of drop outs soon. Even Principal Alexander Philip warned him against this action but he continued his hobby after closing the door from inside and resist to open it till he finish his "lessons." He claimed he wanted silence and full discipline while teaching.

The bar boy Hassan brought Teachers Whisky, soda and ice cubes.

"This is for the health of our ghatti Principal" After raising his glass in his right hand Minguel de Silva announced.

"This is for his transfer." Anand Shenai, the tuition baron hit his glass of whisky with Minguel and laughed wickedly.

"What Paulo? Why are you silent or are you not in favour of this idea?" Language teacher Francisco asked his friend who remained silent and did not participate in the comments.

Still he remained silent and only smiled while sipping his whisky.

"The question is whether you can do something on this?" asked Anand Shenai with little anxiousness.

"This is too much Mr. Anand" He said briefly and continued to smoke his cigarette.

"I think… Brother Paulo… has become a believer… a puritan… Christian" Xavier commented immediately. All of them laughed loudly.

Paulo De Silva did not laugh nor responded.

"What Paulo, can you present our demand to Mr. Braganza Pereira? Asked Shenai impatiently.

"Yes, yes, he will do, he is my brother" Minguel de Silva said affirmatively.

Paulo looked at his brother superciliously but nodded his head expressing his willingness to meet the Education Minister. After taking a full puff of smoke from his classic cigarette he released it bit by bit in the shape of 'O' as if he is relaxing and thinking seriously and after taking a mouthful of air and exhaling it he said "It will be done."

"What?" "What? They asked with curiosity.

"His transfer, Dr. Alexander Philip's transfer"

Everyone was thrilled to hear his comment and they clapped in appreciation.

"But... but... when brother Paulo?" Francisco asked enthusiastically.

"Within three months" he replied with composure.

"Three Months!!?" They wondered and looked each other in surprise.

"Code of conduct." Paulo said in a very low voice with confidence.

"Oh! Elections!! Did they announce it?" Minguel De Silva asked restlessly.

"By tomorrow they may announce it… and no transfers for the next three months… we have to wait" Paulo said.

"But you will do it. Isn't It?" Francisco said impatiently.

Paulo did not respond. He continued to smoke. After a few moments silence he said "I will recommend and he will be transferred to other place, but your problem will not be solved for ever… another person may come… and if he is worse than him what would happen?

"For that Mr. Paulo, we would suggest the name of Mr. Somnath Madkaikar as the Principal." Francisco suggested.

"If he is not ready to join?" Paulo raised his eyebrows in doubt.

"That part leaves it to me" Anand Shenai said with self-assurance. "I can persuade Mr. Madkaikar to join here, it will be beneficial to him, and he can hold two posts, an additional charge of this institution, for that he will agree."

"That is good, he may come here in Gama for three days in a week and three days at Madgao, and he could claim additional TA and DA from the department, since his headquarters are at Madgao, so I think he will agree." Satoshkar Dume said convincingly.

"Further he can roam wherever he wants, he could say he is at Madgao or at Gama, who knows where he is?" An additional benefit of the additional charge. Definitely he will agree." Fillip Francisco Gomes commented and smiled complacently through the corners of his mouth by distorting his lips.

There was complete silence for another two minutes. No one wanted to talk. "For your request I will do that... but one thing, you all should understand... there was no Principal for this institution for the last five years... and our institution became one of the nastiest institutions in our state. This Principal within a few months brought back the discipline and prestige to this Institution... that is a fact... you cannot deny that..." With little irritation Paulo de Silva completed his comments.

"For that... we will give him... a bouquet when he leaves" Said Xavier in a very funny tone and he laughed wickedly showing his exceptionally white beautiful teeth.

"But what about our freedom? What about his harassment to our club members?" One of the members asked.

"Freedom cannot be misused, what about the discipline? We sacrificed the discipline for our freedom... No decent parent would send their children to this institution... any result... actually we are ashamed to say that we are working here in this nasty Institution... we are responsible for it. Isn't it?" Paulo de Silva said with righteous anger.

"Then what I said is correct, cent percent correct!!" Our brother Paulo is a different man now, he becomes a prude" Xavier said sardonically and laughed.

"Please, Please do not pass comments, our aim is to protect our members..." Minguel said in an appeasing voice.

"Do you think only you could move matters? If you cannot, say that... I will do that... we also have connections. "Tuition Baron Shenai announced in a challenging voice. Then there was little commotion and noisy disturbance in the room, everyone started talking and no one was clear what others' were saying. Though Paulo de Silva was not favouring the principal others interpreted it in that direction and Paulo got confused. He thought in his mind: It will be better if the Principal is transferred out, after all he is an outsider and his friends won't allow him to work freely, always there will be clash from Susegaad. Finally he decided to satisfy his friends though his consciousness did not support the idea.

"So we have to wait for another three months" Francisco Gomes said in a very low voice.

"Yes, of course we have to wait" Paulo De Silva announced.

Anand Shenai wanted to say something but he paused in confusion. "Eight months!! "He repeated once again and lost in deep thought. What Mr.Shenai? What you want to say... complete it..." Xavier urged him to say.

"In eight months... he has enough time to change... the time table" Shenai said while yawning. "And if he changes the time table... he stopped for a while... I have to be in time...

and I cannot engage my classes… I have to apply for long leave… that is the only possibility."

"Even I have decided to apply for long leave… Extra Ordinary Leave" Minguel De Silva announced in frustration.

"How many periods do you have Mr. President?" Dume asked Minguel.

"Eleven actually and 21 in time table" Minguel said proudly.

"How many periods you allotted for The Principal?"

"Only 12" He laughed.

"You are great, you are great." Poor gatti did not realise it for the last one month."

"But don't think that you can enjoy fully when he is here."

"I shall get an order from the Department not to change the time table now that is the only solution" Minguel said with self satisfaction. Mr. Diago Dias Carvalho can do it for me. He is very close to the Director."

"I think Filipe Francisco Gomes will be very sad to say good bye to his boss"

Filipe smiled showing his uneven teeth. "Definitely I am going to miss him." He said and again smiled the same smile for few more seconds. Slowly he lifted his bear glass in his hand and stood up and sang:

"We shall overcome"

"We shall overcome"

"We shall overcome some day…"

Satoshkar Dume and Minguel Joined Filipe and Sung:

"Deep in my heart I do believe… we shall overcome some… day." Few more members joined the song in euphoria and danced around the table with the bear and whisky glasses in their hands but the words came out imprecisely and hazily because the alcohol started to act on their brain. With unsteady steps they sang and danced. Soon Minguel lifted the half eaten

Tandoori chicken along with the plate in his hand and sang again:

"Deep in my heart I do believe"

"I will throw him out one… day"

"His annul plan"

"His timetable"

"We will throw it out one day…"

"We will throw it out one daaaayyy."

After the dance one by one sat on their couch as they could not stand steady for long.

"You should find a reason for his transfer" Paulo de Silva requested to his friends.

"We will traaaap him; we need the help of Fatima." Minguel de Silva agreed to meet Fatima the sex mafia queen. Slowly they become silent and started to sleep on their couch. Hassan the bar boy came in and cleaned the room.

# Chapter 15

10th December 6.00 pm.

The students of Susegaad Higher Secondary were busy in organizing their school Annual Day. The freedom to wear their favorite coloured dresses on that special occasion made them happy and gleeful. All were in festival mood. The school compound resembled a February carnival festival. They put on their favorite coloured dresses which were forbidden for normal school days due to school uniform that was introduced recently. Most of the boys were in low waist jeans and coloured T shirts exposing the brands of their under wears and music was on their lips. Many were humming Hindi movie songs, they were moving in a group of three or four. Some wore their imported face mask, though not allowed, for fun and to cheat their friends and also carried expensive mobile phones in their hands. Many of the girls were in their borrowed saris. They looked funny but attractive. Many wore their sari in an awkward manner due to inexperience in wearing that six meters long printed multi coloured long cloth because of their very thin body. Their over sized blouses which they fastened on their bony frame work declared that they were not the real owners of that but were borrowed from someone having well developed body parts. Boys were running helter-skelter without any aim. Some were screaming. Some were dancing. Some of the volunteers were busy in arranging the chairs in a row inside the *panthal* covered with *shamyana*, some were busy in arranging the badges of the dignitaries and other guests, and some pretended that they were very busy. NCC cadets started polishing their old dusty black shoes in a hurry while their officer was shouting at them. They were getting ready as volunteers for the function. An air of joy and tension spread over the students and teachers. Various committees formed for the various functions were reviewing their activities. Reception committee, programme committee, discipline committee, refreshment committee, light and sounds committee were the five major committees formed for that School Annual Day function. Principal Dr. Alexander Philip was inside his cabin and was slightly worried about the function since it was the first such endeavour in this institution. He was not sure about the pace and efficiency of various committee in charges on various duties.

The principal sent a message with his peon to call the programme in charges for a meeting in his cabin. The meeting was informal and very brief. Now he has the first hand information regarding the programme and its final arrangement. The absence Mr. Minguel de Silvia, the in charge of light and sound was noticed by everyone and excused due to his preoccupation.

"Well, everything as per our plans, isn't it? Principal enquired.

After a silence of few seconds the in charges said in one voice "Yes, yes sir, we are moving as per our plans."

"Do we have generators, if the electric supply fails?" Principal expressed his doubt.

"Minguel might have made arrangements" Xavier said in a very low voice.

"Then shall I call the Chief Guest, we can start the function in time, it is getting dark. Principal motioned to the overall In-charge of the Programme committee Anand Shenai. He left the room and fired his corolla city and drove towards the guest house, where the Chief Guest was waiting.

The programme in charge gave instructions to the MC a XII standard girl, to give necessary announcements and instructions to the audience. Nearly 300 parents were waiting anxiously to witness the cultural programme and the prize distribution ceremony. All the front seats were kept for the distinguished guests. Student volunteers and NCC cadets were given the task of receiving the parents and for providing appropriate seats for them. They showed the particular seats reserved for the distinguished guests. Some parents and guests argued with the volunteers for better seats in the front row itself. Some parents complained of the dirty chairs given to them.

"See... how dusty it is... all the chairs are dirty, how you expect us to sit on these chairs" complained one of the stylish ladies in blue dress. The student volunteer ignored the complaint and moved to another corner to accommodate other parents who came late. The parent who complained took the envelope of her invitation card from her blue vanity bag and cleaned her chair herself. Others followed her example. Soon many vanity bags were opened and the husbands cleaned the chairs for their loved ones and threw out the dirtied envelops on the floor. The parents and guests were talking loudly to each other.

"Madam, would you please move to other nearby vacant seat?" Requested one gentle man who came late and looking for an accommodation. "In that case I have to clean all the chairs in this row, just now I cleaned this chair, she murmured, and stood up to give way for the late comer. The late comer took the advantage of the chance and moved in after rubbing his body against her bump. The lady did not show any hesitation and endorsed the act as an unavoidable evil. The gentle man looked around and saw an old associate sitting in the front row. He poked him from behind. In the dim light the man who was sitting in the front row could not recognize his old friend and showed an unfriendly face towards him. He turned his face away without smiling.

"Hello", he uttered in a female voice to attract the attention of his old associate. This time the old friend recognized him from his prominent female voice and smiled at him through the corners of his mouth, and didn't show any interest in further chat.

Time 7 pm. The chilling cold breeze was comfortable for some. Others could not enjoy it. They felt the cold and tried to protect their bare arms by clasping it together. Ladies in saris used it as a thin blanket and withdrawn themselves inside it like a tortoise, to beat the cold winter breeze. The winter sun had burned down in to the Arabian Sea nearly one hour before and it was dark outside the *panthal*. NCC volunteers were looking inside for vacant chairs and guiding the late comers to their seats. The sounds of murmuring voice from thousands of mouths made the air noisy. Parents and students were talking casual matters. Some talked about their sons and daughters who excelled in the exam, others talked about their naughty children who never bothered to study. The girl students were talking about their new dresses or about the brand of perfume or shampoos they use. "Oh, how nice to see your glowing hair, see mine it is so horrible and curly, I do not like my curly hair, I like straight hair as yours, boys are calling me bottle brush because of my hair style, I can't help it, what shall I do, Pleas… e." In a persuasive voice one XI standard student sought advice from her friend.

Suddenly the music stopped and the loud and lively announcement of the compere (MC) heard through the old Philips Ahuja sound box and that silenced the crowd for a moment.

"Dear parents and friends, please be seated and be calm", the MC paused for a moment to give time for her audience to respond. "Within a few minutes we will be starting our function and our chief guest has just arrived… all of you… please rise… and… give him… The MC could not complete the sentence. All of a sudden all the lights went off and there was complete darkness and the amplifier became silent and refused to obey. In that darkness the audience started murmuring once again. No one could hear what the announcer was saying. Sounds of shouting from the four corners could be heard. People saw electric sparks followed by bright light from the nearby green room. That was followed by a shrieking cry of a girl. No one understood what was happening. They were frightened by the sound and the girls' cry from the nearby room. Now they heard the cries of many students. Parents started to ascend from their seats. Principal's request for parents to be seated was not heard by any one in that commotion. In that darkness no one knew what to do. They could hear painful bitter cries of some girls for help. Some parents ran to that corner from where they heard the cry.

"Short circuit", "short circuit" somebody yelled. They saw some figures running here and there in that darkness. Frightened parents started moving out of the *panthal* in haste.

"Kidnappers" "Kidnappers" some boys and girls cried in a frightened voice. "Sir, Sir, they kidnapped some girls from the green room." Some boys screamed at the top of their voice. The parents saw the gradual spreading of fire from the side of the green room towards the stage. The participants in the programmes ran out of the green room in their costumes. A few fell on the floor in that stampede. Others stumped over them while running. Everywhere cries and commotion. Perplexed parents ran out of the cloth *shamyana panthal* with their life. They moved away to a safe distance from the burning *panthal*.

The Nepali watch man ran with a bucket of water towards the green room. Some parents brought small branches of the acacia trees to put out the fire. They banged against the fire with green branches.

"Move out" "move out" the crowd shouted at the children those who were standing near the stage.

"Children… Out… Out… Escape… fast… fast…" they shouted at the children. Frightened children ran out to a safer place and started crying after seeing the fire engulfing their stage and temporary green room. Some NCC cadets were seen helping their colleagues to escape. For them there was no caste, creed or religion. They helped every one. Girls those who escaped from the fire embraced themselves and cried. Many were weeping in despair and fear. They could not bear the sight of their burning stage; their costumes kept in the green room were slowly turned into ashes. Their long waited ambition to perform on the stage also turned into ashes. All their efforts of painful practices of more than a month time and energy gradually engulfed in that fire. The principal noticed the fire spreading to other parts of the *panthal*. The cold light wind of that winter evening spread the smell of burning plastic chairs in to the nostrils of the Principal Alexander Philip.

Soon some emergency lights were brought in and in that dim light the people could see the long black shadows of others on the brown muddy ground. Alexander Philip saw some dark shadows moving away from the green room then that moved across the ground and also heard a vanishing desperate shrieking cry of a girl in the air from a distant place.

"Wait," "Wait" someone said, "The light may come, please wait, doesn't be panic".

Some boys and teachers ran across the ground near to the origin of that desperate shrieking sound. In that darkness they could not understand what was happening. Everybody wanted to move away from the burning *panthal*. Through the smoke they saw a dark maruti van with open doors moving slowly with all lights off. Three men were carrying someone in their hands and trying to enter the slowly moving van through the widely opened doors.

"Idiot, you stop for one second" one of the men cried out at the driver while running slowly along with the moving vehicle with some heavy object in their hand and was struggling to enter the moving vehicle. The driver responded immediately and stopped the van for one second and the three men easily entered inside with their motionless prey in their hand.

'Bang' immediately the doors were shut and the engine roared and sped away into darkness.

The teachers who were looking at the roaring vehicle gazed suspiciously at each other.

"What... was... that? What were... they... carrying? One of the teachers enquired while running. He was gasping and struggled to complete the sentence.

"Look like... they were... carrying someone" another teacher commented while taking a deep breath.

"May be carrying someone to hospital" while panting another boy remarked.

"No man, I don't think they are taking someone to hospital. Their movements were suspicious. Something not expected happened". One of the teachers still gazing at the direction of the disappeared car commented.

Soon many anxious students gathered near the Principal and teachers and they enquired what happened. Neither the teachers nor the students were in a situation to give any authentic explanation. What some of the students said was that two people, one man and one lady, came near to the green room just before the announcements and asked for Ms.Rohini of std. XI. The man was tall and lean who wore a green T shirt; he was very fair and has blue eyes. Around the neck he wore a thick gold chain with a special locket of a small cross attached to an alphabet 'S'. His long hair was tied neatly to form a pony tail behind. His weird and wonderful face was calm and very friendly. He did not enter the green room but stood outside while the other stout lady entered the room and talked to that makeup man. The lady who appears to be in her late thirties was in full make up and was exceptionally beautiful and stout. She was in her tight fit jeans and very attractive. The makeup man talked to that lady as if they knew each other and was very friendly with her and they were talking about something that the students could not hear in that noise inside. She said that she want to pass some important message to Rohini. First Rohini puzzled and bewildered. Then she was informed that her father met with an accident a few minutes ago at the work site and was shifted to Medical College. She also informed that he was serious. She introduced herself as a social worker working among the destitute of Gama beach and she could take her to GMC hospital if she is willing to accompany her. She also informed Rohini that her mother accompanied her father and already left to GMC in an ambulance. After hearing the shocking news she cried bitterly and loudly and went with them crying. Immediately all the lights went off and we saw fire on the main switch board and we all cried loudly in fear. But one of our friends Alisha recognized one of the men who were standing outside as Andrew Akbar, but she was afraid to tell this fact perceptibly to Rohini then. Though Alisha showed some gestures to Rohini, warning her not to go with them she could not understand the meaning of the gestures in that confusion. Rohini was worried about her father and was crying without looking at us. Alisha did not get any time to stop Rohini from going with them. There was no light. We do not know what happened to Rohini after wards. When we realised that it was a trap laid by Andrew's group some of our boyfriends shouted "Kidnappers," "Kidnappers". But because of the explosion and fire nobody could hear what they were shouting.

After knowing this principal Alexander Philip becomes more worried. He had heard about Andrew Akbar and his activities, though he had never seen him personally. He guessed the gravity of this incident. Alexander Philip did not think much to waste the time. Immediately he dialed No.100 and 101. The police control room sent information to City police station immediately. Alexander Philip made many distress calls to No.100 and 101 and gave the full details of the incident. Fire tenders were called and the one fire engine reached the site after half an hour. They pumped water on the already burned plastic chairs and to the ashes of the cotton *shamyana*. Smell of burning plastic and dirty smoke refused to move from the premises for a long time.

There was no causality. Students those who suffered simple injuries were given first aid by the Physical Education teacher and other teachers. Teaches were afraid to comment anything of the incident. A sense of frustration and fear developed among them. Gradually parents took care of their own wards and moved to their own houses. The principal and a few teachers remained near the burned debris of their programme site. They did not talk each other. All were afraid to open their mouth. They witnessed the horrible site of the burned costumes, burned make ups, half burned books, bags, and smoke emitting from the plastic chairs.

The entire programme in charges stayed back in the premises of the school for many hours along with the principal to share their feelings and sympathy. They were waiting for the police to come and write the FIR about the incidents. Alexander Philip sat on a plastic chair near to the burned debris of the stage and could not speak a word. Some teachers and students were standing near to him. He was the one who concerned most. He thought in his mind: 'The programme has to be cancelled.' But he announced it has been postponed. Now there is no time and money to organise everything once again, he thought. The word cancelling will hurt the sentiments of children who worked for it, and spent hours and days for its preparation. He saw many students were crying and sniveling while they were talking each other. Teachers felt very bad about the entire episode. 'A very bad end, someone played mischief to spoil the programme. Teachers may tell the truth afterwards. Even students may reveal it in future. It is better to keep calm now, let the time cure it and bring out the truth.' He thought. He was more worried about the kidnapping incident. He knew that it was his responsibility to protect the children inside his compound. He failed to protect his students. What would be the fate of that poor girl? How shall she and her parents tolerate it? Where will be Rohini now? Poor helpless girl. How to tell her parents that her daughter has been taken away by a notorious gangster? Police is of no use to public. Can we blame the police? They are at the mercy of the corrupt politicians. They are for the political leaders' protection. Police is very indifferent and lethargic to all such incidents that affect the common man. They have no time or interest in solving the problems of poor people. After all what they get if they solve the problems of poor, or if they do something good to the society, nothing, no appreciation, only transfer to difficult stations. They are the real slaves of political bosses. The entire system is to protect the selfish leaders' egotistic motives and their properties. He lamented.

"Was it sabotage?" Finally Principal broke the silence and got up from his chair.

"I don't think" the overall programme in charge said without much concern.

"I had checked all the electrical connections twice, there were no fault" said the Light and sound in charge, Minguel de Silva.

"He cannot be wrong, he is an expert in all electrical connections and especially he works in the electrical lab" Aanad Shenai, the over all in- charge, supported him. He thought in his mind '*sometimes it happens when the head of the Institution is strict. You objected my private tuitions, you changed the time table and compelling us to take remedial classes, so what happened has to be tolerated silently and you are responsible for it*'.

Minguel de Silva thought in his mind. *"I expected at least some casualties, to teach this gatti a lesson. But in one way it was good, if there were causalities more investigations and more trouble. But what ever happened is sufficient and he deserves it."*

Principal noticed the indifference of Minguel De Silva in this incident. The three were moving in and around the stage and viewing the debris inside the completely burned green room.

"But Mr.Shenai, I heard the cry of some girls, they were screaming at the top of their voice, what happened?' Principal asked the programme in charge to know his version of the incident.

"They were frightened, sir." In a very artificial low voice Minguel de Silva replied though principal asked to Mr.Shenai.

"Was there any outsiders present inside the green room?" Alexander Philip asked suspiciously raising his eye brows and was trying to study the face of his light and sound in charge.

"Sir, Some parents were there dressing up their children, and one makeup man was also there inside the green room" one of the cultural committee member informed. The principal did not know that the so called parents were the members of the Susegaad members and the makeup man brought decisively to arrange the trouble.

"And you did not know anything about the Kidnapping?'

"No, I do not know about it" Minguel said as if he was unaware of that.

Principal looked at the face of Shenai and Minguel in that dim light to study their mind and suddenly said, "Mr.Minguel and Mr.Shenai, we have to report the kidnapping case to the police station without wasting time. Now it is already late the culprit should not escape. The person who kidnapped the girl, his height, body colour, the colour of his T shirt, the type of vehicle he used, the colour of the vehicle, the Number of persons involved etc. we know" he added. He himself wrote the complaint and handed it over to the senior most teacher and requested Shenai to accompany him to the police station.

"Now it is 11.p.m. I doubt somebody will be there to record the case, go fast "He said. Reluctantly Mr.Shenai took the senior teacher, Mr. J. Mishra, to the police station in his personal car. Minguel also accompanied him.

After half an hour a police man in uniform with red eyes stood in front of the Principal, who was still waiting near the incident site.

"Sir… Did you…. call…… the… police... Station" The bibulous police men asked the principal in a musical rhythm. With full anger Alexander Philip stared at the police man. I called upon the police station at 7.30 Pm. Now the kidnappers might have fled more than 60 kilometers or more now. Where were you? What are you going to do now?" Alexander Philip questioned the police man who was in a very shabby uniform. He looked like a security guard of some cheap organizations. The Principal could sense the smell of local *Urak* on him. While talking he was struggling to keep his leg steady on the floor and look like dancing in a rhythm.

"Kidnappers?" the police man uttered in shock.

"Yes, kidnappers, they kidnapped one of our students at 7.10 pm."

"Who Kidnapped?" The police man with little interest asked the Principal casually.

"Some people in a maruti van, I do not know them, but students said one Andrew Akbar" with aversion he answered.

"How many were there in the van?"

"I didn't count"

"Can you recognize them?"

"No"

"Then what I can do sir"

Abhorrence and contempt pumped into the Principal's head but he tried to control his anger. There is no use of talking to this man. He is not in his sense, he thought. I have to do something else. By this time he saw some more people coming towards him.

"Sir, Andrew and his group kidnapped our Rohini Kumari." They yelled. Principal was trying to console them. "Yes. I know." He said with a depressed tone. I called the police in time, he lamented but they send this man after four hours. He has no interest in this matter. I am trying to contact the station House Officer in person. He also called the student leader and whispered something in his ear.

Principal drove himself to the City Police Station with one of his lecturers. About fifty students followed his car in their motor bikes and bicycles. Without making any sound the students stood outside the police station and waited outside. The very small police station with few rooms and with no compound wall was dark. It looks like a haunted house with no ventilation or no proper lighting. Very old broken furniture of Portuguese era, dusty fans, broken floor tiles, heaps of dirty files on a few shelves and a few cane sticks in a wooden rack gave the police station a filthy and eerie look. One police man was sitting and sleeping in one corner of a dark room. Some street dogs were lying on the veranda. They did not show any type of response towards the visitors though they were conscious unlike the personal on duty. They had no enemy. Anyone who gives a piece of bread or left out bones or spines of fish was their masters. They do not want to displease anyone. Thieves, murderers and *baboos* were same to them. But they prefer the thieves since they give half of their jail food to them since they were not tasty or good for the standard of a criminal of reputation... The principal and his group were welcomed by this group of stray dogs. They stood up and wag their tails to establish a rapport to the visitors before writing the FIR. They knew who the real criminals are.

The presence of large number of students outside the police station premises put the Inspector nervous and suspicious. He rose on his feet along with his heavy pot belly. He tightened his brown belt and adjusted it properly to bring the buckle in the centre. He looked at the thin tall fragile figure in front of him. He looked up and saw the radiant face of the Principal Alexander Philip.

The principal introduced himself in his heavy Malayalam accent "I'm Alexander Philip, Principal, Susegaad Higher Secondary. I'm the person reported about the kidnapping of one of our students by some anti-social elements about four hours before." He paused for a moment.

"You are from?" the inspector interrupted in between.

"It is immaterial, I'm the Principal, Susegaad Higher Secondary". He briefed.

"What I mean is, Are you a?" the inspector while adjusting his bifocal on his round blunted nose with so many scars and pimples, asked.

"It is immaterial whether I'm a or b or a non…; I'm here to report the kidnapping."

"I know Mr. Principal, you have come to report the case, and I had already sent my constable to your institution to enquire and to report the truth about it." Soon after I receive his report I'll do whatever I could do." "Have patience… Have patience… that is good." You needn't have to waste your prized time to come over here to report it. We will inquire about it, don't worry. Really I appreciate your enthusiasm and interest in this matter. These days we never find sincere people like you. I heard a lot about you. Please sit down." He ordered for three cups of tea for the visitors.

While drinking tea the inspector again asked, "Are you from Kerala?

Alexander Philip nodded his head. "Yes", he said.

"Which part of Kerala?" he asked with curiosity.

"Central Travancore" He stopped.

Inspector realised that the Principal was not interested in his unfit time killing evading talk now. But without showing slightest indication that he had realised the temperament of the person sitting across him, he continued. "During the last summer holidays we were in Kerala for a short tour. We went to Thekkady wild life reserve forest; we could not make the boat trip, on that day all the boat trips were cancelled because of that tragic boat accident on the previous evening. We witnessed the tragedy, more than 60 people died in the lake. Only few foreigners escaped, they swam to the shore and saved their life. Most of them were from Hyderabad. Bad luck, what else to say."

"Yes, I saw the news", Alexander Philip said without showing much interest.

"What negligence from the Government's side. They gave license to a defective boat. Total corruption. Here in Goa really we are lucky. Our system is so effective and efficient. No such tragedy had been occurred or reported for last 50 years. But really I say the land is God's on country. Worth seeing. People are very good. Well educated but could not speak in English. What a funny situation, you might have noticed, Mr. Principal that here in Goa even the fisher folk could understand and speak English well. Any way we actually enjoyed the house boating through the Vembanad Lake." Inspector stopped for a moment.

Alexander Philip thought. Though he is from Kerala he had never enjoyed or realised the beauty of his own state, Kerala. He never had the experience of a house boat journey, through the beautiful Vembanad Lake nor even visited the wild life sanctuary at Thekkady of his own state. He repented for a moment then satisfied himself. No one could see or enjoy everything in this world. Either in his own state or in a foreign land. He knew that the inspector is buying time for the culprit and allowing them to escape. It is midnight, and Andrew might have crossed the border or may be hiding in one of the big hotels of some ministers or waiting for his master with his prey.

Suddenly as if from a shock he said abruptly "Sir, already five hours are passed, I'd reported the incident immediately after that unfortunate fire at about 7.00 PM. Can I expect any news from you? Do you know where the kidnappers are?"

See Mr. Principal, many things are not in our hand. In many instances though we know the culprit we cannot arrest them. The gangsters are closer to higher authority than us. You know it, why should I risk my life. In my capacity I'll help you. I shall inform the developments soon. Further, he continued, today was the birthday of our minister and he asked for all the police personals from here, we could not refuse. Actually at that time, I mean when you called, there were no one here in this station but were on special duty, at the Ministers residence. Our people enjoy that duty, it is party time for them, every one returned in inebriated state." The ASI stopped abruptly and thought himself whether he was supposed to say all these things to an outsider, when he is in the uniform.

"May I know whether the incident took place inside your compound or outside?" The police inspector gazed at the principal's worried face.

"Is that very important?" Principal queried in a curious tone.

"Yes, yes it is very very important. If the incident took place inside your compound, we cannot help much and it is the responsibility of your Institution to provide adequate safety to your students." Again in the same unemotional tone the Inspector said.

"Had it happened outside our compound…?" Principal

"Then it was a different issue. You need not worry much about all the happenings taking place on the public places. We are here to see such things. We are responsible for the safety of people and their property. We would investigate the matter professionally." Inspector looked down and buzzed for the constable.

Then Alexander Philip took an empty seat in front of the Inspector. He was angry with indignation. He looked to his side to see the face of his senior teacher and gestured him to occupy the other empty seat across. With hesitation he sat on the edge of the chair unwillingly. Alexander Philip could see the anguish in the eyes of his senior lecturer.

By this time the students who were waiting outside started shouting slogans.

"Arrest the kidnappers, arrest the kidnappers" they shouted.

"Bring Rohini, bring her immediately" they demanded.

The annoyed ASI looked suspiciously at the tall slim man sitting across him.

"Mr. Principal, I know how to deal with the crowds, I was in the chair for the last twenty five years. Tell your students to keep quiet or I'll make them quite. This is the police station. Not your dirty school." The ASI thundered in a bullying voice.

The senior teacher who was sitting on the edge of a rough wooden chair stood up automatically.

"Mr. Inspector please records my complaint first." Principal said in a firm voice without changing his stand. "You should register the case now, at this moment, otherwise I will be forced to complain against you for protecting criminals, and you are violating rules and the Supreme Court's recent directives. Do you understand?" Principal Alexander Philip shouted back at the same tone to the Inspector.

"An innocent girl was kidnapped in front of everyone, you knew that who was the culprit, and you were buying time for your muddy client, you have already given enough time for that goon to escape, where is the girl? Bring her immediately." Principal shouted in anger without fear. He always has that quality. The very strong moral courage and civic mentality developed from his early childhood days supported by the Syrian Christian religious back ground of his family and his early village life made him fearless. He always stayed fearless against all social injustice. He never had the fear to fight for the truth and the things that he considered correct. His fearlessness and straight forwardness were always wrongly interpreted as an arrogance or village roughness by his superiors including the Director of Education. But he never sacrificed his ethics in life for promotion or for getting cheap trivial popularity. Because of this nature he was always been harassed, penalised and shelved by his superiors. He could not stomach injustice.

The very firm stand of the Principal cooled down the temper of the ASI little bit. He returned to his wits. He lowered his voice and said "Please give your complaint in writing and we will nab the culprit immediately. We already gave the complaint, what else you want from us?' Shouted the Principal. He was not pleased with the promise of the ASI. He suspected the honesty of the police Officer. Alexander Philip and his teacher left the room slowly but the waiting students requested him to wait with them till they get some news from the police personals. He agreed. Principal and about fifty students sat on the veranda of the Police station for the rest of the night. The dirty benches were full of bedbugs and the air with thousands of mosquitoes. In a corner there was a burning tortoise mosquito coil ready to retire from service, the track of its faithful service record was there on the cemented floor as few gray circles of ashes. The very cold wind of the December night almost freezes the students and the Principal. Occasional mosquito stings and bed bugs made the students awake and active. The presence of large number of students inside the police station irritated the ASI and he ordered the students to leave the premises of the Station. But they refused to move.

The Inspector fell on his cane chair and thought "This gatti Principal is going to invite trouble for him, he does not know our position and what our leaders and superiors are telling us, now in the mid night from where I am going to search for that Andrew, in this darkness, at this late night now, unfortunately I accepted today's night duty. What a fate? I would have taken my off and join the minister's birthday party. These rascals are not going home to sleep? If I do anything to nab this criminal next day I will be transferred, if I am not doing anything these students will make more troubles." Why this gatti from Kerala taking too much interest in this case, after all the kidnapped girl is from Karnataka, another gatti, why should we risk our life against the wish of our rulers. It is the practice and unwritten custom here, on the birthday parties of the v.i.p's they need someone to enjoy, unfortunately that rascal Andrew picked up this girl, hope she will not be succumbed by lecherousness and lust of our politicians. Just like any other matter I will handle this matter also. Even though I instruct my police to nab the culprit they won't do it now. They know when to act and when not to act. They get more rewards from Susegaad than the alms from our Department, while thinking about the case he fell asleep. During his short nap he dreamt of a large number of people with choppers and sticks in their hand and they were coming towards him, in the crowd there was a coffin, they were shouting at the top of their voice, then immediately thousands of students join from all corners of the streets, they were roaring at the top of their voice, he was trying to run, but his legs were not obeying his wishes and not moving at all, he struggled very hard to move at least one step but found his legs were very heavy, desperately he tried to ran away from the angry crowd, but he could not do that, something was pulling him back, the angry mob almost reached him, slowly the coffin was opened and a huge hand of a ferocious figure emerged out and it moved toward him, the very huge hand lifted him... then immediately he got up from his sleep and looked around in fear. Angry Students were staring at him. He flushed for a moment.

In the mid night Rohini Kumari's father ran to the police station when he heard the shocking news about her daughter, his wife accompanied him crying bitterly all the way. They waited long for their daughter to come home. When she failed to reach they made enquiry to their neighbors and finally they met a friend of her and got the news. They were weeping with deep distress and grief. The mother after seeing the students and the principal outside the police station, in the mid night, broke out without control and wept bitterly and beseeched them to give her daughter. Rohini's mother fell on the ground and touched the shoes of the Principal Alexander Philip and begged bitterly "sir, where's my Rohini? Who took her? Please help sir, we are poor people sir, sir; please please... while moaning she pleaded. Principal had no words to console the parents. He could understand the parent's agony and pain on this matter. He lifted Rohini's mother from the ground and tried to console her. "We'll bring back Rohini, safely". "I'm with you, all her friends are with you "We will bring back your daughter" he assured them.

The very next day the students have decided to block the national highway to Panaji. The crowd sat on the road. The public was very much annoyed by the way the police handled the case of the kidnapping. This was the second such incident taken place within two months. They knew that police and some politicians are behind this human trafficking. Everybody knew that Andrew Akbar is a government sponsored goon and the kidnapped girls are for the corrupt politicians and their friends. They want to put an end to this dirty business of the politicians and the lust of omnipotent minister's adolescent sons. The police personals with their cane *lathi* watched the movements of the crowd with fear. Wireless messages were sent to Headquarters to reinforce the police personals. Armed police persons were deployed to control the situation.

"We want the police to take immediate action"

Bring Rohini Kumari" they shouted.

Public were confused by the various rumors about the incident. Some spread the news that she actually eloped with her boyfriend. But her close associates and friends knew that it was a forceful kidnapping by the Andrew Akbar, the local leader of the club Susegaad.

The next day the newspapers reported that one Vasco Girl was missing. Also there was a small account of the various incidents and about the picketing of buses by students of Susegaad Higher secondary. One paper reported that the Principal Alexander Philip also participated in the picketing.

On the very next day Alexander Philip was asked explanation for participating in the picketing. All the evidences shown by the principal was not acceptable to the Director of Education Dr. Maria. She was waiting for such an incident to demoralize him, her arch enemy. In his explanation Alexander Philip described all the events happened on that fateful day. He submitted his explanation along with the statements of the senior lecturers and some parents present on that day.

# Part Three

# Chapter 16

That night was unusually chill. The imported car of the minister with special attachments and additions moved through the ghat section towards Ratnagiri at ten kilometers speed. The driver found it very difficult to see the road through the December mist that hindered the visibility very badly in midnight. The strong smell of liquor and smoke inside the car made nauseousness in Rohini. Soon she felt that she was moving and her face was covered with a black cloth. Slowly she was coming to consciousness. The stout lady sitting near to her was also wearing a black burka, she noticed. Rohini Kumari was sitting in between two persons: the stout 'lady' in black burka and another man whose face she could not see properly in that dim light and she knew she was kidnapped and was on move. Through the burka net she tried to see the face of the lady sitting her right side, but she could not recognize her face. Still closing her eyes half, without any movement she sat on the soft seat of the imported car of the minister's son and tried to recollect the events that happened on the previous day. The green room, thundering sounds of the loudspeakers, screaming sounds of small children, suddenly she felt she was in the hands of some men, who surrounded her, she was lifted from the ground in a fraction of seconds before she could realize what was happening, she knew she was screaming then but the thundering voice from the loud speakers devoured her feeble scream, the strong smell of some chemicals pierced through her nostrils, and then she could not recollect anything what happened after words. She knows she is moving in a car along with some unknown people. Now she recollected the face of the stout lady who informed her about her father's accident. Oh! That was a trap to fool me, she thought. She assumed it is early morning because of the dim light inside. She could not understand how far she had travelled yesterday along with these people. Only thing she understood was that she was taken out of the green room by force and she could not resist. She was afraid to move or to cry. She was afraid to open her eyes fully. She pretended as if she was sleeping. She realised slowly that someone had changed her dress. She was in her pink chooridar –the best dress she ever worn – purchased from Narveker's cloth centre, especially for that annual day function. She realized that she wears a black gown now –a burka that she never had. An unexplainable fear developed in her mind as she opened her eyes again to see the face of the person who was sitting on her left. The very same person who was trying to have friendship with her for a long time and the same person who threatened her on several occasions, the local goon who used to visit her school occasionally, the eve teaser who pass comments on girls: Andrew Akbar. The threatening words of him echoed through her mind like a needle piercing in to her body "One day you will be mine" that is happening now, already happened. She wanted to cry but she controlled her fear. She was in the hands of a royal pimp who work for VIPS, the goon of Gama beach. Her palpitation increased and the pulse jumped out and she could hear her heart beat very well. Suddenly she heard someone telling to her in her mind. "Only anger can conquer" "Only anger can conquer". "The only thing you have to fear is the fear itself". The words of her school Principal in one of the school assembly. She was trying to develop courage to face any danger. But the very next moment she found that all the courage drained out of her body. "With fear you cannot do anything or gain anything in your life" Alexander Philip's message echoed through her mind. "Develop courage" she tried to tell herself.

"How can I develop courage now" she thought. They are powerful animals, willing to do anything they like; they have a heart of wolf." She started to think different ways to escape from her abductors, "I should act wisely, and yes I should act now." But the feelings about her home haunted her. The faces of her family members appeared in front of her as if in a movie in her mind and asking her "where are you?" her father, sobbing mother and frustrated younger brother. She suddenly started weeping without any control. The 'lady' in burka opened her eyes when she heard the weeping sound of Rohini. The speeding car jumped over a speed breaker with a jerk and the stout lady positioned back on her seat and looked at her prey gleefully like a satisfied lioness looking at prey.

"Oh!! She is happy now, may be first time she is travelling in a luxury car... she might be enjoying the trip... and she is going to enjoy more, more luxuries and pleasure..." She paused and laughed wickedly.

"We are late madam, we are late" the driver complained "We would have reached Ratnagiri now". The driver said in a very low voice.

"I don't prefer day journey. We have to stay somewhere" The stout lady said.

"I want to sleep at least two hours madam, I could not sleep yesterday, you know". The driver said while yawning.

"Ok. We stay away from the town. I prefer the High Way Kitchen".

"Highway Kitchen?" We passed that motel ten minutes ago madam, Shall we go back?" The confused driver asked his madam while turning back his face to get permission.

"No, no, we will not go back now, I knew the person at High Way Kitchen, that's all" "We shall go to that Madrasi's motel, and we will have *dossa* and *sambar,* I like that, ok. We will go there."

The black Audi was moving very fast as the ghat section was over and they reached a plane land but the December mist made the visibility very poor. Only the lady and the driver were talking and Andrew was in deep sleep. Suddenly the Audi took a sharp turn and enter a small forest road and moved about half kilometers and stopped. The Lady tapped on the shoulders of Andrew and called out his name "Andrew, get up, we reached almost. Wake up my dear" she shouted. Andrew slowly opened his eyes for one second and smiled for a second and again closed his eyes. Then the stout lady looked at her prey and yelled "You bitch get out". Rohini did not answer. Next moment she felt a hard blow on her face. She got up with a jerk and started to cry. "I told you to get out of the car, not to cry". She yelled again. Rohini obeyed her command without any protest and wiped her tears with her slender trembling hand. She was shivering with fear like a small puppy exposed to rain.

"Are you O.K.?" The stout lady asked Rohini Kumari in a very low but rough voice. Her voice sounded like a man. Rohini did not speak but her whole body was trembling with fear like a puppy caught in rain. She felt some one holding her from behind tightly and in seconds she was in the hands of Andrew Akbar.

"Give her some training, let me see, how good she is…" The lady in black burka ordered. Then looked wickedly to Andrew and laughed.

With joined hand Rohini pleaded for mercy "please sir, please sir… only these words came out of her throat.

"Undress her" Johnny roared.

"Johnny doesn't teach me, this is not the first time I'm undressing girls" Andrew replied to his best friend. Andrew held her beautiful long hair in his ugly hands and pushed her down. Her head hit on the side of the car and she cried in loud voice for help. No one came for her help. Not even gods. She was silenced by another hand with bangles studded with diamonds. Her loud cry ceased slowly and ended up in moaning and finally that also stopped as her mouth was filled with her own dupatta. Like a beheaded lamb she shook her legs in utter pain and fear. Her hands and legs were tied together from behind. All courage drained out of her fragile body. She thought that her life has come to an end and these are the last few minutes of her life… last minutes in the hands of a wolf… suddenly she thought of her old father and helpless mother and brother, these feeling made her more distressing and sad. She could not see anything now. Immediately she was blind folded. She heard the tinkling sounds of gold bangles near to her ear. A dirty smelling gunny bag covered her body. She felt she was been lifted again by some powerful hands and transferred to the dickey of that large car. She heard the firing of the car engine and felt the movement of the vehicle.

The journey in the dickey was unbearable for her. She couldn't cry, she couldn't move nor breathe fresh air. The floor was not soft not even flat. She lied inside the dark dickey for many hours. She was hungry and thirsty. Why I was tortured like this, she thought. What wrong did I, what wrong I did against Andrew? She asked herself. She had no answer. She prayed to lord Krishna for help, but no help came, the car moved in full speed tossing her body up and down on every bump. She suffered silently herself without any reason, and she wept but no one listened. The roaring sound of the engine of the car announced that it is climbing a very steep mountain. For many kilometers the car was climbing the mountain without stop. Finally the car stopped. The dickey was opened by Andrew and he checked whether any life is inside the gunny bag. He opened the mouth of the gunny bag and removed the cloth from her mouth and poured some liquid into her opened mouth. The taste was so horrible but she had no option. She wanted to stretch her legs and moved out of the car dickey. But the dupatta returned back to her mouth and the gunny bag was closed once again.

"Slam" The dickey was shut by Andrew. Then there was a long silence. She heard nothing, the whispering sound of Andrew nor the engine sound. She realised that the car is parked somewhere in a forest and she is alone. The darkness inside the dickey and chilling cold bothered her. She does not know how many hours she spend inside the dickey without able to cry or able to move freely. The only free sense organ was her nose and skin and ear. Her motion less limbs felt like a frozen chunk. But she could not help. She wanted to die before the wolves returned.

# Chapter 17

Every minute inside the dickey was an hour to her. Physical and mental torture was unbearable to her fragile little body. She did not know how many hours she travelled in that dickey.

Suddenly when she woke up she felt something cold falling on her body. Her eyes cover was removed already and the dupatta in her mouth was not there. Slowly she opened her eyes and turned her head to one side and then to the opposite side. She realised that she was unconscious for quite some time. She saw through the half opened eyes that someone massaging her legs and she understood she was lying on a bed spread on the grass on the road side. The lady and the Andrew Akbar were standing by her side and looking at her. She had no courage to look at them and she immediately closed her eyes. Some more cold water fell on her pale face. She wanted to cry but she had no energy to cry and thought end is near. She licked the drops of water fell on her face with great thirst. The stout lady in black burka poured more water, without any resistance she tried to drink it, more water fell out through the corners of her mouth. She looked piteously at them for mercy and her eyes were begging for some kindness. Because of the hunger and thirsty she could not move or talk.

"Get up and eat". She heard a male voice shouting at her. She couldn't respond as she was tiered and completely exhausted. She felt someone kicking her and she rolled down to other side. Another leg kicked her from other side and she rolled again with closed eyes with tight lipped mouth to engross the bitter pain and shame. The unreserved humiliation she felt while rolling from one side to other.

"Get up rascal" the rough male voice bawled again. The driver bowed down and lifted her tiered head and shoulder slowly and held her in his arms. The lady gave her an open bottle of cock and she drank it fully.

"Drink fast" Andrew roared.

"Rohini." she heard her name calling out by someone. The stout lady in burka called her in a very soft and loving voice "Rohini…" You are my daughter now… come and eat… See what I bought for you see…, look dear… look… here." She lifted a small packet from her bag and opened the paper cover then she slowly removed the aluminum foil and showed her the hot *pav* inside… come my dear eat… and come with us… if you co-operate with us it is good for you and your family… come my dear eat and follow us" she talked very gently and lovingly. Rohini couldn't resist her hunger. Without saying a word she accepted the food. In her mind she thought, to remain hungry is impossible, I have to eat whatever I get, for energy, energy to live and act when time come.

When she was about to finish the meals, the lady said again in a low but caveat tone "remember, I'm your mother, if anyone ask, you should say that I'm your mother and call me mummy without any trace of doubt." "*kel tuka*" she warned her with a stern scornful look.

"Now we are going to a house, don't try to fool us, if you try to fool us you could see both your parents in Bogda cremation ground, Understood?" Andrew said in a firm and forceful voice, he stopped for a while and gave her a ferocious look. Rohini started trembling and a lightening fear passed though her body. Once again she felt that all her artificial courage drained out of her body. Like a puppy caught in rain she began to shiver and followed them without any resistance.

"Walk fast" Andrew cried in to her ears in a firm but very low but very demanding voice, not to attract any ones attention. The numbness in her legs was still there and she limbed along with them silently with fear. Though Andrew told that they are going to a house they went to a hill station resort. The stout lady covered her face with black veil net and Rohini obeyed her command and did what she said. Though it was noon time the winter sun was not clearly visible. The mist reduced the visibility and Rohini could see tall mountains covered partially with mist everywhere. She crossed her arms around her body to protect herself from the very cold wind.

The receptionist at the counter, a dark complexioned short stout Madrasi of middle age having a prominent pot belly, looked at the tall fair and handsome figure with blue eyes who looked like a foreigner, in green T shirt and blue jeans and the stout women in black burka. The receptionist at the counter in his south Indian English tinged with Tamil accent asked Andrew to write the details of the party accompanying him while looking at the two ladies in black burka with covered face. Andrew with shame informed the receptionist that he cannot write and requested the receptionist to enter the details himself.

"Name?" The receptionist raised his heavy head like a government clerk in a Registrar's office asked.

"Akbar" The answer was spontaneous.

The proud receptionist wrote in his register -Akbar. He again raised his head while rubbing his long slender ball pen on his chin and asked "Age?"

"28"

"Address?"

"R. M. lay out, 3rd Cross, Mangalore South" Andrew responded immediately.

"ID please" the receptionist asked again. He in an apologizing tone said "sorry sir for asking many questions, we have instructions to get full information about all the residents here."

Andrew removed his driving license from his black purse and showed to the receptionist. "My driving license" He said with a tinge of Salcette Konkani accent.

"Yes, yes, it will do, it is sufficient "He checked the name and address on the driving license. He read "Andrew Akbar, Fatima Enclave, and Panaji, Goa". The receptionist looked suspiciously and said, "Sir, here the address is different, you gave the Mangalore address."

"Oh! Shit! See my visiting card, he said without any hesitation and removed his visiting card from the purse and handed over to the receptionist.

Andrew Akbar, Managing Director, Pride Real Estate, R M lay Out, 3rd Cross, Mangalore.

Sorry sir, we have strict instructions to verify the address of all inhabitants. "Please say the name of other parties in your group?" the receptionist asked in respectful voice.

"Smt. Tabassum, age 39 and Remlatbi age 18, that is my elder sister and her daughter, my niece" Andrew introduced them to avoid any more questions.

"Please sign here sir", the receptionist requested the Managing Director with a tone of artificial respect.

After a second checking the receptionist said "Sir, we don't have a vacant three bed room, but I can provide an additional bed, Is it OK?"

*"Oi, Oi"* Andrew said and shook his head in acceptance. But he thought for a second and baffled. The receptionist pressed the buzzer while trying to have a glance at the two ladies who were standing at a distance and facing away from his table. He could not see their face since they had a veil to cover their identity. Immediately the receptionist pressed another button and switched on the CCTV cameras without giving any doubt to the visitors.

"Come, Remla we are going to upstairs" Andrew called his 'niece' in a very kind and affectionate voice. As Rohini turned towards Andrew and to lift a bag from the floor the receptionist could see the one side of her face as the same appeared in his CCTV screen. As Rohini got up she felt light-headedness but followed others out of fear. Her body was very weak and exhausted because of the continuous starvation and torture. Realizing the fact, the stout lady kept a hand on her shoulder to support her. After a few steps she felt the increased salivation in her mouth and she could not see any steps in front of her and she felt the whole staircase is rotating around her. She lost her balance and fell behind and hit the room boy who was climbing just behind her carrying other luggage and room key. The room boy felt some heavy objects on his shoulder and acted on time and immediately supported her while dropping his luggage to one side. If he had not supported her, her head would have hit on the steps. The veil covering her pale face moved to one side and the room boy had a closer look at the beautiful face of Rohini. Even the receptionist recorded the events on his CCTV and could get a full view of 'Remlatbi's face.

"Oh! Jesus" the stout women in burka uttered in a split second without thinking she is in burka.

When this was heard by the receptionist, he raised his eye brows in suspicion. "Oh! Jesus" Christians in burka?

*"Kya ho reha hai?"* Akbar shouted from a distance. He was making some advance payment at the counter while the "stout lady" and Rohini were climbing the steps towards their room. "I think your niece had a fall... or she fainted? I don't know?" The receptionist paused.

"Might be, she was sick, she was vomiting throughout the journey" he commented to assure the receptionist. "We are taking her to a hospital in Mumbai she was sick," while saying this Akbar ran towards his niece to help them. By that time the fainted body of Rohini was brought down to the floor by the room boy and the stout lady. Her fainted body was kept exactly facing the surveillance camera by the room boy purposefully. The receptionist and the room boy noticed the nervousness and fear on the face of the 'mother' and her 'uncle'. The boy ran to bring water to sprinkle over her face.

"Please remove the veil from her face, let her breath freely" the receptionist requested her uncle. Andrew looked at his elder 'sister' for permission. Both of them stared each other in sheer confusion without knowing what to do, both were blaming each other in their look. While the uncle and the mother were staring each other to pass on their fault to another the room boy sprinkled some cold water on Remaletbi's face and the receptionist massaged her sole to increase the blood circulation. Without waiting for the permission he removed the head piece and veil from Remalet's head and opened her eye lids with his dark fat fingers. "torch *kondu vada*" (bring the torch) he instructed his assistant in his mother tongue. The room boy brought a very small red torch and the receptionist inspected the pupil dilation of Remlatbi" and commented *"Sari sari, pennu normal irike" Ellam shariaikolum pedikavenda"* (She is fine, she will become alright now don't worry).

Andrew and the disguised stout 'lady' in burka seemed worried much when they heard the arrival of a doctor. Again they looked each other with anxiety and fear, a fear of being caught, but they remained calm and silent. We should have given her proper food, Andrew thought. The whole plan is going to flop. He even thought of escaping from there after leaving the prey, but that would be more dangerous, in the next moment he thought. Before leaving the place we should clear all evidences. He started planning how to get rid of the evidences against them. Only way out is finish her now itself but how in front of all these employees? The 'lady' in burka thought in a different way. She thought it is only because of Andrew their plan become a flop. How shall we face madam if we fail in our attempt? Johnny the 'lady' in disguise also was trying to find a solution to their problem.

# Chapter 18

*"From whence comes my help? My help comes from the Lord who made heaven and earth."*

Alexander Philip sent messages to all news papers and to all TV stations regarding the kidnapping. Some TV channels telecasted the news immediately. But local prominent papers did not give much importance to that news and they published the news very casually. They gave importance to the killing of the British teenager by her lover at Calangute beach. Kidnapping of a school girl of their own state was not important to them. When all the local dailies gave full coverage to Viola's murder they conveniently forgotten to give justice to genuine local news. Many news papers reported the incident as a missing case. One paper even reported that a 16 year girl of Susegaad Higher secondary eloped with her lover. Susegaad members spread different news that the Principal punished her and did not allow her to participate in certain events and in frustration she left home with some relatives to Bangalore. All these news were the cooked by Minguel de Silva and other Susegaad members to divert the investigation and to give enough time for Andrew to escape. Sawantwadi police reported about an abandoned maruti car at Sawantwadi out post having registration. Police control room contacted the Vasco police station and RTO and found that engine number and the chassis numbers were not matching. The RTO from their records informed the Vasco police that the maruti car having the Reg. No. GDJ 01.7714 belongs to one Alexander Philip.

"Is it belongs to Dr.Alexander Philip?" the ASI Angelo Rebello raised his eye brows.

"Yes, the Vehicle belongs to one Dr. Alexander Philip." The RTO confirmed the news.

"Oh! He is the person who reported the kidnapping case."

"Is there any missing complaint reached in your office?"

"No. not yet" ASI Angelo Rebello kept the receiver back and thought for a while.

A few seconds later the cell phone of the Alexander Philip vibrated and then started to ring. He lifted his phone and pressed the green button to answer the call.

"Hello, is it Dr. Alexander Philip?" a deep base voice echoed in his cell phone.

"Yes, Speaking." He answered casually.

"This is ASI Rebello, City Police Station. Would you please come over here for a few minutes" the voice requested politely.

"Yes, yes, surely" He answered." Do you have any information about the missing girl?" He enquired eagerly.

"Yes, we have" The ASI continued. "Please do come we want your help".

Though he was very busy in his Office, immediately he reported to the City Police Station. He saw some reporters with their camera outside the police station.

"He is there" someone yelled.

One of the reporters came forward and asked Alexander Philip "Sir, Are you the Principal of Susegaad Higher secondary School?"

"Yes, do you have any information?"

"We received important news" The reporter announced.

"What?"

"ASI will tell you."

The ASI was in his civil dress. Alexander Philip sat on the old wooden chair in front of the ASI's office table covered with green felt. The ASI with his left hand adjusted his thick moustache and looked at the principal through his thin silver framed reading glass as if he is going to question a criminal.

Abruptly he asked "Is the vehicle No.GDJ.01.7714 belongs to you?"

"No"

"No?" The ASI repeated suspiciously.

Though the question was not expected he said "No it is not my vehicle."

"But I got information from RTO that it belongs to you".

"One vehicle, a maruti with the same number was with me about six years ago, and I had sold it to one Christopher of Sanguem". Alexander Philip said in firm voice.

"Oh! In that case I have to inquire about it, the RTO office says it belongs to Alexander Philip" He said in confusion. He tightened his lip and started shaking his legs to release his tension.

"What's the matter? Alexander Philip enquired out of curiosity.

While supporting his chin with his right hand and slightly leaning towards the table, the ASI said "Sawantwadi police found this vehicle in an abandoned state, and we are enquiring about it. Eye witness said that they found a girl along with two other people in that car. Sir, did you complete all the formalities while transferring the ownership of that vehicle to that Christopher?"

Yes, I filled up and signed the Form 28 and 29 and gave to one agent, that was about six years ago."

"But in records it is in your name, Mr. Christopher might not have changed the owner ship... It is confusing now. That vehicle No.GDJ 01.7714 was used to kidnap that Rohini up to Sawanthawadi, we doubt."

Alexander Philip couldn't understand much from the statement of the ASI Rebello. He entered into deep thought and became silent.

"Sorry sir, sorry for troubling you, and calling you here" The ASI Rebello said in an apologizing tone.

Next morning the watch man supplied the local daily sharply at 7.30 am, the usual time the Alexander Philip reaches his office. As usual only the Nepali watchman was present there in the office. Some students were running here and there. He gazed the paper to see the present news items. Casually his eyes fell on a news item

**'Principal under cloud'**

He could not believe his eyes.

"The principal, Alexander Philip's car used for kidnapping the school girl is found near Sawantwadi. Principal surrendered to the local police station and he confessed the crime. The minor was holed to Mumbai. Police Inspector Mr. Rebello is investigating the case. Principals' abandoned car was found near Sawantwadi in a damaged condition.

He looked at another paper

**'Minor abducted'** Local Police is investigating the case of the missing girl. Damaged vehicle of the Principal of Susegaad Higher Secondary School, Dr. Alexander Philip was found in an abandoned condition at Sawanthawadi. Police says that this vehicle was used for kidnapping the minor girl from her school campus yesterday during the Annual Day function. The involvement of Principal in that case is established.

Another news paper published the same news in a different way.

**'Missing school girls' mystery resolved'**

Local police has arrested one principal in connection with the abduction of a minor girl. That was the news in another paper. Alexander Philip could not believe his eyes. Immediately he dialed No.100. One lady constable attended his call immediately. "Please connect to the ASI Angelo Rebello" He requested with a disturbed tone. "I have an important matter to discuss with him." He continued. "Sir this is police control room van and we are in Madgao. Kindly call this number." She gave another number. Alexander Philip dialed that number and waited for reply. After 16th ring one constable lifted the phone. "Hello…" he answered "Sir, may I speak to ASI Rebello" There was no answer from other end. Alexander Philip again repeated his request "Sir, May I speak to ASI Rebello." And he waited for the answer from the other end. After a few moments of silence one voice replied from other end:

"*Kon ulaitha?* (Who is this?) "Principal Alexander Philip here", he said in a disturbed tone.

"*Tu hunge yo ani complaint kar, ASI bahar vach' (You* come here and complaint, ASI went out) Alexander Philip heard a click sound on the other end.

He heard the murmuring sound of some students outside his cabin and at a distance some other grown up students were screaming and hauling in protest.

"Principal Go back", "Principal Go back" they shouted. "*Principal chor hai, principal chor hai*" Small children repeated the chorus. Alexander Philip was thunder shocked and sat inside his cabin in a pensive mood. He felt all his courage was draining out of him; he looked down at his own reflected image on the glass top and stared at that image silently with anger. "*Only anger can conquer*" "*Only anger can conquer*" He could hear the sounds of his brother's voice in his ear in that solitude. The original words of Alexander the Great, the

Greek Emperor, who used to tell himself these words when he was in dilemma or in trouble to get some courage to go forward. *"Only anger can conquer, only anger can conquer"* these words echoed in his ears again and again and that gave some relief from that pensive and contemplative mood. To get some courage he folded his fist tightly. The office telephone started ringing ceaselessly. He decided not to answer those calls. With disgust he kept the receiver down and killed that bothersome sound for the moment. He was buying time to think over to reply the inquiries of friends and foes. He had no idea how to react to students, teachers and parents regarding the paper news.

Immediately his cell phone in his front pocket started vibrating and after a few seconds later it started announcing caller by the special ring tone. He identified the caller, a call he can't refuse or overlook… a call that he expected to raise his spirits, and to get some comfort. He identified the caller. He lifted the cell and pressed the green button. He kept the phone very near to his ear and listened carefully. For few seconds there was no voice from other end. Finally he heard the mild, pathetic and anxious sound of Sara, his wife.

"Alex"

Then there was again a silence for few seconds.

"Alex," again that familiar voice called his name. The most familiar sound in the world for him.

"Did you… See… today's… news paper?"

Alexander wanted to say "Yes". But his sound was quite abnormal and incomprehensible, it emitted from the very lower end of his dry throat, and with great difficulty. He himself was not sure what he said- an unintelligent dull odd sound- from his voice box. His response was half dead inside his throat itself.

Sara continued with courage. "Alex, Please read the news-news about you, my dear and what a horrible news!!"

Alexander took a deep breath and sighed, the more oxygen inside the brain made him courageous and witty. He did not want to expose his weakness to anybody, including his wife. In a firm voice, mostly artificial, and cooked with in a moment, he said "Yes, Yes I read, I become famous overnight. My name is there in every news papers today. Dr. Alexander Philip, *the person behind the kidnapping*, we can't do anything now, any way I have decided to call the editors of these papers for clarification." Alright, you don't worry much, my darling. This is Goa. This is the duty of the media. To spread out sensational news… to increase circulation… that is their job… that's all" Now only foolish people believe the news paper news." Switch on the TV and see what they say, you will be convinced then". Bye, bye, see you in afternoon for lunch, Bye" He disconnected the phone and took a file regarding the repair of the school building.

He could hear the murmuring sounds of teachers and students who were in small groups discussing something serious. Their cheerful faces put his morality down. They do not know what they are saying- he thought. Most of the Susegaad members were happy and their joyful faces revealed something-they succeeded in tarnishing the image of an innocent person, at least temporarily. He closed his eyes and entered into meditation. The Bible words he studied when he was young came for his help *"I will lift my eyes to the hills —from whence comes my help? My help comes from the Lord who made heaven and earth. He will not allow your foot to be moved; He who keeps you will not slumber."* These words yielded him new courage and energy. He felt relieved from all his concerns and worries now. He regained his lost confidence. Slowly he got up from his old rusted government chair, while getting up the chairs' spring whined. Slowly he opened the half door and showed his face outside his cabin. He stood straight in front of his cabin with his hands joined behind and remained there like a general who won a battle before fighting it. Students, teachers, and even Susegaad members gradually melted out, complete silence, no murmuring, no cheerful hauling, the small veranda looked deserted, except some teachers, who boldly came forward with a gloomy face towards him and greeted him compassionately. The senior teacher, who was with him on the previous night in the police station, finally said: "good morning sir' to break the silence.

Alexander Philip with his usual calm smile extended his hand and greeted him "Good Morning."

Mishra with a crying face said: "Sir"

Alexander Philip could understand the sympathy and sincerity in his words.

"We will clear it Mr.Mishra" Alexander Philip said.

"Yes sir, we have to. You call me any where I am there…' he paused.

"Now I realised the emptiness of the paper news… it is really bad sir", Wilson, who was of very shy nature commented." I am there Sir, with you in any court or police station" He assured his support in a very soft and assuring tone.

"Mr.Wilson, news papers are doing their business, they have the license to do that, defaming and tarnishing people are one of their businesses. They are the king makers, people those who do not fall in their line, or support them will be targeted and ruined."

"But we have to fight sir" another lady teacher who was standing by the side of Wilson suggested. "I know that Mr.Minguel de Silva is behind all these scandal. Only he knows where Rohini is. He is a member of that gang… they only burned our green room and spoiled that function." While saying this she looked around in fear and checked was anyone listened to her.

"Yes we have to fight, we have to bring Rohini back… that is our moral responsibility" Alexander Philip said in a determining voice.

"I do not know how much help we get from our department and police administration, they are playing double role, and distorting the facts… we will have a tough time ahead, sir…" Wilson said.

"Sir, what they say about your car..?" Mishra asked with curiosity.

"Yes, Mr.Mishra, That was my car six years ago. That maruti van I sold to one Christopher of Sanguem through an Agent. I do not know what happened to that car after that. I think I have the papers of that transfer… the copies of Form No. 29 and 30. I can prove it in the court, but who will wash the mud that these news papers spreads…"

His attention was moved to a group of people standing at the other end of the narrow dingy corridor who were talking to Minguel de Silva and Anand Shenai. Gradually their murmuring sounds become louder and louder, he could not understand clearly what they were talking. But Alexander Philip and Mishra realized their intention and motive. Everyone was holding news papers in their hands.

In a low voice Mishra said to Alexander Philip, Sir, they are the local gang –the members of Susegaad group…" Though Alexander Philip heard what Mr. Mishra was telling, he had no presence of mind to listen to that and he silently nodded his head in approval of the facts.

"It is time for the Assembly, we will talk later". Alexander Philip said all of a sudden and slowly moved to his place. The school assembly was late for five minutes because of this commotion. He could see the suspicious looks of some of the teachers and students but he ignored that totally. Some of them were laughing and passing some comments that were not audible or clear. He also noticed the unusual whispering among children and staff members. The school assembly was brief and many teachers including Mishra and Wilson went to their classes.

Soon after the brief assembly for which the principal did not address them as usual, the members of the local Susegaad club entered forcefully in to the cabin of the Head of the Institution and sat in the chairs kept for the visitors, a few of them stood in front of him. They exposed their club pendent on their bare chest to warn others. Soon six more members entered his cabin. A young leader, an ex-student and drop out of the same school, raised his hand with a copy of the newspaper and shouted to the Principal Alexander Philip:

"Did you see this?"

Without answering directly to their question he questioned: "did you read it?'

"Yes" They all answered together.

"Okay, then what I can do for you." He said in a firm voice without a trace of fear or confusion. His eyes were full of anger and contempt. He noticed the locket with the pendent of the club Susegaad "S" on their chest, the type of locket he had seen a few months ago in an accident scene in front of his residence. "Are you the parents?" he asked.

A short stout goon with full of hair on his chest like a black bear moved forward towards the Principal and showed his golden pendent on his chain and declared "See…, we are the members of the this club-Club Susegaad" He said proudly while expanding his hairy chest with a deep breath and bend his body a few inches backwards, and in this process and he grew one inch more while showing his golden pendent. He was the brother of the local minister.

"You talk only to parents?" he asked in a loud and harsh shrill voice.

"Yes, I prefer to talk to parents" Alexander Philip replied while looking straight in to the eyes of the goon.

"Do you know who am I?" The bear man asked in a thundering voice.

Alexander Philip without showing any shakiness or panic said in a cool and calm voice. "I am not interested to know who you are." He smiled mockingly. His smile provoked the Susegaad members and a person sitting in front of his table across him said in a polite voice "Sir, he is the brother of the local minister."

"Good" What can I do for you?" Alexander Philip said keeping the same contemptuous smile.

The minister's brother, the bear man came forward and cried "I want to know about the kidnapped girl, right now."

"You have kidnapped the girl" another member of Susegaad roared like a lion.

"Police reported they found your vehicle..." Another person screamed hysterically.

"So you know everything, you know better than me, then what else you want to know?" Alexander Philip said while looking at the bear man, the minister's brother.

The bear man started shivering with anger and he raised his short dark hand with a steel bangle on it and hit forcefully on the table top twice, the glass table top cracked with cracking sound. There was a silence for a few seconds. He shouted "Tell… to whom you sold her?"

"That you should know" Alexander Philip replied coolly. "Ask reporters who reported the news that is better." He stopped.

Another member of that self styled moral police belonging to Susegaad group moved towards the small notice board and removed it from the wall and threw it on the floor, the glass case smashed completely and scattered everywhere on the floor. Another boy of sixteen or seventeen with little shadows of moustaches on his upper lips lifted the office telephone up in the air slowly and threw it forcefully on the ground. The old machine broken into pieces.

Not many came forward to assist the Head of the Institution—the Alien Principal, to give him at least the moral support. The very old Indian patriotism, that their ancestors showed to Tippu Sultan, the brave SULTAN who fought single handily, to protect his home land from foreign invaders, when his own soldiers turned traitors and supported the white skinned foreigners, the jealousy of his own one time 'trusted generals', and the courage the Bengalis showed at the time partition of Bengal, the same patriotism their counterparts showed when the Portuguese invaded their mother land with a hand full of soldiers in a wooden ship few centuries ago, their descendants showed the same patriotism towards their head, that they considered, him as an Alien. He, the Alien, sat on his chair calmly without responding. He saw the office files were flying in front of his eyes here and there. That hexagonal blue paper weight, whose edges were broken unevenly because of wear and tear of many years and served many principals faithfully, now knew the strength of Susegaad goons and transformed it to many pieces. The office of the principal looked like a vegetable market with people bargaining and arguing in inhospitable surroundings. The principal remained silent among those young criminals arguing aggressively and violently.

A few meters away a group of jingoists were watching the scene with full satisfaction.

"He deserved that" Minguel De Silva remarked to his close aids surrounding him.

"They will teach him a lesson" Francisco Gomes, the English language teacher commented gleefully showing his yellow plaque teeth. He laughed with a loud blast.

"No. No they are teaching him how to behave in our school... an important lesson in sociology." Satoskar Dhume said. Ha... ha... ha... all they laughed cheerfully to commemorate their success.

At this point another north Indian teacher Mishra, who was teaching Hindi came near to them and intervened "What nonsense it is..." he shouted at them. His English had a tinge of heavy village Hindi. Others in the gang of Minguel de Silva repeated his bad pronunciation... the same words "Nonusense.... Nonusense" in a similar North Indian village tone and laughed again.

*"Hum Principal saab ko madad karna chahiye, aao bhai, hum jakar un goonda lokonko samachenke"* (We should support the Principal, we will go and explain to that goons) Mishra said in Hindi with a persuasive tone.

"Why should we support him?" He does not want our support. We won't support him *"Tu ja* and *support kar"* (You go and support him). Minguel de Silva said in a condescending tone.

*"Sab ne kya galthi kiya?* What mistake did him? Mishra asked. He asked you to teach properly, he changed the faulty time table; he brought back the discipline in the school, that's why you hate him. *Ye achha nahim, vho kuch kiya ye school keliya kiya, hamare or tumara bachhom keliye kiya hoga, tum bilkul galth samchha".* (This is not fair; whatever he did was for the betterment of our school, for our students, you mis under stood him)

"Missssshraaa... jiiii..." Satoshkar Dume screamed at him with irritation and full anger. Without listening to their comments Mishra moved towards the principal's cabin. "Ass licker... rascal....." he heard his colleague's dirty comments about him from behind. He pretended as if he has not heard it.

Mishraji was too late to act. He heard the screaming sound from the Principal's cabin and moved towards it. He opened the half door slowly and peeped inside and saw the horrible looking sight inside. He noticed many boisterous people with exuberant animal spirit inside shouting and screaming at the principal Dr. Alexander Philip. He entered the cabin of the Principal after opening the half door. He was astounded by the crowd inside, the glass pieces, torn files, broken notice board and broken telephone inside the cabin. He saw the Principal sitting on his chair in a thoughtful mood. He had never seen him like that.

*"Are tum log kya kartha hai"* (Hello, what is this? What are you doing here?) Mishraji asked in a very soft and polite manner to the Susegaad members knowing that they are the local goondas and supporters of the local goonda Minister. *"Deko ye baraber nahim tum log bahar jayeeye"* (Please go out, what you are doing is not proper) he requested them politely.

*"Tu konre?* (Who are you?) One of the Susegaad members asked in an aggressive rough manner. Another member caught the collar of Mishra's shirt and pushed him hard. Mishra lost his balance and fell on his back. By that time the watch man, Gangaram Tapa, a Nepali Ghurkha, acquired courage and entered inside with his knife in his raised hand and shouted at the top of his voice *"Bahar, baher, sub log bahar"* (Get out, get out, from here). One of the goons lifted one plastic chair and tried to hit the watch man on his head. Tapa moved away

swiftly and the chair hit on the head of another associate of the S clubs itself. Three of the Susegaad members pushed open the half door of the cabin and jumped out side in fear. Tapa's Gurkha blood boiled and he shouted at the top of his voice *"Marega salenko" Maarega"* (Rascals I shall kill you all) he shouted again and jumped like an ape with his open knife. The unexpected attack from the watchman with his small sharp eyes on his wrinkly red ferocious round face sent waves of fear in the minds of inexperienced cowards and a few more grown up children went outside slowly walking backwards still staring with fear at the curved Ghurkha knife, as if retreating from the court of a Japanese king with respect. Only the bear man, the stout dark brother of the minister remained inside the room. He stared at the watchman like a tiger looking at his prey. But the prey too was smart like a snake in front of a mongoose. Tapa was ready to spit the poison and for a fight. But the principal and Mishra persuaded him and he stopped staring at the bear man. Adrenalin of both subsided below the danger level. Mishra looked at his on bleeding elbow that hit the wall in that clash. The bear man, the brother of the minister looked straight into the eyes of the watchman and raised his golden pendent of 'S' club and said in a threatening voice "You do not know who am I, within few days you will realize the taste of Susegaad..." after saying these words he left the cabin in shame. All his supporters were already left the scene in fear. Alexander Philip was looking at the torn files and scattered glass pieces everywhere on the floor. The threatening sounds of "S" club members were heard for some more time from outside and the sound gradually dissolved in the air.

# Chapter 19

While waiting for the police to come and write the FIR, the principal heard the sounds of another group approaching them. They were a group of migrant laborers. They were the relatives and friends of the abducted Rohini Kumari. They did not enter inside the cabin, but waited outside. Mishraji and Wilson went outside and talked to them first. "Sir they want to meet you" Wilson came and informed Alexander Philip. Unenthusiastically with a painful heart he went outside to meet them. There were about eight people in their shabby clothes that were not washed for weeks waiting outside. When they saw the principal they joined their hands in respect and greeted him and removed their traditional headdress and they looked each other asking or requesting others to speak first. After a few moments of confusion one man acquired some courage and said "*Sab, aap ko milne keliye hum aaya.*" (Sir, we are here to meet you) Their voice was friendly mixed with regards and high respect. Alexander Philip smiled in acceptance of their concern.

"*Sab*" They said to him "*Hum sub aap ke sath hai*". (We are with you) They paused. Alexander Philip smiled and looked at them with gratitude. "*Suchh kya hai hum ko malum hai*" (We know what is the truth). Many of them were talking in Kannada and Alexander Philip could not understand what they were talking but he understood that they came in support of him.

*"Sir, aap ko taklif karne keliye ye badmash log kosish kartha, dero mat, hum sub aap ke saath hai"* (Sir these goons are trying to trouble you, don't be afraid we are with you) One person said.

From the crowd one lady came forward and cried in front of the principal bitterly, Alexander Philip identified her as the mother of Rohini. He does not know in what words to console her. Though he wanted to tell her something, his words stuck in his throat and only some vague words came out of his mouth, he realised that his eyes are being filled with tears, he clasped the hands of Rohini's mother with compassion, and from his eyes, when he closed it gently, two drops of tears emitted out and it flowed down through his cheeks and finally fell on the tiled floor. Rohini's mother cried loudly and it echoed after hitting the walls of Susegaad Higher Secondary school. He noticed some more people among the visitors wiping their tears with their turban edges.

Before the arrival of the police two reporters, of whom one he knew as a person who recommended a 24 years old rowdy's admission in standard XI in Susegaad Higher secondary School and was denied admission stating overage, he returned with some of the Susegaad club members in a hero Honda 100 cc bike with their small camera and a mobile phones and threatened the principal with dare consequences. Then with the help of local roudy MLA he created lot of trouble for the school and tried to burn the cabin of the principal. Alexander Philip could recognize his face. The over aged boy wanted admission only to take advantage of government schemes including the free computers supplied by the Department for Std.XI students. Alexander denied admission to him in view of school discipline. Many teachers informed him that the 24 year over aged boy was a past student of the same school and he had stopped his studies about ten years ago. Now he came as a reporter working on daily wages for notorious news papers that reports hateful slanderous news items and claim money for writing good report or rectifying their own defamatory comments. A portion of the earnings were shared with the local police for the smooth functioning of their business. The new Director General of the Police who tried to investigate the felonious act of extortion by the police personnel gained only the wrath of political masters and he himself became helpless scapegoat and was transferred within months. Though the unholy nexuses between police personals and the various mafia groups was well known to everyone in Goa, except the duly elected democratic Government and its home ministry, the symbiotic association of the two powers made the state the hub of all prostitution and criminal activity. Democracy has become more effective and powerful that no office could function without the help of Susegaad, the grass root power, to that level the democracy has bloomed soon after the liberation and its' growth rate has doubled after statehood.

One of the reporter stood in front of the despoiled office of the Principal as if they have not seen the horrible condition of the office room, and said "sir, we came to know that your vehicle has been caught by the police near Sawantwadi with the abducted girl, Is it true?"

Alexander Philip was silent for a moment, as usual, and was thinking about the paper news about him. The other reporter stepped in "Do you have any comments?"

Without answering their queries the principal rocked his old rusted chair with a contemptuous smile on his face. That smile was very much annoying the other party. He knew their objective, they are here to get some sensational news and to write something different in tomorrow's paper, he thought. He bent back on his squeaking official chair and rubbed his head and asked" What do you want?"

"Your comments"

"My comments!! on what?"

"Yhe…. yhe…, he started to baffle and said…"Of your caught vehicle… and about the abduction of a student from your institution."

"Whether you are here for any sensational news to increase the circulation of your paper or you are trying to find out the truth? He asked abruptly.

"Both are our aims" the young and the smartest of the two replied in seconds.

"If you want to increase the circulation of your paper please go and contact the "S" club members who are standing on the road, if you want to know the truth please go to the police station and find out the truth, or go to Sawantwadi or Tiracol and investigate yourself. If you want to know the feelings of the parents and the innocent public go and contact that people standing there under that peepal tree" after motioning the hand towards Rohini's mother and relatives he said.

"But we want your comments." The reporters said.

"My comments are not important here. Neither culprits accept the blame nor do innocents try to prove their innocence in some cases." His voice was firm and confident.

"So you are accepting that your vehicle was involved in the kidnapping of your own student from your own institution."

"That you said, not me."

"Then how come your vehicle was found with that girl by the Sawantwadi police"

"You should ask the police to find out the truth, not to me" Alexander Philip said with little annoyance.

"Who is the owner of that vehicle No. GDJ-01-7714?"

"Lakhs of vehicles are there in Goa How do I know the ownership of that vehicle No. GDJ-01-7714?'

"But RTO says that the vehicle belongs to you"

"Then, why are you asking me, again?" Please do not waste my time.

Reporters took the photographs of the ransacked office and went back on their 100 cc hero Honda splendor bike.

# Chapter 20

Soon after the departure of that bogus reporters, principal dialed to the office of the Express, the local daily, that reported about the involvement of Alexander Philip in that kidnapping.

One ring, two rings, three rings, finally the call got connected.

"Hello, Express." Alexander Philip heard the voice of a receptionist at the other end.

"May I speak to the Chief Editor… please" Alexander Philip talked in a very mild soft voice.

"One moment Sir… please holds on…" The receptionist while trying to connect to her boss she said in a sweet voice.

Alexander Philip could hear the music at the other end and he waited for the reply.

"May I know who is on the line?" the receptionist asked again.

"I am a social worker; I've an important message to convey, "Alexander Philip paused for a moment. "Please connect to the Chief Editor." He said in a very cool voice. Again he heard the sound of music at the other end for another twenty seconds. Suddenly the music stopped and he heard the voice of another person: "Hello"- this time the voce was of a man.

"Good morning Sir" Alexander Philip send his greetings and after a little pause, he continued "Do you have any latest information on the Vasco abduction case?"

"The police doubt the involvement of the Principal himself… and they found his damaged car near Sawantwadi or Tiracol. One fisher man saw two women in their Burke and a tall person in a car… they were trying to repair their car…"

"Any other information?" Alexander Philip asked with anxiety.

"But they deserted their old vehicle and proceeded towards north in another vehicle."

"Whether the police confirmed that…? That car, the abandoned one, belongs to the Principal itself."

"Yes, yes they confirmed that." The editor confirmed the news.

"But the Principal deny the ownership of that vehicle" the Social worker said over the phone.

"Did you contact the Principal?" the editor enquired.

"Yes, Mr. Editor, the Vehicle No. GDJ 01.7714 was with him six years ago, and he sold it to someone in Sanguem."

There was a silence at the other end… Oh… is it like that? Then we have to confirm with the RTO once again." There was bewilderment in editors' voice.

"And you published that defaming news without validating it, in your news paper. Isn't it?"

"We publish as per our reporters' description and statement."

"Mr. Editor, your paper sullied the reputation of an Officer and you are responsible for it and you have to pay for it." The social worker said. There was a threatening touch in his voice.

"May I know who is that speaking? The Editor enquired in a puzzled voice.

"I am Dr. Alexander Philip, the Principal himself. Thank you Mr. Editor" He disconnected his line.

Soon he called his wife who was waiting for a call from her husband.

"Sara, there is a file No.13 A in my shelf, named Maruti car, and I will be sending my friend to collect it, please hand over it to him."

"Alex any information now" There was panic in her sound.

"No Sara, Nothing, now please searches for that old file and I'll talk to you later." He disconnected his phone.

*******************

The overcrowded RTO office was on the second floor, in the heart of the town and was the centre of criticism of public, a corruption hub where money flows from hand to hand and then finally to the concerned minister; for every transfer and for every registration. Hundreds of dirty soiled and torn files were dumped on the floor due to lack of space. Everywhere files were dumped: on the table, on the shelves and even on the floor. There were so many plastic cups like button mushrooms on the floor. The dark narrow steps leading to the RTO office was used as a waiting room for people visiting that office. People were forced to stand on the steps in queue since there was no space for people to stand inside the rooms. Some of the agents, who permanently occupied the dark corners of the corridors with their small suit cases, always hindered the free movement in the passage. The only shade on the old wall was the colour of the brown pan spit. There was no dearth of pan spit on the wall, people prefer to spit on the wall, not on the floor, so others won't stamp on the sacred liquid, passersby spread that holy liquid on the wall and make beautiful designs inadvertently. Most fortunate agents, preferably the old settlers, have their own small stools that they carry with them, to sit on. One agent who was sitting on a small wooden stool was inspecting his bunch of driving licenses in his hand. Smart agents were going inside the inspector's room like honey bees going to deposit honey they collected, and coming out within seconds; while dozens of people stand in queue for hours together. The serious faces while they go inside turns to a simple smile, without gazing anyone they come out declaring that they have done their job, their innocent smile also declare their contempt to the people on the queues who were not their clients. Soon they were encircled by his clients. He distributed his driving licenses after collecting their fees, some say thanks, while others argue about the exorbitant fees.

"Why this much?"

*"Are gandu* (a insulting word) Rs. 200 for the inspector for signing the documents without delay, Rs.100 for the clerk who has done the basic grass root level work in time, and 200 for me for breaking the queue for you and 500 for the minister for protecting all of us." The agent said with disrespect.

"Okay, the argued person with a disappointing smile retreated shamefully like a boy who received the failed report card in front of everyone in a crowded classroom.

While the most privileged senior agents were breaking the queue frequently as and when they want, Alexander Philip and his friend were waiting patiently for their turn. One inspector in his khaki uniform was busy in reading one Marathi weekly eagerly as if he was given that assignment by his superiors to finish the reading in a specified time. Though many were standing in front of him in a line he was busy in reading the short story printed in black letters. Occasionally he raised his heavy head in response to the sound "Sir" and looked above through the steel frame of his reading glass without much trouble to his heavy head and attend one person at a time and put his initial to that paper and motioned him to show that paper to another clerk sitting little far away to fix his stamp on it. His exceptionally large eye balls looked at the person standing in front of him to see whether he was an agent or an *aam aadmi* (Ordinary man). The inspector looked through his bulged eyes ferociously only to discourage people interrupting him while he was enjoying his magazine.

"He might have paid at least 25 lakhs to buy that chair" Mishraji whispered into the ears of the principal.

One person who overheard his talk replied "This rascal won't do anything without bribing, he is the ministers' *aadmi,* he is not afraid of the public, only we; the public is afraid of him and give what he demands out of fear."

Since they were far away from the Inspector and there were murmuring sound everywhere, their whisper was not audible to others. Another person commented: "Since 9.30 in the morning I was standing in this line, now it is eleven o'clock, I have no hope that I can meet him today." By this time one man who moved towards the entry clerk went straight in front of the queue and tried to slide inside the front portion of that serpentine queue and pretended as if he was unaware of the existence of a queue there and tried in vain to meet the entry clerk, suddenly a cry of about a dozen people from behind stopped him from his action.

*"Are Are gandu Peeche jao, ek dhum peeche"* (You bastard move to the end of the queue) they all shouted from behind. The face of the middle aged man with a hunch and a red turban on his head like the ordinary laborers wear, turned pale in shock and he tried to smile, a lifeless smile appeared on his wrinkled face, he tried to say something, something awkward, not from the heart but from the lips, a smile of simple apology and

shame, and he moved behind and stood behind the 19ᵗʰ person and he almost reached the ground floor on the narrow steps. The queue moved after two minutes and he could climb to the next step after every four minutes. The dingy stair case was with full of people. Just like ants, people moved up and down hitting each other first and turned to other side to give way as if they were trying to kiss each other in vain. A teen ager boy brought tea in a large thermos flask and after serving the tea free of cost to the master who was reading the Marathi paper and later sold it to the people standing in the queue. He filled the very small plastic cup half and given to the tired people standing in the queue and they felt relaxed after drinking that 50 ml tea and dropped the thin white plastic cups near to their own foot without making sounds directly on the floor or on the steps and moved forward as if they have not done anything wrong.

Like smashed white button mushrooms in the field the milky white plastic cups remained there on the steps and on the floor giving the steps a different look. Nearly after one hour the middle aged man who was bitterly trying to break the queue in vain reached in front of the counter and he took a deep breath and sighed. A smile of happiness spread over his creased face, but the emotion of contentment was short lived as the bald headed tall Ghandhian clerk with his round spectacle took his paper in his hand and looked at it suspiciously and looked again at the face of the man standing in front of him and shouted scornfully "Who told you to submit it here?"

"Inspector *saab*" the man with great respect told in a low voice while motioning his hand towards the Inspector who was busy in reading his Marathi magazine.

"This is counter No.6, you should pay the money and this form at counter No. 8, Go." He briefed and took a form from the man behind him to show that he was duty conscious.

The man now confused completely and turned around for help and slowly moved in search of counter No.8.

"I don't know how to work in this office, people are coming here, how I can accept that form, and I accept only forms for renewal of license, not new applications for driving licenses. What the inspector said was wrong or he might have heard it wrongly" The old Gandian clerk expressed his innocence to others and took a *beedi* in his hand and lighted it, took a small puff inside while accepting a form from the next person.

"Counter No. 8 *Kider hai bhai*? (Where is the Counter No.8?)The man enquired.

"It is down on the first floor, go fast they close the counter sharp at 12.30 noon. They are very punctual while closing the counter though they come half an hour late in the morning" another man commented.

The man moved to the down floor and saw a big No.8 written in blue on a glass panel with a round hole in it for putting human hand inside to submit forms and to dig out money from outside to inside. He moved towards Number 8 in a hurry only to be insulted again by another goon "Rascal, can't you see people are standing here, Oh my leg, you stamped on my leg", he pushed him to another side with his shoulder with a slight force.

"Sorry sir" the man pleaded for mercy "*galathi ho gaya, map karo*". (*Please* forgive me) Before he could complete his sentence he was pushed to another side from opposite side "Idiot, why are you pushing me." Be careful don't push people" he warned him. The man with red turban struggled to put his foot on the floor without stamping on others. Here in front of the counter No.8 the queue moved again inch by inch.

The clock on the wall showed 12.15 P.m. Only 15 minutes to close the counter. People standing in line started shouting in desperation. "Fast, fast" they shouted to the cashier collecting the cash. The cashier stopped working and gave a warning look at the people shouting. After 20 seconds, the time fixed by the Indian railway for the local trains to halt at a particular station for commuters to board or alight in Mumbai local railway stations, he slowly he resumed his duty after saying something to the person sitting next to him in Konkani and laughed mockingly with one side of his mouth showing his silver canine tooth. The cashier was looking at his watch frequently after every two minutes and eagerly waiting to close the counter sharp at 12.30 pm. Now it is the turn of the man with red turban on his head, he stood in front of the cashier.

"90 rupees" The cashier demanded the money after looking at the form.

The wrinkled hands of the red turban touched the right side of his shirt, a peculiar thin white shirt worn by some people similar to a short *juba* with side pockets on either side at the lower hip level, to take the money. He touched his right side pocket first, and then he touched his left side pocket to feel the purse. He could not feel anything in his pocket. He bent his body and looked in to his side pocket. It was empty. He again looked to left and searched his left pocket and pulled out the small bag like pocket outside. His left pocket was also empty. He suddenly looked on the floor near to his feet and then to the persons who were standing next to him and yelled in a distressing throbbing voice.

"My purse!! My purse!! He yelled.

He did not get any answer. He saw the person, the cashier, closing the hole on the glass panel just below the blue 8 with his thick brown register from inside. The clock chimed 12.30.

Alexander Philip found very difficult to lift his paining legs to climb the steep steps of the RTO office to reach the second floor. He had to stop on the crowded steps many a times to give way for the people coming down face to face, like the ants stop on their path to give way for their comrades who came from the opposite direction. The small rooms constructed for residential purpose were converted to an office of the traffic cell many years ago when there were only few hundred vehicles on the roads. Now even after thirty years when every house has two to three vehicles and the streets are flooded with cars and two wheelers, the RTO office till remains in their infant stage, with make shift arrangements. One small store room by the side of a toilet was modified and white washed recently to occupy an officer with blue neck tie and grey over coat. He was very lean and his cheek was sunken expressing the starvation and mal nutrition. When all are well fed with ample money from various sources why only this senior Officer was forced to lead a meager life and sitting in a toilet of an old flat, Alexander Philip thought in his mind. The thin whitish skin with numerous wrinkles on the fore head and cheeks also exposed the prominent blue veins in the middle of his forehead. There was no expression on his face. It was very difficult to judge whether he is in a happy mood or angry. He was looking at his files seriously for few seconds and scribbled something on the green noting pages and closed one file and kept it aside. Then again he lifted another from the heap of files and scribbled or signed on the green pages without looking around. A few files were removed by a peon and another set of old files were kept on his table. Alexander Philip stood in front of him for about five minutes but his presence was ignored by the officer with blue tie. When the officer relaxed for a while after finishing a dozen files, Alexander Philip thought of introducing himself and said:

"Sir, I'm Principal of the Susegaad Higher Secondary School" Alexander Philip said.

The Traffic Officer raised his sunken yellow eyes from the file and gazed at the man standing in front of him for few moments and gesticulated to sit in front of him.

Principal sat in front of the Traffic Officer and said abruptly without killing a minute, "News papers of today published news about an abduction case... he paused for a second and continued,... that was about involvement of a maruti car GDJ 01.7714..., I want to know the owner of the vehicle..."

"Your interest?" The Officer asked without any expression on his face.

Principal showed the copy of express and said "This paper claim that the vehicle belongs to me. But actually it is not mine."

The Traffic Officer glanced at the news item and his left hand fumbled for the buzzer switch on the wall. He pressed it two times and took another file from the pile and opened it. He collected the envelope inside the file and kept it in his drawer and immediately scribbled something on the green paper and signed below it. Principal noticed several envelopes inside his drawer. The traffic Officer continued his job systematically with keen interest without looking at the person sitting across him or talking anything to him. After five minutes Alexander Philip repeated his statement once again, "Sir, I would like to know the owner ship of this vehicle No. GDJ.01.7714."

The officer again pressed the buzzer, three times now. A feeble sound of the buzzer was heard at a distance. An exceptionally short and stout dark person with a huge head-disproportional to his body-, appeared in his white dress, he was rude and unfriendly. He had a heavy black brows and coarse features. The Traffic Officer looked at the peon standing in front of him and examined his outfit as if a platoon commander inspecting the dress of his soldier, and raised his eye brows with displeasure.

"Where is your uniform?"

"It is given for wising sir" the peon replied suddenly.

"What did you say yesterday?"

"Yesterday... yesterday… it was raining and I got wet fully."

"Was it raining yester day?" The Officer in a grim voice asked with doubt.

"In our side.., it was raining, sir". The answer was stereo typed and swift.

"There was no rain in... this month in... Goa..? And you are telling it was raining in your side, this month you won't get any washing allowance."

"No sir, please sir, he started pleading… I will change my uniform right now." He tried to persuade his boss.

"What about tomorrow?"

"Surely I will wear my uniform sir" the peon replied.

"How many pairs do you have?"

"Only two sir"

"What about other sets"

"All torn and discarded sir"

"How old is your this shirt?"

"Four years sir"

"But the uniform you got from government wear only for one year"

"Yes sir"

Traffic officer did not laugh. He tightened his thin lips with anger. Alexander Philip thought about his staff. Only

Tapa, the Nepali, was ready to wear the uniform. He was happy and proud to wear that when others were reluctant and felt humiliated to wear their uniform. Many peons claim to the public that they are teachers or clerks. To hide their identity they never wear their uniform.

The traffic Officer instructed the peon to accompany Alexander Philip and to show the records. The peon led Alexander Philip to another room where all the old records were stored. A physically handicapped lady with her stiff neck was in charge of the old records. She could not turn her neck. Her brown and gray hair combined with the stiff neck gave her an appearance of the extinct Neanderthal woman. She rarely looked straight into the eyes of people, but was very stubborn in her facial expression. She instructed the peon to remove one old register with a broken hard cover. She opened the register and turned the pages swiftly and her fingers stopped at one entry. GDJ -01-7714. She read out the name of the owner "Alexander Philip resident of Baina, Vasco." Alexander Philip could not believe what he heard.

"But madam, I sold the vehicle to one Christopher six years ago" Alexander Philip said with great shock and awkwardness.

"Sorry", the women said, "we have no records of that transfer."

"But I have my records with me" He said in a perplexed tone."

"You may have your records but still the vehicle is in your name" The lady clerk said in a firm voice.

"Then I have to verify it, please show the register "Alexander Philip demanded.

"You cannot see our records" she affirmed in a haughty manner.

"Why?" Alexander Philip questioned.

"Sorry, we cannot show our records to outsiders" she said.

"Is that very confidential?" If you show the records is it affect the security of the state? Is it diplomatic secretes?" Alexander Philip shouted.

"I was told not to show the records to any one" She said in a trembling voice. The clerk was silent and utterly confused.

"On what ground you are concealing the records from the public? Alexander Philip asked again. "I know that somebody tampered with the documents, sure." "If you are not ready to show the documents you will be forced to show me the same in the court." He said in a challenging voice.

The clerk put her hand on the closed register and closed her eyes in fear or confusion. Alexander Philip noticed bloodlessness on her face and she gradually turned pale. She was silent but was trying to speak something with her bloodless lips, but no sound came out, only the lips twitched. She was in utter confusion but did not speak a word. Alexander Philip decided to move out. Jagnath Mishra followed him.

A week later the port city heard the news. The watchman of Susegaad Higher Secondary School was brutally murdered and his dead body was found hanging from a tree in the school compound.

# Chapter 21

The hill station motel, the Gulmohar Gardens was away from the city. The receptionist while watching on his small TV set noticed the breaking news: College Girl abducted from Goa: This is the third kidnapping in this month. Abductors abandoned their vehicle at Sawantwadi Goa Border." He also watched the photograph of the girl" immediately he took his mobile and clicked the photograph of the abandoned girl from the TV Screen. His suspicion about the burka 'lady' and the tall young man grew stronger and stronger and without wasting time he fumbled for the buzzer switch under his table and pressed it once. A teenager boy in his brown uniform with red collar and big side pockets appeared after a minute. "Call the lady doctor, very urgent" he informed. The young trainee doctor who was attending Rohini put her in I V injection and reported to the receptionist. Andrew became nervous once again and looked at his friend in disguise vacillatingly. He was planning to escape from the site.

The doctor without much experience saw the photograph of the girl on TV and screamed "Yes, Yes it is She, My God!" She exclaimed in her surprise. The frightened look of the receptionist silenced her. The screaming sound of the doctor aroused more panic and doubt in the minds of the kidnappers though they had not heard what she uttered and the 'lady' in burka peeped her head through the window to see what was happening with the receptionist and the doctor. Neither the receptionist nor the Doctor failed to notice that they were under observation. "Sorry, she said in a very low voice, yes… yes I am sure it is her photo" She reiterated once again with slight fear in her voice.

"Is she out of danger? The receptionist asked with unusual curiosity.

"Nothing to worry but her pulse is very very weak, but she is improving and responding to medicines."

"Keep a close watch on her and do not leave the room without informing me. You understand?"

"Yes, but I am afraid now to be with them. They may even attack me" She expressed her discomfiture.

"OK, we will be here, please go back and say that she in danger and need close observation, you got it? She is a student… now you please go and stay there". Please do not show any trace of doubt on your face. You should act perfectly well. I will do the rest. We should rescue her."

The doctor with a fearful face returned back to Ramla.

Andrew Akbar's distress call for help disturbed the peaceful sleep of Minguel de Silva. He informed that they were trapped inside a motel near to Ratnagiri and need urgent help. He also informed that he could not contact Fatima as she was not lifting her cell phone. Andrew Akbar informed Minguel De Silva to inform personally the news to Fatima at her residence at Gama beach. Her huge castle at Gama beach was forbidden to strangers. Only selected friends were allowed permission inside her house, Minguel de Silva was one among them. The Doberman dogs at the gate recognized the Royal Enfield bike and its owner and gave permission to meet their boss. He knew that only Fatima could arrange some help for Andrew. He didn't know why Fatima switched off all her cell phones. Fatima's wisdom has no parallel. She knew that Andrew would call her on the way and she does not want to give any clue to police about this.

Fatima's huge and ugly figure occupied a wooden sofa while Minguel was standing. Mustafa, her close aid gave her favorite brand cigarette and helped her to light it courteously. She appeared very serious and rough. While blowing out the smoke through the widely opened ape like nostrils she asked "any news?"

"Madam, Andrew had called me in the morning…" Minguel's words vibrated slightly while saying this, and he continued "they were trapped near Ratnagiri… wanted urgent help."

"Expected, fully expected! Nothing strange… as usual". She replied scornfully and spat on the floor. "What did you say? Where are they now?" she cried.

"In one motel near Ratnagiri, Gulmohar Gardens" Minguel said while standing on knees in front of the mafia queen.

"Stupid, why did he go there?" That south Indian hotel never helps us."

"Madam, they informed the police and not allowing them to go out"

"Oh! Good" "Then we have to act" Give me your cell phone Minguel"

She snatched the cell phone from Minguel and dialed a number. "Hello Braganza, Fatima here."

"Hello, Madam," Minister replied.

"Listen, Mr. Braganza our boys are in trouble… while talking she gustered to Minguel to leave that hall and lifted her heavy body and moved to an inner room and spoke." After a few minutes chat she came out and handed over the phone to Minguel.

"Now you may go Minguel, I have made all arrangements, don't use that sim card any more, I have removed it, for you" she laughed wickedly and called Mustafa and asked him to arrange another sim card for Minguel De Silva.

When Alexander Philip gave the news brief on TV he gave his own phone number for contact. When Sara Philip was about to close her flat, 10 minutes to 8' O' Clock in the morning she heard her land phone ringing. But when she reached near the Phone it was already disconnected. Again when she locked her flat to go out for work she heard the ringing of her land phone again. Immediately she opened the door of her flat and reached near the phone only to realize that it was disconnected once again. In fear of missing the bus to her work place she left immediately without waiting for another call.

Alexander Philip returned home after visiting the RTO office in a pensive mood, the tension and the whole day's tiredness made him awkward and morose. He was distressed about the whole day's incident at police station and at RTO office. He lied down with full frustration on his bed and took the day's news paper and searched for the kidnapping news. He read once again the distorted news against him. He closed his eyes to relax. The innocent cannot live in this world, he thought. All sufferings and misfortunes are for the innocent people. Success and prosperity is for the people with crookedness. He remembered the words of Jesus Christ to his Judge the Pilot. "What is truth? The pilot did not answer his question. Is there any truth in this world? He asked himself. Why innocents are being punished? One girl is suffering. The whole world closes the eyes towards the atrocity. Even media is trying to make money out of it. Whether the innocents and trustworthy get any justice in this world? People say truth will win ultimately. After suffering for long if the truth wins what is the gain out of it Ultimately not the truth but the evil wins over the good that is the truth, the history says that. What wrong did she? What wrong her parents did? God gave her beauty but not the power to protect it. A hundred questions passed through his mind, without any answers, unrelated sad thoughts without any solutions flashed through his mind. He did not know when he slept. The metallic sound of a key turning inside the lock and opening of the door has awoken him from his short nap. Sara Philip was in front of him. He smiled at her awkwardly and slept again.

The pleasant smell of Brue coffee brought by Sara Philip put a full stop to his wild thoughts. She sat near him on the same sofa and wiped her wet hand on her own sari tip. She knew that her husband is worried. She looked at his sad face and asked: "In deep thought?"

Without answering her question he lifted the white coffee mug with his left hand and smiled a pensive smile through the corners of his mouth lifting the left upper lips without opening it, as he usually does when he is worried. The smile did not spread all over his face. It died on the corners of his lips-a smile of bitterness, agony and helplessness. He took a small sip of the hot coffee and kept the hot mug on the hand rest of the sofa.

"Whahh! It is really hot" he said. "It burned my lips."

"Sorry I forgot to remind you" Sara apologized. "Did you go to the RTO office to enquire the facts?" She enquired.

"Yes, yes, it is very funny; they say that it is in my name."

"How come?" She wondered.

"It is our democracy". "Everything is possible." "Everything is possible… with money power."

"Now it is very clear that someone is trying to trap you."

"Of course, the fear in the eyes of the RTO clerk and her refusal to show the records are the very evidence for that, someone is after me. She told she had instructions not to show the records to anyone. She was trying to cover up something." Alexander Philip joined his both hands behind his head and leaned backwards and took a deep breath and sighed.

"Alex I forgot to tell you…" Sara Philip said abruptly, "there was a phone call in the morning, someone was trying to contact us, but before I could reach the phone it was disconnected… I was in a hurry… and I had to lock and leave the house…" she paused for awhile. "Two times the phone rang but I could not get connected."

After taking one more sip of the coffee Alexander Philip looked at the machine and searched for the missed call list. "Repeated missed calls, four missed calls… Oh! New number…

he wondered. It is not a local call... it is from outside." After seeing the missed call list he murmured.

"Shall we call back?"

"Yes try"

Alexander Philip checked the time of the calls. 7.50 am; 7.52 am; 8.00 am and 8.10 am". Someone was trying to contact us desperately.

"The first two calls I heard, Sara Philip said "but since I was getting late... I had to leave..., I could not wait... before I could reach the phone the line got disconnected... and I left at 7.55. Please call them now."

"I think I gave this number to the TV personals." He dialed the number and waited anxiously for the answer. "Yes it is ringing..." he kept the receiver close to his ear.

"Good evening sir..." he heard the very soft voice of a lady at the other end. "Hotel Gulmohar Gardens."

Alexander Philip puzzled for a moment "Hotel Gulmohar Gardens?" he repeated the name in a reflex action.

"Yes, Sir, What can I do for you" the lady asked with a professional respect.

"Madam, I received four missed calls from your number in this morning... what is the matter? Alexander Philip asked.

"Sir, had you booked any rooms here?" The receptionist voice echoed over the phone.

"Sorry, Madam, I never booked any rooms with you, but I received some missed calls from your telephone... I don't know who called me... and for what? Only to confirm that I called now..." Alexander Philip stopped for a moment and waited for the response from the other end.

"Sir, may I know the time of that missed calls..." She enquired.

"It was between 7.50 am and 8.10 am, madam" he replied.

"Hello sir, in that case the other receptionist, Mr. Venkatesh might have called you... and my duty starts from 8.30 am. And I will pass the message when he joins at 6.00Pm. May I know your name please" the lady receptionist asked.

"Alexander Philip"

"Alexander Philip?" The girl repeated the name as if she knew the name.

"Are you the Principal, Susegaad Higher Secondary? The girl enquired with great curiosity.

"Yes, madam, How come you know me?"

"Sir I saw your appeal on T V regarding that kidnapping case…" wait a minute please…" she said. There was a long silence at the other end.

Alexander Philip stood up keeping the receiver close to his ear eagerly waiting to hear from the other end and said to Sara after closing the mouth piece with his right palm "I think they have some information regarding Rohini… we could not contact them early…"

"Sir holds on please" the lady receptionist said in between for a second "I am trying to contact Mr.Venkatesh."

Alexander Philip heard the sound of the receiver hitting the table top at the other end and other murmuring sounds of other people that were not at all clear over the phone. He heard the yelling sound of the lady receptionist over the phone calling "call Venkatesh, call Venkatesh." After a silence of two minutes again the telephone became active for a brief period and Alexander Philip now heard the sound of another person "Sir, please hold the line we are trying to call Venkatesh here." Alexander Philip with great anxiety waited for the Venkatesh, receptionist of Gulmohar Gardens.

Few more minutes passed by. Finally he heard the voice of another lady over the phone "Sir Our receptionist Mr.Venkatesh was trying to contact you today morning... he tried many a time on your phone... but no one answered the phone... bad luck... what else to say... I'm doctor Madubala, even I saw your appeal on the TV... I have some information to pass on... the kidnapers with the girl were here for a few hours.... we are very sorry to state that they escaped few hours ago..." she paused.

"They escaped?" in a disgusting voice Alexander asked. "You could have informed the police... very shocking... news... what to do now... did you inform the police? In full frustration he asked.

"Yes sir, we informed the police. I was treating her... since she was sick and unconscious... when they reached here... this place is a very remote hill station and the nearest hospital is about 100 kilometers away... we gave her first aid and she recovered..."

"Then... then... then... how did they escape Madam?" with great anxiety and curiosity he repeated his question. He felt his body is trembling without control. He fell on the sofa and tried to relax... and repeated the words "they escaped... Oh they escaped."

"Sir, listen", Dr. Madubala said patiently "Mr. Venkatesh informed me that the girl was a victim of abduction, and he showed the photograph of her from the TV and I was asked to take special care of her. While I was prolonging the treatment purposefully only to keep them here long and allowing the police to come over here... and at the same time we were trying to contact you. We also informed the police about the suspicious people here with a girl... we also informed your police station as per your instruction on TV... and also the local police. The police informed us that they are sending a team of police people to nab them here... Venkatesh made all arrangements to stop their escape. He closed all the entrance and kept a vigil on the kidnapers without giving any trace of doubts to them. The girl was administered with I.V injection only to give enough time for the police people to arrive. But the unexpected thing happened... they escaped. At about 3.00 pm the police party arrived. There was a lady constable with them. They asked many questions to us and they took the kidnappers along with the girl in their jeep. Actually what happened next wondered us more? At about 4.30 pm another police party arrived and asked about the kidnappers. They said their vehicle got damaged on their way and because of that they were late. When we reported that the kidnappers were already arrested by a police party, they were shocked. They said they did not send any other group to arrest them and suspected some foul play in the entire episode. They said the first group was imposters and the gangsters itself in police uniform.

# Chapter 22

I should find out Christopher. Alexander Philip thought. He spent the whole evening in search of his old files. Finally he got an old file named Maruti 800. Hurriedly he turned the faded pages, the owner's manual that he failed to hand over to Christopher by mistake, photo copies of Form 29 and Form 30 and even the repairing bills, service station bills, date of oil changes with kilometers run etc were intact.

"I got, I got it" he shouted with joy.

"What? Sara Philip asked while cleaning the vessels in the kitchen.

"I got the phone Number of Christopher. I'm going to contact him right now." While cleaning his soiled hands Alexander Philip said with great animation.

"Who is that Christopher? Sara Philip asked in confusion.

"Sara, I sold that old car to him about six years ago. Now the RTO office alleged that I am the owner that, even now. I have to find out the truth."

"Wait for tomorrow, it is 8' O clock now" Sara Philip suggested.

"Not tomorrow, now I am going to call him, otherwise I won't get sleep." He went near the telephone and dialed the old number carefully.

Beep… beep… beep… beep. He could hear the machine trying to catch the signals. He tried again and again in vain. He could hear the same beep… beep… sound. He was frustrated soon. The old number might have changed, he doubted.

The very next day morning Alexander Philip dialed the same number again. He was successful in getting connected to Sanguem.

"Hello, I am Alexander Philip, can I speak to Mr. Christopher, please" he asked and waited for the reply.

There was only silence from the other side. He again repeated "Hello… I am Alexander Philip, from Vasco; Can I speak to Mr. Christopher please?"

"Sir… you don't know…, again silence…, Sir, Daddy is No more" a teenager's painful voice echoed in his ears. "He expired six months ago Sir…"

Alexander Philip was stunned to hear that sad news. He got confused for a moment. He did not know what to talk now. He doubted whether to continue the conversation or to give an abrupt end to that call, he doubted. Finally he said "Sorry to bother you, I did not know about that… I am very sorry to hear that… my heartfelt sympathy to you" somehow he completed his message in worried tone.

"Sir, why did you call now… can I help? I am his daughter." The teenager's voice was firm but mixed with a slight sorrow.

"Dear, I want some information about the car that I sold to your father six years ago, I am in trouble" Alexander Philip completed his message briefly.

"Then, I know you Sir, my dad and I visited Vasco to bring that car, I was in standard six then" the girl said over the phone. "My daddy died in an accident, a car accident, the same car, he died on the spot." The car damaged completely and we disposed it."

"Disposed?" Alexander Philip asked once again.

"The insurance company took it…, I think, and I do not know much about that, Sir, may I call my mummy she knows about it."

"Yes please" He could hear the girls' voice over the phone calling "mummy."

After a moments wait he could hear the voice of a middle aged women "Good morning Sir, I'm Mrs. Christopher."

"Good morning Madam" he replied in a very respectful voice." Sorry to bother you" he continued.

"I want some information regarding that old car, I heard that your husband had a fatal accident… I am very sorry to hear that… and my heartfelt sympathy to you… I never knew about that… really it is shocking news…"

"It is our fate… sir, what else to say…, he was very care less and was coming from a party… late night… as you know… he was drunk… fully drunk… his car hit a truck and it jumped across the side wall of the road and plunged in to Mandovi river near Ribandar and drowned…"

"May I know whether you had changed the ownership of the vehicle at the RTO office?'

"Yes Yes, he changed the ownership, I know"

"I'm asking because, the same car, somebody says, met with another accident yesterday and the RTO says it is in the name of Alexander Philip, my name" He said in an uncertain voice with a slight wavering.

"Very well it was in my husband's name, we claimed for insurance compensation, but the company refused to pay anything to us on the ground that he was drunk."

"Madam Do you have the copy of your RC book with you?"

"Sir I handed over every document to our advocate, he may have it. Since we lost the claim, I was not so keen to take the documents back. And we asked one agent to dispose the damaged car and he might have taken the document from our advocate." Mrs. Christopher paused.

"In case if I want the details would you please help me" he requested with a pleading voice.

"Yes, of course, sir". Mrs. Christopher replied." I shall contact that advocate and agent right now and inform you sir.

"Thank you madam I 'm grateful to you… shall call you later, bye" he disconnected the phone and sat near the phone in deep thought.

The next day Alexander Philip got a sealed envelope. The special messenger from the Department requested Alexander Philip to sign the Register as an evidence of acceptance of the envelope. He took the envelope in his hand and placed against the light to see the size of the paper inside, before tearing the edge of the brown envelope in order to avoid any damage to the paper inside. He had no idea about the content. The peon left his place silently after closing the register in his hand. Alexander Philip pulled out the single sheet with care. He read the content:

No/DE/Vol.II/Tr/ 6070
15th December

## ORDER

I am pleased to transfer the below mentioned officer of the cadre of principal, EEO/ DEO/Dr. Alexander Philip and post him as the Environment Officer with immediate effect. Shri. Somnath Madkaikar, Principal of Higher Secondary School, Valpoi, shall hold additional charge of the Susegaad Higher Secondary until further orders.

The above Officer shall join his duties of posting immediately on receipt of this order. He is not entitled for TA/ DA or joining time. The date of joining should be intimated to this office.

Director

Copy to:  1. The person concerned
          2. Personal File
          3. Shri. Somnath Madkaikar
          4. Director of Accounts

# Chapter 23

Albert Arnold Al Gore, the democratic nominee for the president of USA in the 2000 presidential election had won the popular vote by approximately 500,000 votes, but ultimately lost the Electoral College to republican candidate George W. Bush. Had he won the election the history of the world would have been entirely different. The world wide hatred to USA would not have happened. Had Al Gore won the elections America would not have lost the World trade centre

(?) Man proposes God disposes. God allowed Lucifer to win, for the destruction and they fell into the same pit they made and thousands of innocent people died on both sides. Finally who won the battle? For Alexander Philip, Al Gore was only a Vice President of America from 1993 to 2001. As the Environment Officer he could learn more about Mr. Al Gore and his love for the planet earth. He noticed the huge amount of study materials and environmental kits donated for our children by the United States of America was lying unnoticed and neglected in the junk yard of the Directorate of Education. He was happy to be a part of Mr. Al Gore's GLOBE programme that was launched on the Earth day. These activities on Education and Scientific research among children were treated like Muhammad Bin Tuqlaq's mentality by the Department of Education. Education Officers were only interested in government funds, not in doing anything good for the students nor for the nation. According to Forbes magazine the 'GLOBE' made an extensive use of the internet to increase student's awareness of their environment. Asst Director opposed the proposal stating that it was not feasible in Goa, but feasible in USA. Alexander Philip was sad to see hundreds of Environmental Kits supplied by the GLOBE were gathering dust and moss in the damp corridors of the Department. He came to know that materials were received by the Environment section years ago and no one took any interest to supply the same to the concerned schools. Due to lack of storage facility the same were dumped in corridors. Further no school authorities were ready to lift that valuable kits and cassettes and DVD spending their funds. One full ship of study materials reached India become a waste in the hands of Indian Educationalists and administration.

"Are you ready to take up the matter?" one day Asst. Director asked Alexander Philip.

"Yes, yes" 'Why Not? It is a very good project." He answered.

"You, see Dr. Alexander, It is not so easy to handle the things as you think", Asst. Director said in a confusing tone.

"Let me try", Give me six months time, I shall introduce the same in at least in 100 schools this year." He answered confidently.

"See the Department may not provide any assistance to you for the implementation, no rooms, no infrastructure, no vehicle, no funds, not even the required man power?" Then how are you going to implement it, my dear?" The Asst. Director raised his eye brows and lifted his lower lips and made a sarcastic giggle towards him. He never thought that Alexander Philip would readily accept the challenge. He was trying to discourage his subordinate by projecting out all the negative aspects of the task. Definitely he knew that there were enough central government funds and there were no additional funds required for its implementation. Though Alexander Philip joined as the Environmental Officer, The Asst.Director was illegally handling all central government funds for personal reasons and was not ready to show the files to the concerned Officer. And he did not want anyone to see the accounts or any activity under central scheme.

"The central governments funds are sufficient for that and I shall cut short the unnecessary expenses and save enough funds for this magnificent project." Alexander Philip said in a persuasive and convincing manner. But the reply was not convincing or inspiring or acceptable to Asst. Director. The Asst. Director was silent for a few moments. He did not want to give any central government projects to anyone else in the Office. Though this fact was known to the higher authorities they do not want to make any changes in the status quo. They showed a blind eye to this corrupt practice. When Alexander Philip mentioned about the central government funds a mysterious unexplainable strange expression developed on the fat face of the Asst. Director. As he raised his eye brows some small pieces of the dried sandalwood paste from his forehead fallen down.

A week after this discussion with the Asst. Director, while going through the some of the files, Alexander Philip noticed the embezzlement of central government funds, by some of the officials in the environment section, nearly one year back. One day when his senior Asst. Director was on tour, accidently one of the files dealing with the centrally sponsored schemes has reached Alexander Philip's table accidently. He wanted to see the actual voucher files and other related files to study the matter. He heard from other officials that a huge amount of money has been sanctioned by the central government two years back and the money has been diverted to other projects and a serious misappropriation was done by some of the Asst. Directors by the help of Environment section. But Alexander Philip didn't know the real facts about that gossip.

He pressed the buzzer with his left hand. No one answered the call. After ten minutes he pressed the buzzer once again. As usual peons ignored the bell of a junior officer. The office culture was different. All the senior most people with some authority in their hand or have political connections received attention and respect in the office. Peons and sweepers after the duty time or even during the duty time frequently visits the houses of their bosses to pass information to them and also to attend their house hold works, though they were reluctant to do the office work, during office hours. They were very happy to attend the menial domestic works of the Dy. Directors and Director at their home. Because of this firm symbiotic attachment between the senior officials and the class four employees, the peons never bothered to attend the work of the junior staff, or the new comer 'Aliens' in the office. The class D employees very well knew that the higher officials and the ministers are always there to protect them. Alexander Philip remembered the words of the old Ombudsman regarding the lift Operator. The sixth floor office was not connected to the lift. Hundreds of people were forced to climb up to the sixth floor to attend the BDO's office and Ombudsman's Office at Junta house in the heart of the capital city. The sixty two year old high official, who got an extension of service because of his birth among the ruling caste, commented that the lift operator might be with the minister's kitchen and cleaning fish or sweeping their toilet, and he was not seen as the operator in the afternoon time.

Alexander Philip, the Environment Officer pressed the buzzer once again, but there was no response from any corner. He saw many peons were moving up and down in front of his room. He waited for another ten more minutes and lifted his fragile body from his executive revolving chair and went directly to the section. The section Officer was a great help to all his superiors except to Dr. Alexander Philip. He acted as a middle man between officers and the public, ministers and the printers, officers and business men, for all the illegal and corrupt practices. He was in the good book of the minister of Education and most of the secretariat staff. He was not happy with his immediate boss Dr. Alexander Philip. The sudden appearance of his boss in the section baffled the staff members. OS was sitting with his legs crossed and holding a Marathi paper and was sipping his tea from his large brown cup. Since he was fully engrossed in the reading he did not notice the person standing in front of him at first. He noticed the presence of someone in front of him through the corners of the eyes but did not raise his head to look at him. He thought somebody from the clerical staff is standing in front of him, so he did not raise his 'heavy' head and continued his reading. Other staff members could not resist the humor and started to laugh.

"Mr.OS where is that file No.28?" Alexander Philip who was standing in front of him for a few moments, enquired in a casual way. Office Superintendent recognized the deep base voice of his boss and immediately stood up with embarrassment with a blushing face.

"Sir…. sir"… he murmured in a low voice after keeping his brown tea cup on one of the open files and the news paper on the side of the table. The cup made a brown circle on the noting paper of the file.

"Mr.OS, please give the file of Ministry of Environment?"

A sudden change in the face of the Section Officer has been noticed by the Boss.

"Sir… that… Ahaa… that… file… yha…." He mumbled some incomprehensible meaningless words first and said "Sir that file is with the Asst.Director" he briefed.

Alexander Philip could not believe what his section officer said. He looked at him skeptically for a moment. He knew that OS wanted to cover up something. Without any hesitation he asked "Which is your shelf, let me check your files." He motioned his hands towards one shelf and the Environment Officer moved towards that shelf. There were numerous files inside. They were dumped inside without any order. Alexander Philip took out some of the files and checked.

"Hello Mr.OS, I am asking for the file No.28, the correspondences with the ministry of environment." Again he looked at his section officer doubtingly. Unenthusiastically he started to search for the files along with his boss. Suddenly Alexander Philip's eyes fell on a file super scribed

Ministry of Environment. He also found another file super scribed -Environment Education New Scheme. Those were the two files I was looking for the last two weeks, he thought in his mind, "good I myself have come to search the files, otherwise he would have blot out the same from me."

"Sir... I... thought..." OS wanted to tell something to Alexander Philip. But before he could complete his sentence Alexander Philip disappeared from that room carrying both the files in his hand without showing any expression on his face. The gaze of OS followed Alexander Philip till he entered his cabin. He hit his head in humiliation and frustration. Others who were watching him thought "this time he will be caught, this is his end, and his days are being counted now."

Inside his cabin Alexander Philip sank into his old executive chair, it made an initial squeak sound. As he bends further backwards the old chair made again the same unpleasant squeaking noise. He raised both of his hands above his head and fell back wards inside the reclining chair and sighed. He looked at the files on the table and remained in that position for three minutes. Then he bends forward and took one of the files and opened it. He turned the correspondence pages with inquisitiveness. His eyes fixed on a recent memo from the Ministry of Environment. It was a second reminder letter to submit the utility certificate and accounts details of rupees sixty crores received from the centre. The letter was marked to the Environment Officer by the Director two months ago. But the same was not reached the E.O till date. The amount was received by the Asst. Director about two years ago.

Section Officer Sunil became nervous and scared. He folded his Marathi paper and kept it aside. He crouched down towards his table and kept his hand on the glass top and supported his head with his right arm and started thinking.

He closed his eyes and began to think how to prevent the EO from taking action on those files. Other LDC in the section observed his nervousness but they remained silent. Immediately he lifted his heavy body from the godrej arm chair and went out and removed one Wills cigarette and lit it. He quickly took a few puffs and released it without holding it. He stopped near the door way keeping his cigarette in his left hand looking through the open window. The cool current of air from the river Mondovi snatched the cigarette smoke immediately and brought it inside the section. Some ladies closed their nose to escape from the irritating smell of the nicotine. Through the open window he saw the moving barges with full of iron ores transporting it to the huge ships in the deep sea. His eyes did not fix anywhere. He was deep in his deliberation. He lit another cigarette and smoked slowly while holding the smoke for longer time and exhaled it slowly making a narrow column of smoke in the air. A mild smirk appeared on his fat face, expressing scorn and smugness. With a gleaming eyes and joyful face he returned to his godrej arm chair. He laughed sarcastically to declare to others that he is going to win over gatti EO, the Alien.

After thirty minutes Sunil got up from his seat without wasting much time and went directly to Asst. Directors' room. He knocked gently on the door of the Asst. Director's cabin and waited for a moment.

"Yes, come in" he heard the voice from inside. He opened the door bit by bit and after confirming no one is nearby or inside and entered the room and closed it behind him. Asst. Director looked up and noticed the distressed face of OS. "What happened?" Asst. Director asked anxiously. "Sir… he was struggling to find words and the words chocked in his throat. Then after convincing himself he said with confidence "Sir, Alexander sir got that files"… he stopped for a moment.

"Which files?" Asst. Director asked after putting his pen down on the table till gazing at the fat pot bellied figure in front of him.

"File Nos. 23 and 28" OS took a deep breath and sighed.

"Ministry of Environment files?" He asked doubtingly

"Yes sir" OS said in a worried nervous tone.

"But How?" Asst. Director raised his voice with anger and annoyance. He did not offer OS a seat to sit. "But How?' he again asked with fury." It was with you, it was with your safe custody and I told you not to hand over those files to any one without my knowledge." He looked at the Section Officer scornfully." Now get out and get it back immediately" He shouted in a loud voice.

"Sir", in a trembling voice he replied, "Alexander sir personally came to the section and took it himself, how could I resist? Though I told the file is with you he did not believe that and he himself searched my cupboard and took it away with him."

"And then…?"

"It is with him now"

"Oh shit", he hit his fist on the table and pushed all the files to other corner violently "Now, you see all will be caught, even you cannot escape" In a low voice he cried "it is embezzlement… misappropriation of central fund, you understand… Idiot… that file says everything… it is a solid proof against you and me… we cannot escape… we cannot… be prepared to say goodbye to your family… you may rest in jail for the rest of your life."

"Sir, what I could do to prevent it?" Till date no officer searched my cupboard and I never expected that he goes to that extend. I really apologize for my foolishness and I am really sorry for that…" Section officer said in a very soft and polite manner.

Both of them did not talk for the next two minutes. Sunil was standing all the time in front of the Asst. Director. He was very confused and worried. He was thinking how to ease out the tension and how to solve the crisis.

"Now, what is the way out?" Asst.Director asked his subordinate for advice. Asst. Director knew that OS is more intelligent and cunning than him. He believed in his subordinates' capacities and abilities.

"Sir, I told you first not to bring this rascal here. I heard about his nature, I knew that he will not join in our group and he will be a problem maker here and would be a thorn in our flesh, which happened. Wherever he served he had problem with the staff."

After a pause Asst. Director, said "Do you think that I recommended his name for this post. "I never recommended him or supported his posting here in this department, I knew him very well for many years." He said in very disgusted voice. "That donkey was very much interested in him, out of the four names he suggested Alexander Philips' name for Environment Officer."

"Why? Secretary Education has any special interest in him." OS asked curiously.

"No, No, he has no special interest in him" He is from Orissa and Alexander from Kerala. But he wanted a person with Doctoral degree in Environmental Science for this post. And this alien has a PhD degree in environmental science. Both are outsider gattis." he added.

"Both are gattis" Adharma Pal added that adjective unknowingly.

"Actually three times I omitted this beggar's name, but Secretary returned the file and asked to furnish all the names of officers with their full qualifications. And finally he got through."

"So you were compelled to do that."

"Yes, that was the truth." He lamented.

"Why can't you suggest a transfer sir? OS opened his stratagem box slowly.

"On what ground?" He joined only recently... a few months ago and he has done that state level competition in an admirable way, and that impressed everyone including the Minister. He made all arrangements perfectly well. Seating arrangements, selection of judges, venue, after all comparing by school children, everything were well planned and the function went smoothly till the end. He is a fantastic organizer and orator. That we cannot discard or forget. Only problem with him is he takes everything seriously and sincerely and never co-operates for any illegal things, and never suits for a government servant. How we survived here for many years? We never irritate our superiors nor question them. We are ready to do whatever they tell us to do, and never question them, good or bad". Asst. Director stated.

"Our gentle man does not know how to survive in our club. He is very adamant and straight forward. That is his weakness." OS Sunil expressed his view on Alexander Philip.

"Because of this nature, who suffers? He himself, sees, how many times he had been transferred within two years. Till he didn't realize the fact and adhered to his own strange philosophy for his own ruin. What I was telling, now it is very difficult to transfer him at present. On that day Minister himself appreciated him publically." Asst. Director expressed his helplessness in transferring EO.

"No Sir, It is not like that, Minister will definitely agree to remove him, and I am sure." OS said with full confidence and was looking in the eyes of the Asst. Director.

"But, How can you say like that?" after scratching his head by his left arm he enquired with curiosity.

"Sir everybody knew that Minister got the lions share in that environmental deal. In the name of environmental consultancy one Dr.Cajathan Fernandez was paid at least five crore rupees as consulting fees, TA, daily allowances etc. More than 200 Air trips he claimed for the last two years. The very interesting fact is that none of the officers have ever seen this Dr.Cajathan Fernandez. We all saw some reports and his exaggerated bills for payments. We doubt was there any Dr.Cajathan working in this Department." OS paused for a minute and his face wrinkled in a silent laugh of derision.

"Yes I know these facts"... Asst. Director approved the comments of his subordinates with the same expression and laughed derisively. But we have to obey the orders only... the orders of our democratic smugglers and robbers." Mockingly he again laughed.

"Our appointments are for that, we are changing the R.Rs for that." Is it not a mockery that peons or primary-teachers need some basic qualifications; but a minister doesn't require any qualifications? They have to complete only 25 years and need an identity card proving their age and Indian nationality."

"That is not a problem in India, if they have some contacts even Portuguese or Pakistani nationals become Indians, Chinese and Bangladeshi's can become Indians overnight. You might have heard that an Indian MP was a Chinese citizen. He contested elections from one of the north eastern states and was sitting in the Indian parliament for many years. That is India. We tolerate everyone. We tolerate everything, even injustice. Some of our Legislative Assembly members are Portuguese nationals even in Goa. Our laws are in beautifully printed and decoratively bounded law books and officials are afraid to implement it. It may be because of the fear of losing the chair or losing in elections." OS expressed his view.

"What we need is leaders with determination and vision" Asst. Director commented.

"Fortunately our leaders lack both." OS Sunil laughed wickedly.

"Oh, what nonsense we are talking… we should find out some way to transfer that… E.O… that is important what did you? Say… the minister will support his transfer?" Asst. Director asked with unusual inquisitiveness and interest while cleaning his running nose with a small towel.

"Of course, Sir, He will agree for that. Otherwise he will be exposed completely in front of his rivals and the opposition party. They are waiting for an issue. Though he is uneducated he is sharp and cunning like a fox.. The only essential quality needed for a politician here."

Alexander Philip closed his cabin and put his weight on that very old executive chair discarded by some ex-Directors in past. The chair started to make the irritating screeching sound again. He rolled his chair near to the table and adjusted the desk elevator in front of him and placed the file number 23 and opened it. He turned the pages hurriedly. He noticed one of the nothings of Dr.Cajathan Fernandez regarding his remunerations and submission of reports. He also observed that crores of rupees were claimed by him and also sanctioned to him with the approval of the higher authorities. One thing he noticed was the horrible hand writing of Dr.Cajathan and numerous spelling mistakes he made in his correspondences not expected from a highly educated environmental professional. And the Department had cleared all the claims of numerous air trips that he made from Delhi to Dabolim airport only because he was ministers class mate and friend.. The list of text book writers for various standards, their exorbitant refreshment bills, seminar bills, environmental tour expenses to various places with the family members, numerous sittings to write the books, agreement with the printers, their quotations, comparative statements, approval from various authorities, expenses on special invitees for every sittings, reviewers reports, their bills, printers bill, their revised quotations, escalation rates from printers were placed inside the files. The other file was the correspondences with the ministry of environment. His eyes fell on a letter from the Ministry of environment asking explanation and demanding utility certificates for the expenses made. It was a recent reminder letter. He noticed the date of entry. It was marked to EO. He was surprised to see that the same was never brought to him though he was present on that date in the office. He found out that there was initial order for 25000 books for each standard and the printer supplied only 2500 books. There were two bills one for 25000 books and another chalan for 2500 books. He also noticed a mismatch in entries. It was shown in the file that altogether 150000 books were received in good condition and supplied to different schools. But in fact only 15000 books were printed and no books were given to any schools. The books were printed at the end of the academic year in the month of February, and the school authorities refused to collect the books from the department, since it was too late. From the noting it was found that one Sunil in his capacity as OS informed some of the schools to collect five books per schools for their library and also informed not to teach the books for the current academic year or for the next year because of the numerous mistakes in it. There were letters from the Teachers organizations to withdraw the sub standard green books with faulty statements. Many were baffled and bewildered with the content of environment books supplied to them. He also observed protest letters from various organizations and prominent opposition leaders regarding this environment books scam. They even questioned the need of spending too much on consultancy.

Alexander Philip observed grave discrepancy in the accounts and inflated rates for various items purchased for the section under the environment schemes. A gentle knock at the cabin door alerted him. Immediately he closed the file and kept it in his table drawer and locked it. For the next gentle knock he answered and gave permission to enter. The door was opened by LDC Sulochana.

"Am I disturbing you, sir?' Sulochana asked in a soft mild voice. "Your pay bills for signature."

While Alexander Philip was signing the pay bills of him, Sulochana said "Sir, Adharma Pal is shouting at us. He is worried. He is angry because you have taken his files from his cupboard. Section Officer never showed that files to us, though I am the dealing clerk. OS and that Deputy Director were handling that files alone."

Alexander Philip maintained silence. He pretended as if he is not interested in her talk. But she continued to talk.

At the same time in the cabin of the Deputy. Director, a conspiracy was going on. OS Sunil gave assurance to Asst. Director that he would do all necessary for the immediate transfer of Dr. Alexander Philip. "Okay, since the Minister is involved in this scam, and has personal interest, he will not hesitate to sign" Asst. Director said this and relieved himself. He rocked his chair slowly while looking at his aide. Both of them heard a soft tapping on the door of his cabin. The rocking of the chair stopped immediately. "Yes, yes", Asst. Director gave permission to the visitor to enter, and a lady with long hair and pale face entered the cabin with a file in her hand. Really no one was welcomed inside and the machinators did not want to disturb their private conversation. Asst. Director and OS looked at each other and their gaze conveyed the message to change the subject. Both of them looked at the visitor with little irritation on their faces. LDC Sulochana could read their mind and immediately realized that she was not welcomed by the two and said very politely "am I disturbing you sirs?"

'No, No', both of them said in an embarrassing voice. Then there was grave silence for a few minutes in the room. No one was dared to talk.

Asst. Director took the oval shaped glass paper weight with blue flowers inside in his hand and rotated it on the glass table top to kill time and also to cover his inner feelings. The silence was an indication to OS to leave the room. He got angry with the visitor and thought in his mind *'a time selected to come here, why is she waiting without talking, now I have to leave, they may have some secrets to share.'* And thinking like this in his mind he prepared to leave the room allowing privacy for others. While Sunil was ready to leave LDC Sulochana announced in a hurry "Sir, EO wants to see you. Please report to him by 3.00 pm today." She briefed. OS tried to cover up his nervousness from Sulochana and nodded his head in acceptance of information. A hundred questions flashed through his mind and he looked at his master, his eyes were seeking for help and advice. He left the room with a heavy head of hundreds of doubts inside. "You meet me at 5.00pm today" Deputy Director instructed OS while he was about to leave his cabin. Again he nodded his head in acceptance. He searched his pocket for cigarette. He took one and lit it and walked through the passage.

OS reported to EO sharp at 3.00 pm. as instructed. He pretended to be very polite and loyal to his boss. In a very soft voice he asked permission to enter and stood in front of Alexander Philip. He said in his mind: *this fool does not know who I am, and what I am going to do, he will not be on this chair for long, I will teach him a lesson, time has ripened now.*

"Mr.Sunil, had we received any correspondences from the ministry of environment recently?" Alexander Philip asked directly to the stout person with one dried up tulsi leaf on his left ear and his fore head was smeared with yellow sandal wood paste and in the centre of the forehead above the yellow sandalwood paste there was a red spot of vermilion to express the extreme devotion to the creator, God almighty. Alexander Philip could not see the face expressions of OS because of dim light inside the room. Hardly could he see a huge fat figure in front of him in the candle light. He could smell the strong cigarette smell as soon as OS entered his cabin.

OS crouched down his body about 30 degrees, just like in Japanese custom to express the utmost respect to superiors and replied in an artificial voice, "No sir." His artificial voice and full confidence astounded Dr. Alexander Philip.

"Yeh… yeh…, sir, he was trying to cover his nervousness, I think we were in receipt of… one letter… from Ministry of Environment'… he paused as if he was trying to recollect his lost memory. "But that was a… about… three months ago…"

"Regarding…?" Alexander Philip in his deep base voice demanded.

"I think… it… was regarding… implementation of… Environmental education in… schools" OS said with extra confidence.

'But Mr. OS", Alexander Philip raised his voice little more and in a very authoritative tone he asked "But I am talking about any of the recent correspondences from the Ministry?"

'No Sir'. Sunil said at once without any hesitation.

Alexander Philip opened his drawer and took out the file No.23 and showed him. Is this your file?' he questioned his Office Superintendent. "Whose signature is this? In an authoritative language he quizzed at him.

"It is mine sir, but I have not gone through it." Sunil said as if he was frightened. But in his mind he thought: *what this gatti is going to do, why he is shouting at me, I will show who... I am, wait... a few more days you will not sit on this chair, you die with your ministry's... letter.*

"But this letter was lying with you unattended for the last thirty days." Alexander Philip shouted with a fuming voice. Because of the heavy rain outside no one outside the cabin listened the conversation though it was quite audible outside. He again continued, why didn't you process it?

"Sir I was very busy on those days and afterwards I lost track of it" he said without any hesitation-the very usual readymade answer by the subordinates to superior officials.

"I am asking why you didn't show me this file even after I asked for it." Alexander Philip questioned him in rage.

"It is better to be late, than never, sir...Please give me the file... I shall process it just now" Adharma Pal said casually without a trace of apology.

"Now I know what to do with this file, you need not processes it now" with the same angry tone Alexander Philip responded. "You may go NOW", again he shouted.

After a moment's hesitation, without uttering a word OS withdrew himself after bowing down at 40 degrees twice like a Japanese lady, a system never found in Goa, only to irritate his boss and his boss only could crush his own teeth to quench his fuming rage.

After preparing a detailed note about the events, Alexander Philip took the file Nos 23 and 28 and moved to the Director's cabin. Director's PA informed him that Asst. Director is inside. He stood a few seconds outside the cabin with hesitation and returned after instructing the PA to fix an appointment with the Director when she is free. The whole day the Director was busy with meetings and other engagements so an appointment was impossible. The next day she was out of station. Only after three days Alexander got an appointment with the Director. Reluctance on her face was evident and he noticed the same. She pretended as if she is very busy and in deep thought.

'Good morning, Madam' Alexander wished his boss.

Director Maria without raising her face from the files said something like "good morning" her sound appeared as if she was swallowing a bullfrog. The humming sound of the window AC echoed inside the room. The rearranged table position was noticed by Alexander Philip. The dirty damp smell of the old wet carpet in a closed room was felt. The room was partially lighted; a table lamp from behind was focused on the file in front of her. The reflected image of the Director and the table lamp was clearly seen on the glass top of the Director's table. Some files were kept on the left hand side next to the office telephone. While going through the pages of a file aimlessly she gestured Alexander to occupy the seat. She was trying to find some readymade answers to the visitor in front of her. Immediately she closed the file and looked at Dr. Alexander Philip. Then again she opened another file and started turning the pages aimlessly. She pressed the buzzer with her left hand. The grave silence in the room was broken by the sound of the opening door by a lady peon.

"Call the Office superintendent" she said without looking at any one. The peon disappeared without uttering a word.

"Yes, Dr. Alexander, what is the matter?" Director raised her hollow head and asked.

"Madam, I have an important issue to be discussed with you." He said in a firm voice.

"Alexander, please excuse me, I am very busy toady I have to send a report on SSA today itself, please come some other days. She said nervously. You know our staff, they make numerous mistakes, and I have to go through each and every word. They don't come in time; they don't have a work culture. And most of them are irresponsible and in efficient."

Alexander wanted say that, *"Madam, the last word is more suitable to you than the subordinates."* But he did not tell that and kept silence. After all silence is a method of approval and agreement in India. Even at engagements the silence of the girl is always misinterpreted as acceptance of her future husband, but in fact the girls silence is always a silence of disapproval that no one wanted to agree with.

"Alexander," Director looked at him for a few seconds and said, "Do you know our Office Superintendent, he comes at ten o' clock every day, then how the subordinates listen to him. If he is removed the department will do well I think. But he is the man of PWD minister. Today, I came at nine o'clock in the morning and they came at ten. I do not know how to pull on with this type of people." She expressed her defenselessness to control the subordinates to her one time close friend and paused and sighed. Alexander thought in his mind: *if you were removed from this chair the entire education system of the state may improve, if the superintendent is the man of PWD minister, you are a person of another corrupt uneducated minister Braganza Pereira and the cousin Fatima, and you are sitting in this chair with the help of a mafia queen. You cannot cover the fact that the minister favored you, out of way to select you by changing the recruitment rules over night to avoid me.* But he did not say that on her face. The entire interview process flashed through his mind as if in a movie "Tell me Dr. Alex What is the issue?" Suddenly the Director broke the silence.

The Environment Officer kept two files in front of the Director, files numbers 23&28 and looked at the facial expressions of his superior. He remembered the saying *"if one hey is kept on that chair of the Director, you have to respect that hay, now similar hay is actually sitting in front of him*, he thought. A political hey- a political hey or a politician's hey, or a caged parrot like our CBI (?). Very difficult to understand. He noticed the caged parrot raising her eye brows up in confusion. "Oh it is a very serious matter"-she murmured: 4.5 crores? Where that vanished? Who will take responsibility of this? While going through the files she murmured. Actually we received only very few books? What about remaining books? The printer did not supply it? But we paid for the entire lot. The Director got confused, we placed an Order for 800000 environment books, but you say actually we received only 10000 books. It is a very serious fault from our side. "Now the central ministry asked for explanations and utility certificates?"

"Yes madam, they asked for utilization certificates." "That letter was received nearly two months ago, and this is the reminder letter received one week ago. The Section Head kept me in dark and did not show both these letters to me" he paused.

"Okay, Okay while closing the files she said with much confusion and wavering. "I… will go through… the details… of those files and make necessary enquiry soon and…' I… need time and want to apply… my… mind… on this matter." She said in a wavering voice and laughed like an orangutan showing the pale pink gum.

The old fashioned black phone rang continuously and interrupted the conversation.

Excuse me, Dr. Alex; I shall call you later to discuss this issue. She extended her hand to lift the receiver but paused a while allowing little more time for the Environment Officer to leave the room. Like many Officers Director did not like to speak over phone in front of visitors and subordinates. Realizing this Alexander Philip lifted his fragile body slowly and reluctantly to give a clean air for the Director to speak.

"Hello" she answered in mild voice. May be from some ministers or Officer on Special Duty or any politicians, she thought, usually they call for recommendations or complaints about schools or principals. She was always confused and afraid to answer any call over phone.

"Hello Maria" She heard the familiar voice of her cousin from the other end. The only person who addresses her as Maria, her pet name, is her cousin sister, Fatima. Even after occupying this post she addresses the Director by her pet name. The strong relationship, the blood recognizes the kith and kin and the Director never objected it.

"I told you Fatima don't call me at this time, always I do have visitors at this time, Director spoke in a very mild polite way without a trace of displeasure but she wanted to convey her fear to her sister. "Please call me after 8.pm.at home…" before she could complete she heard a harsh voice from the other end "No Maria, this is very important, and very urgent, I can't wait."

"Fatima you are always welcome, I just casually informed." she paused. Actually she was afraid to talk to a mafia leader in day time though she was a relative. A Very few politicians and her inner circle knew that both are cousins. She even does not like to reveal her acquaintance with a notorious prostitute. "One more thing, I do not know if someone is tapping my phone, please call me from your consigliore's cell. That is safe "Tell me now, what is the matter?' she spoke with slight impatience.

"Your Officer, Dr. Alexander Philip is the problem, Do you got it now? Fatima said abruptly with little contempt.

"Yes, yes just now he was here, luckily I send him out before I attended to you, and I don't understand what the matter is? Say."

'How is he? Fatima enquired.

"He is a very good officer but straight forward and very bold."

"That is the problem with him, he may be straight forward, but why he is meddling with others affairs? I don't understand." She paused for a few seconds allowing Maria to speak, but Director Maria preferred to be silent. Fatima continued over the phone "I heard that he is investigating an Environment issue…? I mean the accounts."

"No idea, Maria," Director wanted to avoid any comment on that issue.

"Yes, Yes, He is after that issue… and I heard he had snatched two files from OS… No 23 and 28 of Environmental Education. Though you do not know what is happening there in your office, I know it. Very well…" she chuckled sarcastically.

Director Maria exclaimed why and how these types of matters are leaked to outsiders. "How do you know that?" she asked with little curiosity.

"Maria, I have feelers everywhere in Goa, I've people in every department, even in the ministry, and again she laughed with pride and satisfaction." Please see that the File No. 23 & 28 should not reach the Secretary Education."

"Why? Director expressed her doubt while looking at file No. 23 and 28 in front of her.

"Listen', there are some problems with that files, I shall call you later in the evening, as you told it is better not to talk over phone, But see, that files should not be moved." There was a click sound and the Queen disconnected the line.

That files never moved from the Office of the Director as instructed. However one personnel file of Alexander Philip moved from table to table and reached the hands of Braganza Pereira within one hour. His officer on special duty one Mr.Crook explained the content of the file to the uneducated Education Minister, after reading the same. "Sir, this is the proposal to transfer that ghatti principal from Environment to south Zone." Bhatia explained the content of the file noting to his master in one line.

"*Chodiyacho…* (Bastard) that Ghatti should be transferred today itself. Where I have to sign?" Minister asked his OSD

"May I write the comments sir" Bhatia asked.

"Yes, yes, why not…?" Braganza Pereira.

Bhatia got a golden chance to express his jealousy and anger to his senior officer Alexander Philip. Poojari Bhatia wrote: "*Officer is inert and untrustworthy he may be transferred with immediate effect.*"

"Please read what you wrote" Braganza Pereira asked in Konkani. "What is the meaning Mr. Bhatia?" He again asked.

"The officer is inefficient and may be transferred immediately" Bhatia explained to the minister in Konkani.

"*Bare, Bare* Good, You are very smart" ask them to issue the order now." While saying this he signed the green noting paper. Alexander Philip has received the Transfer Order and Relieving Order together on the same evening.

No/DE Vol.II/Tr/ 1211
28th February

## ORDER

I am pleased to transfer the below mentioned Environment Officer of the cadre of principal, Dr. Alexander Philip and post him as the DEO, South Zone, with immediate effect. Shri. Somnath Madkaikar, Principal of Higher secondary School, shall hold additional charge of the EO until further orders.

The above Officer shall join his duties of posting immediately on receipt of this Order. He is not entitled for TA/DA or joining time. The date of joining should be intimated to this office.

Director

Copy to :    1. The person concerned.

2. Personal File

3. Directorate of Accounts

4. Guard File

# Chapter 24

The very Old Portuguese building in the heart of the city looked like a ghostly house or a scrap yard, with broken window panes, dusty wooden staircase; wall corners were painted dull red with pan spit. An old sign board read like this 'DO NOT SPIT HERE'. But people preferred to spit on the wall and on the same sign board. The large veranda of the ground floor was filled with hundreds of broken desks and benches covered with all kinds of dirt and paper bits thrown by the small children. Small children in dirty half tore blue white uniform, were running helter shelter with joy. Anyone who enters the premises could easily distinguish it as a government run institution without any doubt or sign board with the first sight because of its deteriorated cleanliness and chaos. The beautifully planned wooden staircase proudly announces the past glory of the Portuguese rule and Portuguese architecture like any other old buildings in the city. Now all the old structures remain on its last legs eagerly waiting for its own pathetic *nirvanha* (death).

'Good… Mor… ni… ng… saaar" one of the peon wished him while he was about to enter his office, he was slightly dancing with unsteady steps. Alexander Philip just looked at him and did not wish him back. Smell of cheap alcohol emitted from his sweat soaked soiled shabby clothes. He noticed the board written in white letters on a black back ground 'Zonal Officer.' His cabin was a small make shift arrangement at one end of a big hall made of partially thin ply wood and hardboard. The door made a loud cry when he opened it. Many files and applications forms were kept on the wooden floor of the Office of the Zonal Officer. The table was full of old dirty files. Hardly could he enter his office through the heaps of files and he sat on an old Godrej office chair. Glass table top was full of dust. Suddenly a thin lady with pleasing face entered the cabin and helped Alexander Philip in cleaning the cabin: LDC Audrey, PA to new DEO.

She was in action. "Sir this is the first list of Schools for Inspection for this year." Audrey showed a list of about 40 schools to him. He selected the names of some the schools and handed over the list to her. He found his new office more comfortable to work. His superior was cooperative. Subordinate staffs were also cooperative. Slowly Alexander Philip entered to his new assignment and forced to forget his environment plans that he nourished for the last eight months.

Driver Suresh was not drunk on that day. He pressed hard on the brake pedal of the old office vehicle, a faded blue colour commander jeep, in front of a low roofed house with a board in front it. The half broken sign board declared the presence of a school nearby, but Alexander Philip could not find any school nearby.

Suresh where is the Model English School? Alexander Philip asked his driver. The driver motioned his hand towards the thatched house in front to him. Immediately a lean figure in long white *kurtha* appeared in front of the house with a wicked smile on his face. Instead of a *pyjama* he wore black tight jeans. The white *Kurtha* extended below his knees. He stood there with an artificial smile on the lips and extended his both hands to greet the new officer who came for inspection.

"Welcome sir", he said instead of saying good morning as usual. He spat on the ground to clean his throat and spat out the remaining pan from his mouth and made a dry cough to clear the throat again. A strong smell of pan entered the nostrils of Alexander Philip. The driver Suresh parked his jeep and opened a small quarter bottle of local *Kaju and* sipped it slowly without mixing it with water. It was his routine. He knew that DEO may take at least three hours to return. He wanted to spend that time wisely and profitably inside the government vehicle. He finished his bottle with few more sips and closed his eyes and leaned back to the driver's seat.

Alexander Philip had never visited such a school with shabby environment. This high school was running in three different nearby houses. In to one of the houses the DEO followed with the gentle man who introduced himself as the Headmaster, "sir I am only the in charge Headmaster, no permanent Headmaster post has been granted yet... he paused for a minute... sir, would you please help to recognize this school... he again paused for a while expecting some response from the DEO. The In-charge Headmaster again spat on the ground before entering his school office. The school office was the veranda of a hut with one steel *almarah*, three chairs and a small table. In one corner in a big steel drum there placed drinking water. A large spoon with a long handle was placed over the drum. As the DEO entered the veranda the clerk and two other people sitting in the office room stood up with respect. The dog which was lying inside the office room was kicked out by the in charge Headmaster himself. The local stray dog growled and went out without much hesitation. The LDC took a dirty towel and wiped out the plastic chair to make sure that it is dirt free.

"Please sit Sir" the In-charge headmaster requested DEO to sit on the freshly cleaned grey coloured plastic chair.

Reluctantly Alexander Philip sat on the chair and looked up and casually asked: "Is this the school?"

"Yes Sir", our infrastructure is not satisfactory... we will be constructing our new building soon. With little wavering he completed his sentence.

Alexander Philip's gloomy look disappointed the LDC and others standing there. But they did not talk anything. After a brief silence DEO Alexander Philip asked "do you have permission to run this institution?"

"Yes Sir" The in charge Headmaster and the LDC said in unison. "Department had given permission to run the School."

"When?"

"Since 19--, Sir."

"Number of students"?

"Forty six"

"For the whole school?"

"Yes, from fifth to ten."

"Tell me do you have permission to run the school with this less number of students?"

"Yes, yes we have special permission to run with less number of students."

"Show me the letter Please"- Alexander Philip.

Hurriedly the LDC turned pages of his file and showed the letter from the Department.

Alexander Philip observed and recognized the signature of the Asst. Director-who had been elevated to the post of Deputy Director recently-the most corrupt officer in the Department.

"Number of teachers?" He asked.

"Six sir."

"Are they getting government salary?"

"Yes sir"

"Is there any other school nearby? Alexander Philip asked in a broody mood.

"300 meters away there is a Government High school" In Charge said hesitantly. "Our students appear Public Exam through that school." He stopped.

"Show me the results of the last Public Exam?" Alexander Philip asked in an authoritative tone now.

In Charge Headmaster and LDC looked each other in confusion." It is written in our inspection proforma, sir."

"Show me" Alexander Philip.

LDC turned pages of the inspection Proforma and showed the relevant page to DEO. Alexander Philip noticed the results of the school for the last five years. Zero percent results continuously for the last five years! There were only four students in standard IX and there are no students in std. VIII Alexander Philip looked up to see the face of the In-charge headmaster. An ignominious expression on the face of the Headmaster was enough for Alexander Philip and he did not want to ask more questions. He sat silently on the plastic chair for another half an hour waiting for the ADEI (School inspector) to come. By that time he checked the student's muster roll, teacher's muster roll, and all other registers. In between the In Charge Headmaster did not forget to inform him about his close relationship with Asst. Director Adharma

Pal. He also informed about his recent elevation to the post of Dy. Director of Education.

While waiting for the ADEI Alexander Philip noticed few students crossed the make shift office room of the institution where he was sitting and they entered into the one of the rooms of the house. The DEO looked at the perplexed face of the Headmaster. Realizing the meaning of the gaze the Headmaster immediately responded.

"They are going to the laboratory, sir."

With the curiosity to see the Science Laboratory of the school DEO Alexander Philip followed the students. They entered into a small room with one fully rusted steel cupboard. There were no stools no chairs or any table for the students. They were standing with heads down. In one corner there was a single bed and one huge person was sleeping on the cot in his knickers and exposing the hairy bare chest. From the soiled cloth Alexander Philip could understand that he is resting after a hard field work in the early morning. He must be a farmer, he thought. Just above his cot on a string tied across the two windows grills there were a number of soiled clothes hanging. In one corner of the room there were heap of aluminum and copper vessels dumped disorderly. The room looked like a villager's bed room cum store room converted to a Science lab. From the thatched roof top rays of light entered here and there making small bright circles on the dark cow dung smeared mud floor. A best place to teach Brownian movements, the DEO thought, to students since the smoke mixed with dust particles from the nearby active kitchen made the light ray's bright grey path inside the dark room. The strong smell of frying dried Mumbai duck entered in to the nostrils of Alexander Philip. The man in his half pant woke up immediately and sat on the cot and opened his mouth widely as if he is going to engulf somebody and started yawning with a loud unpleasant sound to declare the end of his small nap and looked at the tall thin Alexander Philip with little curiosity. The man looked at Alexander Philip and smiled showing his plaque yellow teeth stained with black tobacco. He looked again at the students then at the stranger who was standing with his daughter. He gestured to nearby children asking who the stranger is.

"Papa, he is the DEO, come for inspection" The science teacher who accompanied the students cleared the doubt of the giant sitting on the cot. She concealed the fact that her father had full dose of *URAK* in the early morning as usual. Alexander Philip realized from the conversation between the science teacher and the man sitting on the small cot made of bamboo poles that they are father and daughter. Alexander Philip again asked where the science Laboratory is. Without speaking a word the science teacher opened the steel cupboard silently. The DEO could see a few rusted tripods, a few beakers, some chemical bottles, one compound microscope in its wooden case, another dissecting microscope, half dozen test tubes, rusted iron stands, a few wooden scales of half meter length, a few round bottomed flasks, some specimen jars, some files, one specimen of frog, one plastic model of human skeleton of about two foot length, that was resting in its sealed coffin made of cardboard and some more glass items, mostly broken pieces. All the items looked like old and discarded from some other schools.

By that time the father of the science teacher left the room without making any noise and allowing the inspector to inspect and students to perform their experiments. Alexander Philip had no words to comment. "Please take out the microscope" DEO requested the science teacher in polite words. Like an obedient servant the teacher obeyed the instruction of the Inspector. With trembling hands the teacher opened the wooden case of the microscope and took it out and kept it on the Headmasters' table outside. The dust and oil paper cover of the Microscope revealed one fact: this microscope was never seen the outside world. It was never shown to students. The oil paper that covered the objective lens was intact as it was packed there in the factory where it was born. It was never used. The science teacher struggled at least five minutes to adjust the light in to the stage and diaphragm, but in vain. After many unsuccessful attempts to adjust the light towards the specimen by turning the bottom mirror, the teacher looked helplessly towards Alexander Philip and said in a feeble voice while looking at the In charge Headmaster who was standing nearby, "Sir, it is not working' some problem, I am not able to see anything."

"I do agree with you madam, but the microscope is a brand new one and no one used it before, isn't? The problem is not with the microscope but with you" Alexander Philip said in a low mild voice. The teacher remains silent without uttering a single word.

"Madam, may I ask one question, whether this is a simple microscope or a compound microscope?"

After a few moments hesitation and little wavering in an uncertain tone the Science teacher said "Simple microscope."

"Are you sure?"

There was no answer from the other end.

"Please say, why did you say it is a simple microscope?

The discomfiture in the eyes of the teacher becomes evident on her face. The Alexander Philip asked the students to disperse and started to talk to the teacher who was standing with an awkward face and she was about o cry.

Alexander Philip asked "are you the science teacher?"

The innocent teacher of about 24 years looked down and said "Sir, I'm teaching science but I graduated in Arts. My subject was Marathi for BA. But here I am teaching Science."

"When did you join here?"

"Two years ago, Sir"

"Who was sleeping in that room?"

"My father"

"Is it your own school?"

'Yes Sir"

"How many teachers are here?"

"Six regular teachers."

"How many students?"

"Forty four" The LDC who was standing by the side of the teacher jumped in for the help and answered promptly.

In many schools in Goa in every class there are more than 65 students, now here in this school the total strength is only forty from class five to ten, Alexander Philip thought; many are repeaters and students expelled from other nearby schools.

By this time a Maruti 800 car spotted and stopped about hundred meters away from the school and two people alighted from it. They preferred a short cut and started walking towards the school through the grass fields instead of choosing the long circular path surrounding another house. Alexander Philip, the DEO could recognize one of them as the ADEI of the region, Mr. Surlekar, for whom he was waiting. Mr. Surlekar was a person of medium height with a small pot tummy with a persistent smile on his lazy face. The over sized white half sleeves shirt and the gray pant was distinct from a distance. He was holding a Government file in his hand. His long steps and swinging of only one hand while walking was weird to him. Both of them were walking through the uncultivated paddy fields with wild grass of knee heights. Tiny drops of rain water left after a mild shower on the grass moisten their pants below their knee and discolored their pants below their knee. Both of them were talking loudly but were not clear and distinct. The louder laugh of the ADEI was very audible and students sitting in the class rooms started looking towards them. Alexander Philip could not recognize the second person who was slowly approaching the School. He was a tall figure with dark complexion and with clean shave. He was wearing a long saffron coloured kurtha with two large side pockets on either side. He threw out his cigarette on the green grass carelessly as he approached the School. As he approached the small school veranda of about 10 feet length and 4 feet width, that was the Office room cum headmasters cabin and occasionally teachers resting room, the person in saffron kurtha joined his both hands just like any politicians, in front of him and greeted the Inspector with an unusual zest. Alexander Philip smiled inappropriately as if he was not interested in his greetings but bowed his head slightly to greet him.

The ADEI Surlekar expressed his apology for reaching late. Without any reason he started laughing and while laughing he introduced his companion as his friend and local panchayat member. "Sir... Ha... Ha. Ha... This is... Ha ha... the forth inspection... ha ha ha... ha ha ha... of mine here... There is nothing new... here sir... for me... with closed eyes…. ha... ha... I... could write the report of this school... all in one... Headmasters' room…, Office room…, teachers room…, all in one... ha... aha... aha…, like a hen calling their chickens at the time of danger, he laughed... and in between he uttered broken words and talked... Alexander Philip looked at the ADEI contemptuously, but Surlekar continued without looking at anyone. This school is very special sir... Ha…. Ha... Hi... Hi... Hi... he laughed.

"Mr. Surlekar Please do your work, I am going to STD X for class observation" Alexander Philip said with little irritation… "I have to go"… Saying this he went to one of the class rooms in another room of the house. The very low roofed class room was very near to cattle shed. Few cows were tied inside the shed. They were grazing the dried hey which was kept in front of them. The strong smell of cows' urine and dung from the cattle shed was so nauseating to Alexander Philip. He remembered about his village days in Konni where he used to nurture the cows and hens. But the presence of cow shed very near to a class room was difficult to understand, though the village students may be well adjusted to this situation. He noticed the presence of a fan just above his head, only few inches above. It is dangerous to fix a ceiling fan so low, he thought. Students, they were well grown and over aged and a few were taller than Alexander Philip himself, started laughing as he was looking at the ceiling fan that was fixed on a piece of thick coconut wood that supported the thatched roof. He enquired why they were laughed. "Look sir, there is no electricity in this room and the fan was kept few days ago" all students laughed in a loud noise, even the Inspector could not refrain from laughing. He realized that the fan is a danger neither to him nor to the students, since there was no electric connection at all in that room!

*"Aap ko dikane kelia rekha sir"* (it is kept there to fool you sir) one of the students said in a very low voice. *"Kal fix kiya hai"* (It was fixed only yesterday)

*"Woh kal nikalega, Sir* (it will be removed tomorrow) said another girl. Alexander Philip could not control his laugh, but smiled. There was no teacher inside the class. He asked for note books of different subjects and it was given to him unwillingly. He noticed the embarrassment on the face of the students. The note books were with numerous mistakes and

it was not corrected for the whole year. Hardly ten students were present inside. Alexander Philip looked at the small black Board kept slanting on a small wooden desk against the wall. Total number of students: 12; present 09 it was written on it. By that time a girl in green sari entered the room. Students arose and greeted her "good morning teacher." After seeing the DEO inside the class she moved to a corner and stood there to allow the DEO to interact with students. She informed the DEO that she was not teaching any subjects in that class and it was the period of the In-charge Headmaster and she was send to mind the class.

From the students note books DEO asked some questions. But no one answered any questions satisfactorily. The standard of students was far below satisfaction, he observed. Even in standard ten they were not able to read their own writings nor they were in a position to explain what they wrote. Because of dearth of time he could not spend much time in that class. He went outside and entered another room and noticed some computers were dumped on the floor. There were at least six computers in that room.

"Why are they kept on the floor?" DEO asked the sir present in that room.

"There are no tables to keep them, sir."

"Are they in working condition?"

"May be... yes Sir" He replied.

"Is anyone using this?"

"No sir, there is no computer teacher here."

"Who gave these computers?"

"Government, Sir"

"When you got it?"

"I don't know", he replied.

"Why are they not given to students for practice?"

"Manager told not to give them to students"

"Why?"

"No idea sir may be to save electricity bill."

"Is there any electric connection here?"

"Not in class rooms, only in the bed room of the manger"

Alexander Philip noticed a little dissatisfaction in the words of the Teacher. "When did you join here?" asked the DEO Alexander Philip.

"Six months ago sir"… he stopped for a moment and looked around and confirmed nobody is around and continued in a soft very low voice. Alexander Philip struggled to hear what he was saying though he was standing very close to him. "I was transferred to here from another school" he said.

"Why?"

"Retrenchment" I became surplus in that school, he leaned towards the DEO and continued "actually the management made me surplus, in fact I was not the junior most, but they discontinued my subject to remove me from that school…" 'After removing me they again started the Marathi third language this year."

"What was your subject for graduation?" Alexander Philip asked.

"Marathi"

"What was subject allotted to you here?"

"I teach math in std VIII, IX, & X."

"Are you comfortable with that subject?"

"Yes sir, I studied Math up to Higher Secondary level and I could teach it" he continued "Out of Six teachers here, three are Marathi graduates and no one could teach their own subjects."

During the recess time Alexander Philip returned to the Office room and saw ADEI Surlekar was preparing to leave. With the regular introduction of chuckling Surlekar said,

"I have completed my checking, everything is perfect, all registers are here."

Casually DEO opened the General Admission Register of Students. "How many new admissions are there in this year?" He asked.

"Only six" the answer was from the LDC who was standing there.

"Show me the student's register for std. VII" "Surlekar, Please go and verify the actual number of students in std. VII. He turned towards the LDC and asked "Show me the permission letter from the Department to run the class without minimum number of students." After a little search LDC replied "Sir for this year we did not receive the permission, but for the last year we got it."

With the regular chuckling the ADEI went to the class to check the actual position of students. Within few minutes he returned and informed "Yes, sir, it is correct all students are there in the class."

"Are you sure?"

"Yes, all are present." Surlekar replied with confidence.

"Tell me how many students are in the class" Alexander Philip asked again.

"Fifteen students were there."

"But I saw only 11 students this morning" Alexander Philip.

"Ha... Ha... Ha... he laughed... now all are there... all fifteen... I personally counted.... no doubt... ha... ha... ha... I don't make mistakes... especially when counting... I 'm a math Post graduate."

"Please go and check once again?" Alexander Philip requested again.

"One minute, Sir," He ran out. He came back within few minutes. "Yes, Yes, Ha... Ha... Ha. Wrong mistake sir...

sorry… I counted students of std.VIII not VII. There are only 11 students in the class VII now. You are right sir, I was in hurry; there is a marriage reception now. May I go sir, I have completed all my works, checked all registers and signed, and I shall submit my report within a week."

Alexander Philip got baffled with this request of the ADEI. He looked at him. He thought this fellow had come as if he is a VIP along with some panchayat member and closed the eyes and signed all the registers without checking, in few minutes and wants to go and attend a reception right now. Without answering his request he asked "Have you signed this Admission Register? Did you notice any discrepancy in that?" Why did you fail to notice the overwriting and use of whitener in many places. Did you notice that they have changed the names of students their own without following the norms for it."

"Okay, it is not a mistake, I have noted it and surely I will write in my report." As usual he did not laugh unreasonably.

The In-charge headmaster was apparently disturbed and did not speak. All the queries were answered by the LDC or other teachers. Alexander Philip noticed that the panchayat member and the person who was sleeping on the bed were talking seriously outside in the fields. He called the In-charge Head master and asked him to sit on the opposite chair across the table and he took out his check list and read it out for him. Please tell me, he started:

"Is there any office room separately?"

"No"

"Is there any separate room for the Head of the Institution?"

"No"

"Is there any play ground for children?"

"No", "But, Sir, the fields in front of our house is used by our students as the playground and they play there." The In-charge Headmaster and the elder son of the manager tried to convince the officer in disapproving tone.

"That is alright but now the field is filled with wild grass of one foot height and how you do expect your students play there, even it is difficult to walk through those fields."

"After one month the grass will dry and from November it can be used as playground."

"Is that barren paddy field belongs to you?" Alexander Philip asked.

"No, it is not ours, we are negotiating to buy that land" the In-charge said with without assurance or confidence.

"That is in future, now it is not yours and you cannot claim that. Okay, let me know where the toilet is?"

"What is the need of a toilet here Sir, here in this village!!!? Hi… Hi…, see that forest, all are going there for that job" 'hi… hi… hi…" someone was laughing and passed that comment. Alexander Philip did not pay any attention to that mockery nor did he make any attempt to find out the source of it.

"Is there any well equipped science laboratory?"

"No" was the answer.

"What laboratory sir? Are they going to become President or PM in future? The only vocation available here is selling *pav* (bread) or working in the mines as laborers or farming. For that why they need to study your microscope or Surdas' poem or of Words worth's. All these laboratory, toilets, library and computers are needed for your city children. Ours is a pure *desi* school. While telling this the panchayat member was very strident and harsh.

Soon many locals gathered in front of the school. He could observe the anger in their eyes. He also noticed the S shaped silver lockets representing the Susegaad club on their necks. One of the club member said" *tum kuch bi likho, hum ko malum hai kya karneka, hum vho karenge"* (You write what you want, but we know what to do then, and we will do that) he spat on the ground to express his contempt towards the inspecting officer.

*"Adharma Pal hamara dosth hai, hum uske saath baath karenge, our hum permission le lenge."* (Adharma Pal is our friend and we will talk to him and get our permission) another person said.

Alexander Philip looked at the ADEI who was anxiously waiting to leave the site and to attend the marriage reception at 12.30 PM. ADEI Surlekar looked at DEO and again at the face of his friend the panchayat member in his extra long saffron *kurta* and pants. The wet lower portion of his kurta started drying now and attained a different color there. Two of the surrounding locals showing their bare chest and pot belly took another pan leaf and applied a small quantity of lime paste over it from a small tube then they took a small plastic container with screw cap and turned the lid to open it and took some crushed pieces of *supari* (areca nut) and kept it in the middle of the pan leaves and added a small piece of tobacco and rolled the pan leaf into a small packet and kept the pan roll inside their mouth. The one side of their cheeks looked swollen, with the pan inside their mouth, as if they were suffering from severe tooth ache. Slowly they chewed the pan packet and moved the packet from one side of their mouth to other side and enjoyed the reddish juice from the mixture. Occasionally they spew out the red spit on the ground in front of them and stared at the inspecting officer with a contemptuous look through their red eyes.

Slowly Alexander Philip took his file and water bottle that he carried with him from the Head master's table and moved towards his jeep. Driver Suresh was witnessing everything and was ready with his vehicle. He fired it without wasting time. He asked Surlekar whether he is accompanying him. He informed he is going to attend a marriage party at a different place with the panchayat president.

# Chapter 25

Alexander Philip, DEO informed the authorities the actual facts regarding the Model English School. He wrote about the very poor infrastructure, very low number of students, lack of laboratory, lack of computer room, lack of library, lack of Headmaster's room, office room, play ground and proper class rooms. He also informed that the school authorities have failed to show any account of rupees forty lakhs received as grant for the construction of a new school building, six years ago. They have not purchased any land nor started any construction for the school buildings even after six years. He also mentioned that because of this new private school a government school about one kilometer away with all infra structure is on the verge of closure because of less students. He also mentioned that the school authorities are enticing the students of neighboring Government school to join their institution. He also criticized the report of the ADEI about the wrong information about this private school. Alexander Philip reported that there is no need of a private school in this locality since there is a well equipped government high school about one kilometer away, that was established with the special interest of the first chief minister of Goa about thirty years ago. Giving permission to continue this private institution may result in closure of a nearby Government High

School and a huge amount of public money may go waste. He also wanted to write that a mafia gang is supporting this private school and the Headmaster of the nearby Government High school is under constant threat from this mafia gang for issuing Leaving certificate to his students in order to facilitate new admission to that school. But finally he deleted this part due to lack of clear proof in support of this report. He knew that the pseudo politicians and leaders those who criticize the Government schools are actually killing these institutions with the help of local mafia and also with the help of corrupt officials in the department. He knew that one of the Assistant Directors in the department inaugurates similar private schools in the vicinity of the Government Schools and issues memo to Government Headmasters for not improving the new admissions or for other reasons to demoralize them. He also knew about the involvement of neo political leaders in construction of new schools very near to Government schools, against the existing norms for recognition, only with the intension to grab the public money and create new jobs for their own people, there by jeopardizing and threatening the existing nearby schools.

After a few days Alexander Philip opened old files of the Model English School and accidently his eyes fixed on a report of an ADEI written a few years ago. "The school has no proper infrastructure, no proper class rooms, the school is running in three different houses, huts, the enrolment is very poor, there are no students in std. IX this year, the SSC results for the last five years were zero, there is no drinking water facility, no toilet facility, no laboratory or library." The Recommendations: *"The school may be derecognized."* Smt. Martha Futardo, ADEI. Because of mere curiosity he read the report of the ADEI Martha Futardo once again. 'Marta Futardo?' he was trying to recollect the name. For a few months one Martha Futardo was working in the Old Lyceum he remembered, whether she is the same Futardo? He doubted. After her transfer he never heard about her. His eyes moved down to read the recommendation of the Asst. Director Adharma Pal, *'Recognition may be continued/granted.'* It seems very funny for him to read the recommendation of the Deputy. Director Adharma Pal

: "Recognition may be continued". He read it once again. Then why the ADEIs were sending for inspection? He thought. What rationalization for this recognition? He is the authority, only his words are valid. The school authorities were cheating the public for the last ten years and grabbed all public money and utilized the same for their own personal purposes. Here one authority is supporting the corruption. *"The recognition may be granted"* Why? For what? For not having class rooms? Or for not having toilets? Or for the zero result for several years? Alexander Philip could not digest the words. We should salute her and congratulate her for the bold and clear report about that school, he thought.

He pressed the buzzer. After a few minutes delay one attender in his blue shirt stood in front of him in an inebriated condition. He was very lean with very thin hands and a few veins were prominently projected outside his skinny thin neck. He was struggling to stand steady. He was sweating generously and his blue shirt changed its colour in his arm pits and behind due to his sweat. Alexander Philip could not tolerate his dirty body odor that emits from his soiled clothes. Contemptuously he looked at him and asked him to call Audrey the LDC. Sonu Colvalkar turned his back and disappeared without telling a word and the terrible smell of cheap urak mixed with his sweat followed him relieving the cabin with clean air. Alexander Philip sighed and took a deep breath and waited for Audrey.

Audrey was the new PA to Alexander Philip. She was good natured, hard working with pleasing personality. Audrey may give some information about this Martha, he thought.

"Do you know one Martha Futardo, ADEI? Alexander Philip asked Audrey.

"Yes, sir, she was in our office" Audrey replied at once.

"Where is she? Now?"

Alexander Philip could notice a sudden change in Audrey's face. Her face becomes pale and she was struggling to answer his query. After a moment's hesitation she replied "She is no more."

Alexander Philip never expected such an answer. Even he could not respond immediately. He looked at the eyes of his PA with much curiosity and asked "What happened?"

In a very low and sad voice she said "Sir, she died in an accident... a road accident?"

"When?"

"About four years ago". She paused for a while and continued... police said it was an accident but everyone says it was a murder..."

"No police case? He asked with curiosity.

"Of course! There was a police case, but the FIR was against her, they reported she was on the wrong side of the road on her scooty".

"No witness to this incident?"

"Witnesses were there, they all said she was not riding the scooty when it was hit by a speeding maruti van." Audrey stopped for some time. From her face it was clear that she was perplexed and confused. She was deciding whether to tell the story or not. Finally as if she acquired some courage within herself she started to talk. "Actually what happened was like this... she went to drop her son to school, her eleven year old son alighted from the scooty and walked towards his nearby school, she watched her son crossing the road safely, within seconds a maruti van dashed against her scooty from behind, many school children witnessed the accident, even some teachers saw the accident, but everyone changed their views in front of the police and even in the court. No one was ready to stand as witness."

"Who was behind the murder? Any idea?"

"Sir, everyone in that locality knew who was behind the murder, but no one was ready to become a scapegoat, because of fear. Even the Department refused to help her."

"Any reason?" Alexander Philip asked.

"The only reason was she was bold and sincere to her work, she never accepted any bribe and even refused to accept their request for lunch and to write only favorable report about any schools. All these years she wrote only facts in respect of schools. So many managements were against her. Virtually they were very happy to hear her death, including our Asst. Director of Education. Those Susegaad members even distributed sweets to public on exoneration of the car driver." "Sir you may know that that manager of the school, that you visited few days ago, the Model English School, came here many a time and asked her to change the report favourably, but she refused to write any wrong report other than facts, the prize she received for her sincerity was known to everyone here in this office, first she was transferred to south in a very remote place by the Department, and later this happened when she was on leave and was dropping her son to school."

The DEO remained silent and was listening to Audrey patiently. He tapped his pencil on his executive table to relieve himself from the tension and anger. Finally he responded "Any way it is very sad news to me, we were colleague for few months at old Lyceum, I saw her report about that school and actually I wanted to appreciate her for her boldness and sincerity to profession."

"That you feel sir, do you know what our Department did?, that rascal Asst. Director called her in his cabin and asked her to change her report about the school, but she refused to change her report, the very next day she was transferred to Canacona, in south Goa to punish her, and wrote the reason 'Insubordination'."

"And that corrupt Asst. Director was elevated to the post of Deputy Director now, you might have heard, after superseding five seniors, which was the reward that he got for his recommendation for continuation of recognition for that... school."

# Chapter 26

Through the unfamiliar roads he drove his car. The asphalt on the narrow roads were broken here and there due to a heavy monsoon that year and his car was jumping up and down on the series of pot holes while splashing dirty muddy water on both sides. The road was empty having no other vehicles or people. He felt very lonely and decided to put on the stereo. Now he reached the top of a mountain after driving more than three kilometers of ascending roads. The speedometer showed 15 kilometers per hour. At one junction he stopped his car and waved his hand to a passerby. He approached his car and looked inside with curiosity to see some known friends inside.

"*Ye vatti Kudchire Vaitha?*" Alexander Philip asked the stranger in Konkani.

*"Oie, Oie"*, The man who carried an old plastic pet bottle in his hand was returning from the jungle after answering his nature's call, said with a smile showing his exceptionally long incisors in his rat face.

*"Bare, Bare" Alexander* Philip waved his hand in acceptance and appreciation and drove again another two more kilometers inside the village road. It was a steep climb. The lonely drive bored him. Unexpectedly then started heavy rain and he put his wiper in full speed. Again the speedometer showed a speed of ten kilometers per hour. Now the car stereo was struggling to receive the signals from the FM station and made a clattering irritating sound and he switched off his radio to concentrate on the unfamiliar narrow mountain road. After driving about ten kilometers from Bicholim he could see a small settlement of an old village with different types of roofing for the houses. Some houses with Mangalorian tiles with cemented seats on both sides in front of the entrance. Because of the heavy rain the boy who was selling the bread, the *Pav*, stopped his bicycle on the side of a small shop with his large cane basket covered with plastic and that was tightened with an old cycle tube around the basket rim to keep the plastic intact and to protect the *pav* from the downpour. He made a small opening through the sides of the plastic to remove the pav from inside. He wiped his wet hand with a dirty cloth that was hanging out side from his trouser pocket, before inserting his hand inside the covered cane basket on the carrier of his bicycle and removed a set of six *pavs* from inside and slowly cut out two *pavs* from one side of the set, and gave it to an old man. The old man collected the *pavs* from that boy and covered it with another small thin plastic bag and kept it in his hand and looked outside and waited for the rain to settle. He moved towards one side of shop's small veranda and stretched his hand out side in order to test the intensity

of the rain and looked at another nearby person, who was also waiting for the rain to subside and to go out and smiled and raised his eye brows to express his impatience to move out.

Alexander Philip stopped his car near to that small shop and opened the door waited for two seconds and ran towards the shop without bothering the rain outside, keeping his bare hands on his head to protect himself from the rain, only for a self satisfaction that he was covering his body from the rain outside. Communication will be a little difficult, he thought. He felt ashamed of his weak Konkani. Only three people were there in front of that closed shop, the bread seller, the old man who bought the *pav* and a boy of thirteen years old. To whom to ask about Futardo he was thinking in his mind. He smiled at the old man and the bread seller and they returned the same unfamiliar smile. The boy did not care about the stranger and he was looking at the field where his friends were playing football in that heavy rain. His soiled shirt and wet cloth announced that he was also in the rain and was playing in that mud. He looked at Alexander Philip suspiciously. After a few minutes silence Alexander Philip decided to talk, he looked at the old man thinking that because of his age he may be knowing everyone in that village, a second thought flashed in his mind and thought that the bread seller is going house to house and selling bread and he may be in better position to help him.

*"Pathrav Futardo kutte ravtha?"* Alexander Philip looked at the old man and asked, and then he turned his face to the bread seller and repeated *"Futardo Khoi ravtha?"* Both of them pointed at once to that boy and said "Futardo's grandson." But the boy stared at Alexander Philip without showing any familiarity and he seems to be frightened. But Alexander Philip felt relieved to see the boy and smiled sympathetically and asked him "What is your name boy?"

The boy who was looking at his friends in the field said something inaudible and ran outside towards the field where his friends were playing foot ball.

The old man called out the boy "Aanto, Aanto, come, here is someone looking for your house, come." But the boy without turning back ran towards the field and joined his friends, in the field. The rain subsided significantly by that time.

"Sir, come I will show you the house of uncle Futardo" the old man looked at Alexander Philip and said.

"How far from here? Shall I keep my car here? Alexander Philip asked.

"Yes, yes, you can keep here, otherwise keep it near that jack fruit tree in front of my house it will be safe there, come, I will show his house" the old man volunteered to help Alexander Philip.

Both of them walked through a narrow lane by the side of a large jack fruit tree, the fallen dead leaves of jack fruit tree made a wet carpet under their feet on the lane and a few badly smelling decayed fallen jack fruits hovered by numerous flies welcomed them by their humming songs. Alexander Philip remembered his child hood life at his home town Konni while walking over the damp wet carpet of jack fruit leaves and seeing the similar landscapes, and flashes of thoughts of his home village Konni reeled back in his mind, the same tiled houses, jack fruit trees, coconut trees, other vegetations devoid of tapioca plants, he thought. The heavy summer shower of June had already filled the puddles with muddy water and the roadside small gutters became active once again with running water and green algae and croaking of frogs. After a few minutes' walk they stopped in front of an Old Portuguese villa surrounded by beautiful but small garden. A man in his seventies was sitting in the portico and he looked at the visitors through the thick reading glass with little curiosity and anxiety. He was trying to smile but his smile disappeared in the beginning itself ending with a question mark on his face after seeing one tall unfamiliar person along with his friend. The man who was sitting on the cemented seat stood up with his news paper in his hand he opened his mouth as if he is about to ask something and looked at the visitors. He was wearing an under sized shorts exposing the very thin shank with gray hairs. The black old over coat with a few small holes here and there that he wore announced his old glory of a retired British Railway employee. His bright face with well trimmed bow shaped white moustaches on his thin upper lip below his parrot nose added beauty to his wrinkled tanned seventy year old face. Though his face was bright his small eyes affected partially by cataract rings around the pupil declared a permanent unhappiness usual to many old people who were compelled to lead a lonely boring life.

"Mr. Futardo?" Alexander Philip broke the ice while wiping the hair with his left hand to remove the rain drops.

The old man tried to smile and moved closer to the stranger trying for a closer look to recognize him. He removed his thick glass to have a better look but unsatisfied with that he again kept back his reading glass on his parrot nose and slightly opened his tooth less mouth and remained in that posture few seconds and said "Mr.Cardozo?" Mr. Cardozo?"

"No, Mr.Futardo, I' m not Cardozo, I'm Alexander?"

"Alexander?" Sorry, I don't recognize you, sorry, sir, please excuse me… these days I forget everything…"

"Mr.Futardo, I'm working in Education Department, and you may not remember me, only once we met, that also about ten years ago."

"Sorry Sir, I'm not able to recollect that even" the old man said in an apologizing tone.

"Mr. Futardo, do you remember, once we met in front of the Vasco railway station... I think... about... ten years ago, you had come with your daughter... regarding... your pension papers, do you remember now?"

"I do remember that trip" he removed his black thick framed reading glass from his parrot nose and wiped his wet eyes and kept it back in its place again, yes yes, we... went together..."

Alexander Philip noticed the sudden change in his tone when he talked about his daughter, his words stuck in his throat.

He struggled to complete the sentence; yes... yes... my daughter was with me..."

"Martha...?"

"Yes. Martha... my daughter... Do you know her, sir?" The old man asked while wiping his eyes with his fingers. And he continued... she is no more... now... They killed her sir, they killed her."

"*Yeh, Pathrao owe vaitha*" the other person who accompanied Alexander Philip interrupted their conversation and asked his permission to leave the palace. Alexander Philip looked at him and shook his head in acceptance and thanked him for his help. Both of them smiled at each other and departed.

"Yes I know her, she was with us at old Lyceum for few years, and she was my colleague, then'. Alexander Philip stopped for a second because he knew that Mr.Futardo wanted to ask something in between.

"Are you from railways? "The old man asked looking straight into Alexander Philip's eyes.

"No, no, sorry, I told... I'm from Education Department, newly posted DEO. I have come to see you".

"Are you from Kerala?" the old man asked doubtfully.

"Yes, I'm from Kerala. How do you know that, Sir?" Alexander Philip asked with inquisitiveness.

"In Railways there were many Malayalees, some of them were my best friends, but I do not have any contact with them, now. But their accent is very familiar to me." "Don't mind sir, sorry for asking your name again? I forgot… I forgot… sorry… now a day's I'm forgetting everything…" he said in an apologizing tone.

"Alexander Philip"

"Alexander Philip? Alexander…" She never told anything about you… I have a very poor memory… I don't Know."

Futardo tried to recollect that name but he couldn't. "Anyway, please come inside, please do come inside" the old Futardo invited Alexander Philip, inside his house, very unusual among s who do not entertain strangers inside, especially outsiders. Only very close friends are welcomed inside. Futardo kept his news paper on the cemented seat and went inside along with Alexander Philip. Though the room was not bright enough it was neatly decorated. The floor was cemented with red oxide and it was shining slightly and the four borders were in black cement. In the centre of the room there was the statue of Mother Mary on a small altar and a big rosary of wooden beads was hanging from the wooden frame, well polished very old furniture added the beauty of the front room. Futardo bowed in front of the Mother Mary with full reverence and faith and Alexander Philip followed him in his action.

"Do you know what happened to her? Futardo sniveled." Come, sir, I… will… show her room…. and her photos." Futardo caught Alexander Philip's hand and invited him to an inside room where he could see the life sized photograph of her old colleague on the wall. For a second he thought about his colleague who lost her life for truth and who did her duty, flashed through his mind. Unknowingly a feeling of resentment and bitterness against the corrupt officials in the Education Department entered into his mind. He bit his jaws hard against each other. The indignation and ire was prominent now on his face. He joined his hands in front of his old friends' photograph and remained silent for few seconds and prayed for her souls' rest in peace.

*"Dar uder"* Alexander Philip turned back towards the sound. He saw Aantao peeping in to the room and Futardo staring at his grandson with burning eyes. The boy withdrew himself into another room and started reading loudly a lesson to announce his learning.

Both of them sat on a cot and continued their conversation. Alexander Philip crossed his leg one higher than the other and leaned back and crossed his hands in front of him and took a deep breath and sighed and Futardo leaned against the grill at one end of the cot.

"Uncle, one month ago I joined the Zone and found the report of Martha about one of the schools that she visited." Accidently I went for the inspection to that same school and found the report of Martha was fully correct and based on facts. Then because of sheer interest and respect I asked about that ADEI who wrote that sincere report, I was informed she is no more and died in a scooter accident. But the staff said, that was not an accident but a murder and later I realised that this Martha was my colleague and friend. Then I decided to visit you to find out the truth and also to pay homage to my ex-colleague." He paused for a while after seeing the coolheaded face of Futardo.

Futardo was gazing at the floor without concentrating on any point and was silent. Unintentionally he rubbed his white moustache with his two fingers in order to relieve himself from the stress. His hands moved up wards and touched his wrinkled temple and the veins on his temples throbbed. He remained in that position slightly rubbing his forehead and staring down on the floor with his widely opened small red eyes. Suddenly he raised his head looked onto the eyes of Alexander Philip and said "Aanto was only nine and was studying in class five, and Martha took him to his school one day on her bike, she was very bold, independent and little out spoken. Aanto got down from the bike and crossed the road and waved his hand to her and started to walk towards his school, after few steps he heard a loud sound behind him and turned back, he saw his mother lying on road and her fallen scooter at a distance, he ran towards his mother, he saw the smashed head of his mother, the blood was slowly oozing out through her mouth and nose, she never spoke after wards, her eyes were opened and she lied on that road in that position for more than one hour, no one helped to take her to hospital, all were looking and witnessing the ordeal of my daughter and son,… no one took her to hospital…. they said she was dead… they said she died on the spot… a… Maruti van hit her they said."

"Police didn't come?" Alexander Philip enquired anxiously.

"My son, they came, they came after one hour."

"And…?" Alexander Philip asked in a very low voice.

Futardo took a very deep breath and exhaled. His veins on the temple throbbed again violently.

"You know what our police force is for? They are for protecting the property of their master's, political masters, not for the people… not for the states' interest, many are criminals, and they are the agents for Drug mafia and sex mafia."

"Yes, uncle, I do agree, didn't they help you?"

"They should have showed some sympathy for a dead woman, but they didn't. People would show much sympathy to a dead dog or a buffalo on the road, but not to human…." He began to weep like a child.

Alexander Philip got puzzled and looked at the old fragile man with full of compassion and sympathy. Both of them did not speak for at least three minutes then. The deep silence between them was interrupted by Aanto's reading. The old man occasionally lifted his reading glass and wiped his eyes. After a silence of few minutes abruptly Alexander Philip asked," Uncle, was it and accident?

The old man looked into the eyes of Alexander Philip remorsefully with his sallowed face. Alexander Philip knew that Futardo wanted to tell something, but he was hesitating to tell. Finally after a few moments silence he said, "I doubt."

"Doubt about… what?

"It was not an accident sir. It was a murder." He said in firm voice. The vein on his forehead started beating. Unknowingly he rubbed his forehead mildly to relive himself from the tension. He repeated "Yes it was a murder".

"But the police version was… an accident" Alexander Philip continued.

"Dr. Alexander, even Martha knew that the red Maruti van was following her. She even told Aantao to keep an eye on that red van and he was looking behind and always informing her about the van… while she was driving… but about 300 meters away he told Martha that the van went to another route… by a sub-lane and disappeared. But onlookers said later that a red maruti van hit her scooter from the side while she was taking a turn after sending Aanto to school."

"What? The police could not find the maruti van?

"Yes, yes they arrested the driver and the case was going on for about two years."

"Finally…?"

"Finally… the driver was acquitted."

"Do you know the driver? Uncle"

Yes, we saw each other on many occasions… in police station and even during the trial in the court room."

"Yes, Uncle, please say that why you doubt that it was a murder?"

"Because one of her old colleague from your office confidently told me that… one person… one… Johnny often threatens her with dare consequences because of her report about one school. After that many informed me that, one Johnny was behind her murder… but there was no evidence…"

Alexander Philip's doubt was confirmed. "Mr.Futardo, are you interested in reopening the case?" Alexander Philip asked Futardo with little wavering.

"Why, Dr. Alexander, it is of no use, they are powerful and a group of criminals and the whole administration is with them, what we will do, general public is always at the receiving end." The old man with full frustration and disappointment said in a depressing voice.

"But the guilty should be punished, it should be a lesson for other criminals, see Uncle, all are not corrupt and criminals, always the criminals cannot win, of course what you said was right, the entire administration supports the corruption for their own existence." Said Alexander.

"Do you know Dr. Alexander, the driver who killed my daughter has constructed a huge mansion in Bicholim, and people say it was the reward from that Susegaad club, and otherwise he did not have any other source of income."

The mention about Susegaad club shocked Alexander Philip for a moment. *So he knew everything*, Alexander Philip thought, but he is afraid to talk the truth. He should be convinced the need of fighting for justice. He continued "That is a clue... we will ask the income tax department to trace the source of income... who gave the money to construct the big house... He is answerable... for each rupee... that will reveal the real perpetrator."

"But who will protect my grandson, Aanto, after wards... the Susegaad members would haunt us... any where we go."

"I'm not ruling out that, but we can't surrender to fear always... what does he say?"

"He is a small boy, after that incident he changed completely... sometimes even he becomes aggressive."

"Even Susegaad cannot wipe out all people opposing them, somehow the truth should come out and the Officials who support the criminals should be exposed in front of the public."

"Is it possible Mr. Alexander?" The old man asked with little hope.

"Possible" Alexander Philip confirmed with full confidence. "You or your grand son will not be exposed to danger, since I will be the person fighting for that cause... because I feel one of my colleague who was straight forward and stood against the corrupt practice of the Department should be rewarded... not be punished... that I feel." Alexander Philip took a deep breath and sighed.

# Chapter 27

A tall lean man of about 40 stepped into the city police station in his usual black and white attire and unceremoniously approached the station house officer's cabin and knocked at the half door which covered the room partially and asked for permission to enter inside.

Permission granted. A deep unfriendly rough authoritarian voice from a khaki uniform greeted him from inside.

"Yes, come in" Inspector Dessai.

Alexander Philip noticed the presence of other two persons apparently engaged in unnecessary house matters inside the cabin of the sub inspector. They looked at him unfriendly and suspiciously. Without any introduction Alexander Philip said, "Sir, I've a confidential matter to discuss with you."

"Yes, yes welcome, please go ahead" Dessai.

"Since it is very confidential, if you don't mind can you please arrange for a private talk… he pause for a moment…" Alexander Philip said in a little confusion… for a few minutes… please."

Desai stared at AP in annoyance and said "doesn't matter, that is not necessary, you may please go ahead." He added "they are very sincere and serving here for many years, you can believe them, any way, what is the matter?"

"Sir, I am here to talk about a murder that took place four years ago, one Martha Futardo was killed by a speeding maruti van. I doubt a foul play in that incident, though the culprits were acquitted then I have fresh evidence that it was a murder" AP stopped for a moment and observed carefully the facial expressions of the Sub inspector. Dessai was silent and after a little thought he said, "to… the best of my knowledge… I do not know that case"… he was struggling to find words, "means… much about that case what you are talking about, I have joined recently about one year back, and I have to study the case before making any comment."

"You are right, AP said assertively, but I doubt it as a murder not an accident, and I have fresh evidence for that. I want to reinvestigate the case."

"In that case, please give an application for that, further you shall approach the Court and bring court permission to reinvestigate the case; I am little busy today, our Home minister will be visiting Mupca for the inauguration some barber shop, and I'm in-charge of his security, we will talk later," Desai stood up and took his baton and cap from the table and went out.

"One minute please," AP requested "this is the application for that purpose, for re-investigating that accident case, sign please for entry."

'Okay, then meet me later, sorry I'm late for the function, please give your letter in inward" he instructed his constable to accept that reinvestigation application from AP and went out.

# Chapter 28

Deputy Director Adharma Pal's mobile happened to vibrate inside his neatly pressed cream colored slack shirt pocket and then the famous Sanskrit *bhajan* tune emitted out slowly first then gradually it become louder and louder. Deputy Director who was sitting inside the Director's chamber realized the origin and identified the caller immediately from the special dial tone which he kept particularly for his master. He became nervous and his nervousness was noticed by madam Maria immediately and she wanted to ask the reason for his nervousness but before that she saw him lifting his 90 kilogram body from the soft maroon colored sofa slowly and asked permission to leave the room, "Excuse me madam" in an apologizing tone he said and moved towards the door in haste with his mobile in his hand. Though Director Madam did not like any interferences or hindrance while discussing official matters, but she was lenient towards this Deputy Director and allowed much freedom than any other person inside her chamber. The reason for this freedom was known to everyone. For all official doubts regarding rules and regulations she consulted him for guidance. It becomes practically impossible for her to run the system without him and he knew this fact very well and took maximum advantage of this situation. He used to draft all circulars and even correct the circulars prepared by the madam Director. In return to his services to her he was given an upper hand in the office and even for appointments. When he reached outside the Directors' room he pressed the green button on his Nokia mobile which was gifted to him by the manager of Model English School and kept it near to his ear.

"Hello Mr. Director" Adharma Pal heard the familiar voice of his godfather on the other end. Only his godfather addresses him as the Director, though once he tried to correct him "Sir I am only the Deputy Director." However, his god father said in a forceful and convincing voice then "Don't worry Mr.Adharma Pal I will see that you sit on that chair very soon", but he could not succeed in his attempt and both had to wait, a long wait of many years. The cost of that chair was more than they could expect, Madam Maria outsmarted his competitors. Some of the recruitment rules were peeled off and new ones were added in one sitting of the cabinet in order to bestow her to that post. And Adharma Pal was forced to satisfy with the Deputy Director's post. The price money for the Directors post was flowed out from the sex Mafia queen's personal account to the minister's account. Though he did not get the top post, Adharma Pal was always loyal to his god father and also towards the club Susegaad. "Yes Sir," with highest respect Adharma Pal answered to his godfather. Unexpectedly he heard some bad words from the other end "*Vho Chediacho,* (bad words###) rascal is again creating problems, *kel tuka? Tu sala, kithe karta tumi*? (You fool, did you understand?)

Immediately Adharma Pal understood about whom his godfather was talking, rarely he uses bad words especially when he talks to him. From his tone he understood that he is very much annoyed and angry.

*Kithe dali pathrao…? (*What happened?*) Sang, (*say) Adharma Pal said a very polite manner as if he is talking to a high official.

"*Aikare… aika… (You listen)* that old case of your ADEI… who died... in a road accident…. *kel tuka?* At Bicholim…" he paused for a minute allowing some time for Mr. Adharma Pal to think and abruptly he stopped.

"Yes, Yes" Saab, I know,… what happened now?"

"*Arie…, vho sala……* your DEO that rascal…, gatti… is after that now. Just now I got a call from city police Commissioner that one Dr. Alexander Philip had given a request to reinvestigate that accident case, along with the court order."

"Sir, who said about this, I don't know anything about this" Adharma Pal exposed his innocence in this matter.

"Yes, yes, he gave an application for re-investigation of that, just now, SI Dessai also telephoned to me."

"Ok, ok, I got it, Saab… I…. blab blab... then some meaningless few words emitted from his throat.

Before he could complete the sentence his god father intervened…"Any how you have to stop him, otherwise… you know I will be forced to make one more crime. *kel tuka?*" The telephone was disconnected.

Adharma Pal remained stunned and shocked. He did not know what to do and what to speak to his god father. He was one of the few people who know the real story behind the death of the ADEI Martha Futardo. The Bicholim branch of club Susegaad was assigned the task of finishing that ADEI by his god father. The FIR was manipulated and the case was closed nearly one year six months ago. Many officials knew that she was threatened by the management on several occasions. Her report about the school was there in the zonal office. His involvement in giving recognition is known to all ADEIs in that Zone. He felt that his throat was drying up. He feared, incase if the case is reinvestigated, along with his political boss he also may be questioned and become one of the suspects, he thought. He wanted to sit somewhere and stretched his hand to hold on the railings. He felt the increased palpitation and perspiration.

"Excuse me… Madam," Adharma Pal tried to express his apology for leaving the room without permission while discussion was in progress. "I want to go, just now I got a phone call from my home, I want to go madam, Please, excuse me" he pleaded in an unusual sound and bewilderment.

Madam Director sensed some jeopardy including loss or misfortune in the words of her Deputy Director and her close aid. In utter confusion she preferred to keep silence, unknowingly she began to bite her left hand thumb finger, as usual, to relieve herself from the tension and finally said "Okay… you may go now, we shall discuss later." Soon she realized that she is biting her finger and withdrew it immediately to cover her curiosity and nervousness. After realizing the utter uneasiness on the face of the Asst Director, madam Director was compelled to ask "What is the matter?

Even more confused Adharma Pal thought for a moment: What to tell now? At any cost I am not going to tell about that matter, I have to tell some lies. "Some problem in house, Madam, I have to move suddenly."

Madam Director shook her head as if granting permission to leave. She noticed the sweat pouring off his forehead and his shirt is gradually soaking with his sweat. Adharma Pal felt relieved and he walked away in his own peculiar fashion like a fat duck slowly oscillating his two large fleshy mass of muscular tissues from one side to other side with heavy steps. Then he climbed down the steps without looking at anyone, he even failed to notice the LDC who was staring at him. Looking down with a very heavy mind he directly entered into his cabin and closed the door behind him with a big sound. He pulled his maroon foam leathered executive chair and sank into it impatiently. He gazed at his own image on the glass table top for few minutes thinking about the dark days ahead waiting for him. He began to repent for involving himself in that incident resulting in the elimination of one of his staff member only to please his god father. *"I shouldn't have involved in that"* he thought. Everyone knew that the driver who involved in that incident is working in the office of Alexander Philip now. If he reveals the truth and the conspiracy at the time of interrogations, there is no much hope for escape. The new home minister has no interest in protecting his god father or him. I cannot expect any good from the new ministry, he thought with fright and frustration. He drank another glass of water hurriedly and stood up and increased the speed of the fan to maximum. Again he fell on his chair and got up immediately as if he got some idea to escape from this worry. Gradually he left his cabin and dialed his godfather's number, and kept the phone very near to his ear, the *tulsi* leaf with its flower fell down from his ear.

After a week, Alexander Philip got an envelope from the Directorate of Education. He signed the register and received the brown envelope without any enthusiasm; it was his transfer order to Pariksha Bhavan.

# Chapter 29

When the management issued transfer order to the Principal Apollo, to a distant Institution, who was working in the same institution for more than three decades, decided to take leave for a month in retaliation, and went on leave. The management alleged that Principal has robbed a blackberry from a girl student in the pretext of confiscation and his involvement in black mailing the same student constantly for sexual favor. He was exceptionally fair, one of the Portuguese descendents, with a tall lean stature, his body was bend forward with a hunch, a small face with thick white neatly trimmed beard to cover his sunken cheeks, eyeballs were placed deep inside the sockets, a prominent narrow nose that he inherited from his Portuguese soldier father, the small frameless reading glass that was placed at the end of his nose gave him an appearance of an innocent saint. His under sized shirts barely covered his very long thin hands fully, exposing the hairy hands and a golden wristwatch; students say he is wearing the under sized readymade shirts only to show his expensive golden wristwatch to the outside world. Both of his palms were thick fleshy with small stumpy fingers, clearly indicates his criminal bend of mind as per palmist theory. But he looks like a sanctimonious catholic priest by his soft nature, even a few believed that he was a priest, but one who knows him closely actually knows the real man in him: his wickedness, narrow mindedness and inherent jingoism. He wanted to present himself as a perfectionist in minute things and that was his weakness. He never believed in others ability and did not like to see others prospering in life. Based on the complaints from teachers and students, the new manager, the young priest, decided to teach him a lesson and proposed his transfer. Worried and frustrated Apollo decided to meet the Archbishop for help. When that door was closed in front of him, one of his friends suggested him to approach Fatima the Mafia queen. He was ready to meet anyone to save his skin from shame. The appointment was arranged by his onetime paying guest, one Israeli drug peddler. Fatima could not turn down the request of her close aid and beneficiary.

His appointment as Controller of Examinations raised the eyebrows of many deserving educationalist. However, he survived and flourished under the shadow of Mafia Queen. His oblivious insensible administration and examination reforms ended in chaos and confusion among teachers and students for years together. His superfluous unnecessary interference in every internal matter of school administration and internal examination resulted in degradation of educational standard in the whole state.

Alexander Philip opened different files in front him one by one and entered his comments in that. He did not realize the presence of the Lilliputian woman officer who was standing behind him with her bright green coloured sari and with a smile on her slightly dark face. To attract his attention she said in her mild voice "Good morning sir, I was standing here, but you did not notice me, are you doing any serious noting?"

Slowly Alexander turned his head towards her and said in a cold uninterested tone, "Good morning Madam."

"Am I disturbing you?"

"Not at all" He put his pen down on the opened file on the table and gestured her to occupy the maroon coloured chair with an artificial smile on his face. In fact he did not want to be interrupted then." Any news?" He asked."

"New Controller will be joining today" and she laughed mockingly.

"Who?" He asked with inquisitively.

"Alexander, don't fool me. You know everything and pretend as if you are unaware of it" and after a little pause she continued "Don't you read today's news paper?"

"I read the news papers only in the evening, when I reach home. Secretary says the Office news paper is only for him and the Controller, not for other officers" He said with a little irritation and frustration.

"All the seven dailies he keeps in his custody for the whole day and he turns the pages of only one Marathi paper, I have never seen him reading any English dailies" the Lilliputian officer said.

"Do you know he writes the circulars and noting with the help of another person?"

"Had you ever seen him writing anything in English in front of others? Only fragments, that also with full of mistakes. Whenever he was compelled to draft any circulars or letters he approaches an old retired Secretary over phone and he dictates the draft for him."

"That everyone knows, sir. Our authorities want such 'efficient' people for the higher posts." The woman Officer said.

"How much he had paid to get that promotion?"

"Only seven lakhs. Within one year he recovers that."

"How?"

"Didn't you read that paper news?'

"Sanquelim college authorities received forged certificates of this Office... they even registered a police case... I shall show you the paper." The woman officer said with little contempt.

"Even I noticed the officials are taking home certificates in bulk in the pretext of checking... there is no counter checking for used and spoiled certificates... no officers are allowed to see the accounts of certificates for years... the secretary says it is confidential... the matter is closed there."

"Dr. Alexander, I was here for quite some time, I knew what was going on here, just like you, as you know I am also an alien and the authorities dislike all aliens who question them or try to establish an order for the system, or try to wipe out corruption."

"You are mistaken madam" Alexander interrupted "Not all aliens are disliked..." He paused for a moment and thought whether to complete his sentence or not.

"Yes, Yes You are right, I could guess of whom you are talking... about... I do agree... all aliens are not disliked nor denied promotions... I think you are talking about Adharma Pal, isn't it? The Lilliputian officer laughed.

"He is only one among the hundreds, there are so many supporters who support the malpractice, and they are the agents of politicians in the government. They are promoted and kept in key positions only to serve them, not the public."

While these two officers were talking in the chamber of Dr. Alexander Philip, they saw a white bearded face with thin narrow nose and sunken eyes peeping in to their room through the half-closed door. His eyes were suspicious and he stared at Alexander Philip with full anger. Immediately, the Lilliputian Lady Officer got up from her maroon chair, bowed her head with artificial respect, and said "Good day sir."

The Controller replied mechanically "good day" in a low unfriendly voice, still staring at Alexander who was resting unmindfully on his revolving chair, and left the place after opening the half closed door fully and murmured "keep it open."

"Excuse me, the woman officer got up immediately and followed the Controller calling him "sir, sir." The tall lean Controller looked down towards the Lilliputian Officer after removing his small reading glass from his narrow nose and smiled at her, who was following him.

Before Alexander could open another file, another figure appeared in front of him. He was bald headed, with a very thin moustache as if a line just touching his upper lips, and was about 58 years. He has curly scanty dyed hair behind his head, far below the ears, also showed the true white and gray hairs here and there proclaiming his old age, and his forehead was shining because of the cream he applied in the morning after bath. He was a Saraswath Brahmin with sharp intelligence. He was laughing mockingly like a child without making much noise while pointing his hands towards the direction where the Controller and the woman officer were moving a minute ago with naughty gestures. He was struggling to control his laugh. "Ghana... ghna... ghna" he made some nasal sounds indicating some awkwardness in the fellowship of the new Controller and the Lilliputian woman Officer. "Ha... ha... ha..." he laughed mockingly..." very good combination... ha ha."

Alexander Philip could not control himself; unintentionally he began to smile after seeing the funny gestures of his office Superintend, Mukund who was sarcastic about the new Controller of Examinations." What happened?" he asked inquisitively.

"What to happen?" "I was just watching her –the Lilliput, she is very smart, she is the informer in our office, moves around in all offices and collect all information about all and pass it to the Controller... did you tell anything 'confidential' to her... then finished... she will definitely twist it and pass it... don't worry... sir, ha... haa… haa haaaa... hai." he laughed wickedly and scornfully.

"For me nothing is confidential now." Alexander Philip said with little hesitation. Though he knew that confidential private talks might lead any one into threat in future, nevertheless because of his trust in people and being less cunning in nature, he could not control his tongue on many occasions that led him into further problems in office. He knew that the Lilliput has an excellent tongue, which she may use against him in future. However, he was not much concerned about that. He knows that he is outspoken, however, though he tried many a time, he could not get rid of that habit.

"Sir," the bald headed Office Superintendent continued, "She has a talent to speak and the listener may think that she is a supporter of him, all the Controllers, except this one, kept a safe distance from her to be impartial. Unfortunately this gentle man becomes a prey to this Lilliput... only time will prove..." He did not complete the sentence.

"Tell me, Mr.Mukund, what people say about this Office is correct? Since you were here for the last several years you may know the truth." Alexander Philip asked.

"Better not to talk about all that. Now we are seasoned and lost all efficiency and true spirit and dynamism in life, we are just pulling our days, waiting to get out of this organization for mental peace and dignity, only because of some financial problems I'm continuing in service, we have to witness and also to become a part and parcel of many scams, most of the things are very hurting and disgusting. Many things are about this Office. Once, a Controller of Exam was asked by one Minister to reconsider the result of his nephew. The answer papers were sent to the secretariat and two special teachers were appointed to re-evaluate the answer papers, students were declared pass, however, as you know people cannot keep secret forever, someone disclosed it and the Controller had to resign. It is a known fact to everyone. Another Controller a national party's local secretary, changed his degree certificates marks in order to occupy the post, but rivals went to the court and he was also compelled to resign. Another one just before sitting on that chair was disqualified because it was a case of forged birth certificate. Now this gentle man, everyone knows how he got this post, through the help of that Gama mafia, prostitute, then you tell me sir how our system will improve. All most all on the top people reached there by unfair means. As such because of government interference the credibility of this Office has been deteriorated a lot, and only government puppets could serve here as Controller and Secretary."

"What about the recent scam—the sports policy? Alexander Philip asked only to listen from his mouth.

"Actually the sports policy was introduced in a hurry at the end of the academic year, without the approval of the general body and without any official declaration, only to benefit, not only to benefit, really speaking to make him pass in the public examinations... and that ministers' son participated in college level tug of war and the college principal was forced to give him certificate of participation, awarded grace marks to pass him..."

*"To that level of freedom my father led the state...."* Alexander Philip interrupted his speech. "Now his son could tell like that, Isn't it?

"Absolutely correct... sir, He was one of the twenty member group in the tug of war... he might have touched the tail portion of the rope and claimed grace marks."

"What a funny idea! Only political giants will have this type of intelligence"

"Not only that sir, our secretary's son also benefited in that year..." Mukund raised his voice and continued "in that year secretary's son also got sports merit marks, a below average boy, like his father, also got above ninety marks in standard ten examinations."

"You are not telling the full truth Mr.Mukund, Alexander said in between, Secretary's son got ninety percent marks because his father printed the question papers in that year... a confidential thing, actually he cheated more than fifteen thousand children in that year."

"I know sir, Mukund became talkative, "Secretary and Controller connived together and kept that fact as highly confidential and fooled the public, both of them never revealed that his son is a candidate for that examination."

"Ministers son got a pass class and secretary's son got distinction-a product of an unholy symbiosis between minister and secretary." Said Alexander Philip

"Or, the unholy symbiosis between the Secretary and the Confidential printers" In that year that printer increased the rate of question paper printing two times and the authorities closed their eyes towards the inflated rate and passed that burden to student community... *to that level of freedom my father led my country*... oh what a democracy... what a freedom... freedom for a few... to do whatever they want... the might of the powerful." Mukund paused for a minute.

"Do you know Mr. Mukund, one Dr. Mathur, a RTI activist, reported this recent scam, and asked the government to initiate inquiry about this malpractice, however, he got a reply from the ministry that, the cheating action of the Secretary has no merit for any action against him, means cheating is legalized by the Government." Alexander Philip said disgustingly.

"Sir, how could they take action against him? It was a prevailing practice here for many years, you may not know much about that. I was here in the Office for the last thirty years. Almost all higher officials took advantage of their position, why action only for one Secretary, Government is for the people and for their well being..." He was interrupted by Alexander, *"To that level of freedom my father led this country,"* he laughed ironically. "In Mumbai, you might have heard many old freedom fighters in an Independence day lamented their action, after seeing the pathetic situation of our nation, they said most of the politicians are robbing the nation and amassing wealth for their kids and many parliamentarians are criminals..." He stopped his conversation abruptly when he saw Janardanam, the peon who showed his wrinkled face through the widely opened door of his chamber. He smelt like a pig and was struggling to keep his eyes open, because of the drowsiness, a usual experience, as he suffered from the previous day's drink. He was sweating heavily.

*"Sir,.. aap ko… apaitha,"* Janardanam said looking at Dr. Alexander Philip with his half opened eyes.

*"Khon?"* Alexander asked

*"Pathrov"* He completed his words while struggling to stand erect. (He addressed Controller as *'Pathrov'*, a word for addressing property owners or an alternative of 'sir' to express respect or sometimes disrespect)

"Lilliputian effect" Mukund commented immediately.

"Just a minute Mukund, I'll meet Mr.*Pathrov"* Alexander stood up and walked through the long corridor towards the cabin of the Controller. He had no idea why his boss called him.

The controller was alone in his cage like cabin. Outside his cabin, there was a room for visitors to wait for appointment, before getting permission to enter his cage, however, that room was filled with a truck load of unsold text books, that was printed purposefully after changing the syllabus, only to revenue the printer and the middle man, now the same was waiting another truck from Belgaum belonging to that *aakri wala* for final disposal to recycle the entire lot. Many, including the officers, knew the wisdom of the Secretary and the Controller of Examinations behind this wastage of public money but could not stop it or question it because of the discretional powers of the Controller.

Apollo was on his blackberry, robbed from his girl student, when Alexander Philip approached his cabin. He waited outside his glass cage, allowing his boss to complete his private phone call without interruption. Though he saw Alexander through the glass panel he continued his talk for another fifteen minutes, and showed gestures not to disturb him; the chitchat was a very lengthy one, Apollo was laughing occasionally, and sometimes he was very serious. Alexander heard only fragments what he talked inside in his cage over the phone, since it was not loud enough and clear. He presumed that the call might be from Fatima the mafia queen. He could clearly hear the last few words of him before he was about to end his talk.

"Don't worry, madam, it will be done."

Finally, the call ended and Alexander entered the cage. The Controller was surprisingly and extraordinarily cheerful as if he had won a battle against someone a moment ago.

"Take your seat, Dr. Alexander," he said in a very polite manner.

Alexander sat across him without any expression on his face and supported his chin with his left hand and his elbow rested on the arm of his chair, as if he was in thinking about something or eagerly waiting for some instruction or comments from his boss. He expected something scratchy.

"One thing I noticed here Dr.Alexander" Apollo started his formal talk after removing his small golden reading glass from his long narrow nose and kept it on an open file on the table top, "This office, especially your section is wasting a lot of papers, officers are not careful about the expenditure, I think if you take little care we could save a lot of papers, when we save papers we are saving a lot of forest, and bamboos, am I right?" After saying this, he smiled like a hypocritical catholic priest.

For a few seconds Alexander did not reply, he was thinking what to say. As usual, he kept his left hand first finger on his left chin near the left corner of his mouth and again remained silent.

What do you say Dr. Alexander?" again he asked.

"You are correct sir" he replied without much concern and again remained silent.

"Now we print a lot of drafts for corrections and print only one side of the A 4 sheet, the other blank page can be utilized for other purposes," Apollo continued without waiting for comments from Alexander. "What a waste! No one is concerned" he stopped.

"Now we are doing exactly the same sir, all drafts are printed on the used sheets; we are trying to save maximum papers." Alexander said in a convincing tone.

"Okay, it should be like that, we should not waste our resources, well" he commented.

"Sir, what about those books kept outside?" Alexander asked abruptly. "This office very well knew that the syllabus is going to change and after taking the decision to switch on to the new syllabus in ensuing academic year, you placed the order to print old text books. Is that not wastage?"

Apollo chuckled. He felt discomfited. Again, he chuckled to shutter his embarrassment. He looked into the eyes of Alexander and asked suddenly "I heard that you have been recently transferred here, and also I heard that you were transferred more than nine times in last five years, Isn't it?"

Alexander knew that he wanted to change the topic of discussion to divert his attention to a different subject. He was thinking whether to answer the superfluous question or to keep his usual silence. He preferred to remain silent.

"I am with you Dr. Alexander," Apollo said as if he is sympathetic towards him "Corrupt officials, fully corrupt, I heard that Adharma Pal, Deputy Director is controlling your department and he collects money for every transfer, is it correct?"

"You know better." Alexander did not show any interest in that talk and remained calm. He wanted to ask, "What right do you have to comment on corrupt officials?" but he did not ask. He wanted to tell that many of the officials, who entered the government departments through recommendations of the politicians or by the help of Mafia after superseding genuine candidates, are unproductive and inefficient. The ministers those who shed crocodile tears about the fall of educational standards in the state are responsible for the bad status of the state, he wanted to add, however he remained calm after remembering the bible words-*"Don't throw your jewels in front of swine's."* Finally, after a silence of one minute he said "No idea sir."

"I heard that Food Secretary, one Sushil Kumar, in the government does not accept hard copies of letters written to him and entertains only *e* mails. He makes sure that both sides of the paper are put to use. Further, before lunch break, he walks to the additional secretary's room and checks whether the lights have been switched off." Apollo said this and chuckled.

Alexander thought about Apollo's rounds in the corridors, like a school Headmaster in early morning and afternoon and his chary looks into officer's cabin to check whether they are in place. A slight contemptuous smile gradually spread on the face of Alexander and he said hastily, "Yes, yes, the Week had reported it, a very good example, he continued, "Who knows whether he uses government vehicle for marketing and to transport family members... no idea... better to ask The Week itself. Some may be real patriots; many are hypocrites only to catch the fancy of the media, who knows he is what?" He bunged up.

"Oh, I think you are a cynic-a fault finder" Controller added and laughed softly showing his golden canine teeth. He continued, "People say that Adharma Pal has purchased a huge land property in his native place and also has several flats and bungalows in different cities in Goa."

"All in *benami* names, even Adharma Pal, the most corrupt officer in the department says not to waste paper; officers should have zero tolerance to corruption etc. However, he is the most corrupt educationist in the department, a person who select unqualified candidates against the recruitment rules after accepting bribe, faithfully he transfer a part of it to Ed-mafia gangs." Alexander could not control himself. He noticed the sudden facial expression on Apollo's face when he mentioned about the word mafia gangs. Controllers' face becomes pale as if he has seen a ghost and he remained silent. He did not even see the presence of his PA near to him with some files in her hand. Alexander left the room silently without asking permission to leave. Controller looked at him like a dead man without any expression on his face.

# Chapter 30

Alexander Philip was spending his weekend in his own house after staying away at his work place alone in a rented room about ninety kilometers away at Valpoi. Only one day in a week, he had family life because of his distant posting. Sara

Philip was busy in her kitchen preparing the breakfast for the family. While tying a bandage over his swollen varicose veins on his leg he heard the ringing of the calling bell.

"Sara", he called, "News paper."

He heard the sound of footsteps coming nearer and the sound of a closing door.

"Who is there?" he asked without getting up from his chair.

"Raja Saab" Sara Philip answered.

"Call him inside for one minute." Alexander requested.

"No Alex, he already left "Sara replied from a distance." He kept the paper on the latch and left."

"How is he? He enquired.

"You should actually see him, Alex, he is not a boy now, and he is a man with his moustaches and the white scalp cap on his head."

"Oh! He has grown up well; four years ago he was a tiny little boy of fifth standard."

"He stopped schooling," Sara said while handing over the paper to Alexander Philip.

"He was a good student; even now I do remember his powerful commands with proper intonation during the assembly session in my previous school. Though he was a small boy of Std.V, I chose him for giving assembly commands for the whole school. But it is very sad to hear he had stopped studying." Alexander paused for a while, took a sip of coffee, and kept his cup on the parapet of the balcony wall.

"I heard he lost his father two years ago, a drunkard he was" Sara said.

"Many students are unlucky like that, we are actually lucky; somebody was there to think about our future, someone was there to struggle for us, so we reached here." He said in a sad low voice while remembering about his child hood for a moment. His parents, both father and mother worked hard in the fields and saved some money for his education. "Though we were not rich we had everything we needed, above all they gave us an environment to study, and education was their first preference." While saying this he glanced at his paper.

'Khalida Zia calls off meeting with Pranab.' Suddenly his eyes fell on two familiar photographs that used to appear frequently in all newspapers five years ago. Within seconds, he recognized their faces. Two small stamp sized photographs of S.Keeling and Viola Macke. He read the heading 'Goa drug mafia and Police killed Viola, claimed mother. He read the news with enthusiasm.

London: Eight years after British teenager Viola was raped and killed in Goa, her mother now claims the police and mafia may have killed her daughter after she backed out from smuggling consignments of drugs out of Goa. "Since she knew too much, the local mafia got her killed." Viola was found dead on Anjuna beach. The half-clad body of 18-year-old was found on Goa's Anjuna beach. Investigations had found that the girl had allegedly consumed high doses of cocaine and alcohol and was given ecstasy tablets by one of her friend who allegedly raped her later and left her on the shore. She said Viola may have been planning to smuggle drugs out of India for the local mafia but got cold feet. Police may have actually killed her, she blamed.

Alexander Philip's memories rolled back ten years ago at Susegaad Higher Secondary... that December month's evening... annual gathering... the fire on the stage... his own teachers treachery... a plot to trap him... Rohini Kumari's disappearance... his futile attempt to trace her... Rohini Kumari's parents' grief-stricken face appeared in front of him now... cancellation of the annual gathering... his trip to police stations... his trip to RTO office... court cases... attack on his office room... his transfer after transfer to punish him... finally the faces of Minguel de Silva, the unit president of Susegaad, Braganza Pereira the Minister of Education, Satoshkar Dume, Anand Shenai the math tuition baron, Diago Dias Carvalho the accountant and finally the face of Adharma Pal the wicked politician Deputy, the one who was behind his transfer to grab the public money after eliminating him from all important posts, with help of local Mafia queen and her cousin the Director of Education and finally the emblem of Susegaad club- the S shaped pendent. He felt very uncomfortable with that symbol of Susegaad. An unexplainable fear mixed with contempt and anger entered into his body like a bad omen entering into a woman's body during the tribal witchcraft. Hundreds of wicked faces appeared in front of him, many faces were unfamiliar to him, they were jeering at him, they were dancing, some faces with long canine teeth like that of a tiger but with human like face with pointed nose and sunken cheek appeared dancing in front of him. Unknowingly he screamed with fear, "Sara, Sara,"

"Alex, Alex what happened?" She noticed her husband's face became pale like of a dead body, he was shivering, his eyes were closed. "Alex what happened?" she again asked with fear. When she touched his shoulder, Alexander opened his eyes and stared at her as if he is looking at a devil with fear. He did not speak. After a minutes silence he hold his own head with his hands from behind and shook his head as if he was disagreeing with something. His silence irritated Sara and she shouted, "Tell me, what happened?"

Alexander took a deep breath and showed the paper news to her and said, "Read. Viola's mother is approaching British High commission for her governments' intervention in that case and for justice. I was just thinking about our Rohini's case, and her poor parents, who were not able to fight back, we do have a government, that was ready to protect the criminals at any cost, to protect the politicians' interest and not of the poor... what we could do?"

"Police could not understand a mother's feeling" Alexander Philip sighed and looked at the copper pod tree at a distance. He continued "in our case also they did not show any sympathy, ten years have passed, no trace of abductors, but everyone, even the children knew who were the abductors, but not the police force, what a paradox!!.

"To some extend the Susegaad could mislead the public and diverted the case against you; I don't know what would happen now." Sara sighed.

After taking a deep breath, Alexander said, "Okay we will wait for the court decision."

Sara who was standing beside him commented after a silence of two minutes, "We cannot believe the police here, that's a real fact, almost all are criminal minded, like our leaders. Do you know all our ex-students who were problem makers, eve teasers, those who punctured the tires of the teacher's bikes; who copied and passed in examinations, those who were involved in robbery and kidnapping are in the police force now? The obedient well mannered studious students are still moving around with their university certificates for getting a job."

"A few months back I saw an young police man at old Goa, who came near to me, it was during the feast of St.Francis Xavier, though I could not remember him exactly, he introduced himself as my old student at Lyceum in late eighties, when he started talking I recollected his face, a boy who forged my signature very wisely and accurately in his journal. Now he is in Police. He informed secretly that he paid seven lakhs rupees for that post and was a happy constable. The most interesting thing was he wore a golden pendent of

Susegaad. I thought to keep a safe distance from him though he was friendly to me." Alexander looked at Sara Philip and laughed with a mocking sound.

Sara Philip remained silent. When she heard the 'Susegaad' a sudden fear engulfed her and the fear was evident on her pale face. After a minutes silence she said "Alex, your own friends are your foes now, your juniors whom you helped are trying to tarnish your image and cooking stories to besmirch you, they could not tolerate an alien, a foreigner sitting as their boss."

"No doubt it was evident from Minguel de Silva's talk-he categorically told that it was better to leave the job than working under a *gati* alien: that Mishra informed me."

"No straight forward Officers could survive here, everybody in the government wants corrupt officials, Alex, better you should not pursue the case of Rohini now, I am afraid, and I'm fed up with the dirty telephone calls here. Do not forget that we have a grown up daughter now; are you able to protect us from that Susegaad gang? Tell me, that Minguel de Silva is after us and he makes all that sexy comments at midnight over the phone I cannot tolerate it anymore."

"Why? My dear Sara, why do you talk like that? Why should I change my principles in life? After seeing this paper news, I am much more worried now. All these years I was keen to know the where about of my student-Rohini, I cannot forget her, almost every day I was searching for her, but I am getting only one answer from the police that they are investigating the case and the investigation is in progress, I know they cannot act against the culprit, they cannot charge sheet a ministers' son for kidnapping and rape, the law is only for floating population and for aliens, not for the politicians and for the powerful. They cannot act against the mafia, they are afraid of Fatima."

"Alex, there is a rumor that Minguel de Silva is nominated for state award this year" Sara stopped in hesitation.

"It is not a gossip, it is a fact, he will be given the best teachers' state award for this year, hundreds of sincere teachers were side lined and this mafia man was selected, this is the freedom that our politicians enjoy today, limitless freedom, democracy has been raped here" Alexander said with disgust and contempt.

# Chapter 31

The recently promoted young officer, Poojari Crook, an upper class Bhamin, was annoyed with Alexander Philip, since he was not able to manipulate the office proceedings as he likes, and also on various other issues. He managed to become Deputy Director out of turn after superseding many senior officers. His relationship to ministers and Susegaad Club was well known to everyone. Suddenly he was projected as the most powerful person in the department because of his caste and closeness to government authorities. Poojari Bhatia was a lean person with shrill irritating authoritarian voice, and likes to wear only red slack shirts, unlike other *poojaris* who prefers saffron clothes. In order to cover up his draw backs he shouts at his subordinates without any reason. When he got the higher post in the hierarchy, out of turn, that he never could dreamt because of his poor qualifications, he became very arrogant like anyone who receives something undeserved, and began to use his position to harass his own old colleagues only to exhibit his power in the department.

He was ready to do any dirty things to please ministers and Mafia Queen. He publically declared that he was ready to polish the shoes of ministers if he was asked to do. He agreed that he is a politician; an unsuccessful incompetent teacher of yesteryears became an authority in the department. Soon after his promotion he renovated his office and decorated it with posh kasmiri carpets, expensive curtains, beautiful expensive office tables and high executive chairs. He ordered to disconnect the telephone and internet connection given to Alexander Philip who became a junior officer under him. He relaxed behind his new office table and rocked his new executive chair in style to express his authority. While rocking himself he laughed with content and satisfaction. He pressed the buzzer. One peon appeared.

"Call that fellow here" he ordered.

"Who sir?" The peon asked with little confusion.

"Alexander, call that Alexander." Also call that ADEI and that Headmaster here."

Crook thought in mind: Till last month I had to report to him, now I am the boss, and he will report to me, and I will show who I'm now... Alexander Philip... the Alien Dr. Alexander Philip, the gatti... ha... ha... with much contempt he thought and waited for the arrival of Alexander Philip."

As soon as he saw the ADEI of the zone he began to shout at him "If you cannot do my work don't show your face again here, *Kel tuka.*" The senior ADEI who was working in the department for many years became confounded, after hearing this unexpected demand, though that so common in the Department. The elderly ADEI shook his head without answering anything.

"I want my candidate be selected" He shouted in a firm shrill voice again at the ADEI only to pass the message indirectly to Alexander Philip who was just entering in his chamber. Suddenly a mixture of complex feelings began to express on his clean shaved face, it become reddish, and he tightened his thin lips unknowingly and was trying to say something but no sounds came out and he looked into his papers nervously and started to sign some more papers only to pass time. His pink face because of constant bear consumption became more pinkish now with tension and he was trying to acquire courage to face his onetime superior. He continued to look at his papers without looking at the visitors sitting in front of him. After a pause of three or four minutes he raised his blemished face and stared at the Headmaster who was sitting in a pensive and confused mood. "Did you hear what I said?"

The Headmaster was silent and he looked at Alexander Philip for some response.

"About whom are you talking about? Alexander Philip asked Crook in very low calm voice.

"I mean… I imply… about CM's candidate… he should be selected" He completed his sentence somehow.

"But Mr. Crook…, that candidate you recommend has got a very few points in interview."

"That I don't know… it is CM's candidate you should select him at any cost."

"But tell me how?" Alexander replied politely. "CM's candidate got only 31 points in interview, but there are candidates who got even 87 points… how could I…?" Alexander paused for a while.

"Very simple, change the criteria for selection… and give more marks for interview… fifty… fifty" Crook replied and smiled smugly. He raised his eye brows and smiled mockingly at Alexander Philip through the left corner of his mouth and made a disrespectful gesture, and his pink face glowed with great satisfaction.

"But Mr.Crook," Alexander wanted to convince his young arrogant master, "Is that a criterion has any approval of the department?"

"What approval are you talking about Mr. (?)I am the approving authority now, you submit it that is the end of it, you understood? He began to rock his new executive chair.

'Yes, yes I understood, here all institutions are using their own criteria for selection, minority schools one criteria, aided schools another one, and the government schools yet another… and for us no criteria at all… I believe… only political influence…" Alexander Philip responded with contempt.

The Headmaster who was sitting across Crook was silent and was gazing at the paper weight while listening to the conversation. The ADEI looked at Alexander Philip with astonishment.

There was a grave silence in the room for another two minutes. Bhatia opened one file only to kill his stress and turned the pages aimlessly for another two minutes. Abruptly he raised his head, and stared at the Headmaster in full anger and said "Do you want any lab Assistant?"

The Headmaster who was gazing at the paper weight suddenly nodded his head affirmatively.

"Then you do what I said" Crook raised his voice and the left side of his face twitched twice.

No one talked for another few minutes. Alexander Philip slowly got up from his seat and said "I need time sir" and walked out of the chamber slowly. The ADEI and the headmaster followed him one by one.

"I want the minutes of the interview in two days on my table." They heard a shrill female voice behind them. The half door slammed behind them making a squeaky noise of a rusty hinge.

The Screening Committee members looked each other helplessly while walking towards the class room where Alexander Philip set up his office. Now the senior Officer was given a vacant class room to occupy. Recently disconnected telephone wire was lying on the floor. The dirty muddy floor was with full of dust. All the three occupied broken plastic chairs kept in one corner of the dusty office room of Alexander Philip.

"Is this your chamber sir?" The ADEI asked Alexander Philip.

"Yes, you don't like this?"

"No, of course not sir" The ADEI said unfeigned. "Our Store keeper sit in a far better room… it is very bad"

"This is only a warning to you sir, they are harassing you" The Headmaster who was silent said with a gloomy face. "This is the fate of all those who had worked sincerely for the department for years… all facilities and promotions only for their own people… who are ready to do any nonsense… without any consciousness. What a grave injustice to people… I don't know what to do now… we have selected the best candidates for our school… Now he is telling to select the worst candidate… I'm fed up… really repenting to join here in the department." He stopped for a moment and looked at the ADEI who was looking at the twisted leaf of the ceiling fan above them that was making an irritable noise.

"These young officers do not have any consciousness or like to be criticized, and they do what the corrupt ministers say." The ADEI said. He continued "They only aim at their own positions and promotions. They are with the corrupt ministers for their own benefits." He took a deep breath and sighed to expel the poison that entered his body.

"Why do they conduct interviews? The CM would have selected his own candidate and informed us. What is the meaning of all these formalities and wastage of time?" The ADEI said in a low voice to air his displeasure. "We are spending hours together to check whether the candidates have any employment registration, whether they full fill the RR criteria and their certificates are genuine. Finally, we get one phone call from ministers or speaker or even from local hooligans to select even the candidate who failed or those who do not even attend the interview. Shame less ones, having no ethics or consciousness." He paused for awhile.

"You decide sir; we will come late in the evening to discuss." They understood Alexander is not in a mood to discuss anything then. Both of them left the room without waiting for a nod from him.

Alexander Philip was silent and his thoughts reel back as if in a movie. His previous experiences haunted him. He thought about the ways the administration troubled him for all these years for his straight forwardness and sincerity. The number of transfers he got in last five years amount to sixteen now, but he was contented he did not give in to any pressure till date. He could not bear the pain the way his confidential reports were spoiled by the secretary of Pariksha Bhavan, since he objected the unholy connections of the Secretary with the confidential printers and exposed the mark scandal by the snake in the grass the Hon. Controller. He knew that this Poojari Crook will do more harm than anyone. He is a viper. He got confounded. He was worried about his disturbed family life, when all his contemporaries were given comfortable transfers within the city, from one table to another; he was shunted to distant places. He began to think about his youthful days. The way he was landed in the land of sun, sand and sex. He repented his decision to leave the home town for better prospectus. I would have listened to my parents, he thought repent fully. Next moment he thought that would not have solved the problems; in his home land also the state of affairs were the same, corruption, jingoism, nepotism is everywhere. The mighty one eats up the less fortunate, the might is right, the history says the truth, it is barbarous and malicious. He knows that the Ed-mafia of the state and the Susegaad club is anxiously waiting for his blood and his family. He could envisage a jeering crowd around him. He realised that he is a victim of jingoism and chauvinism.

Suddenly he felt the vibration of his cell phone in his shirt pocket, and gradually it emitted an unfamiliar ring tone. Alexander lifted his cell with his left hand carefully and gazed at it to look for the origin of the call. An unfamiliar number? He thought for a moment whether to answer the call or not. He was bewildered for a moment. The phone continued to ring, first in very low noise and gradually the sound ascended to its maximum. After one minute ringing it stopped automatically. He kept the phone on the table and waited. After one minute again the phone vibrated fist and then started to sing the same unfamiliar ring tone that he purposefully kept for unknown numbers. Finally he took his phone from the table top that was moving in a circle because of the vibration mode. He pressed the green button to accept the call and waited apprehensively.

"Hello, is it Dr. Alexander sir?" he heard a familiar female voice from the other end.

"Yes…" Alexander said in a very low voice as if he was not interested in answering the call and tried to identify the origin of the voice.

"Alexander sir, I am Audrey…, do you remember me… now I'm the PA to the Director of Education." There was a little pride in her voice.

"Sorry Audrey, I could not recognize your voice… now after fifteen years I heard from you… what is the matter? He enquired.

"Sir, Director Madam wants to speak to you… please hold on…" she paused.

Then Alexander Philip heard a soft music for another two minutes. After that he heard the voice of Director "Alexander Philip… this is regarding the minutes of an interview you had attended last month… at that… School… I heard you refused to sign that minutes? Is that true?"

"Yes I refused to sign" Alexander replied instantly.

"Why?" there was a tone of authority in her voice.

"On the ground that they manipulated the criteria for selection… as a rule they had to finalize the selection on the same day itself… Am I right? He replied back with intense dislike. "Now after forty days they are submitting the minutes and criteria sheet after changing the marks to suit their candidate… why should I sign?"

"But Alexander, you forget about the delay and manipulation of marks… sees that they followed the RR for selection."

"I don't think they followed the RR fully for selection… they did grave injustice to other candidate who was highly qualified with a doctorate degree in special education and more than eight years of experience in teaching specially incapacitated children… she was well informed about the need of incapacitated children and knew how to handle them… further she answered all the questions asked by the screening committee and finally that secretary made a merit list giving three marks for her and gave fifteen marks for that boy who did not answer satisfactorily a single question and not knowing any departmental rules and regulations… Is it not injustice?"

he replied with righteous indignation. "Yes I refused to sign that forged document."

"Alexander, forget about injustice and justice, where there justice now? That was an old concept, now the rule is making hey when sun shines *Kel tuka?* We have to protect ourselves first." Director of Education tried to appease Alexander Philip.

"Hello Madam, I'm a Syrian Christian and I have a consciousness and my consciousness does not allow me to sign that forged document and there by doing grave injustice to a deserving candidate" Alexander Philip said in a convincing tone.

"Alexander what nonsense are you talking, consciousness and all that things, I told you,... that are all old philosophy, now with your consciousness you cannot live here in Goa. After all you should realize the fact that you are an outsider and though you have stayed here for more than thirty five or forty years you are still and outsider... are you listening... they can do anything they want... they even finish you and your family... better you sign that papers. That chairman is very close to CM, do you know that? The voice sounds like a warning and Dr. Alexander Philip heard a click sound at the other end.

Alexander Philip remembered the words of his late mother Mariamma Philip's advice, when he had decided to continue in a foreign land as an alien. Though she was not much educated like him, she had a practical knowledge, and once she advised him: Alex I know your nature, not to be adamant my son, you should protect yourself first, and should listen to the authority though they ask you to do wrong things. He wanted to think in that way, only to protect his family from the Susegaad gang. He knew that his fate will be like anyone who stood for justice or like anyone who received bullet on the chest after signing the documents for the opposite party. Anything could happen, he thought. He also thought about the case of Durga Shakti, the young IAS officer who was suspended for her honesty. The fate of mine also will be the same, he thought. In her case at least the IAS and IPS officers association were there to protect or to support her at least morally, whereas in my case even the Officers Association is supporting the corruption and the all the office bearers are the secret agents.

On the next day when Alexander Philip was about to have his lunch an young man in a golden yellow slack silk shirt hurriedly walked into his make shift office room with heavy steps. Immediately Alexander recognized him as the chairman who was present for the interview about forty five days ago. During the interview one thing what he observed was his unrefined mannerisms and his dress code. During that interview he unbuttoned two upper buttons of his shirt to expose his unattractive chest like any other loafers. A closer look revealed his locket – a thick golden locket in the shape of an S and a small cross attached to it. So he is a member of Susegaad, Alexander thought in his mind.

Abruptly he asked "Did Director call you?"

"Yes, yesterday, so you approached her" Alexander replied unfriendly.

"The person whom we had selected is the CM's person; you have to sign these minutes." While handing over the file towards DEO Alexander, he demanded.

"I knew very well that you are very close to CM" Alexander Philip smiled gawkily and said while opening the file. He looked at the merit sheet and found the corrections made in that sheet to bring the second person to the first position. His marks were intact. The Expert's marks were also changed, but he signed on the sheet. "Educated rascal, he gave almost the same marks what I had given during the interview, but now he changed the marks to please the CM and Susegaad," Alexander thought in his mind.

"Why can't you submit these minutes without my signature?" DEO Dr. Alexander Philip asked to the Chairman of the School who was sitting in front of him.

"That secretary says DEO is the ex-officio member of the departmental screening committee and as such without your signature we cannot process it" Chairman of the school said while staring at Dr. Alexander Philip through his bifocal spectacles.

"Then in that case I will sign this document with protest" Alexander Philip said.

"Director might have informed the consequences of that to you, I believe." Without much concern he warned Alexander Philip. "Better you do it now."

# Chapter 32

"Sara, the supreme court is planning to punish the judges of the lower court for endless adjournments of cases." Alexander Philip announced the paper news with little enthusiasm. "Good, if they implement it" Sara replied back while she was arranging the breakfast. "Lakhs of poor Indians may get a relief from their endless trouble." She commented without much concern. "Do you know our *Suriyanelli* case in Kerala happened when the girl was 16 years old and now she is 33 years old and the culprits are central government law makers and cabinet ministers? Whether our court could take unbiased judgments in that case? I doubt. It is still going on in different courts, only adjournments and new dates, no decision yet. Rohini Kumari was abducted when she was 16 or seventeen. Till date no one knows about her whereabouts. Police has only one answer the investigation is progressing; progressing at snails' pace, only to save that ministers son and Susegaad gang. Now more than nine years have passed that ADEI Martha's case is still in its infant stage, only adjournments no decisions. In many cases the judges are incompetent to take a decision, sometimes they are at the spell of political pressure, or at threats from local mafia gangs. Whatever may be the reason the law is for the powerful ones. How many scams? Cattle scam, coal gate scam, mining scam, mark scam. An endless investigation, only to fool the people, one scam engulfs another scam. Common people will not get any justice here. To that level of freedom our democracy decays day by day." Alexander talked to himself in indignation. Soon his eyes fell on a small news item in one corner of the inside paper. One sex worker escaped from a famous hotel was harassed by two constables in a moving police jeep. One of the police men forced her for oral sex and his companion took a video clip in his mobile phone and circulated it to his friends. Later the young woman was severely beaten up in the police lock up for immoral activity by other lady constables. He read the news and cursed the fate of the state's democracy. Since similar news was so common so he did not give any importance to that news.

News papers publishes different hot news every day, about ministers' involvements in drug mafia, ed-mafia, land mafia, coal gates, illegal mining, kidnapping, sex scandals, extortions, rape in schools, shameless enticements, food poisoning and so on. But society never changed much. Ministers remained in the same mind set to loot the public money at any cost.

They were least bothered about the paper news or the law of the land. All were trying their best to loot or grab others' money or property at any cost, including news papers. News papers compete among themselves to publish topless and bottom less photos of celebrities to lure the sex craved public. Adult entertainments! But what about the healthy teenagers? How could the society penalize them for trying the real entertainments (?) instigated by the pornography in news papers, TV shows and obscene advertisements and films? The rapes, killings and abductions of innocent girls increased tremendously. Who should be blamed for this? Unethical news papers? Corrupt ministers? Or the senseless Sensor board? Or the foolish public? There was not a single day without the news of rape or kidnappings. Alexander Philip attributed all those to vulgar scenes in the movies and TV. Ministers' direct involvements in all the cases or the involvements of their party men and relatives blind folded the sincere police officers though they are ready to book the culprits. Ministry out of fear of being toppled by the anti social legislative members always tried to protect their own interest and allowed the common people to suffer. For the CM the common people were mere puppies accidently crushed under the wheels of his bullet proof Mercedes Benz car? Black cats with AK 47 rifles to protect the antisocial elements, law breakers and those who loot the government treasury? Why do people time and again vote for a TV set or for a computer? Alexander Philip has no answer to all these like lakhs of common law abiding citizens. How far the governments fool the people? He was disturbed by all these thoughts.

The calling bell chimed. Slowly he got up from his old rattan chair. Arthritis has almost eaten up his health now. He struggled to walk near to the door to answer the call. He saw a young tall man with a smiling face.

"Sir, good morning" while smiling he said with a bright face.

Alexander Philip paused for a few seconds to respond. He was struggling to recollect that face. The young man realised that his teacher is struggling to recollect him. He again said "Sir I'm Chandrasekhar..."

"Sorry Chandrasekhar I could not recognize you... I'm very sorry"

"Sir ex-student of Susegaad Higher Secondary"

Silence from Alexander Philip baffled Chandrasekhar little more. He continued to introduce himself more. "Sir during that Annual day function in our school... when that fire broke out... I was there sir with you... at the police station to give the report... about that kidnapping."

"Along with sir Mishra...?" Alexander Philip continued the sentence.

"Yes sir..." Chandrasekhar said in a low voice.

"Sorry Mr. Chandrasekhar, I am very sorry, time has made lot of changes in you, that is quite natural... It was my mistake... Please do come in" He invited his ex-student warmly with great pleasure.

"Sir, I joined the police service soon after my education"

"Good, I am very happy to see my old students... especially students like you... you were..." Before he could complete his sentence Chandrasekhar interrupted "Sir now I'm posted at Mapusa, and I have brought some good news to you..."

"Good news... You got promotion?"

"No sir, the news is partially good and to some extends very sad too."

Alexander looked at his ex-student eagerly who was very thin and pale with very delicate physique about ten years ago. Now he is a grown up man with good personality. His thick moustache suits him very well. "Tell me Chandra what is the news" Alexander enquired.

"Sir, I saw our class mate Rohini Kumari" He said abruptly and paused.

Alexander Philip received the news with great excitement and curiosity. His face brightened and his eye brows were raised a little in excitement "Where?" He enquired.

"She is in lock up sir, now"

"In police lock up? Why?"

"She was arrested a few days ago from Calangute"

"Arrested? Why?" Alexander became very impatient to here the details.

"Sir, you might have read the news in today's paper about her… the police arrested her from Calangute under mysterious circumstances…" Chandrasekhar explained the news with great grief. The worst thing happened to her, actually she escaped from a five star hotel, a foreigner helped her to escape from there, but she was caught on the way by our police and what happened in the police jeep was true that you might have read in the paper… very sad thing and very horrible thing happened to her."

Alexander recollected the paper news what he read a few hours before. He became silent in anguish. The news disturbed him fully and he began to shiver unknowingly as the adrenalin pumped into his blood stream. He could not control himself. Again he looked at the paper news and read it again.

"Chandra, I read it today morning, even I thought about our Rohini while reading the news paper… and even told about it to my wife… really a horrible news… very sad thing happened to her, really terrible… I tried my level best to save her from the beasts… but I could not… I could not… is she alright now?"

"No sir, she is almost mad women now, not even talking to anyone and refused to meet any one… and the way my colleagues treated she was unimaginable… I repent… I could not do anything… the culprit was my immediate boss… a father of three daughters… he is a beast not human… a monster… Sir, really I repent now… I should not have joined the police force… Now I realised that the police force is the most corrupt department in the state… really with good intention I joined the force, but every day we are forced to do dirty unlawful things… as you know police is the friend of criminals and drug mafia here… they are behind all nasty things I am afraid… I do not know what to do and how to escape from these mafia web."

"You cannot escape from this mafia labyrinth of corruption and atrocity, Chandra… if you want to continue. A few days back our Director of Education telephonically warned me… and reminded me that still I am a *ghatti*… though I was staying in Goa for more than thirty five years… still I am treated an outsider by my own department, and he admonished if I am not signing a forged document to favor CM… he warned me, the Susegaad may even finish my family… that was the threat I received for not selecting a member of a Jingoist Party man for a government job." After few seconds pause he asked "Tell me Chandra what we could do save her now."

"Sir, when I recognized her I tried to contact her family, and I came to know that their family left Goa after that incident and even her father is no more now, he died one year ago, and her younger brother is staying near that Zuari Jerri colony in a small rented room. I contacted him, but he is not ready to accept her, even he refused to visit her in lock up… someone should help her… she in a very distressed mood now…"

There was a grave silence in the room. No one talked. Alexander was gazing aimlessly outside through the open window and was in deep thought. Chandra looked at the floor only to kill the time and was waiting for some response from his ex- principal.

Finally Dr. Alexander Philip broke the silence. With determination he said "OK Chandra I will come and release her, before that once again we will contact her brother to convince him."

"I warn you not to stick your nose in that case again" Sara who was listening to the whole conversations shouted furiously with red eyes. "You are inviting only trouble to us… don't forget that we have a daughter… and we are aliens here." She started to sob bitterly. She snatched the newspaper from her husband's hand and threw it on the floor with resentment.

Alexander could hear the sounds of vessels falling on the floor. He remained silent and holds back.

When the trio visited the Police station they saw Rohini behind the bars, sitting on the bare floor in one corner of a small dark room. Through the rusted iron bars Alexander Philip saw her. She looked like an insane lady. All her teenage beauty had gone forever. Her beautiful hair was not combed for days together now. To protect herself from flies and mosquitoes she covered her body with a torn sari. She sat on the floor like a criminal having no courage to look at people because of utter shame while the real criminals were moving boldly here and there in their khaki uniform. The lady constables who thrashed her mercilessly on the other day for immoral act looked at her like saints. Without meeting Rohini Alexander Philip met the SHO along with Chandrasekhar and completed the formalities to release her while her brother Mallappa was waiting outside. Rohini did not realize the presence of her brother and teacher nearby because she was gazing continuously down on the floor in depression and was not bothered to see who was around her.

A fat lady constable opened the door of the cell and demanded her to come out of it. A hysterical cry with full of fear and agony that emitted from that young lady was the answer, who was shivering with fear. Rohini ran out of the room and looked at her brother with blank eyes struggling to locate a familiar face among the police people. She couldn't recognize her younger brothers' face that she has not seen for the last ten years. A tall young man with strong muscles with tears in his eyes was not the picture of Mallappa in the mind of Rohini Kumari and she never expected her brother or any known person around her. She thought that it is the beginning of another ordeal and the same thought made her to cry loudly.

*"Augirao Chediacho"* The lady constable shouted at the lady who was bitterly screaming with fear. Though Alexander Philip wanted to give a befitting answer to that lady constable's dirty remarks, he kept quite purposefully and turned to Rohini and called by her name "Rohini… we are here to take you home." Suddenly Rohini recognized her ex-Principals deep base voice in seconds and looked at his face and immediately fell on his feet and again started to cry bitterly "Save me sir, please save me she cried."

"Get up Rohini, get up, no one will harm you now" While saying Alexander Philip lifted her from the floor. They embraced each other for a few minutes till she calms down completely.

"See your brother" Alexander slowly murmured in to her ears. She looked at the tall young man with tears in his eyes and puzzled. She could not believe her eyes. Suddenly she fell into his extended arms and wept sorrowfully.

One police man asked Alexander Philip *"Ye Chedu khon?"*

Alexander Philip immediately replied *"Vo mera betti hai"*

# Chapter 33

It was Johnny who called Andrew Akbar, *Paklo* for the first time while they were playing on the muddy Gama beach, when they were children. Now the public like to call him as Paklo Dada, with respect and fear. He slowly established his real estate business and named it Paklo Constructions Ltd. A huge four storied building with full view of the Arabian sea near Gama beach next to Fatima's castle with its own private terrace garden was the seat his empire. He decorated his office room with expensive Italian marbles, chandlers, imported wall paintings and wall fittings to impress his valuable foreign customers. His conference room was superior to vidhan sabhas decorations and he always boast about his posh interior decorations with pride. He imported all the leather finish sofas and furniture from Honkong and Singapore. Only a few trusted members were allowed inside his office with secret passages and secret hide outs. Ministers, high profile police officers and government secretaries were his usual visitors in his posh office. From his office he could see the entire Bogda hill. He always dreamed of constructing his own hotel project after evacuating the entire inhabitants from that hill. Gradually he became the keeper of all black money from the government officials. Most of the evenings he spent his time in casino games along with ministers and other business people. Though he crossed his forties he did not get time to find a spouse for him. Same was the case of his friend Johnny. Both of them lived a happy gay life together with all vices.

Paklo Dada's brand new Audi stopped in front of his real estate office on beach side. Immediately one body guard opened the door for him with reverence and as Paklo came out and two of his personnel body guards escorted him to his most expensive modern office. One of his escorts again opened the office door for him and other one stood outside the huge gate at the entrance and another assistant accompanied him with some files in his hand inside. Paklo dada walked like a modern Indian political leader with black cat security as escorts.

Paklo Constructions Pvt. Ltd grabbed all prime area in the city and became the successful competitor for all government tenders throughout the state. The land owners who refused to negotiate with his price were handled by the Fatima's boys and Johnny. The Gama beach where he had grown up was partially cleared by the authorities by force. Andrew wanted to set up a five star hotel on the hill top of Bogda with beautiful view of the sandy Baina beach and to show the public his power. The horrible unpleasant memory of his early child hood days always haunted Andrew Akbar. He remembered the way he was treated by the public and the police when he was a young boy and he was waiting for a chance to retaliate and revenge. He has not forgotten the raids in their cubicles; for any theft happened in the city, and very often their belongings were thrown out by the police to find out the theft articles among them. Very often he remembered Indian nationalist party's meeting on the beach and the way he was running naked in fear of khaki uniform. Now he knew that all local khaki personals are his friends and there is no need to fear them anymore. He dreamed of his ambitious hotel project overlooking the Gama beach. He was not satisfied with the hotel plan submitted by the Indian architects and then he invited foreign architects and finally he was pleased with a plan submitted by a Korean architect. He had plan for secret passages and secret rooms to cater his drug and flesh trade and he feared an Indian architect may reveal his cunning ideas to public sometime in future, so he preferred a foreign architect and passed his secret plans to him. He also made arrangements in the plan for a secret escape tunnel to sea in the event he was caught any time in future. He knew that for his ambitious plans political power is a must. He decided to contest and win the municipal elections. He trusted his childhood friend Johnny for everything. His childhood friend Johnny was with him always as a shadow. Because of his feminine nature and female voice he could easily dress up like a female and cheat the public. Born in a respected family he was hated by his own family members because of his involvement in antisocial activities. Johnny wanted only bear or a bottle of whisky occasionally girls. That was plenty at the Susegaad club house; the number two room of hotel Sumitra, the infamous beach side hotel. Hotel Sumitra and Jesus bar was acquired by Club Susegaad from its previous owner. In the bar he dressed like a pretty women to attract the customers. He rarely visited his home and supported his elderly mother. It was Johnny who encouraged Andrew to contest the municipal elections. Just two months before the municipal elections he arranged free sari distribution to poor people in his ward followed by rain coats and free note books to children. He printed special notebooks with photographs of Paklo Dada and also with brief notes of his social works carried out for poor people. He and the Susegaad members arranged street cleaning programmes in Vasco and video clipped it only to air the same through the local TV channels. Soon after the photographs and video clipping the members left the garbage collected on the road side in different places only to repeat the same cleaning action and to blame the government for inaction. The action of dumping the garbage on the road side by Paklo's people and Susegaad group members were aired by some social media supporting Alexander Philip resulted in fresh enmity between Paklo Dada's Susegaad and Dr. Alexander Philip. Susegaad was angry with the Alexander Philip and was waiting to take avenge since he bailed out Rohini Kumari from the police custody.

Seventeen year old Mallappa chalked out his own plans. He took membership in a new organization aimed at the welfare of poor and helpless unfortunate people. He did not forget his own health and exercised two hours a day to improve his physical powers and walked ten kilometers regularly. Gradually his friendship circle increased. He had to support his ailing mother who moved to her village soon after the death of his father, who died of depression and frustration. He secured a small job at Verna Industrial estate to feed himself and Rohini who started her own tailoring business at their one room residence. Both of them spent their free time with a local NGO group run by missionaries who work among destitute and AIDS patients. Slowly with the help of loving neighbors she began to lead a normal life.

One day Mallappa took her sister Rohini to a Kali temple at an isolated place inside a dense forest near Neturlim. The temple was on its last legs and it was partially demolished during the Portuguese regime nearly hundred years ago. However, many worshiped this Kali Devi and locals have full faith in the powers of the Devi. In the past children were sacrificed in front of the Devi for receiving favors by the locals. Rohini was nauseated by the sight of blood of animals sacrificed in front of the *Kali Devi*. Mallappa bought a cock from the nearby vendor and asked her to catch it firmly. "You should kill the cock in front of Kali Devi in one strike." He told his elder sister in a low voice to her ear. Rohini looked at her brother in hesitation and little fear. There was a pool of blood in front of that idol of Kali Devi made of black stone. Devi's red tongue was protruded out and her dreadful blue eyes were glowing like of a beast. The idol has a long sharp triad in her hand. Devi's frightful face would surely make a sense of fear in anybody's mind.

"Why?" She asked her brother.

"It is to please the goddess" Mallappa uttered in a firm voice.

"I can't kill, I can't" she replied.

"Then, why did I bring you here?" he asked with little irritation.

"To pray to Kali Devi" She murmured.

"Devi won't listen to your prayer without shedding blood; which is the rule" He tried to encourage her.

"I'm afraid, *chotu*" She again said.

"With fear you cannot do anything" he whispered.

"I know *chotu Bhaiyya*, our Principal Dr. Alexander Philip always says the same. Once he said "the only thing what we have to fear is the fear itself" and on another occasion he quoted the words of Alexander the great "Only anger can conquer.""

"Finally only he was there for your rescue Rohini, do you know that?" Mallappa with sorrowful eyes continued "Even I feel guilty, Rohini, I was not ready to come to your cell at Mapusa... I feel guilty now. When that Chandrashekar, your class mate police man, informed me about your condition actually I was worried and afraid... only because of your Principal I came to meet you." Mallapa paused for a minute and looked into the eyes of his elder sister which was glowing with tears. As she closed her eyes two drops of tears fell through her cheeks. Immediately she wiped her eyes with her left hand. She remained silent for a minute looking at the frightful face of Kali Devi. "Because of me he suffered a lot, *bhaiyya* the entire Susegaad become against him and still troubling him… I will pray for him first…" She joined both her arms together and stood in front of Devi and prayed. Tears started to roll down through her sunken cheeks. Mallappa waited patiently till she finished her prayer and at the end when she opened her eyes Mallappa asked her, "What did you pray?"

"I prayed for my sir, If he were not there I would have ended my life in frustration and in shame, I prayed for his good health, I heard he is suffering from severe arthritis." Rohini said with gratitude.

"You should sacrifice this cock to Devi, now for your sir, are you ready?"

She was silent for a moment and as if she had determined something she took the cock from her brother and held by its two wings. "Now what to do? Tell me" she asked for help.

"Now you hold its both legs together, like this" Mallapa showed how to hold a cock by its legs. The cock flapped its wings three times and stopped as if it was ready to be sacrificed for Devi. Mallappa took a long knife of one and half feet long from the feet of Kali Devi and gave it to Rohini and said "Now you keep the head of the cock on that log in front of Devi and with one strike you should separate the head from the body and pour the blood on the floor in front of Devi's feet, that's all" he paused and waited to see the action. "While cutting the head you should think about that beast-Andrew Akbar in your mind." Her brother reminded her. When he mentioned the name of Andrew Akbar, her face became red in anger and she looked at the glowing facing of Kali Devi and raised the sword in the air and chanted loudly:

"*Om Durgayami namaha… Om Durgayami namaha… Om Durgayami namaha*"

She knew something happened to her body and she felt her heart beats stronger and pumbing it faster than ever and in seconds and started to shiver, she raised the sword in her

hand and with one strike she separated the head of the cock
from its body. The headless body of the cock began to tremble
again and again splashing blood from its neck like a small jet
and finally settled near the feet of Kali Devi, as if asking for
favour. The headless body rolled thrice and failed during the
fourth attempt and lied still without life near the feet of the
idol.

"One day I will kill that beast like this... and I wanted to
see his headless body lying under my feet... like this." Mallappa
determined in his mind. He banged his right fist on his left palm
and shouted in anger "I will do that, I will do that... He began
to chant the same *"Om Durgayami namaha... Om Durgayami
namaha... Om Durgayami Namaha"* He roared in anger. Rohini
Kumari could not understand what he was doing. What *Chotu
Bhaiyya* what happened?" she asked. Mallappa shook his head
twice in anger but did not reveal what he decided in front of his
Devi. He collected the cock's body in a plastic bag and returned
home and left the head for the Devi.

Every month on the new moon day after sunset they
visited the same temple and sacrificed one cock to Devi and
returned home with the headless body of the cock. Rohini
Kumari's fear and hesitation disappeared gradually and she
performed the sacrifice without any demur. At the end of
every sacrifice Mallapa closed his right fist and banged against
his left palm and shouts in full anger "I will do that, I will do
that... Maha Kali helps me." He pledged it for three times.

During the fifth instance he bought a goat in front of the
Kali Devi and asked Rohini to kill it while thinking about the
beast–Andrew Akbar. He advised when she hesitated to kill that
animal "Rohini think that you are killing the beast, which spoiled
your life, in front of the Devi and get satisfaction. Strike Now,
Strike now" he yelled while holding the goat firmly. The animal
tried in vain to move, but it was not a match to powerful Mallapa.

First time Rohini separated the head with three to four strikes. On the seventh instance she cut off the animals head with one strike. "Good, Very good, you should cut of his head with one strike... you are fit now. Now you pray to Devi to give courage, this is the last visit in this year..." said Mallappa.

# Chapter 34

In October four engineering students checked into a hotel near Baga beach and decided to go for a walk at night to enjoy the sandy beach and clear moon light, without knowing the fate waiting for them. They lied on the clean sand and gazed at the sky and cherished the sweet memories. One of them said "This is the fulfillment of my teenage dreams." Another said "after my marriage I will return to this same beach and stroll here along with my wife." The third one commented "I shall come here again but not with my wife, with some travel girls and enjoy here in Baga." Forth one was silent. Immediately they saw someone approaching them. First they ignored the strangers and continued their talk. Two police men stood in front of them.

"Get up rascals "one of the police men shouted.

The boys without doubting much slowly got up and sat on the sand.

"Stand" the other man in police uniform shouted.

While the students were struggling to get up, the police men caught them by their collar and announced, "You are under arrest."

"Under arrest?" Why?" one of the students asked with little confusion.

"You will come to know… soon" one of the police man in uniform cried and pushed the boy to the ground.

"Do you have drugs with you?" the police man enquired.

"No, we are students from Bangalore, we don't have any drugs with us" One boy acquired courage and said.

"Don't play much, we have information… you are drug traffickers… come along with us" one of the police man in mufti announced and dragged one of the students

The innocent boys looked each other in panic without knowing what to say. One of the students, who were silent, took his mobile and tried to dial a number. The police man acted immediately. He snatched his mobile and slapped on his face. "We want to search you… we know that you are drug traffickers." One of the police men started searching the pockets and took out a small packet with white powder. The boys wondered. At the same time two more persons reached the site and they caught the boys by force.

The new comers announced, "We have got the *mal* from you and you are under arrest and you remain 20 years behind the bars". The innocent boy's faces became red in fear. The faces of the police men were not clear in the moonlight. The boys started pleading their innocence and they knew that the drug was implanted by the police men themselves.

"Cool down boys…, cooldown" the first police man in uniform changed his tone and said.

"We will save you, but you have to shell out Rs.50,000."

Students do not know what to do. One of the boys said "We don't have money".

"If you don't have the money, stay behind the bars for twenty years… now come to the police station with us, we will talk there." The police man threatened them again while holding them tightly.

"Sir, please leave us… leave us free, you take whatever we have" one of the boys requested in fear. He handed over his wallet to the police man. The police man took the wallet and counted the money "this is only three thousand… who want this… we want Rs.50, 000, nothing less than that." The police man was adamant. Others also followed their friend. One boy removed his gold chain and gave and others removed all their valuables and gave to the protectors of law.

It seems the police men were happy and they released the boys and disappeared in the darkness. They threw the starch powder packet on the sand and left.

At the hotel they immediately telephoned to their parents and described the whole episode and asked them to send money for their return journey and also to pay the hotel bill. One of the parents contacted their relative, a Superintendent of police at Bangalore and informed the robbery. He immediately contacted his counterpart in Goa and on the very next day the robber police men were caught during an identification parade at police station. The news paper reported this news also reported that the Goa police men have demanded a bribe for shooting a film 'Anjuna Beach' on murdered British teenager Scarlett Keeling. The boys after their return decided not to visit Goa in their life, out of fear. The suspended police men were reinstated soon. People say club Susegaad was behind their reinstation and immediate promotion.

# Chapter 35

Paklo Dada joined CDP to contest the assembly elections well before its final announcements. A party stood against the corruption, mafia and prostitution selected a notorious kidnapper as their candidate. People say Paklo paid three crore rupees as cash for his candidature to the party president. The president was not bothered to dig the origin of the bribe. A party which was on its last legs need not worry about the ethics for which it was founded by someone to fight corruption. The money derived from smuggling, drug trafficking, assassination, prostitution and extortion has no difference to the CDP leaders. News papers were flooded with 'well-wishers' congratulations and greetings to Paklo Dada. Many gave the greetings in fear of the gangster for their own protection and survival. Many were forced to give full size photograph of Paklo Dada in the national dailies to impress the voters. The number of paid workers for Paklo Dada increased day by day. All local goons were recruited by Johnny for his master. A wave of terror engulfed the port city. People were afraid to talk against prostitution and corruption. The crime rate rose twenty times and police reputation reached all time low. People who talked against Paklo dada were silenced by the goons.

Assembly elections were fast approaching and Paklo dada had many ambitions. His hotel projects on Bogda hill, to acquire prime lands in the city to construct sky scrapers and a huge mall in the heart of the city. Johnny the election manager prepared a large number of Susegaad emblems in brass, copper and silver as a locket for members and sold at a huge price and in return he assured protection from police and other gangs. All shop keepers were compelled to buy that Susegaad emblem, and out of fear many purchased the same and hanged it next to their god's image. City was flooded with the huge cut outs of Paklo dada the mass leader. As planned by his election manager, in one December evening he planned to start his election propaganda on a new moon day and decided to visit the Zuari nagar slums. He made all arrangements to distribute free items like saris, bicycles and home appliances in the morning and he was confident that he would get vote's equivalent to the number of items he distributed. He arranged for liquor distribution at night. After the liquor distribution he decided to visit at least 100 huts on that day itself to demand votes. Paklo dada never believed in requesting for votes, instead he demanded it.

At about 8.30 PM in the evening Paklo Dada along with Johnny and a few club Susegaad members reached the Zuari nagar slums, one of the largest slums in Goa with thousands of small huts and cubicles. Complete darkness in that area made it difficult for them to see the path. Dirty stinking smell of garbage's and filth welcomed them. Ray of lights coming from a few kerosene lamps through the slits of rusted tin sheets of the cubicles were the only light on the muddy path. They found it difficult to keep their legs out of human shits and dogs excreta on the way. In some places accumulated drainage water and slurry spoiled their footwear's and legs. Smell of cheap alcoholic beverages, and smoke and smell of frying Mumbai duck and other fish items increased the suffocation in that slums. Thousands of people in those cubicles without any water supply or electric supply depended on wood and charcoal for cooking. Because of the freezing cold in the month of December, the smoke refused to move up and remained near to the ground and that made the area foggy. The visibility through the fog was very poor. Radio music from distant huts, arguments between brothel owners and clients, helpless girls sobbing sounds, sounds of beating, quarrelling between neoghbours, and women's shouting's at their boozer husbands followed by their loud cry made the slum a hell. Some stray dogs woofed at the strangers and followed them. Such environment was not unfamiliar to

Andrew Akbar. He remembered about his child hood while passing through the narrow passages in between the cubicles. His child hood and teenage was spend in that environment till Fatima came forward to protect him and provided with a decent accommodation in return of his services as a pimp. But Brother Johnny, who was born and brought up in a decent family till he joined with the mafia gang, found it very difficult to adjust with the filthy environment. However he followed his master without complaining. The election campaign party of Andrew Akbar entered a cubicle where they saw a police man in a compromising position with a young girl. Without asking anything they closed the door and moved to the next hut. The police man grunted, but remains silent after recognizing the mass leader Paklo dada in front of him. He covered his face immediately with a shawl. In the next cubicle the people welcomed him with joined hands. The lady's eyes were glinted with gratitude for the free sari that she got in the morning and promised full support for his candidature. Almost all hut dwellers welcomed him and promised support out of fear. Already Susegaad boys spread the news that anyone who vote against Paklo Dada would be tied up to a tree and thrash to death and would burn their huts. In another hut the door was made out of bamboo mat and it was loosely attached to the crude frame made out of Bamboo. Johnny hit the tin sheet wall two times to alert the people and announced the arrival of Dada Paklo. But there was no response from inside. Paklo saw a shadow moving behind him while Johnny was peeping through the half opened door of the hut to check whether anyone inside.

As he put his head through the half opened door he felt some powder fell on his face, the powder forced him to close his eyes as it started acting immediately within a fraction of seconds; a severe burning sensation, the smell of red chili powder entered his nose and he cried in pain while covering his eyes within his hands. Before he could come to senses he felt something hard hit on his head one after another, then he felt a hard blow on his belly and also below his knee. While touching the burning eyes he tried to open his eyes for a second, but he quit from his attempt because of the severe burning sensation in eyes.

"Paklo, run run, we are tra… pped" Johnny cried out with pain.

Next moment he fell on the ground with a grunt. He tried to say something to his master, but because of severe pain on his head and knee only a groaning sound emitted from his throat. Paklo could not see clearly what was happening to his Johnny. At the same time he also felt that a tall shadow was standing just behind him. Paklo tried to turn his head to see who that tall man was. Within seconds Paklo felt he was being lifted from the ground by that powerful shadow just behind him and in the next moment he was thrown inside the hut. Immediately another person smeared the red chili powder on his eyes. He was forced to close the eyes. In the next moment a series of blows fell on his face and belly. Paklo fumbled for his pistol from his waist while closing his burning eyes. A severe blow from an iron bar on his hand prevented him from his action. "Johnny" "Minguel" "Augustino" Paklo Dada cried out with pain from his broken hand. He heard the sounds of people's footsteps running away from him through the gullies. Party workers ran for their life leaving their master in darkness. Andrew could hear the painful cries of his friends from a little distance. Johnny was lying on the floor with his eyes closed. Suddenly he got up from the floor and was trying to stand on his feet. A powerful kick on his groin spoiled his attempt to hit back at the shadow. Paklo felt both his hands were motion less and someone from behind was holding it firmly. With all his strength he tried to escape from the grip of the powerful shadow, but in vain. Now he knew that his strength is no match in front of a teenager boy. He yelled for help and cried out "Johnny", who was laying motion less on the floor. Johnny, when he was gaining consciousness heard his master's cry for help, but he could not see anything clearly in the dark and he was helpless. Johnny felt that someone was tying his hand with a plastic rope and he failed in his attempt to release himself from the clutches of that powerful shadow. The other party workers who were accompanying Paklo ran for their life through the gulley and some of the shadows followed them and hit them from the back. No one tried to resist. Through the unfamiliar paths they lost their way out and struggled to escape.

Slowly Paklo Dada realised he was surrounded by more than five powerful people with mask on their head and his mouth was fastened with wooden log and rags. Soon he was tied to a central pole of the hut.

"Kali Devi, I got him" the tall shadow cried while holding Paklo's neck in his powerful hands.

"Devi... accepts my sacrifice" another female voice echoed inside the hut through the darkness. Andrew could hear someone chanting *"Om Durgayami namaha... Om Dugayami namaha... Om Durgayami namaha..."*

Paklo wanted to scream loudly but no sound escaped out from that jammed mouth.

"Dada, may I please...," a female voice murmured with a tone of vengeance in to the ear of Andrew Akbar who was tied up to a central pole of the hut.

Paklo recognized the voice and he jerked with fear.

"It should be a lesson for all other rapists and pimps" the female voice again muttered in to the ears of Andrew Akbar. Akbar recognized the female voice. He tried in vain to escape.

"Act now" one male voice shouted. "Now it is your turn."

His attempt to open his burning eyes even failed. In the darkness Andrew could not do much to save himself....

One elderly lady murmured into Paklo's ear. "You thought that you could cheat the poor by giving us a free sari or bicycles to our children... and you dreamed of becoming our leader... at the cost of our girl's virginity... it should be lesson for our politicians, present politicians who are criminals and smugglers... who plunder the public money and live in palacious houses... and look down at us after winning the elections... it should be a lesson... natural justice... it is mere natural justice... we know that you could escape from all punishments when you become a minister... don't think that you could fool us any more..."

"We know that you escape from the law and all punishments because you have money and you may succeed in twisting the law in your favour... this is the punishment you deserve... dada" another female voice murmured.

The grunting and moaning sound from Paklo Dada slowly reduced and finally stopped.

The mafia queen heard the news with great shock. She was not sure what was actually happened. Dada Augustino and his boys returned to the slum within one hour to retaliate. It was about one' o'clock in the morning. Most of the slum dwellers were fast asleep and did not know what happened during that night to 'the leader of masses' from whom they received free saris on the previous day. In the mid night they heard some sounds of shouts and scream and immediately they found their huts are on fire.

Johnny who regained consciousness could not tolerate the dirty smell around him. Soon he realised that he was lying on a heap of waste. He struggled to get up from the place. With the bleeding head he sat on the waste for some more time. He did not know what happened to him on the previous night.

Immediately he heard some screming sounds of slum dwellers running for their life. At a distant place he noticed a hut on fire. Gradually the fire spread to the nearby areas and within a few minutes more and more huts were on fire. He tried to make some sounds to attract their attention. But he had no strength to call out their name. "Minguel... Minguel"... he cried" But his voice was not loud enough to reach Minguel De Silva in that commotion. Minguel with a torch in his hand passed that way without noticing his friend lying on the dirty garbage hill. He was busy in torching the huts. Mafia queen sent hundreds of workers with fire arms to retaliate the attack on Paklo dada. The night sky flamed with the burning huts.

# Chapter 36

"Dear brothers and sisters, Brother Johnny is not with us now... I am sure his soul is with the Christ and listening and watching our prayers from distance... though he is not among us in the flesh, his deeds and memories are here with us... he was a good friend a good singer and a good organizer..., we remember him for his deeds... let us pray for his soul... let his soul rest in peace.. we also pray for his mother... please all rise" The stout and short priest extended both of his hands in front slowly as if he is about to receive something precious and everybody in that four hundred years old ancient church ascended as the Church choir played the sad drum beat, except Johnny's old and weak mother. Her small cataract affected eyes filled with tears and as she closed her eyes to pray, two drops of tears fell like two pearls on her old and worn out black dress that her late husband gave her ten years ago on her sixtieth birthday. Her sisters-in-laws all were there sitting by her side in their new expensive black dress, and looked at her scornfully while they crossed themselves bending their heads along with others in the church. Minguel de Silva along with Fatima was sitting in the second row to pay homage to their faithful worker. The slow and sad drum beat was followed by some songs sung by the church choir, while the priest stood motionless in front of the altar with his hands up in the air. Then suddenly the music was stopped, and the priest occupied a chair in the middle behind the table and his body was hidden by the table. A beautiful young lady in black dress with a prominent nose appeared on the side of the altar and opened the Bible and read a lesson from book of Isaiah. Susegaad members those who attend the church service first time in that church looked at the various paintings on the wall, the expensive fully lighted and marvelous imported crystal chandeliers hanging from the high roof, and at the statues of baby Jesus in the arms of Mother Mary in golden casket on the left front side of the huge church and the statue of crucified Jesus Christ on the right side.

In between the statues in front of the church, Johnny's coffin was kept with his head raised little as if to show his face to Jesus Christ, with his hand tied together above his chest with a small wooden cross kept in between the dead fingers that projected out to show that he was a Christian at least after his death. He has gone, gone forever. Except his mother and a few of his close friends of Club Susegaad, all others felt a relief. Now the girls could walk free to schools for some more years till someone else fill the gap created by the death of Johnny, the gangster; parents thought and they sighed and took a deep breath of relief.

Suddenly the church choir started a new song in the background music of the organ as if to awaken those who were sleeping or gone away with their wild thoughts. After the song the priest made some more prayers and the portion of the crowd murmured something in response, most of the words were half pronounced and not clear and they said it in a haste to cope with others or to compete with others to finish it first and then they bowed their head and crossed themselves. Then again silence dominated for a few more moments.

Then another girl, dark complexioned with black dress appeared in front of the pulpit and read another lesson from Corinthians II. After the bible reading the stout and short priest in purple gown stood up and ascended his hands slowly and the crowd stood up for the mass. He raised the small circular Host (bread) in his hand and said and Jesus said "this is my body, and who ever eat this will live forever," he paused a little and continued his mass. He took the chalice from the alter side shelf with reverence and wiped the inside portion with a white clean towel three times and poured the sacramental wine inside and prayed. He broke a piece of bread and put it in his mouth and tried to swallow it without biting on it. He was taught when he was young not to bite the Host but only swallow, by the elder priests, and he never he tried to bite on the flesh of Jesus Christ to avoid any further injury to him and also in the fear of blood oozing out of it. He drank the sacramental wine himself for the sake of Johnny's soul who was lying motionless inside his newly polished coffin that was apparently looking at the priest with his dead eyes. His chin was tied with a clean white tape to keep it in its place. He was sleeping… the final eternal sleep… that no one could prevent… he slept in peace when only his mother wept for him, though she was humiliated and tortured by her own only son… now he is no more. Even she thought Johnny is lucky to die before her death... a death... that she never thought would happen... she never thought to witness it with that cataract eyes. Everyone thought he may die with his enemies hand or in the police station. But he was lucky; he lost his both kidneys and liver when he was forty years old. Nobody was really interested in his life, not even his mother nor his family members. Only the minister of Education Pereira Braganza felt that he has lost one of his slaves who were ready to do anything he commands. Now he is no more.

"Now the coffin may be shifted to the grave yard" the priest announced. A teen aged boy in his black suit approached the priest and said something in his ear. The police in black suit in mufti identified Susegaad members among the crowd and positioned behind them. Hundreds of criminal cases were registered against the Susegaad members by the new administration, and they were looking for Fatima for the last few months. One of the tall and stout lady constables in their black civil dress positioned just behind Fatima. Since the new DIG does not believe the local police he personally arranged the CRPF force to nab the Susegaad group. Susegaad members did not identify the band members even at a later stage. The DIG was controlling the entire operation from the terrace of a nearby tall building very near to the Church and grave yard. He kept fifty strong CRPF Jawans inside the church compound to help the CBI officials. Local police was unaware of this operation.

The teen aged boy who talked to the priest returned to the pulpit and the priest motioned the parishioners to occupy their seats once again. The boy read out a neatly worded condolence message "Uncle Johnny", he started, we know that you are watching us from heaven and we believe that you are with Jesus Christ, though you are not with us today in flesh, the sweet memories of you are with us and we remember you in coming days… we remember your great contribution to our association, thank you uncle Johnny, may your soul rest in peace." He stopped.

Again the priest stood up and moved near to the Johnny's coffin. The crowd gathered on both sides of the aisle to have a last vision of Brother Johnny's face, which had molested several dozens of school girls. When the coffin was outside the church there was a little commotion, people started hurrying and pushing the row of people just in front of them only to see the coffin once again. The tall and stout lady constable who was deputed to nab Fatima walked just behind her. The huge figure of Fatima moved along the crowd like an elephant among the herd of wild buffalos. Suddenly the crowd stopped moving and Fatima also stopped moving front. People was stamping recklessly on the fresh mud tomb of a recent burial.

"No place to stand" Fatima murmured and looked around. "Everywhere mud" after looking at her expensive and stylish shoes she murmured. The unexpected rain in the early morning made the grave yard muddy.

"Madam, come we shall stand there…, there is little grass over there" The lady constable tried to entice her near to the CRPF personals standing there. Suspecting no danger she moved to that grass land very near to central force.

Before she could reach her destination she was surrounded and caught. "Madam, you are under arrest" the lady who was accompanying her said to her in very low and soft voice. Madam, Fatima queen was concentrating on her shoes getting dirtied and was trying to avoid the mud as could as possible. She realised what she heard only when one of the CRPF personnel caught on her hand and put the hand cuff on it in seconds. She looked perplexed and tried in vain to release herself from the metal ring which was already on her hand. "You are under arrest" the lady constable who was standing nearby repeated with a smile on her face. Like a big buffalo surrounded by lion and lioness she looked helplessly for help. She saw Mustafa her driver looking at her from a distance. She saw two people were running behind Minguel De Silvia. Satoshkar Dume fell on the ground after hitting a marble plaque in the grave yard while trying to run away. Immediately he was overpowered by strong central forces. He tried to show his artifice once again but the strong blows on his face one after another cooled him down. The people started running helter-skelter after seeing the fight between people. After some time they realised the arrest of a notorious gang along with its stalwarts. The priest concluded the last rituals in a hurry. Only Johnny's crippled mother and the teenage boy who read the condolence message stood by the priest till the end of the service. Fatima could see the faces of Minguel de Silva, Francisco and all her loyalists inside the police van with their hands tied on poles. They looked like lambs waiting for the butcher in a slaughter house. Fatima was locked to a central pole inside the vehicle. She was gasping and asked for water to drink. But instead of water she was given hard blows from all sides. Throughout the years she never received the taste of blows herself but only given to innocents. Dada Augustino pleaded for his queen but his pleading fell on deaf ears. Screaming and moaning of Minguel and Francisco were also heard inside the speeding van with every blow from police personals.

People read the next day's news paper with great enthusiasm.

Mafia queen arrested. People sighed in relief.

All happiness of the public vanished with the next news: "DGP shunted out of Goa."

# Epilogue

Alexander Philip was summoned by the Minister of Education, Mr. Adharma Pal, Mr. Crook and others were in his cabin. They accused him of insubordination.

"I am not a patriot" Alexander Philip said to the minister. "Only people who occupy political posts like you are patriots and also those who had spent some time in jail are considered as patriots; doesn't matter for what purpose you were sent to jail, may be for fodder scam, extortion, smuggling, mark scandal, human trafficking, prostitution, drug peddling or even stealing others rights. No common men like me who served the public for a life time are considered as patriots, sincere Officers are being targeted and demoted. Ofcourse we were paid for the job. But you were trying to demoralize all sincere officials who worked for the society. If the standard of education is low and our students are no were in the main stream, it is only because of your selfish policy that promoted jingoism and hatred. You wanted all faithful corrupt servants who dance as per your tune in your department and not efficient people to occupy important posts. You wanted to fill up your department with your own party workers. A hundred thousand corrupt beneficiaries will escort you when you go to jail and another thousands people will be there to receive you when you get a bail. Netas and diplomats have immunity; immunity to break laws of the land, immunity to steal our natural resources and they enjoy immunity inside and outside the jail with all comforts. Learned advocates are here to protect the thieves', murderers and molesters if they have money. Lakhs of people who serve the public like me are not considered as patriots, only jingoists and chauvinistic leaders are patriots; not A*am Aadmi*. We are mere public servants better to say slaves of pseudo-patriots like you." Minister did not speak a word. However, his supporters' face proclaimed their anger and again a cold war has begun between evil and good. They swayed their closed fist in the air in protest and shouted slogans praising their mass leader and the Mafia club Susegaad.

The RTO officer was busy in collecting his envelopes on every evening and divided each ones share and distributed faithfully. The drug peddlers deposited the politician's share in Swiss bank or at their Dubai account without fail. *Lal bati* officers and Ministers moved fearlessly through the streets in their most expensive cars available and enjoyed their immunity fully and spend their nights in Casinos. Minister's son waited outside the city college to select his next pray. Ministers visited District Hospital to enquire the health of Andrew Akbar. Slum dwellers collected half burned tin sheets to protect their huts once again. The scar on the tar road of the burned tyres in the middle of the railway station road started to fade out. The Mafia Susegaad members called an emergency meeting at Gama beach to chalk out their future plans. The two sister rivers run slowly to the Arabian Sea as usual to dump the sins of politicians of Goapuri. The sun of Golden Goa drowned into the sea as usual.